CREW

A Novel

by

Greg Gilmartin

Kyle —
You time is now!
Go Fast! Pass Boats!
Tell Stories!

Greg

This novel is a work of fiction. Any references to real people, events, establishments, organizations or locales are intended only to give the fiction a sense of reality and authenticity. Other names, characters, places and incidents portrayed therein are either the product of the author's imagination or are used fictionally.

First printing December, 2007

Publisher:

Pet Rock Films LLC
85 Oswegatchie Road
Waterford, CT 06378

Printed in the United States of America

Cover Design by Mardy Pryor, Shoreline Graphics.

For the crew. My friends. My family

Acknowledgements

Friendships help make our endeavors more enjoyable. Good to share with someone, good to have them watch your back and good to have them believe along the way. The inspiration for Crew came from friendships, most in sailboat racing but, the process of writing and publishing a novel brings others along who play an equally important part. Thanks to those who helped, the crew who never saw it coming and those brave enough to nurse the manuscript along. There are many, fortunately, but I want to offer special thanks to Marty, Tony, Hutch, Ken, Billmo and Pat, who believed without condition.

Greg Gilmartin

December, 2007

Crew

By Greg Gilmartin

PROLOGUE

The old man peered through the blinds into the darkness outside his second floor apartment. The house two doors down and across busy Boylston Street had new owners. And the new owners seemed to have a lot of friends. A rookie cop could have figured out the scene.

He had seen them the last two nights. A growing stream of faceless folks had come to his Worcester neighborhood, where old triple-decker homes shared the boulevard with storefronts and closed gas stations. College kids, professionals, factory workers, blacks, whites - all types - walked up the steps, paused at the door, went inside, and exited a few minutes later, their pockets, their nose, their lungs no doubt, full of cocaine. Or crack. He knew what was happening.

The blacked out BMW parked in front was not just another one of the visitors. The old man could make out the license plate in the glow of the streetlights. "SNOWGO" it read. Stupid! The punks who make the money on the body poison just don't know how to handle it. They advertise, for crying out loud!

Twenty years on the Providence police force and another twenty as a private investigator had taught him a thing or two about people. So many jerks lived as if they were untouchable. He had put his share of jerks behind bars. The drug dealers were especially bold, he thought, and often stupid.

He watched a smallish man come out of the house, a briefcase swinging from his arm. The guy wore a wide brimmed hat and a suit with a string tie. He slipped into the back seat of the car and it immediately sped away, heading toward downtown.

Twice retired, seventy-two years old and living alone, the old man picked up the TV remote, clicked the mute button and returned to the late movie. Someone's got to do something about those drug dealers, he thought.

~~~

CHAPTER ONE

C aptain Jorge Pizzaro was right in the middle of Colombia's war on drugs and that war was in the jungle. Poised at the doorless opening of a small twin engine Cessna, the wind tugged at his jumpsuit. He adjusted his goggles, checked his chest pack and turned to his partner's backpack chute. He gave it an affirmative slap and Lieutenant Pedro Cepeda returned the favor for his captain. They nodded to each other and looked out at the expanse of green rolling by 5,000 feet below.

Pizzaro pointed at the blue ribbon of the Guanapanaca River snaking its way through southeastern Colombia toward Brazil. Cepeda's goggled gaze followed. A double twist in the river matched the three-day-old photo Pizzaro held in his hands. He studied it once more. Snapped from a U.S. spy plane, it showed a narrow clearing cut into the jungle big enough for a runway.

He looked at his watch. 1415 hours. Friday afternoon. September 21. The noise of the rushing air and the engines killed any thought of talking. He held up three fingers and Cepeda nodded.

Pizzaro preferred not talking before a jump. He liked to think about his first step into the air, the rush of wind, and the effortless fall. Yelling would have broken his concentration and, frankly, would have required too much energy. He was beginning to feel the aching effects of the three earlier jumps that day and the five from yesterday. Before that, he had lost count.

It had been a week since he had joined the *Rapidero Fuego* unit, but to him it seemed like a month. As forward scouts, he and Cepeda were the first into the jungle, followed by an attack force of forty men with one mission in mind - destroy the cocaine processing labs of Colombia's *narcotrafficantes*.

For years, the jungle had provided good cover for the drug makers. It was an isolated, unfriendly environment that kept the police and other nosey parties away. It also supplied water, an essential ingredient in the chemical laden cooking process that turned cocaine paste into snortable cocaine hydrochloride.

However, for the first time in the twenty-year drug war, the full scale of the jungle operation was exposed to the authorities. High-flying spy cameras from the U.S. found the isolated labs. Long strips of black and white and infra-red film had been turned into 20,000 photographs, each covering ten square miles of jungle. Two photo analysts from the CIA taught young Colombian analysts how to spot dirt airstrips, chemical caches and anything larger than six feet that looked out of place in the jungle.

It was a massive undertaking, but the war had taken a new turn. In the first week of the *Rapidero Fuego* operation, fifteen of the twenty-five sites pinpointed and attacked had been producing cocaine, no longer were.

Three minutes passed and the pilot of the Cessna cut the engines to idle and signaled to Pizzaro and Cepeda. They were already out the door, diving with their arms and legs swept backward, letting gravity pull them downward at 120 miles an hour.

Their free fall lasted fewer than forty seconds. Pizzaro felt the snap of his nylon para-wing open at 1,000 feet, looked up at its proper rectangular shape and then searched for the chosen landing site down river from the suspected lab. Cepeda's chute opened a second later and the two soldiers silently floated under their light blue "squares" toward the jungle.

Pizzaro took a last look around at the tree tops and then killed his speed with a nicely executed flare, landing gently in a walk just five feet from the river's edge. He pulled his cutaway cable to release the chute, turning to gather it before the cloth touched the ground.

A wind gust forced Cepeda to make a sudden turn to avoid a tree in the last fifty feet and he landed hard in the knee-deep grass on the riverbank, but jumped to his feet unhurt and gathered his chute. Both men did a rough pack, fully expecting to use their chutes again before the day was over.

Armed with two M-16s, one equipped with the M-203 grenade launcher, extra ammo, a pair of binoculars and a radio, they set out under cover of the dense growth, carefully moving along the tree line twenty yards from the river.

It took them nearly thirty minutes to cover two miles, and several more to cover the last fifty yards as they silently crept toward the riverbank. Both were drenched from the day's heat by the time Pizzaro signaled a halt and they settled into position under the broad green leaves.

They were opposite a clearing Pizzaro estimated to be 100 feet across and 2000 feet deep, cut into the jungle from the river's edge. Through his binoculars he saw a pair of ten-man tents, and a pavilion with a thatched roof that appeared to house the cocaine vats and supply storage. White piles of powder lay drying on a tarp next to the pavilion.

Dozens of fifty-five gallon drums were piled along the jungle's edge. He counted four men working around the processing tables and vats.

Nearby several men stacked duffle bags. Pizzaro counted twenty-seven of the dark, canvas sacks. It looked like a shipment was ready for pickup.

Pizzaro did not see any posted guards, though he was sure there were weapons nearby. He positioned his small radio headset with the built in microphone and keyed the transmit switch on his belt.

"Vigilar, this is Corneta. Class A. Ten plus. Hot zone. This is a go. Repeat. Go." He spoke softly, but clearly.

"Roger, Corneta. Vigilar. Copy a go," came the reply from the Cessna, circling down river. The pilot relayed the message to a staging base in Lerida, fifteen miles away.

"Rapidero this is Vigilar. Class A. Ten plus. Hot zone. Go. Repeat. Go."

In Lerida, the warm turbines on five Huey helicopters began to whine. Colonel Jesus Cesar's force of forty men loaded up and they were airborne inside of five minutes, heading for the lab in the jungle.

The Colonel rode in the lead helicopter grimly watching the dense jungle whiz by just a dozen feet below him. He was a tired man of fifty-two, a life-long soldier, trained by the U.S. military. A veteran of numerous conflicts, his brown face was etched with painful memories, too many worries and too much fear. His country was fighting for its life mired in a desperate civil war driven by violence and greed.

He thought of the seemingly unstoppable plague of white powder that funneled through his tiny country into the bloodstream of the rest of the world. Like the weather, it seemed no one could do anything about it.

Half a million kilos produced and smuggled each year, over five hundred tons, worth over twelve billion dollars. And that was only an educated guess. It was a fact, however, that the massive profits from the white drug were unmatched by any other form of contraband that had ever found its way through this smuggler's haven, including gold and emeralds. In two decades, a new generation of Colombian smugglers, *narcotrafficantes*, was well rooted and had grown to unimaginable levels of prosperity.

They were ruthless. The untouchables, thought Cesar, the rich in a nation rife with poverty, the strong in a nation full of fear, the self-proclaimed kings who offered their countrymen only two choices, *Plata u Plomo*. Silver or lead. Most took the silver, bribed to turn their heads. Those who dared fight took the lead.

The *narcotrafficantes* murdered the police, the politicians, the press, the public, and even each other, battling to protect their markets and their profits from cocaine. Bullets, bombs and blood were a way of life in a county that had survived outside invasions, but were unsure of surviving an enemy from within.

Colonel Cesar was one of the driving forces behind a small core of determined Colombians, loyal to newly elected Presidente Ferdinand Barranqui Gomez. They were fighting back. In the first few months of Gomez's administration, there had been successes. Six leaders from the powerful Medellin and Cali cartels had been jailed or killed. But there was much more to do.

Cesar's thoughts drifted to his hand-picked unit, each lost in their own nightmares as they prepared for battle. They were loyal veterans selected for their fighting ability. More importantly, they were men who had each suffered the violent loss of a loved one at the hands of the *narcotrafficantes*. It was sad how many qualified!

He thought of his own dead wife and son, killed by a car bomb six months ago. Vengeance is mine, sayeth the Lord, but his *Rapidero Fuego* force from the sky had brought a little bit of hell into the drug makers' lives in the past week and there was more to come.

The colonel keyed his radio.

"Alberto, from the north this time. Everyone else from the south. Twenty second intervals."

"Yes, Colonel," came the reply from Alberto, the one they called *Acalorado*, the Enflamer. He piloted the last helicopter in the loose formation and watched the four ahead peel off to the south to circle around the target and come in from the riverside. He slowed his speed a fraction and held his course. The clearing was several miles, dead ahead.

The first four Hueys, painted in olive tones of jungle camouflage, were stripped for combat. Each carried six soldiers, a gunner with a swivel mounted M-60 machine gun in the right side doorway and two flight crew. Alberto shared his chopper only with his co-pilot, Esteve, in a Huey specially outfitted for this mission.

"Corneta, this is Rapidero. Two minutes," Cesar spoke into his radio. The colonel heard two clicks in his headset in answer. Now we begin again, he thought.

On the ground, Pizzaro and Cepeda sat perfectly still looking straight down the box canyon framed by jungle trees. The dirt runway was empty but he now counted six men working at the pavilion. The captain checked the second hand of his watch and took aim with the grenade launcher.

"*Ffoofpt!*" came the muffled sound from the rocket as it exploded out of the wide mouth barrel and arched its way through the thick jungle air to land in a bright red explosion on the pavilion roof. Like a powerful Molotov cocktail, it exploded in flames.

Pizzaro let loose another rocket, this one landing on one of the tents.

There were men running and stumbling, stunned by the sudden intrusion of flames. Some went looking for their weapons while others ran for the safety of the trees.

Just as the second rocket exploded, Alberto's specially equipped Huey came flying in at tree top level through the black smoke at the far end of the clearing. The noise of his engines had been lost in the exploding confusion around the lab workers, but now over the clearing, it reverberated loudly off the wall of surrounding foliage.

He slowed his momentum with a sudden nose up flare and then spun the copter 180 degrees, hovering at twenty feet. He pitched the nose down and aimed at the wooden pavilion in front of him. A hissing sound came from the copter, just audible above the sound of its rotors, and suddenly the hiss turned into a roar as a 150-foot stream of liquid fire shot out of a nozzle mounted just under the cockpit.

The stream of burning fuel turned the pavilion into an inferno. One man died instantly as the flames enveloped him from head to foot. Another ran in terror, his clothing on fire. One man managed to get off a burst from his machine pistol, but he, too, disappeared in a ball of flame.

Alberto gently slid the copter sideways to bathe the entire pavilion in flames. The drying cocaine began to burn. The stream of hell stopped as suddenly as it started, leaving just the hissing of compressed air and the crackling of orange death eating the pavilion and nearby jungle.

Alberto spun the copter again, rose up and disappeared over the trees as the four other Hueys came swooping in from the river. The soldiers jumped from the hovering craft and spread out as the choppers flew off to circle overhead, their M-60s punctuating the air with cover fire.

Incendiary grenades went off near the tents and the cache of fifty-five gallon drums of chemicals on the other side of the clearing turned into a fireball. The stack of duffel bags fell victim to a soldier with a backpack flamethrower. The lightweight canvas burned away, revealed white bricks of cocaine that turned brown then black and filled the clearing with an acrid smell.

Some automatic weapons fire came from the workers but that resistance was quickly silenced and the former jungle lab became quiet with only the crackle of flames and the steady thump of the circling helicopters filling the steamy afternoon. It had taken four minutes from the first burst of Pizzaro's grenade.

Colonel Cesar counted five bodies at the burning pavilion. Five more were dragged in by his men and laid in a row. The colonel checked their pockets for papers, found nothing useful and waved his hand toward the burning structure. Without a word, the soldiers added the five bodies to the

---

conflagration. No one felt remorse for those already dead.

A movement on the edge of the clearing caught Cesar's eye. A man dressed in white hiding in the dense undergrowth turned to run when he saw the dead men tossed on the fire. The jungle swallowed him in a blink.

Cesar held up a hand to his men who had their weapons ready.

"Let him go. Let him tell the story about the bomberderos."

He smiled at what the man might say, and then he keyed his radio. "This is Rapidero. LZ clear. Come get us."

Chopper One picked Pizzaro and Cepeda off the far riverbank and went after their parachutes while the other choppers landed on the smoky airstrip, followed by the Cessna. Cesar estimated 600 kilos of coke had burned in the pile of smoldering duffel bags, about a week's production from this small lab - a $12 million hit at current prices.

But which syndicate? And did it really hurt them? Of course it hurt! Cesar practically shouted out loud. He wasn't going to start second guessing his plan. They had inflicted damage this week and they had to keep at it until the war was won.

In ten minutes, Pizzaro and Cepeda were back on the ground, hunched over the floor of the Colonel's chopper comparing a map with another set of black and white photographs, the latitude and longitude of each photo etched along the picture's border. They were confident they could hit one more lab site about forty miles to the north on the Yapurari River and still have enough fuel to get back to the staging base at Araracuera by nightfall.

Three hours later a lone pilot in an old Beechcraft twin, low on fuel, and one engine already feathered, touched down on the dirt runway along the Guanapanaca River. He had faced severe headwinds on his flight from the south and had miscalculated his fuel reserves.

The second engine sputtered quiet even as he bounced to a stop and the pilot sat in his seat surveying the charred scene. Nothing moved, except a tiny trickle of smoke from the uneven pile that was the pavilion ruins. He saw barrels everywhere, cracked open, the contents either burned or spilled on the ground. His gas supply was in that mess!

He slowly climbed out of the plane and checked the barrels up close to confirm his fears. The lab had been totally wasted and he was stranded with a planeload of coca paste from Peru and not enough fuel to take off again! As the night dropped around him and the noise of the jungle filled the dark, he crawled into his plane to wait for the dawn, unsure of what he would do then.

CHAPTER TWO

P eter James McDonough, his feet firmly planted on a stone wall, looked north across the expanse of San Francisco Bay toward Sausalito and then west at the majestic Golden Gate Bridge spanning the mile-wide gap in the coastline. He was about to embrace his addiction to speed. Today, it would be in a sailboat.

A steady wind licked at the grey-green water, spawning whitecaps atop the choppy waves. This was to be the racecourse. The breeze pressured his face and tousled his brownish-red hair. Behind him the stucco and orange tile of the St. Francis Yacht Club glowed in the September morning sun.

His alert blue eyes squinted, accentuating the crows' feet at the corners, premature for a man of thirty-five, unless he had spent a lifetime outdoors. A boyish smile spread across his tanned face as he turned to the man and woman standing with him.

"Right side favored?" he asked. He had already convinced himself it was, due to the wind direction, but wanted to hear their thoughts.

"If the breeze holds, PJ. Right side of the course definitely favored," answered the older man.

Friend, mentor, surrogate father, racing tactician, Jester Miller had been sailing with PJ for the last twenty of his fifty- nine years. In the lone reversal of roles in their relationship, it was PJ who had taught Jester how to harness the wind in the sails. The two of them had held this same little talk before every race and they rarely disagreed.

"Actually, guys, the left side will be favored by the time we head for the finish line."

PJ looked at the woman standing next to Jester. She was the new addition to their pre-race ritual. Kathryn Byrnie was striking with long black hair, black eyes and a smooth, brown face that looked like the ultimate tan. She was a month older than PJ and more than a little exotic, PJ thought to himself. More importantly, Kathryn was a lifelong sailor on San Francisco Bay.

She was about to head east with PJ and Jester to join their Fast Car Caravan in Mystic, Connecticut. There, her computer and design expertise would help them build and test revolutionary plastic engines for cars, planes and boats. On this Saturday, however, she was their navigator.

Her hiring had delighted PJ, coming a week before the start of the Great Bay Series. The five race regatta involved twenty boats from the Fabulous Fifties Association, a friendly organization of successful businessmen and sailors who built fast fifty foot boats and raced them against each other at the world's best sailing venues. PJ was a founding member and loved nothing better than gaining an advantage with some local knowledge on board.

The mere listing of sailboat racing and flying under hobbies had separated Kathryn's resume from the dozens of other applicants they had been reviewing. Her portfolio of fine industrial designs had won her the job. She possessed a rare combination of engineering and artistic perspectives that attracted both PJ and Jester to her.

"The current, PJ," Kathryn said, as if reminding him. She was a full head shorter and looked up at him with a crooked little smile, her eyes squinting in the brightness. "It will be flooding when we turn at Blossom Rock and head for the finish line. We have to go left or we may never get there."

The tidal flow in and out of San Francisco Bay funneled millions of gallons of water under the Golden Gate Bridge every six hours. In the process, the water level rose and fell as much as six feet, creating swift currents that could play havoc with boats. For sailboat racer, a foul current was slow.

"Oh, yeah," PJ said, his smile now a sheepish grin, "I guess we can't forget the current. I knew that."

"What time does it change?" Jester asked, looking at the water, his shock of white hair wild in the wind.

"One-thirty," she offered, checking her small blue notebook with the figures she had jotted down the night before. "The full moon makes it especially nasty. The tide log has it as the strongest flood current of the year. It'll be over five knots late this afternoon."

"Three knots against by the time we get to the right side," Jester said.

"Go left," Kathryn pointed. "The south side is protected by the Presidio and Fort Point. And there's shallow water along the shore, so, I expect we would see less than a knot there."

The two men and the woman stood silently for a moment, looking out on the bay. PJ let out a small laugh. He was used to race car speeds over 180 miles an hour and could deftly maneuver a plane moving at 400. Here he was trying to salvage less than one mile per hour. Well, that's sailboat racing, he thought.

"So, the left side favored?" he repeated his question.

"Left side definitely," Jester answered, a big grin on his face.

"I agree," Kathryn chimed in with a big smile that showed off her bright white teeth.

"I guess that is why we asked you to navigate, Kathryn Byrnie!" PJ laughed, his eyes locking onto hers. "You'll keep us honest." She looked very confident, he thought.

The three of them turned toward the small marina basin behind the yacht club and joined the rest of the crew already on the boat.

* * *

It was a little after two that same afternoon when Brett Lesco reached the vantage point he had selected on the Golden Gate Bridge. His one-piece coverall read "Golden Gate Bridge Authority" over the left breast, partially hidden by an insulated vest. A Giants' baseball cap sat on his head. He carried a long toolbox in one hand and a key in the other.

The travelers in the steady stream of cars filling the six lanes of concrete were much too busy gawking at the overpowering structure to notice a lone workman. The two dozen or so joggers, bikers and walkers on the sidewalk also gave little more than a glance as he slipped the key into the lock on a red metal door that extended a few feet above the bridge railing. The key came from a diminutive man named Rogo who had helped him prepare for today's job.

The door opened easily revealing an enclosed ladder that went straight down under the roadway. He paused long enough to register the size of the Pacific in front of him and the small crowd of tourists on the Marin Headlands, then firmly grabbed the ladder and swung himself over the bridge railing. He balanced the toolbox on a rung while he reached behind to close the metal door. It clicked shut and he found himself in a darkened closet, the only light leaking in from the water 220 feet below.

Lesco was on one of four work scaffolds that permanently hung from the bridge superstructure. However, the ironworkers who performed the daily chipping and painting routine that kept the massive bridge glowing California Red were not working today. It was Lesco's good fortune to find the southern scaffold near the mid point of the main span. An ideal location for his plans.

The toolbox made it awkward, but he managed to descend the ladder to a steel platform thirty feet below and then crossed to the bay side on a narrow walkway. He found the spot he had scouted two days earlier where the walkway turned sharply left and he set down the box. The view was stunning. His eyes immediately glanced at the white buildings of the city and he thought of Athens, with its white boxes on brown hills.

A large motor yacht bobbed quietly over her anchor in the chop of the water several hundred yards from the bridge. The bow of the boat and an inflatable yellow ball bobbing about fifty yards to the north appeared connected by the giant shadow cast from the bridge. For the moment, the arc on the water marked the finish line of the Great Bay Series sailboat race.

The breeze blew out of the west, just as Lesco expected. He saw the group of sailboats three miles to the east, working their way toward him. He had plenty of time. Cars and trucks rolled overhead, their rumblings creating a gentle vibration that he could feel through his feet.

Lesco's thin fingers opened the toolbox and carefully removed two smaller cases. From the felt lining of one he lifted a black metal gun barrel and locked it onto its plastic stock with a twist. He released the shoulder rest from the stock and it quietly clicked into position. A Leupold telescopic sight came from the other case and slid smoothly into the custom grooves on top of the barrel and also locked with a click.

He scratched his beard and shivered in the breeze. Under the roadway there was no sunshine and he zipped up his vest. Then he pulled three pieces of a plastic antenna from the toolbox, screwing them together to form a rod about five feet long. To one end he taped a two-foot strip of orange surveyor tape and the other end he taped to a support bracket under the metal platform, extending the rod below the bridge. The orange streamer went stiff in the breeze. Still from the west, he thought after watching the streamer for a moment.

The boats were close enough now to distinguish the color of their hulls. He watched the leading blue boat turn away from the red hull. Splitting tacks, he thought. He looked down between his legs at his homemade wind vane, but there was no noticeable change in the wind's direction.

He next carefully loaded five 7.62 mm match rounds into a clip, licking the end of each one, and slapped the clip into the chamber. The familiar metallic taste of the bullets calmed him. He took a sixth bullet and slipped it into his breast pocket next to a photo cut from a local magazine.

"This will be an easy payoff," he said aloud, his voice lost in the dull roar of the traffic overhead. Through the scope, he picked up the sail number 50001 on the red boat as it continued on starboard tack, hugging the San Francisco shore.

***

PJ McDonough was at peace with the world. His new fifty foot sailboat, *Poly Rocket*, slid gracefully through the white-capped water, driven by an unseen fuel. His strong hands gently held the carbon fiber steering wheel and felt the pressure on the rudder as it kicked aside the water, pushing the stern to the left. He eased the waterborne thoroughbred into the groove, the ever-changing and sometimes elusive sweet spot where sails and crew are in harmony with the wind. It felt good in his hands and *Poly Rocket* moved at maximum speed, hard on the wind.

The Blossom Rock buoy was behind them a mile and the current had started to flood as predicted by Kathryn. They were short tacking along the waterfront to stay out of the worst of the flow. Staying close to the shore meant dodging the cruising sailors coming out of the harbor marinas, as well as the steady stream of ferries that gave the tourists a small taste of PJ's playing field.

At one point they had come so close to the Pier 39 shopping district that PJ's mainsail trimmer, Lenny Cain, had asked one of the tourists if they had any Grey Poupon, which brought peals of laughter from the pier and the crew. Lenny was the boat clown, always looking for an audience. PJ and his crew put up with his banter because no one could match his touch on the large mainsail that powered the boat.

Lenny was one of a crew of nine PJ assembled for the Great Bay Series. Except for Kathryn, all of them had sailed with him for years. Each was hand-picked for their sailing skills and attitude. They worked smoothly on the boat, melding their different personalities into a formidable team.

"A little lift here, Dutch," PJ said to his closest friend and port jib trimmer, Dutch Winslow.

"Easing some," he said and eased the kevlar jib sheet attached to the headsail a few inches. The line groaned loudly under pressure as it reluctantly slid around the large drum of the winch. In response, the sail subtly changed its shape, keeping *Poly Rocket* in the groove.

"Coming up to the lift now," PJ intoned, turning the wheel slightly to move the bow to the right a few degrees.

"Trim on," Dutch said to the pair of winch grinders.

Dave Bender and Ray Winston, both over six feet tall, one bulky, the other lanky, hunched face to face over the twin handles in the middle of the cockpit. Connected to gears below deck, the "coffee grinder" multiplied the sailors' power ten fold and they easily spun the big winch drum, grinding in the few inches of jib sheet that Dutch had just eased out. Again, the jib changed shape.

"Stop," Dutch commanded and the two grinders instantly did so.

Simultaneously, Lenny made a small adjustment to the position of the mainsail, the two sails working together to power the boat.

"On target speed," Jester said to PJ a moment later, watching the array of instruments on a cockpit panel. He was sitting just to the left and behind PJ on the low slung cockpit combing. It was the traditional position for a tactician and a helmsman, allowing good visibility of their own boat and their competition.

"We should continue on starboard here and hope we get lifted right along the shoreline," he said, feeling the wind blowing from the right.

"We can safely go within two boat lengths of the beach, PJ," Kathryn said from the narrow companionway that led below. One of her jobs was to keep track of how much water *Poly Rocket* had under her nine-foot keel.

"I think we can get to one boat length, maybe twelve feet on the depth sounder," PJ said. *Poly Rocket* was brand new, fresh from the wrapper only ten days ago, but PJ had come to win. Putting his million-dollar boat close to the rocks was part of it.

"It's only money, right?" he laughed.

"It's only *your* money!" Lenny answered.

"Twelve feet it is," Kathryn grinned. A folded chart in one hand, her range-bearing compass in the other, she resumed scanning ahead for any wind shifts and unusual current lines, visible to the trained eye as slight variations in color on the water's surface.

PJ watched the jib telltales, eight-inch lengths of videotape sewn on the sail that indicated the airflow over the synthetic cloth. He kept up a litany with Dutch and Lenny in response to changes in wind direction and strength, which were both subtle and often. Jester chimed in when boat speed and target speed didn't match. The rest of the crew, Mickey, Crash and Stoney, joined by Dave and Ray, sat to windward as railmeat. Their legs hung over the side to help stabilize the boat.

PJ looked over his right shoulder at Stick Ketchum's blue-hulled fifty, *Sally Goose*, sailing away from *Poly Rocket* on the opposite tack. Ketchum had been sailing on the bay for nearly forty years and knew its changing moods intimately. PJ was unsure why Stick had tacked away and was now heading toward the middle of the bay. *Sally Goose* had been in the lead, two boat lengths ahead of *Poly Rocket* when she changed direction. The rest of the fleet was behind and close to shore.

"What's with Goose?" he asked to no one in particular.

"Looks like she has a big wind shift out there," Jester suggested. Indeed, Ketchum's blue-hulled fifty was sailing closer to the wind and appeared to be pointing right toward the finish line.

"Should we follow?" PJ asked. He needed more input.

"We knew he'd get a big lift, but Stick's gonna' start losing half of what he gains to windward when he hits the teeth of the current." It was Kathryn speaking, her hand bearing compass pointed at the blue hull. She looked right at PJ, flashing her crooked smile.

"I think we stay here," she said with confidence.

"There's more wind to the right," Stoney Bullard suggested from the rail.

"And more current," Kathryn countered.

"It's the Sausalito Sucker Punch," Lenny laughed. "Go for the pretty side and end up at Alcatraz."

PJ smiled. Lenny was right. Despite more wind, which meant more speed, Ketchum would be pushed to his right, right toward the former island prison, by the strong current rushing through the middle of the bay.

"We stay," he decided. "At least to Anita Rock. Hell, let's ring the bell at the Coast Guard station!"

"What about that three footer," Kathryn reminded him. There was a rock near the Coast Guard dock.

"Well, we'll just miss it, okay?" PJ replied. "We've decided to go deep to this side, so, let's go deep."

"I hope you're right," Jester said and PJ laughed.

"So do I," he said. Kathryn just smiled and resumed her scan of the water.

"Another little lift, Dutch," PJ intoned and the trimming and tweaking continued as *Poly Rocket* glided past the orange tiled roof of St. Francis, the host club for the regatta.

They passed between Anita Rock and the shore and stayed on starboard tack. Jester had been right. The land caused a continual wind shift in their favor.

However, PJ's concern was boat speed. Staying in close meant less wind and they had slowed considerably once past the yacht club. More than once he wanted to tack away and head for the stronger winds visible in the middle of the channel. Other boats had joined Ketchum out there. He fought the temptation until they ran out of water.

"Hey, Pitbull! I need some main halyard tension on the tack," Lenny called to pitman Mickey O'Mara.

Mickey, a freelance writer, was without a vicious bone in his body. He smiled, snapped a quick photo of Lenny with a small camera that appeared from a pocket in his foul weather jacket and gave him a thumbs up from the rail.

"Easy. We're not tacking just yet," Jester said. Lenny nodded. Jester looked at the finish line about three-quarters of a mile to their right and at Ketchum's *Sally Goose*, still plowing through the water toward the other end of the bridge. Ketchum had more wind, but didn't appear to be gaining distance on the finish line. The current was hurting him.

"Okay, Peej, let's go now," Jester said as the Coast Guard dock loomed in front of them. The depth sounder read eleven feet and PJ nodded with a small grin. He noticed the dark shape of the three foot rock slide by, visible underwater half a boat length to starboard.

"Ready about," called PJ and he shifted from the soft horseshoe seat to stand behind the wheel. The rest of the crew moved quickly from the windward rail to their positions, preparing the lines for the all important tack.

"Tacking," and PJ turned the big wheel slowly to the right about a quarter turn, then faster another half turn and the bow of the boat passed through the eye of the wind.

As the wind pressure on the jib eased, Dutch released the sheet that held it tight. It went slack for a second until Stoney Bullard, the starboard trimmer, took up tension on the new sheet and started hauling on it, grabbing large sections of the line with a sweeping hand over hand motion.

Stoney stood only five-five, but pound for pound he was the strongest man on the crew. The line came in quickly with the help of Dave and Ray on the coffee grinder.

Christina "Crash" Clarke, the only woman working the bow in the Fabulous Fifties fleet, stood just forward of the mast and made sure the sail swept cleanly through the foredeck. Pitman Mickey gave a quick crank on the mainsail halyard winch as he slid across the cabin top. In a matter of ten seconds, the tacking maneuver was complete and *Poly Rocket* heeled over as the breeze filled her sails and she began to accelerate in the new direction on port tack.

At first it appeared they had sailed too far and had overshot the finish line. But, PJ and Jester expected to be swept right by the incoming current to the near end where the committee boat marked the finish line. As they came out from behind Fort Point at the south end of the Golden Gate Bridge that's exactly what happened. *Sally Goose* tacked a full minute later and trimmed in smartly, also lined up with the committee boat end of the finish line. The water rushed past both hulls as they cut through the white caps on opposite tacks.

"It will be close, PJ. Steady on your course," said Jester. He watched Ketchum as the two boats drew closer, their paths aimed at the same point in the shadow of the bridge.

"Speed is even, relative bearing is not changing, Peter." Kathryn pointed her hand bearing compass at *Sally Goose* every few seconds. The boats were dead even and on a collision course. The finish line was still half a mile away.

***

From his lofty perch Brett Lesco tracked the symphony of movement on the water. He made a mental note of the slight direction change in the orange tape still flapping stiffly in the breeze. He pulled his head away from the scope and inhaled deeply. He enjoyed hunting men and went out of his way to make the challenge as difficult as possible. No one could do it his way, he thought. His record spoke for itself. The money was also nice - $250,000 for a few hours in the fresh air of San Francisco Bay.

He pressed his face against the eyepiece again and easily swung the rifle to the left to pick up the blue hull of sail number 50234. A towel wedged between two bridge cross supports provided a stable platform. He swung right and found the red-hulled boat.

He focused on the two bodies behind the steering wheel and slowly tracked them as the sleek boat drew closer, moving from right to left across his vision. He estimated the distance at seven hundred yards. His right thumb reached up and flipped off the safety and his index finger felt the trigger guard and then moved onto the trigger.

For a moment the rumble of the traffic overhead filled his ears, but he was relaxed, his breathing already in a natural rhythm. He felt the slight vibration of the scaffolding and tried to fall in synch with it, becoming a part of the bridge.

His world narrowed down to the few essentials he was taught in Marine Corps Scout Sniper School. Soon, even the blood beating in his ears dissolved from his mind as the target filled his eye.

He took another breath, exhaled half of it, extended the pause before inhaling and squeezed the trigger. With practiced movements honed over years of sniping, Lesco re-cocked the single action bolt, re-aimed and squeezed, repeating the sequence until he had emptied the clip in a matter of ten seconds. The sharp report that exploded from the rifle with each squeeze of the trigger was lost in the afternoon wind as a convoy of circus trucks rumbled by overhead on their way to San Rafael. And five high-powered bullets rained down on the sailors in the red-hulled boat.

They were a team without fights, a group of fast friends, focused on the same goal - to make *Poly Rocket* go and have a great time doing it. They were having a great time right now, as the fifty foot red hull slashed through the water, the fresh breeze now full on their faces.

"Starboard!" cried Stick Ketchum on *Sally Goose*, demanding right of way as she bore down on *Poly Rocket*.

"Hold your course!" PJ shouted at Ketchum, eyeing the distance the two boats had yet to travel and their respective speeds. "I think we have them," he said confidently. He planned to hold aggressively on port tack. If it worked, they would win.

"Starboard!" Ketchum's voice sang out again over the wind and water. "You can't make it, PJ!" The two boats, a total of twenty tons were rushing toward each other at a closing speed of about seventeen knots.

"Hold your course, Goose!" shouted PJ. Four boat lengths.

"Oh, man, I love it this close!" Lenny said with excitement, a big smile on his face. He was not convinced *Poly Rocket* would make it in front of *Sally Goose*.

"We are making trees," Jester said in a steady voice, watching the distant Angel Island shoreline behind *Sally Goose*, a stationary reference point matching her speed against *Poly Rocket*. He never liked close crossings, especially with million dollar yachts, but unlike Lenny, he did think they could sneak in front of *Sally Goose* without fouling.

PJ shifted from his seat on the edge of the cockpit and ducked behind the wheel so he could see the fast approaching *Sally Goose* under the mainsail boom.

"We got'em!" he said.

And then chaos split the day.

The first bullet from Brett Lesco's rifle slammed into the horseshoe life preserver where PJ had been sitting a split second before. Jester heard the dull thud of it hitting. He turned his head toward the sound and saw the odd hole that suddenly appeared in the yellow horseshoe's canvas cover.

"What the hell!" was barely out of his mouth when the next bullet ripped into his left shoulder, knocking him off his seat into the tilted cockpit behind PJ. His left arm went dead and, unable to cushion his fall, his head banged into a cockpit winch, knocking him unconscious. His limp body landed on the lifelines.

PJ did not hear the first two bullets hit, but heard Jester's cry. He turned to see his friend falling when the third and fourth bullets hit the deck and something flew up and struck PJ. He was momentarily stunned and felt a burning sensation above his eye. The fifth bullet smashed into his left hand, knocking him away from the wheel.

"What the...?" PJ started falling on the tilted deck, pain shooting up his arm. Reaching out instinctively for something to stop his fall, he grabbed a spoke with his right hand. His falling weight turned the wheel hard and instantly the big rudder spun the boat to the right.

On board *Sally Goose*, Stick Ketchum had angrily accepted his failed gamble. Less current had won out over more wind. He aimed to pass behind *Poly Rocket* when he saw the red-hulled boat suddenly turn right at him.

"What the hell is he doing?" he yelled and turned his wheel hard to the right.

"Tack!"

His crew had only started to react when the two fifty foot hulls collided bows on. *Poly Rocket's* composite hull hit fiberglass and punched a hole in *Sally Goose's* left side just aft of her bow pulpit. *Poly Rocket's* momentum carried her bow up onto the blue boat with a sickening screech, ripping Ketchum's jib and taking out two lifeline stanchions along the rail before clipping the port side shrouds that held the mast in place.

A single, loud *twang* was heard as a stainless steel rod pulled out of the deck fitting. This was followed by a sharp *crack* aloft as the suddenly released pressure on the shroud caused the tightly strung aluminum mast to snap thirty feet from the top of its seventy-five foot height. In slow motion it toppled like a tree, bringing the jib and mainsail down with it.

Poly Rocket fell back into the water and was now lying abeam of the wind, her sails trimmed in tight. The twenty-knot breeze hit this wall of kevlar and pushed the boat slowly over on her side.

The collision jolted *Poly Rocket's* crew on the rail and knocked the unconscious Jester off the lifelines and into the water.

"Jester's overboard! Man overboard!" Crash shouted in horror, pointing at him from the rail. Kathryn, her knee and ribs shooting pain from contact with a bulkhead, started to move back across the sharply angled deck toward the vacant wheel, her hands grabbing for a handhold. She had to get control of the boat, which had begun to move again.

PJ was dazed. He lay against the lifelines and looked up the tilted deck at the blue sky and the Golden Gate Bridge shining in the background. He thought he saw white wisps of fog tickling the upper towers of the bridge. At the moment of impact, he had watched Jester's still form fall into the water.

This is not happening, he thought, as the alarms began to ring in his head. He fought off the confusion, and the pain that seemed to shoot up his arm and reach his head. He grabbed the horseshoe life ring under him and rolled backward over the lifelines into the water after his friend.

"Peter!" Kathryn yelled as he went over. She grabbed the steering wheel, struggling to keep her balance. Dutch, nursing his left arm, broken against the coffee grinder, stepped over the unconscious Lenny, released the mainsheet and let off the jib sheet, easing the pressure on the sails. The boat straightened up, coasting flat on the water with the sails flapping noisily

The shock of the cold water shot right through PJ, but he stayed afloat and kept his eyes on Jester's face down body a few yards away. He swam to him and was able to turn him over on his back, slipping the horseshoe under his arms.

Jester's eyes were closed and his body was limp. His foul weather jacket was ripped and there was blood coming from the hole over his shoulder.

"He's been shot!" PJ blurted dumbfounded seeing the torn jacket hole. "We've been shot!" he said as the full realization struck him.

He wiped his hand across his eyes revealing the blood that came from both his head wound and his hand. The salt water added to the constant pain. His body pumped adrenalin, and he rhythmically kicked at the water, holding Jester on the surface.

"Don't you die, damn it!" he shouted, trying to get a response from his lifeless friend. "Don't you die!" He could see *Poly Rocket* trying to approach them, but the swirling currents under the bridge had them going in different directions.

A Coast Guard patrol boat shadowing the race came into view. Arms and hands reached over the side to fit a life sling over Jester and haul him on deck.

"Watch his left arm!" PJ shouted from the water, his strength just about gone. A few moments later, he felt the deck under his own back and hazily looked up at two uniformed young men.

"He's been shot. Somebody shot at us," he mumbled.

His whole body began shaking. He was cold and felt weak from the loss of blood. He knew he was going into shock. Just before the darkness of unconsciousness overcame him, PJ saw those wispy fingers of fog over the bridge again. And then he heard the wind carrying the noise of confusion away to quiet.

~~~

CHAPTER THREE

The wind pressed against the boy's face and the engine roar filled his ears. His mother's arms, wrapped tightly around his legs, held him on the front seat. His head poked over the windshield into the slipstream of his father's new Shelby Cobra. His eyes narrowed to slits. His cheeks pushed out. His teeth bared in a wide smile.

"I feel the need for speed!" chanted his parents, a lullaby of fun for their son as the houses and trees blurred.

The speed and all its sensations were intoxicating for five-year-old Peter James McDonough. A high that had, so far, lasted thirty years. His friends called him a speed freak. He preferred speed artist. Deep down, he knew he was just a driver.

"Nothing artistic about the way you crashed your new boat, McDonough!" a voice snickered from some dark recess in the puffy clouds.

"Speed kills those who don't know how to handle it," he heard himself say. It was spoken brashly by one who understood the mastery of arms and hands on the controls. Who was he speaking to? A reporter?

The white wisps changed to a black spiral of smoke on the road ahead. It came up very fast and in another instant he saw the mangled racecar upside down straddling the guardrails, the flames licking at the inverted number five on the blackening once white side. Track workers in red and white suits frantically tried to get close to the wreck.

"DeLorenzo," he muttered. A wave of guilt flashed through his body. He was convinced he had made a good pass on the number five in the last lap.

"Sure, auto racing is more dangerous than sailboat racing." The brashness continued. "But for both, you need a fine tuned sensitivity and fast reflexes to maintain harmony between man, machine and the environment they travel through."

Was that a grin or a grimace on the reporter's face? No, there were many faces, a sea of anger, all pointing their fingers at him. He was drowning!

Jester floated by, his lifeless body drifting on the cold waters, the hole in his foul weather jacket edged in blood. He had to jump into the water. Jester would have drowned if he hadn't been there. Jester had been there before for PJ. More than once.

It wasn't his fault!

Someone touched him and the wisps of clouds suddenly evaporated. His eyes opened to a blinding white light. A pair of eyes immediately replaced the glare, staring intently at his forehead.

"Welcome back," came the man's voice under the eyes. His hands were busy on PJ's face. "Just another minute and I'll have you closed up. What kind of a sailboat race were you in, anyway?"

The doctor smiled grimly as he focused on the five-inch gash above PJ's left eye. PJ closed his eyes again and saw Ketchum's boat looming large, the sudden pain in his head and hand, the crash, Jester going overboard and the cold water.

"How's Jester?" he asked, afraid of the answer.

"He was barely alive when he went into surgery," answered the doctor in a professional tone. "He'd lost a lot of blood, swallowed a lot of water and was unconscious...but they had a pulse."

Tough bastard, thought PJ.

"I would say you were very lucky, Mr. McDonough," the doctor said, turning to set his instruments on a small tray. PJ opened his eyes again, the doctor's practiced movements appeared in slow motion.

"A bullet or a bullet fragment nicked your forehead. Less than an inch, a fraction of a second, it could have been your eye or worse."

The doctor pointed at PJ's bandaged hand.

"Your hand took a more direct hit, but the bullet grazed the meaty edge just behind the pinkie knuckle on the metacarpal. I'm afraid it took a good chunk of flesh with it and some bone fragments."

PJ looked at his bandaged hand. He felt nothing.

"It will heal," the doctor continued. "Probably leave a permanent scar, where the flesh was ripped away. As far as nerve damage, we'll have to see how it goes after a week or so."

"There's nerve damage?" asked PJ, suddenly very much awake.

"Some. It's limited to the pinkie area. It might heal completely. You, ah, won't lose use of your fingers, but I don't want to soft sell you either. There is damage. Time will tell."

PJ wondered for a brief second if he would be able to type at a computer keyboard again and laughed at the thought it might not be so bad if he couldn't.

PJ sat up on the hard table and realized he was in the Emergency Room at the end of a row of half a dozen examination tables separated only by sliding curtains. Nurses and doctors were in constant movement around him. There was another man lying half naked on a medical table next to him with a bloody bandage on his shoulder, a nurse attending to him. Apparently another gunshot victim from another battle somewhere in the city, thought PJ.

"Can I see him? Jester?" PJ asked the doctor as he wrapped PJ's throbbing head with some gauze.

"As soon as the surgery is over," nodded the doctor. "I'll check for you."

"Thanks, ah, doc. Say, what's your name?" asked PJ.

"Dr. Preston. I'll get you some painkillers. You'll probably start feeling your hand in twelve hours." And with that the doctor went through a pair of swinging double doors, only to be replaced by Kathryn Byrnie, still dressed in her red and white foul weather gear. PJ saw a slight limp as she walked over to the exam table. Her eyes fell for a moment on the bloodied man on the next table, and then she looked at PJ.

He slipped off the table and stood as she gently put her hand on his forehead, her eyes filled with concern.

"How you doing?" she asked. She had a momentary bout of embarrassment when she realized they had never really touched before. It passed, helped by PJ's smile.

"A few nicks, but I'll be fine," he lied. He didn't feel so hot. He reached up with his right hand to lightly touch her arm. He was mildly surprised, but pleased at her concern.

"I don't know about Jester," he said.

"He's in surgery. We saw them wheel him past the doorway," she said, holding his gaze for a moment and then pointing with a wave of her hand down the hall to the right.

"How long have I been out?"

"Over an hour." She backed away and looked at the man in the next bed, then quickly turned back to look at PJ.

"Dutch is here, too. He broke his arm. It's in a cast already. Lenny, too. The rest of the guys are still at the boat. They are all pretty shaken up by this thing. Lenny's got a big bump on his head, but he'll be all right."

"Maybe knock some sense into him," PJ laughed weakly.

"Why would anyone shoot at us, PJ?" she asked, her eyes wide with anger and confusion.

"I haven't the foggiest idea, Kathryn." He looked down at his bandaged hand and saw the bridge looming over the tilted deck. He looked up at her. "It had to be from the bridge."

"Yes, the police are saying that, too. They've already questioned most of us, even talked with Stick Ketchum and his crew," she said quickly. "God, the boat is a mess, PJ! Both of them. The police found three bullet holes. *Sally Goose* lost the whole rig...no one can believe what happened...!"

She stopped. The words were rushing out of her much too quickly and the adrenalin was starting to pump again, just like it had when the two boats collided.

PJ lightly touched her elbow, as if to say everything will be all right, though he didn't know exactly what it was that was going to be all right.

"Let's go find out about Jester," he said quietly and led her through the double doors. The shots in the middle of the bay had spawned a terrible feeling of insecurity in his mind. His eyes were alert as they left the emergency room.

Dr. Preston gave PJ some pills and a prescription, and then directed them to a third floor waiting room. In the elevator, PJ and Kathryn stood quietly. He leaned back on the wall, staring at the floor, lightheaded. In the small cubicle, the smell of the hospital, of sickness and death, overwhelmed his thoughts.

He remembered when his father had died. PJ was only eleven. His mother had been working only three months for Jester at Fast Car Caravan when the news reached them.

Regret to inform you. Phantom shot down over the Mekong Delta. Commander James Patrick McDonough died a war hero. No hospitals, no blood, no body. Just two Navy officers at the door of their Mystic home.

He felt the loss again, that emptiness that stops hope in its tracks. There is only now and only nothing. He remembered how Jester had stepped in to fill that void. Jester designed and built race cars and PJ fell easily into the world of motors, chassis setups and speed. And Jester fell easily into their family.

In high school, they built a go-kart from scratch. It was a simple metal frame with a suspension and a motorcycle engine. To PJ, it was an Indy car. He spent hours racing it around the parking lot of Fast Car Caravan, lost in his world of races and rallies, swerving around potted plants he used for turning marks, the plants taken from the front office when his Mom went to lunch.

Jester watched him drive with amusement that quickly turned to keen interest. PJ's touch on the controls was evident from the beginning. One afternoon, Jester presented him with a set of orange cones to replace the plants. PJ reacted as if he had received the keys to Indianapolis. Mrs. McDonough was also pleased.

PJ thought about calling his mother and the office, about his boat and his crew and about Jester. He wasn't a religious man, but at one point felt a strange sense of regret he didn't believe in a higher being to whom he could direct prayers.

They sat in the waiting room. He half listened to Kathryn recount her first meeting with Jester, his eyes focused on the bloodstains on his boating sneakers.

"At first, I thought he was some dirty old man who had followed me to lunch and he then he plops down this photo of a sleek car and then a drawing of *Poly Rocket* and he says, 'Does any of this turn you on?' I looked up at him with that shock of white hair and that intense look in his eyes and was about to call the cops. But, then I looked at the photos and they were just great! I *was* turned on... by the lines, the way they gave off a feeling of speed even standing still."

PJ allowed himself a small smile thinking of Jester's irrational exuberance when he became passionate about a project. Coupled with his hirsute continence, it had frightened more than one.

"He pulled out a chair, sat down and said, "I'm going to change your life...."

The last word trailed off in mid sentence and PJ looked up, only to see a doctor he didn't know. Dr. Preston was standing next to him.

He was acutely aware of Kathryn's hand lightly touching his leg. He knew immediately and closed his eyes. He wished he could close his ears as well.

"Mr. McDonough, I'm Dr. Hodge, Chief of Surgery. We did everything we could."

Kathryn let out a small gasp.

"The bullet severely damaged arteries around the heart and we just couldn't keep up with the bleeding. I'm terribly sorry. Jester died just a few moments ago on the operating table."

PJ wanted to crawl into a corner, pull the covers over his head and dream about race cars and sailboats. He stood up abruptly and looked at the doctor. He was unsteady for a moment as the blood was slow to reach his head. He blinked his eyes real hard, and then took a deep breath, forcing himself still.

"Did he drown?"

"No. He was breathing right up to the last. His heart kept pumping, but we just couldn't contain the blood. I'm very sorry."

"Thank you, Doctor. Dr. Preston," he said, nodding toward the two. He felt like stone.

Then he started walking.

"PJ?" he heard Kathryn call after him, but he ignored her.

"Mr. McDonough!" he heard Dr. Preston, but did not turn.

He pushed through the nearest Exit door and stumbled down the steps, moving faster, taking them two at a time. He didn't hear the door open and close above him or Kathryn's call.

"PJ! Wait!"

He needed air, he needed sunshine, he needed to be free from the confines of the stinking hospital. His mind was numb. Then that spiral of black smoke appeared, reminding him of another hospital of death so far away and so long ago.

Jester's face flashed through his brain in a flood of images. A warmth filled PJ as suddenly as if someone had turned a switch. The quick smile, the wild white hair, the soft spoken, but strong words of encouragement, and guidance. The solid touch of his hand on PJ's shoulder, the gleam in his eyes, the love of a friend.

He reached the lobby, burst through the stairway door, startling those milling around, and headed for the main entrance. Dutch and Lenny stood in a circle by the wall with some of Ketchem's crew, but he didn't stop. He ignored their looks. He heard, but did not respond to Kathryn's call as she came out of the same doorway several seconds behind him.

His friends started to follow him into the sunshine. His head throbbed and his heart pounded as he crossed the city street, dodging cars. He turned east toward the waterfront, horns honking in his wake, his eyes glazed.

He moved blindly along the pedestrian-clogged sidewalk. He was running now. Running away. But the faster he ran, the quicker he came to the reality. Jester is dead! his brain shouted, but he did not want to listen.

He was weak from his own bloodshed and trauma. His head was filled with a rhythmic pain. His breath came in gasps. After many blocks he found himself at the waterfront, the Bay Bridge to Oakland overhead. He slumped against a thick round piling, his flight useless. He remembered Jester's last moments on the sailboat.

"I hope you're right," Jester had said as they decided to hug the shoreline. "So do I," PJ had replied and they shared that look they had shared so many times before when they had made a choice, taken a chance and hoped it would pay off.

"You're making trees!"

The tears broke free at that moment as he gave in to the gut wrenching reality. Jester was dead. And he sobbed like a child, his anguish dripping into the water, their playground, suddenly and mysteriously turned into a killing ground.

~~~

CHAPTER FOUR

P J awoke with a start, his body stabbed by pain. A nightlong battle with his dreams had ended with him rolling on his bandaged hand. He slipped groggily out of bed and swallowed two pills from Dr. Preston, hoping they would quell the hurt.

The dreams had left him sweaty and disoriented. Or was it the pain? He was awake now, but the images lingered as fading scenes from a silent movie. Monstrous waves tossed and turned him on a confused sea and a black spiral of smoke beckoned from the horizon. A signal of refuge? He could not go there. And who was the white-haired man standing knee-deep in white powder flashing metal in his hand?

He stood unsteadily in front of the hotel room mirror and remembered pleasant images that lingered as well - sunlight on snowy mountain peaks, waterfalls and the face of Kathryn Byrnie. She also had been a part of the night illusions and her dark, lithe form had stirred him.

San Francisco Bay filled his hotel window. The sunshine made it a bright postcard picture. The clock read twelve noon, Sunday. He had slept for fifteen hours! Then he remembered.

Jester was dead!

He sat back down on the bed, his will to move, even stand, suddenly sucked from him. New images, these real and painful, rushed forward - the tears of the night before, the shock on the faces of his crew as they sat in the hotel, unsure what to do, unable to accept the missing white hair of their friend. The anguish of his mother on the phone was fresh in his ears. She and Jester had grown very close.

He knew he had to move. But he didn't.

The clock read 12:15 when a knock at the door stirred him. He opened it and faced two men, one in a leather overcoat and fedora, the other in a windbreaker with a large manila envelope in his hand.

The man in the leather coat flashed a gold shield from the San Francisco Police Department.

"Good morning, Mr. McDonough. I'm Lieutenant Josh Wingate, this is

Sergeant Russo." The lieutenant's eyes looked past PJ into the room. "Could we trouble you for a moment or two. I know this is a difficult time, but we would like to ask you some questions about yesterday's incident."

PJ sighed and stood aside, waving them in. He hadn't given much thought to the police.

The two entered, their eyes roving like cops, scanning the room. Russo stuck his head into the bathroom. Wingate moved toward the window and sat on the arm of a stuffed chair.

"I'm real sorry about the death of Mr. Miller," Wingate started. PJ nodded automatically. Condolences meant nothing to him at the moment.

"We shared a love of the water and sailing," Wingate continued, sounding congenial. "I do some buoy racing myself in a J-29. I followed the Fabulous Fifties in the magazines. He will be missed."

"Thanks," PJ said dryly. Nothing anyone could say would bring Jester back.

Wingate pulled a small notebook and pen from his coat pocket, looked right at PJ expectantly.

"So, maybe you can tell me what happened?"

PJ looked at the detective and spread his hands, the white bandage sweeping an arch through the room. He offered the detective a thin smile.

"Hey, Lieutenant, I don't know what happened, except someone shot at us, probably from the bridge, and my friend is dead."

"You were Mr. Miller's partner, weren't you?" Wingate asked.

"Yes. Fast Car Caravan. We build engines in Connecticut. I own a third of the business."

"This morning's paper suggests you get control of it now. Is that right?" Wingate asked.

"Yes, I do," PJ nodded, realizing that fact himself for the first time since the shooting. "Well, most of it." Jester's real son, Harold Miller, would inherit half of Jester's portion of the business. PJ would get the other half and hold 72% of the stock. The long suppressed feeling of hate toward Harold suddenly surfaced along with an image of the nattily attired bureaucrat. Just as suddenly, the feeling was gone, evaporated like a midday cloud. It all seemed trivial in the face of Jester's death. PJ forced himself to focus on Wingate.

"What makes you think the shots came from the bridge?" Wingate asked. "Did you see any movement, a puff of smoke, a color... anything?"

"Where else could it be from? We were practically right under it." PJ paused for a moment trying to remember the details.

"I didn't see anything. I didn't really know we had been shot until I saw where the bullets had ripped Jester's jacket. And my hand," he added, holding it up as evidence. Wingate nodded and wrote in his book. Then he looked up.

"Mr. McDonough, do any of your crew members like to get high?" The question caught PJ by surprise.

"High? On Drugs? Jeez, what is this?" he said, standing up. He felt lightheaded and steadied himself against the desk.

"We have reason to believe the shooting might have a drug connection," Wingate said matter of factly.

"Pardon me, Lieutenant, but that's crazy!" PJ laughed. Wingate's serious expression didn't change.

"There are no drugs on my boat," PJ said calmly, trying to figure out where Wingate was going with his questions. "I am not aware of any. These people are my friends. Maybe you can explain what you mean!"

Wingate took the manila folder from Russo and pulled out an 8 x 10 black and white photo.

"Do you know either of these men?"

Wingate gave the photo to PJ and watched his reaction.

PJ saw two men standing in what appeared to be a marina parking lot. The taller, thin-faced man was facing the camera, his eyes hidden under a pair of wrap around sunglasses and a Giants' baseball cap. He wore a suede jacket and a white turtleneck. Tufts of black hair spilled from under the cap and onto the back of his turtleneck. A scraggly beard covered his chin, but his upper lip was clean-shaven.

The other man was smaller, with short hair and a thin mustache, and a very prominent nose. He appeared to be explaining something to the taller one.

"No idea," PJ answered honestly after studying it.

"Does the name Carlos Quintaro mean anything to you?" asked Wingate.

"Quintaro? No, nothing," said PJ. "Who are these people?"

"The little guy's name is Rogo Alvarez Esteban," explained Wingate pointing at the shorthaired man in the photo. "Know the name?" PJ shook his head.

"Why are you tailing him?" he asked.

"He's a Colombian, a shipping broker. Let's say his activities have attracted our attention recently," Wingate volunteered.

"He's a drug smuggler?" PJ asked Wingate.

"Maybe."

"Who's the other one?"

"Brett Lesco."

It was Sgt. Russo speaking for the first time.

"Ex-Marine Corps. A specialist in the elimination business. He's a nasty one."

"A hit man?" asked an incredulous PJ.

"An assassin, Mr. McDonough," Russo corrected. "This guy *likes* to kill people from long range and beat an easy getaway."

"Why hasn't he been arrested?"

"No one has been able to catch him," was Russo's simple reply. Wingate reached into his pocket and withdrew a bullet still in its casing.

"Know what this is, Mr. McDonough?" Wingate asked.

"A bullet," PJ shrugged. "I don't know, for a high-powered rifle? It's not M-16 issue."

"It's a 7.62 mm match round, the kind used by military snipers. It was found on the bridge along with this."

He produced a folded piece of paper. It was a magazine photo and story about the Great Bay Series. A hole had been torn in the middle of the face in the photo, but PJ quickly recognized the white shock of hair that was Jester's.

Russo took the bullet from PJ, and the photo from Wingate, placing the bullet through the hole. He held it up in front of PJ.

"Sniper's calling card," Russo explained. "Traditionally, a sniper leaves a fresh bullet on the body. Unsettles his buddies. You know, 'next one's for you'. One of our men found this, bullet in photo, on the bridge."

PJ nodded slowly. He had heard of the tradition while in the Navy. Russo's words only confirmed what he already knew, but he still didn't understand. Seeing his friend like that sent another stab of pain into his heart. He pushed the photo away and sat back on the bed.

"Why would someone want to kill Jester?" he asked simply.

"That's the question of the day, Mr. McDonough," Wingate sighed. "Lesco's been seen in the last two years, in Miami, Houston and New York. At first, he was just a face next to others under surveillance. But, one of the guys at DEA noticed every time Lesco showed up in a photo, someone nearby showed up dead a few days later, shot from a long distance."

"The DEA's looking for this guy?" PJ interrupted.

"Yes," Russo answered after a pause, then nodded for Wingate to continue.

"One of the victims was a key witness in the trial of a cocaine dealer in Miami, shot through a window fifteen stories up at the Fountainbleu. Another was a drug dealer, taken out at an amusement park. No loss there, right? And the third was a New York banker visiting the Hamptons. Two shots in the head on the beach. Calling card photos like this one were found nearby in each case," said Wingate. He held the bullet and photo up, waving it at PJ.

"He's killed others," added Russo. "And now Mr. Miller is shot and killed in the middle of San Francisco Bay." He picked the photo out of Wingate's hands and brought over to PJ.

"This photo was taken two days ago at the Sausilito town docks. That's Lesco with the beard. He's been in town, and I'm betting he's the triggerman. That's why we came to see you."

"So, once again, Mr. McDonough," Russo asked. "Do you know of any possible connection between your crew and drugs? I have to ask you, was Mr. Miller involved in something?"

PJ's head was throbbing now.

"You son of a bitch!" PJ said angrily. He knew he would have popped Russo if he wasn't a cop.

"Jester was clean, damn it!"

Jester was not involved with drugs. PJ would not allow himself the thought. Maybe someone on the crew? Unlikely. He had sailed with them for years, to Bermuda and back, up and down the East and West coasts. They were his friends. He knew their habits.

Except Kathryn Byrnie. They met only a week ago, at the start of the Great Bay Series. She brought impeccable credentials to Fast Car Caravan. She had been impressive on the sailboat. He liked her.

"Lieutenant, Sergeant. Let me make it real clear to you. There are no drugs in this picture. My crew is clean. It has to be something else."

"Well, maybe, Mr. McDonough," Wingate said, closing his notebook.

"Understand, we will be checking out your people anyway, just in case."

Russo zipped up his windbreaker and stood up.

"Mr. McDonough, keep your eyes open, okay? You may have been a target as well. I know this guy Lesco. He doesn't like to miss."

"This all seems very unreal, Sergeant," said PJ. "Drugs, murder? I'm having trouble believing it."

"Mr. McDonough, I've counted enough kilos and enough bodies to know the two often go together. It's a deadly game and a very real game. Human life means nothing to these people in the face of tens of millions of dollars."

"So, who's Quintaro? What's his connection with this?" asked PJ.

"Don't know, exactly," Russo sighed, feeling the frustration one gets from chasing clouds. "Another Colombian. He owns the shipping company that employs Esteban."

"Where's the connection with drugs?" PJ asked.

Russo just looked at him blankly and shrugged. "Well, I'm sure your aware of Colombia's reputation. We're working backwards from Esteban. We believe the two have been in contact."

"That's enough, Sergeant," Wingate stopped him, flipping shut his notebook. "Thanks for your time, Mr. McDonough. When are you planning to head back east?"

"Tomorrow," PJ said numbly. "They're preparing Jester's body today. I'll be flying him back tomorrow."

"You're a pilot?" Russo asked.

"I am. All of the crew fly, most have their own planes. Lenny leases a couple of Citations for his sporting goods distribution outfit," PJ answered.

"Lenny?" Wingate asked, flipping through his notebook. "Cain, right? Who else is a pilot?"

"Stoney Bullard. He works for Grumman. Dave restores bi-planes and flies them. Ray's got a small Cessna. And Kathryn. She has a commercial license, lots of hours, no plane."

"A boat load of pilots," Russo said with a smile.

"Sailboats and airplanes need air," PJ said.

"Any of them made flights out of the country recently?" Wingate asked. PJ looked at him for a moment. He didn't like Wingate's tone.

"I don't believe any of them have made the kind of flights you're thinking of, Lieutenant," PJ said flatly.

"Well, I hope not, Mr. McDonough," Wingate answered, closing his notebook again. "How can we reach you after tomorrow?"

PJ fished a business card from his wallet on the dresser and wrote his home number under the office number.

"I'll be there late Monday," he said, handing the card to Wingate. "I hope you'll call if you find out anything."

"We will. Thanks again for your time," Russo said. "We're real sorry for your loss." And the two left.

PJ wandered back to the window and watched a large freighter approaching the U.S. Navy Supply Depot on Yerba Buena in the middle of the bay. He found himself questioning his friends' integrity, and then hating the two cops for planting that seed. He took it personally, as if suspecting them of drug smuggling was a slap at his own judgment. There's no way....

The phone rang, its loudness surprising him.

"PJ, what do we want to do about *Poly Rocket*?" Dutch's voice was asking.

"Jeez, Dutch! Let's just sink it," PJ answered sourly.

"I know, PJ. I feel the same way." He paused for a moment. "The crew will be splitting to the four corners later today. If you want to get it ready for the Carib next month, we have to do it in the next few hours."

Sailing was the last thing on his mind, but he knew the *Poly Rocket* project had taken on a life of its own. The boat was a test bed for Fast Car Caravan's new plastic technologies. Jester had developed many of the composite materials that went into the million-dollar racer. It was part of PJ's future.

The final sailing regatta of the Fabulous Fifties season was scheduled for Tortola, BVI, in three weeks. The Fifties were designed to be dismantled and shipped by truck or freighter to the next venue. It was quicker and safer than trying to sail them across open ocean.

"Dutch, I guess we have to do it," PJ sighed. "Jester would want us to sail hard. We still have a chance to win the championship."

"He would, the old goat," Dutch answered with affection.

"Okay, let's do it. Alert the crew. About an hour."

PJ hung up and sat for another few minutes, trying to remember how he had dealt with death in the past. Not well, he thought.

After his customary cold shower, he dried himself with one hand in front of the mirror. The bulky bandage on his left hand made it difficult to move his fingers. The pills had not killed all the pain. The gash above his left eye was red and puffy, the black threads garish on his tanned face. His brownish-red hair was a tangle, spilling over his ears, but his blue eyes were clear. There were a few scrapes on his shoulders and upper back.

He scratched a faded scar on his right thigh out of habit. It was a decade old memory from a bayonet accident during an intense Navy SEAL training exercise. That hadn't been his fault either, he thought.

He dressed as fast as his wounds would allow, applying a fresh bandage to his head, and left for the marina. His mind flip-flopped between self-pity over the loss of Jester, and avenging Jester's death. For now, self-pity was easier, since he had no idea where to begin in the other direction. But something Russo said gnawed at the back of his brain, just beyond his grasp.

~~~

CHAPTER FIVE

W hen PJ arrived at the St. Francis Yacht Club Marina, *Poly Rocket* was gently swinging from the end of a crane. Christina "Crash" Clarke was at the controls, her touch honed as a young girl in her father's marina. Some of the crew were scattered on and around the sleek racer, carefully guiding her with long dock lines to the cradle on land.

Crash's shapely five-foot body, blue eyes and pixie blonde hair hid her tomboy nature very well. She was a physical woman who enjoyed the hands on work of sailing as much as she enjoyed off-road motorcycle racing. Only twenty-four, her experience with boats and bikes was well beyond her age. She had joined PJ's crew when she was nineteen and quickly assumed a paid position as the team's boat manager. *Poly Rocket* was the third machine they had campaigned since she came on board. PJ and the crew followed her lead when it came time to ship the boat to the next race.

Dutch was on deck, the blue cast on his left forearm an instant reminder of what had happened in the bay. Dave, Stoney and Ray were on the pier, leading the hull toward the cradle with long dock lines. Mickey was taking pictures.

The damage from the collision with *Sally Goose* was limited to the bow pulpit, which now appeared as a twisted sculpture, and the underside. The red and white hull was etched with blue paint where she had climbed up on *Goose's* deck.

"A two day fix, at most, PJ. And maybe ten grand," came a voice behind. PJ turned to see Lenny walking from a cargo container with *Poly Rocket Sled Shed* painted on the side in colorful red and yellow graphics. It housed a traveling workshop and storage area.

"Looks like it might take you longer," he added when he saw PJ's bandages. Lenny forced a smile from under an old military helmet, faded captain's bars on the front.

"Maybe never," PJ answered, throwing a mock salute with his bandaged hand. "Expecting a war?"

"Snipers," Lenny said, half-serious. His remark hung in the air as they

---

watched the boat settling into the cradle.

"I can't believe he's gone, PJ. We lost a good man," Lenny said after a few moments.

PJ looked right at him. "We did, Lenny. A good friend."

Jester's unconscious body floating in the water was a haunting vision that would stay with them forever.

"Any leads?"

"The police stopped by about noon. I think they have a suspect in mind. A hit man who might be connected to a Colombian drug dealer," PJ said. He could hardly believe the words he was speaking.

"A hit man?! Drugs?" Lenny looked at PJ. "What the hell are you talking about?"

"I don't really know," PJ answered. The two of them just looked at each other.

"Sheeet! With this bunch of boy scouts?" Lenny said, pointing toward the crew, "Beer smugglers, maybe, but drugs! Sounds like the cops are snorting up in the evidence room."

Kathryn walked up and joined them. Her hair was tied back in a ponytail showing off her dark face, high cheekbones and the black pupils set in her white eyeballs. Her shorts revealed black and blue patches around her knees.

"Afternoon, guys," she greeted them both. "We thought you were going to sleep all day," she smiled gently at PJ. She flashed her slightly crooked smile again, more open to the left side of her face.

"I almost did," he started playfully, but it was forced.

Every morning during the past week his first glimpse of her had been special. Her appearance momentarily suspended his thoughts and he found his entire being focused on her. This morning was no different, and he thought how she had moved through his dreams the night before. But the reality of this morning was different and brought him back quicker.

"Nightmares kept me tossing and turning. I woke up at noon and found the nightmares were real," he said slowly.

Most of their tears had been used up the night before, but he put his arms around her in a friendly hug. His face briefly touched her hair and the light scent of her perfume reached his nose.

"Did I hear you say hit man?" she asked when they separated.

"It's pretty off the wall stuff. Colombians, hit man. I don't know what to believe. Jester's dead. It's hard to find much else that matters."

The three of them fell quiet, until PJ broke the silence.

"Lenny, let's check out the rig before the boat goes south. You had it strung pretty tight yesterday."

"Tight is right, baby!" sang Lenny, glad to be talking about something else. "We had that sucker tuned to C sharp!"

He made a twisting motion with his hand, emphasizing the tension on the composite plastic rods that kept the seventy-five foot mast upright. "I've already been up the stick and found a cracked strut. It's all coming out for a close up eyeball, Peej."

Lenny headed off with a wave toward Crash in the crane. PJ shook his head in admiration. He knew Lenny ran his sporting goods company with the same breezy attitude he displayed on the boat. His company was called Fun and Games Unlimited, a name perfectly suited to his personality.

"We still have life and it must go on," he said softly to himself as he watched Lenny and Crash talking.

"What?" Kathryn said.

He looked at her for a long moment before he answered.

"It was something I heard Jester say once or twice. We have life and it must go on."

"Yeah, it must," she agreed. She let out a sigh. "It's hard, but it must." They started walking toward the boat.

"So, how are you feeling today?" he asked.

"I've got some awful bruises on my knees and ribs, but mostly I feel kind of empty. Sad," she said, looking at his forehead. "How's your head and hand?"

"A constant dull ache, but nothing serious," he dismissed it.

She put her hands into her pockets and looked toward the Golden Gate Bridge, visible through the high fog moving quickly into the bay.

"What did you mean about a hit man a moment ago?" she asked.

"Police theory. But I'm not ready to play cops and robbers right now. Let's get the boat ready, okay?" said PJ grabbing a nearby ladder and propping it against *Poly Rocket's* side. He felt the need to do something constructive, to move.

"Sure," she answered.

He stood aside and gestured up with his thumb. She smiled a "Thanks!" and climbed. PJ followed. They went forward and joined Dutch at the bow, surveying the twisted bow pulpit.

"Pretty tough stuff, yes?" said Dutch.

"It's called silitonium. We first used it for the oil pan on the Miller. Your cast is made out of it." PJ looked at his long time sailing buddy. "You holding up?"

"Oh, hey, doin' just fine, Pete. Put me in, coach. Throw me the ball!"

PJ smiled. Dutch was never down, he thought. No, he corrected himself. He had seen him down the night before, when they had wept for Jester. He seemed himself today.

Dutch and PJ had met as teenagers when they enrolled in the same sailing class at the Mystic Seaport. Through their twenties, while PJ was in the Navy and then racing cars, and Dutch was catching footballs, they would try to get away once a month to race each other in Sunfish and Lasers. They were tireless in their efforts to beat the other.

Dutch had a short but splendid career in the NFL, catching 101 passes in 75 games. Tired of the weekly pounding, he quit the game, spent a year with a New Zealand sailboat crew in the Whitbread Around the World Race, and then settled down in Connecticut to open up a restaurant in New Haven. He called it *Dutch*. That was ten years ago. He had since opened three others in Mystic, Newport and Provincetown.

Six feet tall, as tall as PJ, blonde hair and mustache, trim and ready to run, he liked to think of himself as the fastest restaurateur in New England.

"Unless you, Stoney or Dave can bend this thing back into shape, let's replace it," said PJ looking at the bent pulpit.

"Why? It's still solid," Dutch asked, giving it a kick. "It will make the competition think twice before they try to cross tacks with us."

"Are you doubting the strength of America's biggest small man!" came the voice of Stoney Bullard as he poked his head over the bow at their feet. He had climbed up the docking line used to guide the boat into the cradle.

With swift, sure movements, he grabbed the lower rail of the pulpit, reached up for the upper rail and hung from it. He fully expected his 150 pounds, most of it muscle, would move the silitonium back to its original shape.

"No way, Stoney!" laughed Kathryn.

Stoney did five quick chin ups, forcing his weight downward on each rep, but the bars didn't move. He looked at the immovable plastic as if it was the enemy, shrugged his shoulders and swung his leg up onto the deck.

"I must be getting old," he muttered, climbing over the rail.

"Stoney, you've always been old," said Dutch playfully.

"Yeah, Dutch, about as old as your last original thought," he snapped back with a grin cutting across his rugged face.

Stoney looked up at PJ's bandaged hand and head and then square in the eye.

"You steered a hell of a race, PJ, right up until the point where those bullets started flying. You got any ideas why?

"I haven't got much to go on, Stoney," looking at his friend. "Can we talk about it after we clean up the boat?"

"Yeah, well, I'm not so sure how safe it is right now," Stoney said, his eyes darting around the marina. Docked boats, parked cars and people walking in the nearby park made for a busy background, and easy hiding places.

"We sitting ducks, PJ. Jester didn't get killed for no reason. Something you guys are involved in pissed someone off. That is sure," he said seriously.

"Jeez, Stoney!" PJ snapped. PJ didn't want to think about it. But part of him believed Stoney was right.

"Just thinking out loud, PJ," Stoney continued. He looked at Dutch and Kathryn. They were both looking around, suddenly aware of how open they were standing on top of the sailboat's deck.

"I suggest you cover your six. Maybe they come back for you," Stoney finished with a steely look at PJ.

PJ couldn't help smiling at his diminutive friend. Stoney spoke the lingo of a fighter pilot where the enemy's location was always referenced by the face of a clock. It was right in character for him to point toward some unknown enemy, especially from behind. He tested planes for Grumman, but PJ knew the shadowy rumors of his military past. The crew often joked that Stoney was their resident spy. He played along, without giving away too much.

"Anyone working around here or do you want some coffee and donuts sent over!" interrupted a voice from above. They all turned to see Lenny hanging from a harness on the crane, swinging toward the mast.

"This thing is coming out. I suggest you undo the turnbuckles or we'll lift the whole rig!" he yelled.

"Now, Dutch, let's see if you remember anything I taught you!" Stoney

---

said. He grabbed Dutch by his good arm and led him away, leaving the suggestion of danger hanging in the air as if it wasn't his problem any longer.

"You never taught me anything worth remembering, you half baked flyboy!" Dutch said, following him.

PJ joined them, grabbing a screwdriver. He bent to the fumbling task of disconnecting the starboard mast shrouds from the deck with one good hand, while they worked on the port side. He found himself looking up every now and then at the surrounding grounds and the water. He was glad he was bending down. Soon, however, the routine of dismantling the boat occupied his full attention.

Kathryn ducked below decks and unplugged all the electronic wires that connected the instruments on the top of the mast with the navigation equipment below. Ray, Dave and Mickey hauled the bulky sail bags from the boat to the container. When the shrouds were loose, Crash maneuvered Lenny close enough to attach thick nylon-web straps to the mast and then she gently pulled the carbon fiber stick out of the boat, laying it on the ground next to the cradle.

In less than an hour, the broken strut had been replaced and the mast secured to the cradle. The container was packed and *Poly Rocket* was ready for her 4000-mile trek to the next race in the Caribbean. PJ finished off the task by covering the winches with custom-made canvas.

"Let's get everyone together," he yelled. "Up here!"

"Crew meeting!" yelled Dutch, flashing a case of beer he had stashed below.

The entire crew climbed the ladder and assembled in the cockpit. It was like their usual pre-race meetings, but this time they were out of the water. And they were missing one man.

"Mickey, are you going to write this up?" PJ asked as Mickey O'Mara snapped away with his camera.

"You bet, PJ," Mickey said seriously, clicking one final picture. "*Speed Machines* cover story, easy."

"Just print the facts, Mickey," PJ asked simply. He was used to publicity, both for his exploits on the water and on the racetrack, but the glare of publicity suddenly seemed very intrusive.

"Always," Mickey said, putting away his camera, sounding as if his pride was hurt.

"And what are the facts, PJ?" asked Dave Bender.

Crash knocked over a beer, spreading a small puddle on the deck just as Dave sat in it. He jumped up with a curse and picked her up as if to throw her overboard. At six-five, 265 pounds, Dave was the crew giant. His big hands and explosive power made him a powerful force at the handles of the coffee grinder.

The crew started hooting and hollering, half wanted to see Crash fly, the others wanted the meeting to begin.

"Hey, she's a lady! You got no class or what?" yelled Stoney.

At Dutch's urging, Dave finally put Crash down on the deck.

"You're lucky I love you, you big lug," she yelled at Dave. "Or I'd kick your lights out."

"Yeah, lucky me, Crash. I forgot what a sweetie you are," Dave answered while the rest of the crew laughed.

"Knock it off!" PJ barked. The crew was not used to hearing him yelling on the boat and they settled down immediately.

PJ looked around. He searched for the words, where to begin. He didn't want to be there, but he was their leader. He was the guy who had brought them to this place. He looked in each of their eyes, making contact, one by one. Then he raised his can of beer into the air.

"Jester was our friend. He's dead, but I know he lives. Inside each of us. Take his spirit, his love of life, his love of sailing and make it part of your own." He drank heartily, the cool liquid washing down his throat.

"Jester!" said Dutch and followed suit. The rest of the crew did the same with a word or two in honor of their dead friend. A simple eulogy to punctuate their grief. They, too, drank the beer as if it would ease their pain.

They tossed their empty cans into the cockpit. They fell on the deck with a hollow clink, followed by the pop of new cans being opened and the crew settled down again. Stoney and Lenny did not open second cans. Both were flying out that night.

"I think Stoney sees more shadows that all of us," PJ started again, bringing a few snickers from the crew, "but he may be right. We may be in some danger. I have no idea why Jester was murdered." The word stuck in his throat. "The police seem to think he was the only target, but I just don't know."

Everyone shifted in their spots. The traffic noise from nearby Marina Boulevard seemed suddenly louder, a reminder they were out in the open.

"Life goes on," PJ continued. "We grieve, but we keep living. We're bringing the body back tomorrow. Jester's funeral will be Friday. I know you will all be there. Lenny is flying back tonight and has room if you need a ride."

Dave, Kathryn and Dutch would be flying home with PJ tomorrow morning. Everyone else said they had their own transportation plan.

"I will be in the Caribbean next month," PJ said firmly. "Jester would have wanted that. We still have a good shot at the overall championship if we have a good week. *Poly Rocket* is still a test bed and there's more to learn."

"We'll kick some butt for Jester," Lenny said.

"Will it be safe in the Caribbean?" Ray asked.

"Ray, I don't know," PJ answered.

"So what if it isn't safe! We have to stick together in this and help PJ if we can."

It was Crash, speaking in a rare loud voice.

"Thanks, Christina," PJ said sincerely. He was the only one who called her by her given name. He felt close to the young woman, although he admitted she brought out a schizoid attitude in him. At times, she was an attractive young nymph, and at other times, she acted like a younger brother.

"I don't expect any of you to put anything on the line," he said, smiling at her. "We don't even know who we're fighting."

"So, why don't we try to find out?" Dutch asked. "I have no problem putting it on the line for Jester."

"Me neither," Mickey concurred.

"You're ready to take on drug dealers and assassins?" Ray asked.

Dutch just shrugged.

"Why not? Let's find out who's behind this and give them a little hell!"

Most of the crew nodded, a couple offered hearty agreement.

"What are you going to do, Dutch, serve them a batch of poisoned quiche?" Lenny's voice dripped sarcasm. He wasn't so sure. A half full beer can came flying across the deck as a response from Dutch.

"Serve this, joker!"

Lenny caught the beer in the shoulder and it sprayed Ray and Mickey sitting next to him.

"Hey, guys, come on!" PJ yelled above the din. "I'm angry for what happened to Jester. We're all angry, but for now, this is a cop thing."

"Lenny said this might have to do with Colombians, right?" Dave asked. PJ nodded.

"What about the mine?" Dave asked innocently.

The mine!

"Slug in a ditch!" PJ muttered. "Of course!" It had been gnawing at him since Wingate and Russo questioned him. The Miller Mine in Colombia. PJ thought of the chunk of Goshenite sitting on his desk in Mystic.

"What mine?" asked Dutch.

"The Miller Mine in Colombia, Dutch," PJ said excitedly. "I can't believe I didn't think of it sooner. Jester owns a mine in Colombia. It produces Goshenite for our engines."

"What the hell is Goshenite?" Ray asked.

"It's a crystal, like an emerald with no color," PJ answered.

"An emerald? For engines?" Dutch asked confused.

"Yeah. No. It's clear, no color. Right in the middle of developing the Miller, we were having problems with the hot spots in the engine. The plastics were melting under the heat. Jester found that a coating of treated Goshenite kept the engine core cool. He spent some time researching it and found a source in Colombia. Hell, I remember he was gone for two weeks and came back with a lease to an abandoned Colombian mine that was loaded with the stuff. We still get shipments every two weeks!"

That mine was Jester's little secret, thought PJ.

"How does that connect with drug dealers?" Christina asked.

"I don't know," PJ answered slowly, though his mind was racing. "But, that's surely a connection with Colombia." It had been sitting right there in front of him, but he hadn't looked beyond Jester's dead body.

"If the police are right," Mickey suggested.

"What would a drug dealer want with Goshenite?" Christina asked.

"Good question, Christina. It's basically worthless unless you're making plastic engines," PJ answered.

"Maybe they found a way to make it into a drug," Lenny said straight faced.

"Good, Len, keep it serious," PJ said sarcastically, as some of the crew snickered.

"But why shoot at Jester over a mine?" Dutch asked.

"I have no idea," PJ answered.

"PJ, I hope you figure it out, but I have to catch a plane home and cut some grass." It was Ray, the lanky grinder, who earned his living cutting lawns. The fact the lawns were on the estates that clung to the sandy cliffs of Long Island Sound made it a very comfortable living. He slid his thin frame off the low cabin top and headed for the ladder.

"I'll see you Friday at the funeral, PJ. Take care." He shook hands, disappeared down the ladder, and drove off in his rental car to the airport.

"What's next, PJ?" Dutch asked.

"I guess it's time I found out about that mine. It's somewhere in the mountains of Northern Colombia."

"I gotta catch a FedEx flight, Peej. I'm out of here, too," Lenny said, getting up and taking off the helmet he had been wearing. "I have to be in Boston tomorrow bright and early."

He was about to plop the helmet onto PJ's head but the white bandage stopped him. He shoved it into his hands instead.

"Stay low, friend," he said, looking right into PJ's eyes. "I'll be near a phone if you need me." PJ thought he saw Lenny's eyes begin to mist up.

"Gotta go," he said abruptly and left.

PJ watched him go. Mickey and Stoney left right after Lenny, heading for Los Angeles, Mickey's home.

"Soft pedal this, will you, Mickey?" PJ asked, hoping his bandaged face wouldn't appear on the cover of some sailing magazine.

"It's already news, PJ," Mickey answered and then paused. "I'll probably do a piece on Jester, say you expect to be in the Caribbean next month for the finals. Promise you'll let me know if you find out anything else before Friday?"

"Promise," PJ answered and they shook hands.

"Hey, Peej," Stoney whispered. "I was serious about covering your six. If you need some protection, or maybe information, let me know. I can make a few calls."

Stoney had a way of looking at trouble as if it were just another game to play and win. PJ half believed that if, in fact, he wanted an F-18, Stoney could get it.

"I don't know where the war is, Stoney," PJ said as he waved goodbye to his friend. "Not yet."

Kathryn and Dutch were cleaning up below decks and Dave and Crash

---

were closing up the container. Crash would accompany *Poly Rocket* and the workshop on the truck caravan to Florida with the other boats. She would catch a flight to the funeral at the end of the week.

Suddenly, PJ was alone on the deck, with his thoughts. Most of the crew seemed ready for a fight, but he wasn't sure where to direct their anger. Or his. However, he knew he was the one who would have to find out.

~~~

CHAPTER SIX

Carlos Octavio Quintaro laughed out loud. He was delighted with his country's war on drugs for it was sure to make him a billionaire. At least, so he planned. Flying cocaine right up the nose of the coastal watchdogs would be his greatest achievement as a smuggler.

His lanky, six foot two inch frame draped over a leather couch in the spacious upstairs office of his home outside Riohacha, Colombia. The sound of the blue green waters of the Caribbean drifted through the open doorway. Outside security lights illuminated the brown tiles of the back porch, the white wash stucco walls and a portion of the well-kept lawn of his villa. Beyond there was only the night and the sound of water lapping at the rocky coastline.

Quintaro suddenly jumped up, threw his right arm high in the air, and released the dozen photographs he had been studying. They fluttered around the room, floating every which way, some gliding out the doorway, others catching an air current and flying across the room to hit softly against the panes of glass that offered a floor to ceiling view of the water to the west and the Sierra Nevada mountains off to the south.

"*Fantastico!*" he shouted, laughing wildly as he strode onto the porch. He climbed atop the narrow ledge, balancing himself twenty feet above the ground, and stood with his arms outstretched, open to the dark sea as if beckoning all within his gaze to come and pay homage to his genius.

Sergeant Jairo Sanchez, a young soldier of the Colombian Army, dressed in civilian clothes, stooped to pick up the fallen photos. He found himself grinning at the outburst by the man known as Quintaro. To see him in such an expansive mood was rare. The sergeant had been to visit Quintaro on three other occasions, none as relaxed as this one. He plucked the last photo from its landing place behind a tall copper urn in the corner and followed onto the porch.

Towering over the soldier, white ruffled shirt open almost to the navel, face golden brown, wavy hair cascading behind his ears, as white as the perfect set of teeth that smiled broadly, Quintaro looked like a movie star. Sanchez thought a Colombian version of Errol Flynn. He smiled again in surprise at this unique moment.

"Jairo, you have brought me a grand day!" Quintaro beamed, jumping off the ledge and landing lightly a foot in front of Sanchez. He put his hand on the young soldier's face, a fatherly gesture, tapping him three times.

"You did well. The timing of your transfer to the photo recon unit has been perfect." He grabbed Sanchez by the wrist, raising up the hand that held the photos.

"It appears our Presidente is having success with his *Rapideros* at the expense of our friends to the south in Medellin and Cali." The word "friends" was spoken in such a way as to convey to Sanchez the exact opposite meaning.

"I knew this would happen. They have grown soft from their profits and are ripe for the picking." Quintaro nearly spat the last, then reached for an orange from a bowl on the table. His slender thumb punctured the skin and the round fruit disappeared in his hand. Quintaro's grin took on a look of menace, thought Sanchez as he watched the man squeeze the juices from the orange into his mouth.

"And to see our own labs in the Mesa de Yambi targeted for later this week means we have moved just in time. They will find insects, trees and animals. But, nooo cocaine!"

Quintaro drew out the last, clearly in a childish mood, full of the power of his plan. He loved the rush that came with playing on the wrong side of the law. It was the same feeling he had experienced forty years ago. He, a ten year old street urchin, had carried gold teeth through the dusty alleys of Bogota' for his undertaker uncle. He had been paid fifteen pesos for that task and another fifteen to keep it a secret. Pennies. But the shear thrill that flushed his body as he moved on his secret quest had hooked him for life.

He laughed again, a wide-open, hearty laugh, taken at the expense of someone else. From his pocket came a gold and ivory money clip with a large emerald set in the middle. He peeled off five one hundred American dollar bills, folded them lengthwise between his fingers and handed them to Sanchez.

"Here is something extra. Buy something nice for your beautiful wife, Rosalita and your bambino, Ana. They deserve it. Thank you for your work," he said sincerely, his green eyes looking directly into Sanchez's young face.

Sanchez felt the power of his gaze, as if Quintaro looked right into his soul. The Sergeant closed his hand on the money, but Quintaro did not let it go, offering instead a slight tug of resistance.

"Remember, no one must know that you came here. Ever." The tone of Quintaro's voice was no longer fatherly.

"Keep your ears and eyes open, contact me in the usual way if something of interest crosses your desk. Do you understand me?" The last spoken sharply. His green eyes seemed to glow and Sanchez thought for a fleeting moment they might burn a hole in his skin.

"Yes, jefe. I understand."

"Keep your mouth shut. Not a word even to your family."

Sanchez nodded and Quintaro let go of the money.

"Good, I know you will do well. Now, off you go. Bernardo will show you out. I have much thinking to do before it is time to sleep." He tapped Sanchez on the cheek one more time, turned and walked back onto the porch, humming an old Indian tune.

The sergeant pocketed the money. As if on cue, Bernardo Luis Quintaro, Carlos' brother, appeared at the doorway and led the young soldier out.

Small, but strongly built, Bernardo stood on the porch and watched Sanchez drive his rented Escort down the gravel driveway that looped through the grounds in front of the sprawling house. The two armed guards opened the iron gate and Sanchez drove through, turning onto the main road for the ten-minute ride to the Riohacha airport. Bernardo did not move from the porch until the sound of Sanchez's auto had been replaced by the sound of crickets in the surrounding trees.

On the way to the airport, Sanchez could feel the five folded bills in his pocket. It was a nice bonus in addition to the $5,000 he had already been paid for the recon photos. He needed the money and it had been well worth the risks he had taken. But as he drove on, intent on catching the last flight back to Bogota', he realized he could not rid his mind of the burning image of those green eyes of the man they called Quintaro.

The phone rang twice deep in the house before it was answered. Carlos was studying a flight chart of Florida and the Bahamas on the second floor when Bernardo buzzed him on the intercom.

"It's Simka," his brother voice said on the speaker.

"Good, good. I'll take it in my room."

He skillfully walked the dividers across the thin red line he had drawn along Florida's east coast, connecting West Palm Beach to Jacksonville. He jotted down the distance and smiled with satisfaction, in no hurry to answer the call. No harm in letting Rex wait a bit, he said to himself.

A full minute later, he walked into the next room and picked up the hand receiver sitting by his bed. He flipped a switch on a black box under the phone and then pressed the blinking light.

"Rex, my friend! Are you well?" he said with genuine enthusiasm.

"Don Carlos, I am very well. The news from San Francisco is also good," came the voice on the other end. It had a metallic sound, filtered through a scrambler in the basement.

"I'm happy to hear that. There were no problems?"

"A professional job. The subject is out of play," Simka answered after a slight pause.

"That is good, Rex."

Quintaro trusted Simka to get results.

"So, we can move tomorrow as scheduled, yes?" Quintaro asked

"Yes, Tuesday," Simka answered. "I expect a delivery early from Mario. Then we will move to the valley and set up operations. The weather is marginal, but I do not expect trouble."

"Rex, that is good news! I am pleased so far. And can we expect to be ready by Saturday?"

"Four days is pushing it, Carlos," Rex said.

"We must be ready by Saturday," Carlos answered firmly. "There are new customers waiting and we cannot disappoint them the first time."

"We will do it, Don Carlos."

"Good, good. Have you heard from Luis?"

"Yes, he is here now. He assures me the island is ideal. Supplies have already arrived and everything will be ready."

"Good, Rex. I trust it will happen. Julio and I will join you in three days."

With that, Carlos hung up. Bernardo stood in the doorway.

"Rex says the balance sheet will be brought up to date tomorrow," Carlos told his brother with a smile. "He will make the deliver here. It is the final three million from the New England shipment. I expect you will be here to receive it?"

Bernardo nodded.

"Good. I must go to Santa Marta for the day. We will have a clean slate when production commences in the valley."

"I am not so sure keeping all the cash here is a wise idea, brother," Bernardo said. "We might use it to open up that connection in Venezuela I spoke of last week. It might be a good time to take advantage of the unstable political situation."

"Bernardo! For the last time, NO! We will have many expenses in the next few days. We need the cash here," Carlos explained for the third time that day. "You should relax. There will be plenty of opportunity in the next three months for you to exercise your financial genius."

Bernardo was only two years older than Carlos, but they were very different. Bernardo was the nervous one, Carlos the cool one. Bernardo's nervousness led to temper tantrums that were more annoying than fearsome for those who worked with him. They knew that Bernardo would not hurt a fly.

Carlos seemed always to be in control, but his temper tantrums, rare as they were, sent chills through those around him, including his brother. At the far ends of his criminal network, where the stories of his temper had grown in the retelling, he was feared.

Yet, mostly, Carlos Quintaro was a charming man, civilized in his tastes, respected in the community. In the light of the public eye, he was a shrewd and generous businessman who had turned a small import-export company into QUIMEX, the largest shipper in Northern Colombia.

His respectability hid a dark side driven by greed, power and violence. QUIMEX was a grey web of legal and illegal practices, the ideal front for his growing network of smugglers and distributors.

Cigarettes, stereos, bicycles, refrigerators, diamonds and emeralds, marijuana and cocaine moved through his network. There was always someone, somewhere, who was willing to pay top dollar for merchandise difficult to buy on the open market.

Carlos learned that murder, kidnapping and intimidation were a necessary part of doing business, if only to protect his own life, as much as to stay out of jail and to expand his influence. He often left the dirty work to others more inclined to spill blood, but he did not hesitate when his turn came.

"Well, then. If you do not wish to discuss Venezuela I am going to bed, Carlos. Good night," Bernardo said, somewhat annoyed.

"Good. Sleep. I am expecting another guest shortly. Sleep well, Bernardo Luis. Soon you will be wealthier than even you can dream about! Hell, maybe you can buy Venezuela!" Carlos laughed after him and went back to his work.

Not long after, Carlos heard the high-pitched whine of jet engines. The noise drifted through the open office doors, barely loud enough to be heard over the pounding of the surf against the rocks.

Acarapi Gonzales, he thought. The "Cocoman" from Peru.

He imagined the smiling, hirsute man, wearing a traditional Peruvian stove hat, waving a gun in one hand and a machete in the other, looking right at home in the jungle. He shared the name of Peru's great aviator hero, Captain Jose Quinones Gonzales, but not the heritage. Quintaro had not seen him since the two of them had smuggled cigarettes into Peru from Panama seven years ago.

The whine grew louder as the plane approached from over the water. Quintaro walked out onto his second story porch to peer into the darkness. A grove of orange trees planted just behind the house blocked the view of his private airstrip about a half-mile to the north, but he could clearly hear the plane's engines working on final approach. A twin, he thought, trying to match the engine's whine to the sound of others he had heard. He couldn't find a match. He checked the wind and was pleased the prevailing southerly breeze was in fact blowing straight out of the south and down the runway he had designed and laid out himself.

"Ha, Mother Nature is behaving tonight!" His loud laugh underscored his confidence.

A strip of blue runway lights appeared, dots through the trees. Seconds later the landing lights of the jet appeared as three white dots in the sky. He was mildly surprised. From the quiet sound of the engines he had thought it was farther away.

The plane's approach dropped it behind the trees and out of his sight, but the squeal of tires and the roar of reversing jets signaled a safe landing. He took the porch steps two at a time to his waiting jeep and sped off along the dusty, tree lined road that lead to the airstrip.

Immediately, a second jeep pulled out from it's parking place in the shadows, where two of Quintaro's bodyguards had been waiting. They followed about 150 feet behind, the man in the passenger seat cradling an AK-47 in his lap. The driver's weapon of choice, a MAC-10 machine pistol, was within arm's reach in the backseat. Their job was to stick close to Quintaro and see that no harm came his way.

Quintaro glanced in the mirror at the following jeep. No one is sleeping tonight, he thought. That is good. The Cocoman could be a dangerous fellow if pushed the wrong way.

The airstrip was one of Quintaro's first projects when he moved to his ranch. In Colombia, air travel was the only way to go, especially for such a man who loved to fly. At five thousand feet in length, it could handle cargo planes and small jets. The paved strip was complete with a radio beacon, two hangars, a fuel storage area and a guard tower that doubled as a control tower from its vantage point next to the runway on the edge of cliffs above the Caribbean Sea. Just the kind of backyard facility a successful business man would have, one who cherished his desire to come and go on his own schedule.

The QUIMEX offices and the main shipping docks were in Santa Marta, as were other interests. The other commercial seaport was in Barranquilla. Both were only a twenty-minute commute by helicopter. Bogota', the seat of the Colombian government, was only two hours away in his personal plane.

It was a trip that took several days by car on Colombia's twisted and tortured highway network that snaked through the tropical jungles and over the mountains. Quintaro's need to access government officials could not wait that long and the telephone system was no way to conduct his private business.

Quintaro's jeep sped toward the plane as it swung around. The landing lights winked off as the jet stopped with a jerk on the tarmac in front of the two hangars. Painted in jungle camouflage, it was hard to see more than a silhouette. The red light on the high T-tail blinked, the red and green safety lights glowed from the ends of the overhead, sweptback wings.

Quintaro recognized the shape from photos in a flying magazine. It was a BAe 146 with four especially quiet Avco Lycoming turbojet engines. He smiled, as a horse trainer might when looking upon a champion thoroughbred for the first time. However, this beauty was more like a muscular mule.

Quintaro stopped twenty yards from the jet, his headlights shining on the door behind the cockpit. The jeep with his two bodyguards hung back. Both men jumped out and stood beside their vehicle, their automatic weapons cradled in their hands.

The engine turbines were still spooling down when the plane's door opened. A man dressed in military green poked his head out, looked around and then disappeared. A moment later a ladder unfolded from the fuselage and extended six feet to the pavement.

Quintaro could see the pilot watching him through the cockpit window. Two uniformed men, both with rifles slung over their shoulders, quickly exited the plane and stood next to the ladder, staring straight ahead. A small gesture from Quintaro brought his bodyguards quickly to his side, their weapons at the ready.

The blackness in the doorway now filled with a rather large man with scruffy hair and a beard, also dressed in military green, who, with some difficulty, eased his large bulk backwards down the ladder. On the ground, he turned to face Quintaro.

"Carlos?" The man shouted. He blinked into the headlights of the jeep and waved uncertainly.

"Gonzales?" Carlos responded, also with some uncertainly. He stood up in the jeep to look over the windshield. "Cocoman? Is that you?"

"In the flesh, jefe!"

"My god, the man is as hairy as ever, but he has doubled in size since I last saw him," Quintaro said in an aside to his bodyguards as he jumped to the tarmac and walked swiftly to greet his friend.

The man named Gonzales weighed 300 pounds and he lumbered forward to greet Quintaro. "Carlos, it is good to see you!" he said, a big smile on his lips. He threw arms around the taller man in a friendly embrace. Quintaro could smell rum on his breath.

"Acarapi, it has been a long time, no?" Quintaro said, accepting the big man's gesture with a friendly, though not quite as enthusiastic, embrace.

"Seven years, my friend. They have been kind to you. You look excellent! No more hacking through the jungle for el jefe, eh?" He let out a large laugh that echoed off the nearby hanger.

"It has been good for me," Quintaro admitted with a small smile. He patted the Cocoman on his belt buckle. "And you? Are you the new model soldier for Peru?"

"Air Force, my friend. Colonel Acarapi Gonzales, Peruvian Air Force at your service." The fat man gave him a jaunty salute that did nothing to help his military bearing. "Fortunately, I am no model for a soldier, jefe. But I can still drink these young turks under the table!" He waved at the two men standing by the ladder and his laugh boomed out again, filling the night. "Have you a drink for an old comrade?"

"Of course, Acarapi. We will drink and we will talk about the old days, but first, may I have a tour?" Quintaro asked, pointing at the plane.

"For a drink, I will show you my mother's underwear," Gonzales laughed. He turned toward the open door and yelled at the man who had first appeared in the doorway. "Sergeant, open her up for my friend!"

"Yes, sir," came the response and the sergeant disappeared into the plane. A moment later a hatch was unlocked with a *thunk* and a ten-foot section of the fuselage behind the wings rose up, revealing a large, empty cabin.

"British Aerospace has done it again. Whisper quiet jets, heavy payload and short take off and landing...everything a smuggler could want, no?" laughed Gonzales.

Quintaro stood quietly by the opening. Gonzales had a sly smile on his face. He watched Quintaro scan the expanse of the cabin quickly. Small lights along the walls illuminated the interior. Quintaro estimated it was sixty feet long and ten feet wide. Three rows of small metal wheels could be seen sticking up from the cabin floor to help ease the movement of cargo pallets along the cabin.

Gonzales began to chuckle softly, as if he had just revealed a great secret, and his laughter became louder as Quintaro looked at him and also began to laugh. They both shared the unspoken understanding that this plane would more than suit their needs.

Later, in the comfort of the main house, Quintaro and Gonzales shared a bottle of Arguardiente, the anisette laced elixir of Colombia, and talked of their smuggling exploits of the past. In an adjacent room, two pairs of bodyguards sat and waited for their bosses.

Quintaro stood with his back to Gonzales, as the fat man told a story about smuggling marijuana along the Amazon River. He listened with one ear while inspecting his own collection of knives, daggers and bayonets that filled two walls. The display was so extensive it could just as easily have been a museum exhibit on the history of hand-to-hand combat since the 15th century. Every type of blade was on display from a small palm knife to a Turkish yataghan with a double curved blade.

He absent-mindedly rubbed an old wound on his left shoulder that bothered him only when he drank too much Arguardiente. He gazed over his collection, taken by the pinpoints of light dancing on the still sharp blades. He reached for one particular machete, somewhat nondescript except for the deep gouges in the two-foot blade, and wrapped his fingers around the rough tape on the handle. He lifted it from the wall, feeling its comfortable weight.

"Cocoman," he interrupted Gonzales, quickly turning and in a smooth, back handed motion sent the sharp weapon flying toward his fat friend sitting on the couch telling his story.

"Do you recognize this?" Quintaro shouted playfully. The blade spun three times as it crossed the fifteen feet to Gonzales, making a sinister swishing noise. Gonzales was overweight, but his reflexes were sharp. With hardly a pause in his story, he shifted his glass and reached out with his right hand, catching the flying blade firmly on the black handle.

"Iquitos!" he shouted, naming a major port along the Amazon River just south of the Equator in Northern Peru. "I remember, jefe. The vines were as thick as table legs!"

With a wicked smile, he deftly twirled the machete in his hand and then swung it mightily over his head and brought it down on the coffee table in front of him, slicing through a leg as though it were butter. The bottle of Arguardiente hardly moved so clean was the cut. He looked at the blade in satisfaction, surprised himself at the ease in which it cut through the one-inch leg, and then threw it across the floor where it landed at Quintaro's feet.

The table teetered for a moment and Gonazales neatly grabbed the bottle of liquor as the table toppled on its stump of a leg.

"You bastard," Quintaro shouted at him, "that was an expensive table!" But there was little anger in his voice. Maybe a little surprise at the strength of Gonzales's swing. The fat man reached for the Arguardiente and poured himself another round, that low, chuckling laugh coming from his body.

"And it would have been expensive for you, jefe," Gonzales said through his growing laugh, "If my eyes and hands did not have their old form, eh! My men would not have left here unavenged if something happened to me."

Quintaro picked up the machete and replaced it on the wall. He walked to the fatman and grabbed the bottle from his hands and poured himself a glass of the clear liquid, finishing the bottle. He grabbed a fresh bottle from a small bar near the window before he sat down across from Gonzales.

"Do you remember how you felt when we moved that load of cigarettes right past the military roadblock in Iquitos seven years ago?" Quintaro asked.

"I thought we were going to die," Gonzales said solemnly, his brown eyes looking right into Quintaro's green eyes. Then a smile broke through his shaggy beard, "But I am named for luck. Acarapi! I was excited. And not by those pretty cha-chas who rode the mules in front of the army."

"It excited me, too, my friend. I love that feeling, that tingle when you know one slip, one shift of the wind, ha, a soldier's whim, will suddenly put you around a bullet or a blade."

"But I didn't like the jungle, jefe," Gonzales laughed. He shuddered at the memory of the thick green vines, the insects and the heat, oppressive and complete, overwhelming to the body and spirit. "That really scared me." He drowned the remains of his glass and reached for the fresh bottle.

"No more jungles for me, Cocoman." Quintaro was speaking quietly. "No more dirty risks. The time is right for the major score. A clean risk, but the biggest of your life."

"I'm listening," Gonzales said, watching the clear liquid fill his glass.

"As you know, our friends to the south in Medellin and Cali have their hands full," Quintaro started. "There has been much bloodshed, the military is in the jungle burning coca labs and there is turmoil in the distribution system due to new radar sites along the U.S. borders. Seizures are up. Costs are mounting. Markets are short on supply. Heroin is making a comeback."

"It is tough at home, too," Gonzales nodded. "The Presidente is cracking down on the guerrillas and the cocoa growers."

"I understand," Quintaro smiled. "There is much confusion and concern. That is why I want to expand immediately. To use the confusion to our advantage."

"You think that is wise?" Gonzales asked, his drink suspended at his lips. "Salazar will kill you." Juan Samuel Salazar was the head of the Cali drug cartel. He controlled much of the cocaine production in Colombia.

"Salazar is too busy fighting the government and the animals from Medellin. By the time he realizes something has happened, it will be too late."

"I am not so sure, Carlos," Gonzales shook his head.

"Acarapi, for years I have been happy with a small share of the pie. Big enough to make me a wealthy man, but not big enough to attract much attention. But I have been busy. I have made some useful contacts at home and in America. Europe is opening up. I want more. In fact, I want to take control of the market in the next three months. I want to flood the streets in America and Europe with a new, powerful strain of cocaine. No one will expect a player such as myself to attempt that now. That is why, my friend, I think the time is perfect."

"What about the government? I hear they are using U.S. spy planes to find the labs?"

"I have taken care of that," Quintaro smiled.

Gonzales looked at Quintaro for a moment. He saw a man who believed he would succeed.

"What can I do?" Gonzales asked.

"I want paste, my friend," Quintaro said, reaching for the bottle. "It must be Bolivian, the best and purest you can find. That is essential to my plan. I want 10,000 kilos a week for twelve weeks. I want it delivered here in that jet you have. One shipment a week, in and out in one hour. You land at my strip here and we unload. You return with cash."

Gonzales took a swallow of his drink.

"That is a lot of paste, my friend," he said.

"Can your plane handle it?"

"No problem, but it will cost."

"How much?"

Gonzales calculated the figures. He had been smuggling goods in and out of Peru for over twenty years. He and Quintaro had worked together on half a dozen lucrative deals involving a variety of products, including pot, cigarettes and auto parts. They both had a knack for delivery, concealment and schemes.

Cocaine paste was merely the latest product and the fat man had not received his nickname for any other reason than his ability to move it from the high mountains of the Andes. The paste was the first step in the production of street cocaine and crack. He had supplied most of the drug makers in Colombia at one time or another. However, his largest one time shipment to date had been 2000 kilos.

"300 a kilo, American dollars," Gonzales said, ending a thirty-second silence.

"250 is my only offer, friend," said Quintaro.

"No one has the delivery capacity that I do," reminded Gonzales. "Bolivian coca means higher transportation costs. Besides, there is the pressure at home. The American DEA is involved, things are tightening up."

"That is why I gave you such a good price!" Quintaro laughed. "I can make it easy for you," Quintaro continued. "How do you think your plane flew through Colombian airspace so easily tonight?"

Gonzales nodded slightly and took a sip. He had bought his way into a position of power inside of Peru, which allowed him easy access to the government's military assets, but he could not carry that power outside his country's borders. It was Quintaro who had obtained flight clearance over Colombia for Gonzales's jet.

"American dollars?" he asked to confirm the price.

"Of course. Two and a half million each week, in American cash loaded on the plane as soon as we unload the paste. Oh, yes, and it must be an exclusive contract between you and I. No one is to know what we are up to. Is that agreed?" Quintaro smiled, feeling the power of the Arguardiente and his position.

"That is thirty million by the New Year, my friend," Quintaro continued, pushing his deal. "A lot of money."

"And it is a fraction of what you will realize, my friend," said Gonzales.

"I, too, have many bills, Acarapi. I will have to take many risks.

Besides, you choose to do what you do best. I choose to do what I do best."

"It is enough for me, jefe," Gonzales smiled, lifting his glass toward the white haired man. "To the jungle, to the future, to early retirement, yes!"

"To the power of cocaine!"

"To the profit of cocaine!"

Quintaro raised his glass and the two old friends clinked their drinks in the night. The pact was sealed and Operation Snowmine was underway.

~~~

CHAPTER SEVEN

The Starship 4000 flew through the darkness, her black plastic body buried in clouds at 33,000 feet, looking like no other plane in the sky.

The long, cantilevered main wing sprouted from the rear of the fuselage in a thick delta shape before tapering off to thin, blade-like wings which abruptly went vertical at the ends, turned into tip sails that housed the dual rudders. It looked as if some giant had simply snapped the wing tips upright. The stubby tail section extending downward from the tapered cabin added to the unusual sight.

The two turboprop engines faced backward, each one housed in a slim nacelle attached to the main wing close to the cabin. The pair of five blade propellers spun steadily, pushing the plane forward at a speed of 400 knots.

Just forward of the cockpit, a canard wing swept back from each side of the bullet shaped nose, looking very much like a pair of eight-foot whiskers.

The brainchild of the design engineers at Beech Aircraft Corporation in Wichita, Kansas, this blacked out version was on loan to Fast Car Caravan and outfitted with plastic engines in the hope of improving the Starship's performance.

Inside the warm, quiet cockpit, PJ's bandaged head was back on the headrest. The persistent throbbing only magnified his sense of emptiness. He felt the presence of Jester in the back of the plane, the metal coffin in the aisle a haunting cargo. He tried to divert his mind by watching Kathryn fly the plane from the right hand seat.

Her fingertips worked confidently on the trim controls as she made small corrections in the turbulence. Her dark eyes reflected tones of blue, orange and green as they scanned an array of information displayed in colorful numbers and graphs on small television monitors.

She flipped a switch on the Global Positioning Satellite receiver to check their current position. GPS calculated latitude, longitude and altitude every second. It told her where she was on the planet, accurate to within fifteen feet. The digital readout read 70.5 miles from the Groton-New London airport in Connecticut.

"Starship 3-7-9, this is Boston Center. Switch to Providence Control, 119.7. Have a nice evening."

"Roger, Boston. Good night."

Her voice filled PJ's earpiece and he smiled. He found himself enjoying everything about her. The deep but soft timbre, soothing yet confidant, even sexy, brought life to the most basic radio chatter. Kathryn punched in the new frequency, then looked at PJ before opening her mike.

"Want to take her in?" she asked.

He rolled his head slightly on the headrest.

"No, I'm content to sit and watch. I'll be right here if you need an extra hand on final. I can give you one," he said, holding up his bandaged left hand.

"You big baby," she teased. She had seen him handle the plane with one hand on the first leg of the flight from San Francisco to Wichita. But, she wasn't going to ask him twice. She was having a ball flying this new aircraft and was happy to be at the controls.

"I don't normally let anyone fly my plane," he said to her as she cut back on the power to begin the descent. Except Jester, he thought, who normally sat in the right hand seat. The noise in the cockpit changed immediately as the plane began to slow and the digital altimeter started clicking off the feet.

"You like to be in control, right?" she said as she punched up the Groton weather frequency.

"I do," he admitted. He thought ruefully how things had been out of his control the last forty-eight hours. "It's nice to give it up to someone as competent as you."

He cringed at his choice of words. You're a dope, McDonough!

"You think I'm 'competent'," she replied with a small smile, saying the word exactly as he had said it.

"Well, let me put it another way," he said, hoping to salvage the moment. "Your touch on the controls is as delicate and fine as your beauty," he said broadly, sweeping his bandaged hand in the cockpit.

"I like that better!" she laughed, looking over at him.

"Good. I mean it. You have a nice touch. Hmmm, looks like the weather's marginal at Groton," he said, changing the subject.

The computer screen displayed the weather information, labeled Echo. It indicated the ceiling was only 2000 feet, visibility two and a half miles with thunderstorms to the southeast and light rain over the airport.

"Ceiling below 3000. ILS approach," he said. "You want it, you got it."

She nodded and pressed the mike button on the wheel.

"Providence Control, this is Starship 3-7-9. Through flight level three zero for 15-thousand. We have Echo."

"Roger Starship 3-7-9, this is Providence Center," a female voice answered. "Groton altimeter 2-9-8-6. Continue to 7000. Decrease speed 2-0-0."

"Roger, Providence. 7000."

"We should be able to beat the worst of the weather," PJ said as he leaned forward and keyed in several numbers on the navigation computer with his good hand.

The main monitors in front of both pilots went blank for a second before a graphic display of the Groton airport appeared, with a series of vector lines to indicate the proper flight path for their approach. These were overlaid by the green and yellow returns of the radar. It showed clouds all the way with thunderstorm cells southeast of the airport. A red blinking V indicated the Starship's location. The digital read-out from the GPS indicated they were now sixty-five miles out.

"Just like a video game, Kathryn," he said. "Keep the V on the vector line on the lower screen, and keep us on the horizontal glide slope on the upper monitor and we should come out of the clouds on the downwind leg about two miles out."

Kathryn nodded, looking outside the cockpit at the void that alternated black and white as the Starship's strobe flashed against the clouds. She remembered the rush from her very first flight nearly twenty years ago as she and her father cleared the trees at the end of the little airpark near her San Jose home. She was having as much fun right now.

She also remembered the teen-age agony of having to wait until her sixteenth birthday before she was officially old enough to receive her student certificate, even though she could already handle a plane with aplomb.

Her obsession with flying led to a commercial pilot certificate with instrument and multi-engine ratings and her log book totaled nearly 4000 hours in the air. But descending through the clouds still bothered her. She had to make a conscious reaffirmation of her belief in the instruments every time the weather went soupy.

"We become such a slave to these gadgets," PJ said quietly, as if reading her mind. He adjusted the contrast on the monitors. "But without them, we can't really extend ourselves into the unseen and the unknown, can we?"

"I suppose not," she answered. Then she laughed. "I'm always imagining there is a mountain that has suddenly grown at the end of the runway since the last time someone looked. Pretty stupid, huh?"

She thought of the snow-capped peaks that often appeared in her dreams.

"Mountains of the mind, right?" said PJ. He laughed too. He put his hand on hers for just a moment, feeling the plane's vibration through the wheel and her hand. He looked right at her.

"Kathryn, there are no mountains in Groton. Only flat water, next to a flat runway, ready to welcome us home. Your new home, actually."

She smiled and nodded, enjoying his warm but brief touch. She moved her thumb over his finger and gave him a small squeeze.

"Well, I like it so far, PJ." She scanned the instruments again.

"Passing through fifteen thousand. No mountains."

"Believe in the numbers. No mountains," he smiled and let his hand fall back into his lap and his head back on the headrest. The digital clock on the instrument panel read eight o'clock. They had been in the air for almost four hours on this leg from Wichita and had made good time, but PJ was tired.

Sitting there in the darkened cockpit, anger swelled up in PJ again. He accepted it and found it an acceptable mask for the emptiness he felt without Jester. He seemed to be teetering on the edge of a dark abyss, a bottomless well of inaction. He used the anger as a crutch to strengthen his resolve to avenge Jester's murder. Revenge didn't feel comfortable on him, but it felt better than emptiness.

There was much that awaited him in Mystic. The funeral on Friday, his grieving mother, who was making all the arrangements, and Jester's papers, charts and photos of the Colombian mine. The task of keeping Fast Car Caravan, now his company, on the edge of technology also awaits, he thought. The realization he would have to see Harold again. The anger was good. It let him believe none of what lay ahead would overwhelm him.

"Providence Control, this is Starship 3-7-9. We're at 7000," came Kathryn's soft voice, interrupting his anger. They were right on course.

"Roger, Starship. ILS runway 5. Switch to Groton Approach, 125.6.

"Roger, Providence. Switching to Approach."

As Kathryn switched frequencies, and turned easily onto the new course, she noticed the engine temperature in the right hand engine.

"See engine number two?" she asked PJ.

"I just noticed," he nodded. "It's only up 10 degrees. Try cutting back

RPMs."

She slide the right-hand throttle forward a fraction and watched the display expectantly as she contacted approach.

"Groton Approach, this is Starship 3-7-9. Heading 1-4-5, through 6000 for 25-hundred."

"Roger, Starship," intoned a new controller's voice. "Crossing traffic on your nose six miles at flight level 2000. You are number two in the pattern behind the C-130."

PJ looked at the rectangular landing pattern around the airport as it was displayed on the monitor. The blip of the military transport showed on the downwind leg flying parallel to the runway, preparing to make a wide 180 degree left hand turn onto final. They would follow a similar course, their approach taking them over Fishers Island Sound south of the runway.

"Groton, we have radar contact on traffic." Kathryn answered. Then to PJ, "Number two's temp is up ten more."

They both watched the temperature gauge displayed on the screen.

Just then a new voice joined the airwaves, the deep, all business tone of a military cargo pilot.

"Groton, Guard 2-9 out of clouds at seventeen hundred. On final. I have visual on the runway." The military jock was practicing for war, thought PJ.

"The ceiling's closing in," PJ said out loud. He was sitting up now, alert for the landing. He eased the throttle some more, watching for a decrease in the engine temperature. When it didn't come, he peered out of the cockpit window at the impenetrable cloud cover. The new engines were Fast Car Caravan's first effort to break into the aviation industry. Maybe it's an electrical problem, he thought.

His eyes returned to the instrument panel, saw the altimeter pass through 4000 and continue its steady drop. The engine temp did not decrease and was now reading about 30 degrees hotter than number one.

"Are we there yet?" came a voice from behind. PJ turned to see Dutch stretching in his seat in the main cabin.

"In the pattern, Dutch. ILS."

"Where's the bottom of this stuff?" Dutch asked, looking out his window.

"1700," PJ answered.

"Wonderful!"

Dave's big body was still sleeping in the seat across the aisle, looking very cramped. PJ smiled at the thought that no airplane seats were made for a six-five giant.

"Groton, Guard 2-9. We have the outer marker."

"Roger, 2-9. Cleared to land," answered the approach controller. "Starship 3-7-9, turn left course 0-5-0, continue to 2500."

"Roger, Groton. 3-7-9 turning left 0-5-0. Passing 3000. Still...."

Kathryn's transmission was cut short by a muffled thump from the rear of the plane followed by a sharp crack. A second later, a beeping alarm began sounding in the cockpit.

"What the hell was that!" she asked shooting an uncertain glance at PJ.

The Starship lurched to the right and PJ instinctively grabbed the wheel to help Kathryn get control. The red fire light came on for engine two.

"I have a fire light on number two," Kathryn said, her voice steady. "Wait. All readings on two are dead. We've lost the meters." The wheel was alive in her hands as they began to lose altitude.

"Killing two. Mixture to idle cutoff. Fuel control off. Throttle off. Extinguisher activated," PJ ran the litany of the procedure as if it were a practice session while his good hand moved quickly over the engine switches between the seats. The depressurization alarm was beeping, but at their low altitude the cabin pressure had already been equalized with the outside air. It only indicated the cabin seal had been ruptured. He switched off the alarm.

Other alarms continued to sound as the Starship yawed to the right, her nose pitched down. Kathryn worked to pull the nose up without stalling.

"Wing forward?" she asked.

PJ reached for the handle that prepared the wings for landing. The nose wing moved from its swept back cruising position to its straight out landing position, giving the plane more lift at slower speeds. The lever also controlled the flaps, but PJ saw the indicator light was not lit.

"Wing forward. No flaps indicator," he told Kathryn.

She nodded. "Do you smell smoke?"

"Yes, from the rear. Feathering two." He flipped the switch that stopped the prop from spinning and angled the blades into the wind. Just then Dutch stuck his head in the cockpit.

"A little smoke in the cabin, captain. Keep flying," he said evenly as he grabbed a fire extinguisher from behind Kathryn's seat and turned back into the cabin.

Dave was already up, snapped out of his sleep by the noise. PJ could see him flailing with his jacket in the rear of the cabin. Light smoke had reached the cockpit. The out of place silver casket in the aisle triggered the word sabotage in PJ's mind, but the smell of the fire turned his attention back to the instruments.

Their air speed was down to 140 knots and decreasing. The trend meter indicated airspeed would continue to drop to 90 knots, below stall speed. Worse, their altitude continued to drop.

Suddenly they were out of the cloud cover, the lights of the runway shining to their left about a mile. Beyond, PJ could see the Gold Star Bridge that carried the interstate over the Thames River between New London and Groton.

"Full power on one," said PJ as he pulled the throttle back to the stops. The five-blade prop on the lone working engine bit into the damp air and they felt the immediate acceleration. The airspeed began to hold around 120 knots and the click of numbers on the altimeter stopped, settling at 1200 feet. The temperature gauge on number one held steady in the green.

"Groton, Starship 3-7-9," Kathryn spoke steadily into the mike. "Making short approach. Have visual on runway. We've lost an engine."

"Roger, Starship," came the reply. PJ noted a keener interest in the controller's voice than before. "You are cleared to land. C-130 is just turning off runway." The controller paused, then added, "Do you want the emergency equipment?"

"Negative," Kathryn replied as she turned the plane to the left.

PJ's bandaged hand cradled the wheel, but it couldn't do much. He could feel the sluggishness of the controls as they banked steeply toward the runway. He worked the throttle with his right hand, letting Kathryn concentrate on the wheel. They said nothing, responding to the needs of the Starship as she clung to the precious air lifting her wings.

They needed to stay in the air just a bit longer. The lone working engine was keeping their airspeed up, about 115 knots now and the plane was responding.

"Fire's out, PJ," yelled Dutch. "The right engine is gone."

"I shut her down, Dutch," said PJ.

"No, I mean it's gone. The prop is not there."

PJ looked back at Dutch trying to understand the impact of what he had just said. A distinct whistle could be heard as the wind rushed through a hole in the cabin rear on the side of missing engine.

"The wing looks okay, best I can tell," Dutch said. "And Kathryn's books are toast in the luggage compartment," he added, almost smiling.

"What books?...oh, yeah." PJ remembered her showing up at the plane that morning with two boxes of books, a big suitcase, a lap top computer and a travel bag full of clothes. All her personal belongings in the world.

"Is that all?" PJ asked.

"Best I can tell," Dutch answered, sitting back in his seat.

"Well, she's acting real soft, so buckle up for the landing," PJ said and turned his attention forward.

With the right engine gone, the left engine wanted to push the plane to the right, while the decrease in power rolled the plane to the left. The automatic rudder trim wasn't working, leaving Kathryn with her hands full on the control wheel, trying to stay with the Starship's squirrelly motion.

Her eyes bounced between the air speed indicator, the altimeter and the runway lights ahead as she guided the plane through a steep left hand turn. She leveled off with the end of the runway less than a mile away.

"Gear!" PJ remembered, feeling stupid that he had almost forgotten. He felt much better when he heard the secure "thunk" of the tricycle gear locking in place and the instrument panel lights showing green for all three wheels. The drag of the gear dropped their airspeed to 105 knots, just above stalling speed.

"3-7-9, Approach. You're a little low and to the left of center line."

The big blue structure of the Formula Yachts factory caught PJ's eye just ahead. Kathryn's short cut to the runway had taken them a lot closer to it than he would have liked. Three sailboat hulls fresh from the mold were clearly visible sitting on their cradles in the parking lot as they passed overhead not 100 feet above the ground.

"Roger, Groton," Kathryn answered. "I have visual on the runway."

"A little right, Kathryn," PJ said quietly. "Easing throttle."

"No, I need it all!"' Kathryn responded immediately, her hand reaching to the controls and touching his already there. He stopped moving the throttle, her hand like an electric jolt. The Starship crossed just 30 feet above the chain link fence that surrounded the airfield, it's right wing down.

"Level, baby. A touch left now," he urged, using body language to straighten the wings, not daring to take his hands off the throttle. They both saw the last bank of red runway approach lights, rising up from the ground on their metal lattice. PJ thought they were going to hit it, but Kathryn had already responded, correcting the wheel to the left.

PJ was sure the red lights were close enough to reflect on his face as they flew over them and then the right landing gear touched down hard not twenty feet from the end of the concrete, giving off a puff of blue smoke.

The plane bounced back into the air, the wings rocking left, even as PJ cut back on the throttle. Kathryn corrected with a dab of right rudder this time and the weirdly shaped bird leveled off at ten feet and then settled down, both tires touching together, sending off a sharp squeal and more smoke.

As the left gear touched down, the blades on the lone engine automatically flattened against the on rushing air, slowing the plane down. As the nose wheel gently touched, Kathryn slowly applied the brakes.

The anti-lock carbon pads took hold and Kathryn turned off the runway well before the end, smartly taxiing the Starship past the main terminal and to a halt in front of the Air Exec Service Center as if nothing unusual had happened.

With the plane parked, Kathryn just sat in her seat as PJ shut down the engine. She let out a long, quiet sigh and took her hands off the wheel for the first time in two hours. Then she patted the wheel gently.

"Nice plane."

Behind her, she heard Dutch and Dave slowly clapping their appreciation.

"Good one, lady," Dutch called, hiding the relief in his voice. "Now, can we try it again without the bouncing?"

PJ was grinning at her.

"Welcome to Connecticut, Kathryn Byrnie. No mountains here, just plenty of excitement."

She laughed at him, a big grin breaking out on her face. "Thanks for letting me fly your plane, PJ. Jeez, that was real interesting!"

"You did a nice job. Very cool. I'm glad you're on our side." PJ was all smiles as he rubbed her shoulder.

"Thanks. My first genuine emergency with an audience," she admitted.

"Really!?" PJ was surprised. She nodded her head.

"I'm even more impressed, especially the way you kept your cool on the radio. You can fly my plane anytime."

"I was just trying to keep her in the air," she said modestly.

"You did a hell of a job." He unbuckled his harness belt and slid out of the seat. "Write up the log while I take a look at what happened, okay?" and he was gone, following Dave and Dutch out the door and to the rear of the plane.

They were amazed at what they found. The nacelle that contained engine two was still attached to the wing, but the side closest to the cabin looked like it had been hit with a rocket. The business end of the engine, the prop and exhaust cowling were missing leaving just a blackened hole and a tangle of splintered plastic turbine blades and other engine parts.

There was a small gash in the fuselage that went through to the luggage compartment at the rear of the cabin where the fire had started. PJ thought the prop might have caused the hole when it separated from the engine.

"What do you think, Dave," PJ somberly asked his chief mechanic.

"Looks like someone tried to blow us up, PJ," Dave answered evenly. "No way a turbine blade or unseated shaft could do that, not with this composite nacelle. Had to be a bomb of some sort."

"A bomb!" asked Dutch incredulously. "You can't be serious, Dave."

"First guess, Dutch. That's all," Dave answered.

"We were over water when it happened," PJ said quietly. "Oh, man! I hope the prop didn't hit anyone."

Kathryn's face appeared in the hole from inside the cabin.

"My books!" she called to them. "They're all burned!" Then she got real quiet as she saw the empty engine nacelle for the first time. Her face disappeared inside and she reappeared a few seconds later joining them by the wing.

"Oh, PJ," was all she could say. "The prop!"

She looked at him wide eyed.

"We were just off Mumford Point, PJ, I'm sure it was over water," she said, remembering how the chart looked. They shared a similar, horrifying image of the five-blade prop spinning out of control in a local neighborhood.

He nodded, "I think you're right. What's that?" he said, pointing at what she had in her hand.

"This was sitting in the luggage compartment," she said.

PJ thought it was a piece of the engine exhaust cowling, blackened from 100 hours in the air and whatever else had just happened on their approach.

Dave agreed as he turned it over in his hand. "It shot right through the cabin skin," he said. He looked at PJ.

"Or went in through a hole the prop ripped," PJ suggested.

"I'm still thinking bomb, PJ," Dave said.

"PJ, I think you had better reassess the police theory that Jester was the only target," Dutch said. "Somebody doesn't like you."

"Or us," Kathryn added.

PJ was tight-lipped as they stood staring at the empty hole. Dutch was right. The sniper's calling card indicated Jester was the target, but now he wasn't so sure.

"Nice job, Kathryn," PJ finally spoke. Then he turned to Dave.

"Dave, get a good night's sleep and then bring in two guys who can keep their mouths shut and help you pull apart what's left of number two and give me a full report on what you think happened. I'll get Matt Brewer from the NTSB to clear it tonight so you can start first thing in the morning."

There was enough damage, especially with a wayward prop somewhere south of the airport, to be considered "serious". That meant the National Transportation Safety Boad had to be informed of the incident. However, PJ hoped to keep it quiet for as long as possible. The last thing he wanted right now was the media spreading the story that Starship engines were falling off.

Brewer was the New England region coordinator for NTSB and had been PJ's first flight instructor. They had kept in touch over the years and PJ was sure Matt's usual backlog of paper work would delay official reaction for a while, at least until the Caravan mechanics could get a handle on what had caused the apparent explosion and fire.

"I'll use Sandy and Gary," Dave said. "We'll lock up the Starship in the old Air Exec hanger. No one will bother her there tonight."

"That's great, Dave. Look at number one while you're at it. Carefully. It might have been tampered with, too. I'll call Wichita. I want to rebuild ASAP, so they'll have to send some assorted parts. And I want to find out more about the guy who did the refueling job there."

"We've only got the one spare engine ready, PJ," Dave reminded him. "It's still got some tests scheduled this week."

"Let's push those tests to priority and finish them by the end of the week," PJ ordered. "We'll need to repair the holes in the nacelle and cabin."

"Okay," Dave nodded. "Looks like a job for the Weldstic formula."

"Good idea, Dave," PJ said. "I certainly didn't want to test it this way, but give it a shot." Weldstic was a new product from Fast Car Caravan's chemists. It acted as a bonding agent to reconnect the molecular components of composite fibers that had been splintered or cracked under pressure. Without it, a small crack often forced the replacement of an entire section. PJ stood there trying to reconcile the fact his own troubles were actually helping business.

Then he heard the sound of approaching cars splashing through the puddles on the pavement. It was a hearse, his mother's car following.

"Guys, can you lend a hand with the casket?" he said to Dutch and Dave, but his mind was on his mother.

A tall woman stepped from the car, her long, reddish-brown hair visible in the hangar lights. She was wearing jeans and a flannel shirt, the sleeves rolled up.

PJ rushed up to her.

"Thank God!" the woman said as they embraced. Kathryn remained standing under the blackened engine mount, but could hear the woman quietly crying in PJ's arms.

In her sixty years, Ann Elizabeth McDonough had seen her pilot husband killed in combat and was a few days from burying her closest friend and companion, mysteriously murdered while sailing. Yet, her tears were a release of joy that her only son was alive and home again.

"Are you in pain?" she asked quietly, holding his head in her hands, her eyes searching the bandage on his forehead.

"Pain of emptiness," PJ said.

"I know," she said, resting her head on his chest, the words muffled. "Empty and hopeless. But you're standing here. It helps. I didn't think I had any tears left," she laughed gently, wiping her eyes. She looked over PJ's shoulder and saw Kathryn.

"Hello, I'm Ann McDonough. You must be Kathryn." She let go of PJ and stepped forward to greet her.

"Yes, Mrs. McDonough. Kathryn Byrnie. Nice to meet you." Kathryn took her hand. "I'm sorry we couldn't have met under more pleasant circumstances."

They shared a small hug.

"Call me Ann. I've been doing a lot of hugging the last day or so. And crying," she said.

"Me, too. I only knew Jester briefly, but I'm so sad he's gone," Kathryn said.

"He had a way of winning hearts, he did," she said.

A few years after his dad's death, PJ sensed Jester and his mom had grown very close. Though she said they never would marry, she did not hide the fact he was her companion and good friend. As the relationship grew, so did her involvement with Fast Car Caravan. Today, she ran the company on a day-to-day basis and knew as much about it as Jester and PJ, probably more.

The casket was gingerly maneuvered through the narrow side door of the Starship and placed in the hearse. The three of them stood and watched quietly. Once it was in place, Ann walked to the rear of the vehicle and briefly touched the metal box. She stepped back and stood motionless until the driver had closed the rear door and driven out of the airport.

PJ touched his mom's shoulder and she turned, her face impassioned, only the tears glistening in the light betrayed her grief.

"Let's go home, Mom," PJ said quietly and she nodded.

"I'm okay, Peter," she said softly and walked to her car.

"I'll be over as soon as we square away the Starship," PJ said as she climbed behind the wheel. She sat for a moment, her hands on the wheel. He could see her fighting back more tears. Then she nodded again, gave him a smile. "I'll have the coffee ready," she said and drove off.

Dutch and Kathryn walked up next to PJ.

"She okay?" Dutch asked.

"You know Ann," PJ said. "She'll manage." Then PJ turned to his friend.

"Dutch, it looks like you might get your wish. We have a fight on our hands."

"PJ, I don't know. The odds suck when we don't even know who it is we're fighting," Dutch answered. "Maybe it wasn't a bomb." He didn't sound convinced. "Hell, they, whoever 'they' are, already have us down two-zip. And we haven't even found the ball park!" he said.

"Well, my friend, tomorrow we start looking."

"You look. I have to run a few restaurants," Dutch said and started toward his car. Then he turned with a smile, calling back as he walked, "But if you get lost, give me a call."

PJ waved, turning to Kathryn, "He loves a fight."

"I guess this one found us," she said, looking at PJ and then the plane.

Dave chugged up in the tractor. They three of them moved the damaged Starship into the old wooden hanger where it joined a canvas

---

bi-plane Dave was in the middle of restoring. He said good night and headed home, while PJ made two quick calls from the outside pay phone. He left a message on Brewer's answering machine at home. The second went to the Groton police who reported a quiet night. PJ felt better about the missing prop. He would wait for NTSB to go public with the incident.

He then took Kathryn by the arm.

"No motel for you tonight, Miss Byrnie. Your stuff stays put until the feds can analyze it, so you're coming home with me. I have plenty of room, plenty of things you can wear, if you like late 20th century fashions. You deserve some of the comforts of life tonight," he said with a weary grin.

She did not put up a fight and they walked over to a sleek coupe.

"There's as much glass as there is metal," Kathryn said, admiring the polished black finish.

"Actually, there's no metal at all. It's all plastic, Prototype number three of the Miller," he said with some pride.

"Of course," she said quietly as she ran her had over the smooth surface. "Like the hull of *Poly Rocket*." She realized it was the same car in the photo Jester had shown here when he tracked her down at lunch in San Francisco.

"Exactly. Plexiglas for windows, rubber tires. Everything else is composite plastics, with a touch of Goshenite in the engine core," he explained as the motor came to life with a throaty drone.

She buckled up, sinking back into the leather seats.

"This version handled better than the others, so I kept it. You should see them on the road next fall. Ford bought the design two years ago."

"Jester told me when we first talked, but seeing is believing," she said.

"We modified this particular engine to run on a methane- ethanol fuel mixture. It's made from rotting garbage. We think we can get it on the market in a year or two," he added with a smile.

"So, this is the kind of things we'll be doing," she said. The prospects both intrigued and excited her.

"A short stop at mom's and then we can call it a night," PJ said as they turned onto a narrow road that snaked its way through a thick stand of pine trees.

She sank deeper into the seat, enjoying its smell and feeling a calm returning to her after the adrenalin rush of the landing. She was happy he was driving.

~~~

CHAPTER EIGHT

Ann McDonough's home gave off a warm glow despite the spacious room on the first floor, open front to back with a high ceiling. A sunken sitting area in the middle of the room faced a fireplace. Dozens of photographs lined the walls except across the back where plants waited for sunshine under a row of windows. Kathryn was immediately drawn to the photos. PJ joined her.

"Family history, frozen in living color on a wall," he said with a smile.

"It's amazing. You're in every one!" she said, scanning one wall.

"Well, not quite. There's some of Jester here and my dad and the crew in Bermuda." He looked along the walls realizing it had been a long time since he had stopped to look at each photo.

"Is this your dad?" Kathryn asked.

"Yes. He was killed in Vietnam," PJ said quietly.

The photo showed a pilot standing on the deck of an aircraft carrier in front of an F-4 Phantom jet. PJ had looked at it many times and each time he thought he saw the hint of fatigue around his father's eyes. Or was it fear?

"Oh, I didn't know," Kathryn said, looking up at PJ. "His smile is just like yours."

"You think so?"

"Yes, definitely, and the eyes. He has that McDonough look about him."

"What McDonough look?" PJ asked.

"Oh, a look of readiness. Eyes that see everything."

She was smiling at him.

"It's a look that says there is someone very awake in there."

"You think so?" he said, returning her smile. "Well, honestly, this someone is hardly awake right now."

"Maybe some coffee will help," Ann McDonough said behind them, holding a tray of filled cups.

"Oh, thank you, Mrs. McDonough...ah, Ann," Kathryn said. They each took a cup and continued to look at the photos.

"This is a lovely wall," Kathryn said. "These photos are just wonderful!"

"Thank you, dear. I think I went overboard a bit, but it is nice to pause and look at the past."

"As long as we don't get stuck in it, right, Mom?" PJ said.

"That's right, Peter."

"Who took the pictures?"

"There are some publicity shots. A few news photos, but I took most of them. Of PJ, at least. When you are surrounded by men who do exciting things you have to try to become a part of it," Ann said.

"They're very good."

"I've always liked that one," she said, pointing to one a couple of feet over their heads.

It was a photo of a young PJ, maybe ten years old, standing on the side of a capsized sailboat, trying to right it. His bathing suit had come half off when the boat went over and his bare ass was the focus of the photo.

"Great, Mom!" PJ laughed.

"Nice buns, PJ!" Kathryn laughed.

There were photos of Jester and PJ with the Miller Motor Car on the day it was unveiled to the media. And Jester working with engines and Jester with chassis frames, even one with him in protective gear working around a vat of molten materials.

There was a twenty-year old PJ, holding a parachute in front of a small plane, and another of PJ smiling behind the plane's controls. Another with PJ on a military watercraft with a big fan on the back. Sailboats held equal space with race cars. Kathryn recognized most of the crew crouched around a large silver trophy that stood three feet high, the pink walls of the Royal Bermuda Yacht Club filling the background. An aerial shot of a large sailboat under spinnaker and blooper was next to it.

"We won Newport to Bermuda that year on a boat we called *Camp Hobo*," PJ said with excitement. "Six hundred thirty eight miles downwind in twenty-five knots and big following seas. What a ride!"

"I remember reading about it," she said.

One section had several photos of PJ and Jester around a low-slung race car with rear wings. It was shiny red, plastered with stickers from a dozen sponsors. The powerful centerpiece of the section was a close-up of a driver in the red car caught in the middle of a turn. The helmet shield was flipped up, and it was covered with a sheen of oil, as well as the top of the helmet, the driver's fireproof balaclava, and the short windshield. However, the photographer had been perfectly focused on the driver's blue eyes. They were clean and dominated the photo.

"That's you, isn't it. I recognized that look again," Kathryn said. "Formula One?"

"Yes. I did Formula One for a year," PJ said slowly. He made it sound unpleasant. He silently wished his mother had not hung these photos.

"Only one?" Kathryn asked innocently.

"Only one," PJ said and moved on.

Kathryn didn't pursue it.

"PJ mentioned you're a pilot?" Ann McDonough asked Kathryn with interest. She knew PJ didn't like those photos.

"Damn straight she is," PJ said, before Kathryn could answer. He was happy for the change of subject.

PJ moved toward the sitting area, while Kathryn quickly scanned the remaining photos. He began to tell his mother about the emergency landing only an hour ago. He praised Kathryn's performance to the point she felt some embarrassment.

"Oh, PJ, it wasn't that dramatic!" she protested mildly.

"Nonsense, you were brilliant."

"PJ, what could have happened? I didn't even stop to look at the plane," she said.

PJ hesitated for a moment. He knew he couldn't hide anything from her.

"Dave thinks it was a bomb," he said reluctantly, then added quickly, "But, he isn't sure."

"A bomb, PJ?" his mother said. Her calm demeanor changed as PJ told the story and she now looked worried.

"Oh, this is terrible. I don't understand! Why would anyone want to bomb the plane?" Her eyes went wide as she began to put things together. "Oh, my God! Does this have something to do with Jester's shooting?"

"I don't know, mother. Probably," he admitted.

"Why you? Are you in danger now?"

She was trying hard not to cry. PJ moved close and put his arm around her.

"I can't rule that out," PJ said honestly, "Hey, we're safe here. It may have something to do with the mine in Colombia."

"The mine? Laguna d'Vacio Esmerelda?" she said, looking up.

"Mom, this can wait," PJ said. Her lip was trembling.

"No, it's okay, Peter." She stood up and walked to the desk in the far corner of the room, removing something from a drawer. She stood at the desk for a moment before returning with a photograph, and her composure.

"Sometimes I am doing just fine and then out of the blue I remember he's gone," she said softly, a tissue in her hands. "I don't know if I could handle anything happening to you. Here."

She handed the photo to PJ.

"You know how he loved having his picture taken," she said. "This was taken at the mine last year. I've been meaning to get a frame for it."

Jester stood in the foreground, surrounded by vertical cliffs and a snow capped mountain peak in the distance. His white hair was blowing in the wind, a yellow bandanna around his neck. He leaned on a shovel, his foot propped up on the blade in a classic prospector pose.

"He never told me much about the mine," PJ said looking at the photo for the first time.

"It was his little secret," she said quietly. "I think the Indians didn't want him to say much about it. Besides, it's one of the richest sources of Goshenite in the world."

"What did you call the mine a moment ago?" Kathryn asked.

"Laguna d'Vacio Esmerelda. The Lake of the Empty Emerald. The Indians call it the Valley of Codazzi. An Austrian first worked the mine, looking for emeralds. All he found was Goshenite and named the glacial lake in the valley when he abandoned it."

Ann walked to the mantel over the fireplace and picked up what looked like a rock made of glass.

"Goshenite," she said to Kathryn, handing her the piece. "Shaped like an emerald, but no color."

Kathryn turned the rock over in her hand, then held it up to the light. Up close, she could see the six sides of the hexagonal shape. The light was refracted inside the Goshenite, but Kathryn thought it rather dull looking and understood immediately the empty emerald reference.

"Green emeralds are much more interesting," she said, replacing the rock on the mantel.

"Too bad there aren't more uses for it," PJ said absently.

He was looking at the man standing next to Jester in the photo, a short, powerfully built man, with straight black hair, and a sleeveless shirt open to the navel. A black hat sat on his head and a gold pendant hung from a chain, shining in the bright sunshine against his bare, bronzed chest. He held a black rock with a clear, hexagonal crystal sticking out of one end.

"Who's with Jester?" PJ asked.

"Eduardo, the mine boss," his mother said. "He's a Kogi Indian, like the rest of the workers. That piece of Goshenite is the piece that ended up on your desk, PJ. I brought all the files on the mine I could find in the office, like you asked," she said, gesturing to the corner.

PJ smiled and passed the photo to Kathryn. He stood up, kissed his mother on the forehead and walked over to the desk area, returning with a short stack of file folders, a thin book and two rolled up maps.

"Why would Colombians want the mine?" Kathryn asked.

"I just don't know, Kathryn," he said sifting through the papers.

"They must," Ann McDonough suggested. "A man from Colombia tried to buy out the lease earlier this summer, but Jester didn't want to sell."

"Someone tried to buy it?" asked PJ surprised.

"Yes. It was June 25th. I remember because it was on your birthday, PJ. A well dressed man met with Jester at the office and then left in a hurry." She let out a small laugh. "Jester called him creepy."

"Did he give his name?"

"I wrote it down." She picked up the thin black appointment book and turned a few pages before she found the correct date.

"Luis Caron, Colombia Precious Metals," she said. She flipped to the back and removed a business card from a plastic liner. "Plaza de los Conches, Cartegena, Colombia, S.A.," she read from Caron's card.

"Colombia Precious Metals!" PJ said, looking at it. "Are they for real?"

"And why resort to murder over some dull rocks?" Kathryn asked.

PJ opened one of the folders, while Kathryn picked up another. In a matter of minutes, the three of them were pouring over the papers, photos and maps that told the story of the Miller Mine.

They discovered that Jester had signed a personal twenty-year lease for $25,000 a year. He had received a one-page document signed by the Director General of INDERENA, the agency that ran the national parks and controlled mining in Colombia. A topographical map showed the mine's co-ordinates as Latitude 10 degrees 40.33 minutes and Longitude 73 degrees 33.57 minutes, putting it right in the middle of the Sierra Nevada de Santa Marta mountains in northern Colombia.

"There are no roads to this place," PJ said after studying the map. "It's surrounded by mountains."

Other photos confirmed the isolated location. They showed a brown, rock strewn valley with a lake, surrounded by high cliffs and a hole cut into the side of a rock wall with several men working outside it with shovels, picks and wheelbarrows.

"Who is this man?" Kathryn asked, showing a photo of a man in his mid 30's, resplendent in a blue suit, his face caught between a grin and a grimace. The Washington monument stood on the horizon. It seemed out of place among the shots of mountains, lakes and mine workers.

"What's the hell is that doing in there?" PJ asked, more than a little annoyed. He reached for the photo, glanced at it for a moment, then threw it back into the pile in the middle of the table. He looked at his mother with open hands.

"What the hell!" he snapped.

"PJ, I'm sorry, I didn't know it was there," apologized his mother. "This is all Jester's stuff. They're all his papers."

PJ sat back on the chair, resigned, shaking his head.

Ann picked up the photo and looked at it for a moment and then placed it gently back on the table.

"He did work out the permits for the mine," she said softly, looking at her son.

"He knew?" PJ moaned, almost whining. His shoulders slumped and he suddenly felt very tired.

"Knew? He swung the deal. You know Harold. He knows who to call, how to get people to say yes!" Ann said it with a hint of pride.

PJ just sat there slowly shaking his head. He heard a voice smirk, "He certainly got one girl to say yes!"

"Whose Harold?" asked a puzzled Kathryn. She had not seen PJ so deflated since they had met just a couple of weeks ago.

PJ looked at his mother. She could see the pain in his eyes.

He turned toward Kathryn and gave her a tight little smile that soften very quickly as he met her gaze.

"Jester's son," he said. "Harold Miller."

"Jester has a son! I had no idea, no one ever mentioned him," Kathryn smiled, looking from one to the other. Blank stares were all she saw. No one spoke for several seconds.

"It's a little complicated." Ann finally broke the silence.

"No, you know what? It's not, Mom," PJ interjected, leaning forward on his chair. He looked at Kathryn and sighed. "It's really very simple. He was my best friend and stole my girl friend." He felt a sense of calm as he spoke the words. "This is easier than I thought it would be," he said to himself. "That was three years ago. We haven't spoken since. He was a prick and she was a bitch and they deserve each other!" That felt real good, he thought and smiled.

"Oh, my!" said Kathryn, caught by surprise. "I'm so sorry!"

"Hey, nothing to be sorry about, Kathryn!" PJ laughed. "Stuff happens to everyone."

Ann looked at her son with a curious smile. She had never heard him speak of the incident until now. She had heard the story from Harold and Jester, but never pressed PJ to open up and he never did. She just quietly suffered along with him, because she knew he did suffer over it.

"PJ, are you okay?" she asked. PJ nodded and went to his mother's side.

Kathryn watched them share a hug. "I didn't mean to pry," she said and turned back to the papers in front of her.

"Hey, it's okay. It's been a long couple of days," said PJ. He sat back down. "Let's spend ten more minutes with this and then we'll call it a night."

Silence overcame the room as they focused on the contents of Jester's files. Kathryn picked up a group of photos in a plastic container and was immediately drawn to the mountain scenes pictured around her. There was something about the puffy clouds and snowcapped peaks that tripped a memory. She gasped at one labeled Pico Codazzi on the back.

"What?" asked PJ, happy to change the subject.

She just looked at the photo, not hearing him.

"Kathryn, did you notice something?" PJ persisted.

She looked at him with a weak smile.

"It's nothing. I just thought the mountains looked familiar. It's so beautiful there," she said, showing him the photo. She put it down and picked up another, lost in herself. "So stark. I've seen this before."

"Have you ever been to Colombia?" Ann asked.

"No," Kathryn answered as she studied the new one.

It showed the miners in the native garments of the Kogi Indians, according to Jester's notes. In contrast, there was another photo of the miners on the lake sailing five small sailboats.

"Sailboats?" Kathryn laughed.

"Hey, I thought it would be good for morale," PJ said. "They're Sunfish, sailing dinghies. I shipped them down on the fourth anniversary of the mine. Jester said the Indians loved them."

PJ found a photo of a rough looking runway. There were only two photos taken inside the mine itself. PJ could see spots of light that marked the edges of the cave and estimated the cavern might be as much as 100 feet across.

Kathryn reached for the first photo of Jester and Eduardo again and held it for a long time, even lightly tracing her fingers over Eduardo's face.

"Who's Barney Devlin," PJ asked his mother, waving a document.

"Barney Devlin, Air Lift South America. Those are bills of lading. He flies supplies into the mine and brings the Goshenite out."

"Devlin. Now I remember him. I spoke to him once, when the Sunfish were shipped in," PJ said.

"He gets a check every month from us," Ann added. "In Santa Marta, right?"

"Yes, looks like he has an office at the airport there," PJ said, studying the papers. "I should call him." He looked at his watch. It was after eleven. He looked at the maps again and then moved to the couch.

"Well, the mine is real, that's for sure, but I don't have any better idea why someone would kill Jester for it?"

"Or try to kill you," Ann said quietly. She held her coffee cup tightly, her head bowed. PJ couldn't think of anything to say to ease her fear. He just put his arm around her again and held her for a few moments.

"PJ, this has been a terrible two days. Please don't let anything happen to you!" She was crying big tears now, the worry running down her cheeks onto PJ's shoulder.

Gilmartin

"I'll be extra careful, mom. I promise," PJ said. He held her tightly, rocking her as she had rocked him when he was a young boy.

"Try not to worry, Ann," Kathryn said, touching her hand.

The three of them sat for a few moments and then Ann sat up, smiling through her tears.

"Thank you, dear," she said and dabbed at her eyes with a tissue. "You know how mothers are."

"Do you have a place to stay tonight?" she asked Kathryn. "I have room here."

"Well, PJ offered," she smiled. "My stuff is still in the plane, kind of burned up, and he said he had a few things..." she paused.

"That's fine. You'll like his place," Ann said with a smile. She got up.

"There's nothing set in concrete here. We could stay here." PJ put a hand on his mother's shoulder.

"No, go. You both need some sleep. We have a company to run. I have more calls to make tonight for the funeral. Some of the IMSA guys are at Laguna Seca. They're probably just getting in from the track out there. Don't worry about me."

PJ started to feel better about his mother. She was sounding like the organized business manager that she was. She had regained her composure again and walked them to the front porch. She looked at her only son.

"Just be careful."

"Don't worry about me, Mom," PJ said.

"You know I will anyway," she answered. "And, PJ. I think you should talk to Harold. He wants to talk to you."

"You've talked to him?" PJ said with some surprise.

"Of course, dear. He was one of the first calls," Ann responded, sounding more than a little disappointed in her son. "Not everyone hated him like you."

PJ felt like he was getting a scolding from his mother.

"You have to tell him what's happened. He deserves to know what happened to his father first hand from you."

She handed him the photo of Harold Miller and showed him the phone number in Jester's handwriting scrawled on the back. PJ looked grimly at her.

"He did swing the deal at the mine," she reminded him.

"Of course. He must know about the mine," PJ agreed. "I'll call him." The thought of dealing with Harold had been as distasteful as he could imagine up until a few minutes ago. Now, it seemed he was one of their best leads.

Later, in the car, PJ looked over at Kathryn, gazing out the window, lost in thought. She met his gaze.

"Do you think we are in danger right now?" she asked.

"Well, if we assume the worst, yes, we probably are," he said, looking at the darkness around them. "But, I'm not ready to assume the worst. I think we'll be safe tonight and then tomorrow, we'll try to find out more. I'll call Wingate and Russo tonight and update them on the mine. Then Barney tomorrow."

They drove in silence for a couple of minutes before Kathryn asked, "I'm sorry about what happened between you and Jester's son."

PJ looked over and felt a growing affection for her. It may have been only a sense of calm and comfort. At that moment, he wanted to tell her everything.

"Sometimes you are just so ripped apart from something you think you need, and maybe even think you deserve, or maybe even think you own, that you are turned into some irrational monster and can find no way to forgive or forget. That's how I felt about my good friend Harold who lied to me, disrespected me and basically let his lust for my girl get in the way of our friendship. I was ready to kill them both or turn them into stone if I could and, while I didn't, I ended up bottling up all that emotion for three years, turning it inside, putting it in a box where it just grew into a stinking, rotten chamber of angst and heartache, ready to spill it's ugly contents over anyone I was near if I should even as much as see a blonde walking down the street or in a love scene in the movies...even commercials, for pete's sake! I was a closet basket case and really screwed up until yesterday, when it all seemed so trivial in the face of Jester's murder."

"Oh!"

Her small exclamation sat out there between them, and quickly died along with her prying. She wasn't quite prepared for PJ's response. She didn't feel very confident exploring the mysteries of human relationships. Kathryn knew the pain of breakups, but hers had always been a slow, subliminal dwindling of the spirit that ended in mutual agreement that each party should never see each other again.

In ten minutes, they pulled up to an old shack covered with lobster buoys. A small hand painted sign shaped like a lobster read "Halsey's

Dock".

"Is this your home?" she asked, looking toward the three piers that jutted from the rocky shore.

"Not quite, but it seems like it sometimes."

He smiled and took her hand, leading her down the dock and onto a small cabin cruiser with *Water Wheels* painted in red across the transom, the Fast Car Caravan logo in the lower corner. He climbed up two steps to the bridge deck and in a moment the exhaust fan came on, followed shortly by a muffled roar as the dual engines bubbled at the stern.

"You live on the boat?" she asked, climbing toward the bow.

"No, but it's close," he smiled, watching her smartly clear the bowline. He was particularly attracted to women who knew how to handle themselves around a boat.

"Leave it right on the dock," he said. PJ released the stern line and slowly edged the boat out of the slip into the Mystic River.

"My all weather taxi," he smiled as they accelerated. He pointed the boat towards a flash of lightning to the south. It was an unusually warm September night, and the thunderstorms were about to reach them.

The breeze felt good on her face as they motored. She stood next to him, holding on to the top of the windshield, the wind blowing her hair.

"Where are we going?" she asked.

"Over there," he pointed off to their right. "Ram Island. Home."

"You live on an island!" she laughed. She looked where he had pointed and could make out the low profile of a landmass about a half-mile away. A light beacon on the western end of the island made a slow sweep across the horizon.

"Oh, how nice. An island," was all she could say as she shook her head. "All the comforts...."

He smiled, keeping his eyes forward as they motored through dozens of sailboats anchored at their moorings. He gave the boat a little more power and steered right for the island. Kathryn thought they were going to hit the shore, then saw the small channel that cut through a low section.

"Only at high tide," he said with a grin.

They came out on the other side and PJ pointed a remote control at the shore and two spotlights came on, lighting up a small dock.

They secured the boat and walked up the slate path. The house was a wooden, two story affair, cedar shingles on the sides built around a stone lighthouse rising three stories at the core. The light Kathryn had seen from the boat swept over their heads again.

A real lighthouse, she thought.

Inside, the natural wood walls gave it a warm, cozy feeling. A comfortable living room was to the left of the entrance with a fireplace on one wall and a high angled ceiling. Windows on each side of the fireplace opened onto a wooden deck that ran around the house. It looked as if the water lapped at the edge of the planks.

They passed an office to the right with computer equipment on a desk in one corner and shelves of books around the outer walls, through a stone archway into the kitchen in the base of the lighthouse and then to the other side of the house and up stairs. He led her to a room on the second floor with a large window that looked out on the Mystic River to the north.

"Please make yourself at home," he offered. A moment later he returned with a white terrycloth robe, some clean sweatpants, a pair of woman's jeans and two cotton tops, one red and the other blue.

"These should get you through the night and tomorrow until we can rescue your luggage," he said, tossing the clothes on the bed.

"Is this the she?" she asked with a smile, holding up the jeans from a woman almost two sizes larger.

"Leftovers from that chapter I spoke of early. It's long finished," he shrugged. He was glad he hadn't thrown them away, only because Kathryn would use them now, rather than any feelings he still had for their original owner.

"Her name was Cindy." He still enjoyed the sound of her name, if only for the briefest of moments.

"Thank you," she said simply.

He looked at her. Her long, black hair was windblown, her shirt and leather jacket the same way he remembered it on the tarmac that morning in San Francisco. She stood there, a picture of athletic grace and beauty, yet soft and warm. The word alluring crossed his mind. He liked her standing in his home.

"I'm going to take a shower in my room," he said, pointing down the hall. He pointed to a door in the corner. "There's a shower for you right here." He hesitated as if to add something, but thought better of it.

Later, he felt refreshed despite another battle trying to keep his hand and head dry. He left a message for Wingate on his answering machine and wondered down to the kitchen.

Kathryn had opened a new bottle of Sebastian's rum and he mixed a healthy dose with some tonic for himself and took a sip. Then he went looking for her and guessed correctly she was in the lighthouse tower.

Although the light had long been taken out of official government service, it was still listed on charts as privately maintained. He had remodeled it when he first moved onto the island, moving the light to the roof and creating a quiet room for himself that offered a 360-degree view of Fishers Island Sound and the Mystic River.

She stood there, sipping her drink, wearing the white robe and looking to the west where the white light of the Dumplings and the red light of Race Rock traded winks in a steady four-second rhythm. He walked up behind her and stood very close, almost touching. She didn't move. He could smell her freshly washed hair and smiled at the aroma of his own brand of shampoo.

"It's so beautiful, PJ! So serene, so...perfect, isn't it?" she said quietly. She turned her face toward him and smiled. "Do you entertain up here a lot?"

A flash of brightness filled the room and he looked at her crooked little smile and dimples. God, he loved that smile, he thought! The clap of thunder that followed gave her a start and in seconds the copper roof was alive with the sound of rain.

"No," he smiled. "Actually I haven't spent much time up here in over a year." PJ watched Kathryn turn away and walk toward the northern window. "Too many hours at work!"

"Is that Mystic?" she asked, pointing with her glass at the orange glow up the river.

"Yes and no," he answered mysteriously. "Mystic doesn't really exist, you know, except as a river. It's officially Groton and Stonington, with the river up the middle. But for those who have found refuge in her sheltered harbor, Mystic is very real. It has a quiet beauty in the fall, winter and spring. It's chock a block boats and tourists in the summer."

"Really?" She stood still, looking at the lights along the shore and the dim outline of the moored sailboats they had just passed through.

"Mystical Mystic. Magical, mystical Mystic," she spoke softly. The noise of the rain hid her words and he moved quietly behind her again, taking in the view over her shoulder. The rain was heavy, pounding the roof and running off in streams. Thunder rumbled every few moments, the lightning flashes illuminating the river. Inside the little room, the two of them stood quietly listening to the sounds.

"I feel safe with you, PJ," she said after awhile.

"I haven't done such a good job keeping you out of danger so far, have I?" he said.

"Well, it has been scary. But, I felt something good from it all. About myself. About reacting under pressure."

"You've certainly done that," he said.

She turned and looked into his eyes. It was hard to see their color, but she knew they were blue. Honest eyes, she thought. Strong, clear and sharp. She thought of the eyes in the racing photo at his mother's house. She suddenly wanted to know more about him. A flash of lightning lit up their faces.

"Why did you leave Formula One after one year?" she asked quietly.

He looked at her and didn't answer.

"I don't mean to pry again," she said.

"I'm not used to talking about it," he said and walked to the other side of the room.

"Okay. But now I'm more intrigued. Is it a big secret?"

"It was a part of my life that didn't turn out as I had hoped," he said after a few moments of silence.

"I would think you would be good at it," she said.

He didn't like to talk about it, but for some reason he found himself wanting to tell her the story. He wanted to tell her everything.

"It was in Brazil, the Grand Prix," he began. "Jester had developed this top notch suspension system for his Superline 2000 and it was dialed in pretty good. Half way through, I made a pass around a driver named Flavius DeLorenzo. He was driving a Brabham. The video showed we never touched, but he lost control as I passed. He spun, flipped, hit an emergency truck and caught on fire. They couldn't get him out."

"He died?"

"Yes, he died, and so did a track worker on the truck."

PJ sipped his drink, his eyes focused on the winking Latimer Lighthouse a mile to the southeast.

"How terrible! It wasn't your fault, was it?"

"I didn't think so, but the Brabham team owner led a campaign to bounce me from the circuit. He blamed the aerodynamics of the Miller and my lack of experience. A lot of the other drivers went along. Formula One is a tight little brotherhood and I was one rookie they didn't want around."

"That's terrible!"

"I survived," he said, then laughed at the unintentional irony of what he said. "DeLorenzo didn't."

"How unfair," she said quietly and sipped her drink.

"Tell me about it! I don't like to relive that year because it leaves me very angry at what might have been. The Miller was brilliant! I had already won two races and we could have challenged for the championship, but...hey, it wasn't to be."

He felt the anger rising again. Then he cut it off.

"It's funny how life works out. I still get angry at how unfairly I was treated, but you know what eventually happened?"

"What?"

"Jester pulled the car out of Formula One and we started working on the plastic engine. In five years, we sold the design to Ford and I'm probably wealthier today than I would have been as the World Champion. Maybe a little less famous."

He smiled warmly.

"That's great! Mr. Destiny, right?" she asked.

"Mr. Lucky, maybe!" he laughed.

"Hardly," she said.

They were silent for a moment.

"That's why I loved Jester like a father," he said almost in a whisper. "He took care of me at every turn. He could have found another driver to race, but he decided to try something else and revolutionized transportation in the process. He made me a part of it."

Another flash of lightning lit up his face, revealing a grim expression.

"And it's up to me to see his dream lives on."

"That's exactly what you'll do, PJ McDonough," Kathryn said and put her arm around him. He returned her embrace and they hugged for a moment.

"So, Kathryn Byrnie, tell me about you," he said, leaning back to look into her eyes.

"Oh, who said anything about trading secrets?" she laughed.

"Hey, life is unfair, right? So, tell me how a Byrnie such as yourself has such a lovely bronze complexion and black eyes and hair and looks more like a Mediterranean princess than a Scottish lass."

"I tan easily?" she asked with a smile.

"Not!"

"Okay. You're right. I am not a Byrnie by birth. I'm adopted. Taken off the streets of Brownsville, Texas by Estelle and Tom Byrnie when I was four years old."

"Adopted. Really?"

"Really."

"I think you're the first adopted person I've had the pleasure to make the acquaintance of," he said grandly, holding out his hand. She took it in the dark and shook it warmly. He could hear her giggling.

"Brownsville? Are you Mexican?" he asked.

She turned away and looked out the window again, playing with her drink.

"Do I look Mexican?"

"Well, yes, I guess so. I don't know."

"Actually, PJ, neither do I."

"You don't? How's that?"

"There was no birth certificate when I was adopted, no record of my nationality."

"That's strange. It bothers you, doesn't it?"

"It used to. When I was growing up in San Jose, the kids at school used to call me names. Wetback, brownie, Chiquita. God, I hated them!"

"Name calling was more vicious with our generation," PJ said. "My dad grew up in a melting pot in New York City. Micks, Wops, Kikes, Darkies, Polacks...everyone had a nickname, but he said there was no malice."

"Well, there was malice coming from those kids I had to grow up with. But, I got through it, put it behind me. My parents loved me and I felt like an American." She paused. "I hadn't thought about it in a long time, until tonight."

"I didn't mean to force it on you with this silly game," PJ said.

"No, not here. Earlier. When we were at your mom's house. I saw that pictorial record of your family. The photos of your father. They really touched me," she said quietly, turning away from him. He wanted to reach out and touch her, but he didn't.

"I don't know who my real parents are," she said and turned back to him. "Then when you showed me the photos of the Colombian mine, I almost freaked out."

"How come?"

"I felt drawn into those pictures, PJ, as if I was not looking at them for the first time. It was very strange, but I had a reaction. I don't know what it was exactly, just a feeling, a very distant feeling that drew me toward the mountains, toward Eduardo."

"When I was a little girl, I used to dream about the mountains, rushing water, and happy faces, and snow on the rocks. I was always playing by the water's edge and then I would run through the forests, big green leaves above me that blocked out the sun. Ha, I was always so happy in those dreams! I figured I was dreaming about the mountains around Lake Tahoe. My mom, dad, and I used to fly up there on weekends to camp out. I loved it!"

She paused for a moment.

He met her eyes in the dim light filtering from the kitchen below and suddenly thought she looked very fragile.

"When I saw those photos from the Miller Mine I realized the mountains I had been dreaming about were in the Valley of Codazzi," she said, her voice real soft, her eyes misting. "I'm sure it was those mountains."

"Really?" PJ said surprised. He could see she was trembling. Now it was his turn to put his arms around her shoulders. She allowed him to pull her close, her head nestling on his chest. Her body was warm under the robe and seemed to melt against him.

"Mountains are mountains, Kathryn. Snow caps, rocks, blue glacier water...they could be from anywhere."

"Mountains of the mind, right," she said softly.

"Yes, mountains of the mind."

"Hmmm," she said, but was not convinced the answer was so simple. The photos and her dreams seemed so real to her.

"Look, I think we both need a good night's sleep," he said after a few moments. She looked up at him and nodded, stepping away and wiping her eyes with the back of her hand. She still held her drink in her hand and finished it off with a big swallow.

"Sleep sounds very good, PJ," she smiled and he led her down the spiral stairs to the guest room.

"Sweet dreams," he said in the doorway and kissed her lightly on the forehead, holding her gaze once again before turning to his own room and the welcomed coolness of the sheets of his own bed.

It was PJ who did the dreaming that night.

He saw a bearded, white-haired man with green eyes standing on a jagged, rocky peak, the wind tugging at his long hair. The man's hand held a silver object and it was pointed at him.

Suddenly, the vision shifted. He was outside an airplane, looking in the cockpit windows at Kathryn hunched over the wheel. Smoke was coming from the lone engine and the plane was pitched downward. He banged on the window in vain to wake her, yelling, "Kathryn! Kathryn!" She didn't move.

The smoke then moved into the distance, now a long black plume that rose through the bright day. And he was racing toward it, the highway rushing under humming wheels.

He woke with a start and lay there staring at the ceiling, the distant rumble of thunder and the ever present gurgle of water running past his island home the only sounds in the night.

He was acutely aware of her presence in the other room just fifteen feet down the hall. He remembered the smell of her hair and felt a wave of lust flow over him, strong enough to make him sit on the edge of his bed and think about slipping into her room, sliding under the covers and holding her body close.

But the moment passed, replaced by the image of Jester's lifeless form floating face down in the water and the passionate desire to avenge his murder. A desire that strangely felt as comfortable as it felt strong.

~~~

CHAPTER NINE

Eduardo Nevita, the superintendent at the Miller Mine, heard the airplane first. The buzz of its engines bounced off the canyon walls and rolled its way up the plateau toward the mine entrance where he was working. A moment later, the camouflaged, high winged cargo plane, a C-123 Provider, appeared over the ridge two miles to the south, descending into the Valley of Codazzi on its final approach to the dirt runway next to *Laguna d'Vacio Esmerelda*.

Eduardo had a bad feeling about the plane. The regular supply flight from Santa Marta was not expected for several days. This plane was different. Eduardo had seen news reports of the Provider in use by the Delta Nine guerrillas who controlled the Colombian Llanos over 500 miles to the southeast. The guerrillas did not have any business in the Sierra Nevada de Santa Marta Mountains. Or so Eduardo thought.

He waved to his assistant, Felipe, and they jumped into a jeep and sped off down the hill toward the airstrip. The other men working in and around the mine entrance heard the plane now and paused long enough to watch their bosses drive off before continuing their work.

The work was like all mining work, slow and dirty. But, high in the mountains, surrounded by rock, no one was going anywhere very quickly. The men transported chunks of black granite from the mine to a cleaning area. There men chopped at the hardened metamorphic ooze with hand picks, the ground around them ankle deep with chips of rock. Others used steam hoses, removing more of the blackness. They were careful not to damage the clear hexagonal crystals of Goshenite embedded in the mother rock.

Once freed, crystals were then packed in plastic bins and carried to the nearby refining house, where chemical solvents finished the cleaning process before they were packed for shipment to Mystic, Connecticut. There they would be melted back into liquid and enhanced by a powerful jolt of electricity to coat the hot spots in the core of the plastic engines built by Fast Car Caravan.

The workers went about their jobs quietly and happily. The pay was good and three times what they could earn farming in their small villages.

They had plenty to eat at the mine, decent accommodations, even organized sports, including soccer, volleyball, and sailing on the lake. Each miner worked under a six-month contract and most had signed up two and three times.

The lure of finding a crystal laced with chromium among the colorless crystals was incentive for some of the miners. It was accepted policy at the mine that any emeralds found belonged to the finder. However, this had yet to happen.

The miners often joked about Klaus Luki, the Austrian prospector who first mined the valley. They said his failure had driven him crazy and he still wandered the mountains in search of precious gems, his howls of frustration mixing with the nightly winds that swept over the isolated area.

That isolation appealed to the miners. They were Kogi Indians. These were their mountains. They believed it was a magical land alive with the spirit of their ancestors, the Taironas. Their beliefs were rooted in *aluna*, the seven levels of nature that blended the spiritual world and real world. The Kogis called the Sierra Nevadas the "Heart of the World" and themselves, the "Elder Brothers", the protectors of the fragile balance between man and nature.

A 200 square mile microcosm of the world's climates, the Sierra Nevada de Santa Marta Mountains was rival to the Himalayas in steepness, if not in height. They rose sharply out of the Caribbean Sea along the northern coastline of Colombia, reaching nearly 18,000 feet, with varied vegetation, wildlife and terrain.

On the lower mountainsides coffee, bananas and marijuana shared the humid warmth that rolled in from the sea. On the higher slopes, the greenery gave way to a brown and barren landscape, dotted with small, windblown trees and bushes, surrounding deep blue lakes of sparkling glacial water. Animals and birds of many species thrived, but the valleys, peaks and steep slopes in between were mostly unexplored.

Eduardo was the son of a Kogi *Mama*, or chieftain. As his jeep sped toward the runway, he thought of the days when he and his father first explored the stony unknown together, a rite of passage for a ten year old. They had walked for several days and soaked in the serenity of the rocks and the company of father and son. He learned much of the special world in which they lived. And the special relationship his father had with nature.

Eduardo remembered one night. The last embers still glowed in the fire and he drifted in and out of sleep, tired from a long day of walking and no food. He saw his father sitting in deep meditation by the fire. Suddenly, before his sleepy, young eyes, his father's body was transformed into the body of a jaguar. He thought it was a dream, but the next morning there was fresh meat to eat from a mountain deer killed by a sharp-toothed animal. His father never said where the meat came from, and Eduardo dared not ask, but he was forever respectful of the strong powers possessed by those of pure thought among his race.

Five days into their walk, they came upon a narrow pass between two ridges, wide enough for a man to squeeze through. On the other side, they both stood in awe. A long, narrow valley, hidden more than a mile above sea level stretched before them, protected as far as the eye could see by mountain peaks that rose three miles high, their tops unseen in the clouds. To their right, a deep blue lake reflected the sky, fed by a rapidly moving river that ran the length of the valley along a nearly vertical canyon wall.

Opposite that wall, beyond the lake, a plateau gently sloped upward for about a mile before it ran into near vertical walls of another ridge that climbed to a snowcapped peak. In the distance, a break in the clouds revealed Pico Codazzi stoically guarding the north end of the valley.

It was Eduardo's destiny to return to the Valley of Codazzi twenty-five years later when Jester Miller hired him to re-open Klaus Luki's abandoned emerald mine and dig for Goshenite. Fourteen men had joined him, the sons of his tribal brothers. They were family, and despite the occasional hard conditions at the mine, they were a productive and happy team. They felt very much a part of the mountains, and that was good. Eduardo was their leader and as he watched the plane approach the end of the runway, he felt protective of them.

***

Rex Simka, at the controls of the approaching aircraft, was relieved when the plane broke through the bottom of the clouds. His calculations had been correct. The valley was visible ahead, just over a ridge. In the seat next to him, his co-pilot, Luis Caron, let out a sigh, happy to see out of the cockpit again.

"Pretty ballsy, my friend, no?" Simka laughed with glee at his co-pilot.

"Insane is more like it!" Caron answered.

Both were dressed in the dark brown uniform of the Colombia National Police. Two lines of men in grey and brown mufti, twenty-five in all, armed with automatic weapons, were crouched in the plane's cargo bay ready to do battle.

They crossed over the ridge and Simka pushed the controls forward, dropping low over the lake, lining up just to the left of the canyon wall. A rough diagram was strapped to Simka's knee and it proved accurate. Simka could see the rushing water that showed white where the river joined the lake, and a small orange cone that marked the end of the narrow runway, just a few feet from the water's edge.

A sudden cross wind gust lifted the right wing, but he quickly leveled off and the oversized wheels touched down on the hard dirt surface. He reversed the pitch of the props and revved the engines, slowing the loaded craft. The runway was less than 3000 feet long, but Simka had the plane rolling easily within 2000 feet. He taxied past three barrack-like buildings to his left and toward a peaked roof structure standing at the far end of the airstrip. The big doors under the plane's high tail began to open.

Jose Salazar, the mine's business manager and cook, watched from the second floor of the peaked roof building used as the Ops Center. The plane taxied right up to it, spun around and stopped. Men with guns came running down the plane's unloading ramp. He thought it unusual that the plane had no markings.

The armed men spread out in several directions and soon he could hear footsteps inside the building. He switched on the short-wave radio transmitter and a low crackle of static came from the speaker as the dials came alive. A soldier burst through the door before Salazar had a chance to send any message. One burst from a MAC-10 machine pistol blew apart the transmitter, cutting off the Miller Mine from the outside world.

Eduardo heard the gunshots as he and Felipe arrived at the Ops Center. Before they could react, several soldiers pulled then from the jeep. Four others jumped in, turned the jeep around and gunned back up the hillside toward the mine, leaving Eduardo and Felipe to watch the rest of the soldiers deploy around the grounds. Several ran toward the barracks to Eduardo's right. A moment later, Jose came stumbling out of the Ops Center, pushed by another armed man, and the three of them were held at gunpoint near the plane.

Simka stepped from the rear cargo bay, followed by two men carrying MAC-10's at their sides. Simka was a tall man with a thin mustache. His face was brown from the sun and he carried himself well in a uniform, even though he had never served in the military. He was an American and his background was in law enforcement with the FBI and the Drug Enforcement Agency.

Working out of Miami, Simka had enjoyed the chase for drug dealers, but the longer he chased, the louder came the call of its dark side. Three years ago he had succumbed, drawn to the Colombians by the lure of the money, the power it buys, and the drugs.

In a brash statement, he killed his DEA partner during a major sting operation in Key West. The set up would have netted the feds 100 kilos of cocaine valued at $2,000,000, and two key players in the Medellin cartel.

When the deal went down, Simka shot his partner, the two drug traffickers and kept the drugs and cash, fleeing the country in a stolen plane. He used the murders, the money, and the drugs as his resume' when he came to Carlos Quintaro and asked for a job.

Quintaro at first denied any involvement in drugs or any interest in Simka. However, Simka persisted and was eventually hired. Quintaro admitted Simka's knowledge of U.S. drug interdiction plans would be most valuable. Simka did small jobs and soon gained Quintaro's trust. His insight into the workings of the American law enforcement gave Quintaro improved success with cocaine shipments into the U.S. Simka was promoted to a bodyguard, where Quintaro could keep a close eye on him. They came to enjoy each other's company.

In turn, Simka showed respect for Quintaro, and worked hard, using his talent for planning operations. Simka also exhibited a ruthless demeanor that put fear in the hearts of those who spent any time around him. Quintaro liked that and used Simka to boost his own reputation. On this day, Simka was spearheading the takeover of the Miller Mine and would supervise its conversion into the center for Quintaro's cocaine smuggling operation.

Simka stopped in front of Eduardo and looked him over. The Indian was dressed in dusty tan pants and a sleeveless work shirt made of leather, open at the chest. Simka's eyes stopped on a two inch gold pendant hanging from Eduardo's neck. It was the likeness of an ancient Indian deity in full war bonnet with hands on hips, striking a defiant pose.

"This is very old, yes?" Simka asked Eduardo, fingering the heavy pendant. His Spanish was flawless.

"It has been in my family for several generations, sir," Eduardo answered. The proud Indian stood unflinching, his black eyes watching Simka's every move, his body language unwittingly mimicking the deity.

"Are you in charge?" asked Simka.

"I am the mine superintendent," Eduardo answered firmly but politely. "Eduardo Nevita. And you, sir?"

"I am Lieutenant Commander Pedro Rodriguez, Colombian National Police." Simka reached into his breast pocket and pulled out an official looking document embossed with the seal of the Colombian Government. He held it up in front of Eduardo.

"I have here an order from Presidente Ferdinand Barranqui Gomez placing this mine and its property under my command. All mining activities are to cease immediately and all persons at this mine evacuated to Valledupar."

Simka spoke with an official tone. He did not wait for Eduardo to agree, but simply gestured toward the plane. Eduardo wasn't quite ready to leave.

"This mine is leased by a foreign company, sir, by Jester Miller of the United States," Eduardo tried to keep his voice even. "I must speak with him before I can allow you to take it away."

"Mr. Miller has already been spoken to," replied Simka. He started to move toward the operations building, but Eduardo's voice stopped him.

"I have heard nothing from Mr. Miller. Your piece of paper is meaningless until I hear from Mr. Miller!" Eduardo spat in the dust. He did not believe this brown uniformed man. "You are not police. You are more like guerrillas. Or *contrabandista*!"

Simka turned and moved up close to the Indian, staring him straight in the eye. The ruthless streak in Quintaro's agent seethed through his false words.

"Sir, I am a representative from the Colombian government and I have direct orders from the leader of this country to close this mine, remove the workers and then move on to my next project, which will likely be something deemed very important by our Presidente. I don't have much time and I am prepared to use force to accomplish my task. Do we understand each other?"

Eduardo eyes shifted from Simka's face to the men standing in a small circle around him with automatic weapons ready. His was a proud, brave man, but not foolish.

"What about the rest of my men?" Eduardo asked, resigned to the takeover.

"Good. We understand each other!" Simka flashed a short smile that masked his annoyance. "You and your men will not be harmed. You will ride in my plane to Valledupar, where upon you will each receive $500 in cash. That should be plenty to get you and your men back to your villages."

Enough to live on for most of a year for many of the Indians, thought Eduardo. But why Valledupar? That was a town on the southern edge of the mountains. The Kogi villages were to the north.

His suspicions grew as the jeep returned, joined by two of the mine's pick-up trucks filled with the workers and Simka's armed men. The trucks came to a halt in a cloud of dust next to the plane and the men forced out.

Escape seemed useless. Eduardo knew his men could survive in the mountains, but it was doubtful anyone could even run twenty yards without drawing a rain of automatic weapons fire.

"May we get our personal belongings?" Eduardo asked Simka, trying to delay the inevitable.

Simka looked at the three low buildings about 500 yards away, the living quarters of the mine crew. Too risky, he thought. He wanted it quick and clean and any more delays would just muddy the plan.

"No. We must leave right now," he answered abruptly. Simka turned to Luis and they spoke briefly. Luis in turn barked orders to the armed men and the mine crew was herded toward the plane.

"You can buy what you need with your new money!" laughed Simka and he strode toward the Ops Center, several soldiers trailing behind.

The miners were ordered to sit forward in the cargo bay, huddled together on the metal floor. All the armed men left the plane except for two guards.

"Hugo! Santos! You stay with these men. See they are comfortable," Luis said loud enough for Eduardo to hear. Then he opened the cockpit door and climbed the short ladder up to the flight deck.

Moments later Simka's tall figure entered the back of the plane and the hydraulic ramp immediately began to rise up with a whine, sealing the plane shut. He moved through the Indians with a stony gaze and up into the cockpit.

The engines coughed to life and the plane taxied to the far end of the runway, pirouetted just yards from the lake, and without a pause began to roll into the wind as the engines roared to full power. It picked up speed and the canyon wall raced by the windows, as if ready to reach out and clip the right wing tip. About 2000 feet down the strip, air speed indicating 105 knots, Simka gently pulled back on the controls and the nose wheel easily lifted off the runway, followed seconds later by the rest of the aircraft.

The bumpy takeoff roll was replaced by airborne smoothness and the engines pulled the old plane into a climb over the end of the runway and the river. Simka banked gently to the left to follow the riverbed and keep the plane from hitting the high cliffs on the right side. He continued to climb slowly, following the river until it turned sharply left. Once they had cleared the ridges on both sides, he gently banked left toward the west and the plane entered the clouds.

At 12,000 feet, they broke into sunshine and Pico Colon and Pico Bolivar, the highest peaks in the Sierra Nevada de Santa Marta, appeared ahead through the cockpit window, their snow capped beauty glistening in the sun. Beyond the mountains, the clouds ended and the Caribbean Sea was visible.

In the co-pilot seat, Luis pointed to a lower peak just to the right of the airplane's nose.

"Codazzi," he said. Simka nodded and changed course slightly so they

---

were flying directly for it. The altimeter read 16,000 feet.

In the cargo bay, Eduardo felt the chill of the metal deck as the plane climbed higher. He fingered the gold pendant around his neck and worried. He knew something was not right. The Indians sat huddled together, several munching on coca leaves, kept in small mochila bags around their necks.

Eduardo sensed they were heading west, when they should be heading southeast to reach Valledupar. Huddled there in a tight group, with the two guards not fifteen feet away, his mind raced. He felt foolish for leading his men right into this trap without as much as a struggle. It may already be too late, but he had to do something. The odds might be better against the guards up here. He turned to his assistant next to him.

"We have been tricked, Felipe," he said, switching from Spanish to Iki, the native tongue of the Kogis. Felipe was surprised, but listened intensely. The rumble of the plane's engine vibrated through the big cabin, forcing Eduardo almost to shout.

Eduardo spoke so all the men could hear him. He smiled, acting as their leader, as if asking each one how they felt.

"Be alert," he warned in Iki, "We have been tricked. Be ready. Wait for the signal." Then quietly to Felipe. "Distract the guards. Start a fight."

Felipe looked up at the two guards sitting on jump seats on each side of the flight deck doorway. Hugo was looking out a porthole and Santos was fiddling with his gun.

Felipe gave a rough shove to Victor sitting in front of him. Victor, one of the youngest and strongest of the miners, turned sharply. Felipe pushed again and Victor stood up quickly.

"Fight me, you pig!" shouted Felipe in Iki. Victor was hesitant, but Felipe, all five foot five inches, rushed toward him and tackled Victor. They both stumbled backward over the others and across the cargo deck.

Hugo and Santos jumped up, shouting and pointing their weapons, while the other Indians grabbed at the two combatants. Eduardo watched both guards wade into the fight and he jumped on Hugo's back, knocking the gun to the deck where it slid toward the rear of the plane.

Santos had his hands on Felipe, but four new pairs of hands grabbed the guard and began to pommel him. Hugo staggered with Eduardo around his neck and fell backward against the cabin wall, smashing Eduardo and breaking free. Eduardo ended up on the deck, the wind knocked from him. Hugo turned for him, but three Indians jumped him from behind and they all fell in a heap.

Everyone was up and moving, either fighting the strong guards or cheering on their friends. The shifting of all the men, over a ton of cargo, was felt in the cockpit through Simka's hands as he held the plane's control wheel. He looked at Luis, jerking his head back toward the cargo bay.

"See what's happening back there. We are almost in position," he said, looking at the peak of Codazzi just a few miles away. "And put on your cargo harness," Simka added, as his co-pilot scrambled out of the cockpit. Luis pulled out a .9 mm pistol from his holster and climbed down the ladder to the cargo bay. He opened the door slowly and saw two separate fights as half of the Indians grappled with Hugo and Santos.

Jose had grabbed Hugo's fallen gun and when he saw the cockpit door open, he let out a short burst of gunfire. Everyone went diving to the floor as the bullets started ricocheting around the cabin.

"Jose, no!" shouted Eduardo. "No guns in the air!"

Luis slammed the door shut and heard the bullets bouncing off the bulkhead.

"The Indians have a gun!" he shouted up to Simka.

"Dump them now!" Simka yelled back and put the plane into a slight dive.

"What about Hugo and Santos?" Luis shouted back.

"Do it now, Luis! There is no time," came Simka's hard reply.

Crouched in a the small space behind the door at the foot of the cockpit ladder, Luis looked at the cargo loading control panel just above him and punched the green button under the word "DOOR". The hydraulic motors began to whine, pumping hydraulic fluid into pistons on the clamshell doors and with a sharp clang, the rear of the plane began to open.

The noise of the thin, cold air rushing into the new opening at 180 knots was deafening. The Indians, still hugging the deck after Jose had turned the cabin into a hornet's nest of bullets, stared as the cabin filled with bright sunshine and the brown and white of the rocky peaks below.

Luis flipped a second lever marked "LOAD LOCK" to unlock the slab of metal deck the Indians lay on. It was a sliding deck on rollers used for easy unloading.

"Unlocked!" Luis shouted up to Simka.

Immediately, Simka pulled back hard on the wheel and pushed the throttles on full. The nose of the plane came up at a 30-degree angle and shouts of terror came from the Indians as they felt the deck move under them. Slowly, then with frightening speed, the deck slid toward the opening at the back of the plane.

Jose, standing closest to the door, turned when the doors opened and was pitched forward when the plane went into its steep climb. He tumbled down the unloading ramp and into the sunlight. Then the rolling deck slammed to a stop at the end of the ramp, sending twelve Indians and two guards into wingless flight.

Their screams filled Eduardo's ears as he grabbed for a loose cargo strap hanging from the side of the plane, stopping his fall short of the ramp. He was buffeted angrily by the wind, his gold pendant painfully smacking him in the eye with its weight. He twisted to look in horror at his friends turned into tiny dots falling toward the rocks below.

Felipe was still in the cabin, on his hands and knees sliding toward Eduardo, reaching in vain for another cargo strap. Eduardo reached out and managed to grab hold of his leg as he slid by, but the extra weight of even the small Felipe was too much and Eduardo's handhold on the strap slipped, and they were both carried out the cargo bay door with Eduardo's hand firmly clutching Felipe's leg.

The blast of cold air rushing past Eduardo's face sucked his lungs empty. He separated from Felipe and watched the plane flying away, the noise of the air filling his ears. He saw the burnished Codazzi peak. Close enough to almost reach out and touch. Colon and Bolivar he had climbed, but not Codazzi, he thought. As he fell, he felt strength building inside his body.

"We are one with nature, my son, we are a part of her boundaries, so there are no boundaries. Be one with the other and you can fly, you can be a rock or a rush of water. Be pure of mind and spirit and lift your soul and your heart to the great Mother."

Eduardo heard the words distinctly in his father's voice and felt a calm descend over his mind and body as he fell. He slowly turned in the air and saw the white snow on the peaks rushing towards him and thought very hard about his life as a Kogi Indian, his father's words and the seven levels that bind the spiritual and real world together and make them one. And then there were only the voices of his brothers who had gone to the mountains before him, the mountains he loved so much. And then only whiteness and the sound of the wind.

~~~

CHAPTER TEN

T wo days after the takeover of the Miller Mine, supply pilot Barney Devlin broke through the clouds at 15,000 feet. His darkened cockpit suddenly flooded with light and he lifted his eyes from the instruments, squinted through the windshield and marveled at the view. After thirty-one years in the pilot's seat, he never ceased to be amazed at the sights to which he was privy.

He had entered a world known only to flyers. A world confined by vastness, domed in blue, floored in cotton, baked by the yellow sun. Jagged peaks poked through the whiteness, erect and snow covered, sentries in a kingdom that seemed to have no end.

In a second he had his visual bearings and felt at home, silently naming the peaks spread across the horizon. Bolivar, Ojeda, Colon and Codazzi, the peaks of the Sierra Nevada de Santa Marta mountains. Their harsh faces were familiar friends from the comfort of the cockpit. Barney shivered at the thought of standing on the top of one for even as long as it took to down a shot of Arguardiente.

Barney drank in the beauty of nature three miles up, yet he knew it was to be short-lived. His destination was hidden under the clouds, surrounded by immovable rocks and tricky winds, in the Valley of Codazzi.

Barney Devlin was a soldier of fortune who had settled in an exotic country. His sagging jowls sported a scruffy white beard that seemed to flow down to his chest where tufts of white hair spilled out of his open flight jacket, the leather cracked and faded, as dark as his tan. His bald head hid under a floppy brimmed hat that touched the bridge of his aviator sunglasses. He looked every bit of his fifty years.

Except for the eyes.

Deep wrinkles at the corners and the heavy bags underneath, his eyes shone ice cold blue. They revealed a man with years of experience, maybe not enough sleep, and a youthful yearning for more.

Barney was an American by birth who had not been home in thirty years. Instead, he had logged thousands of hours flying across Colombia, Central America and the Caribbean, hauling cargo of every description, from people to pickles, into small airstrips he categorized as desolate and remote. He had landed on islands, in the jungle and on the sides of mountains. His ability to land where others dare not provided a decent income, a nice beach apartment in Santa Marta and three squares a day.

The creases on his face changed ever so slightly as his lips broke into a small smile, revealing straight, but not so white teeth. It was a career and a home he hadn't planned on when he took off from Miami as a twenty-year-old mercenary piloting an ancient twin-engine bomber in the Bay of Pigs invasion of Cuba.

Shot down by Cuban gunmen, wounded in the arm, he parachuted into the jungle and evaded Castro's soldiers for two days before escaping from the island in a stolen fishing boat. Delirious with fever and soon out of fuel, he was plucked from the Caribbean Sea by a freighter bound for South America.

Sitting above the clouds, Barney thought of Eduardo down below in the Valley of Codazzi. He was close to the young man, their history together recorded years ago when Eduardo's father had saved Barney's life and nursed him back to health. Eduardo had been only a child then.

He smiled at the irony of Eduardo's desire to leave the mountains and learn about the outside world, only to return to the isolated rocks years later. A Kogi's destiny was among the mountains, he guessed.

And his sister, Azulmora? Well, maybe not all Kogi's were destined for the rocks, he laughed, looking at her dark, young face smiling up at him from a photo taped on the instrument panel.

Barney checked his GPS readout again. The landing approach to Codazzi was a test for even the most experienced pilot. Most of the time the approach was blind through layers of clouds that formed between the rocky peaks. There were no FAA controllers to guide him to the airstrip. He relied on a systematic series of checkpoints in the air. Numbers in his navigation receiver that created a three dimensional electronic map.

The twin turbo engines hummed in unison, the props biting into the cold, thin air with confidence, pulling the plane through the sunlight. A warning buzzer went off, indicating he had reached his first checkpoint.

On this Thursday morning at the end of September, he was flying an unscheduled supply run to the mine. Five hundred pounds of food and equipment were strapped down in the cargo space. They would be exchanged for two tons of Goshenite destined for Fast Car Caravan in Mystic. The real reason for this flight, however, was to check on the mine.

The phone call 48 hours earlier from PJ McDonough was his first clue something was not right. Barney had never met McDonough, but knew of him. They had spoken once before and he recognized the voice straight away.

"Barney Devlin, PJ McDonough calling from Fast Car Caravan in Connecticut. Can you hear me?" came the distant voice. The satellite transmission that beamed PJ's voice from the U.S. to Colombia still had to travel the final few miles over the somewhat primitive Santa Marta telephone system.

"McDonough, yes. This is Barney, I hear you fine. What's happening in the states?"

"Not good, Barney. I have terrible news," PJ had answered. "It's Jester. He's dead."

"What! Jester? That son of a bitch! I can't believe it! What happened?" he had asked dumbfounded.

PJ described the shooting in San Francisco Bay the previous Saturday and the early police investigation. Barney listened in disbelief.

He knew Jester well. They had met when Jester first came to Colombia looking for the Goshenite mine. It was Barney who had put him in touch with the Kogi Indian who guided him into the Valley of Codazzi. It was Barney who had made the first landing at the small airstrip there, but only after Jester convinced him he could do it. Barney remembered it had taken a couple of days of talking and some late nights in a few of Santa Marta's watering holes. They had grown close.

"Barney, we need to get some answers," PJ finished.

"Hell, PJ, Jester was my friend. Tell me what you need," Barney had said. "What's the shooting have to do with Colombia?"

"It may have something to do with the mine in the Valley of Codazzi," PJ said.

"The mine?" Devlin was surprised.

"Do the names Brett Lesco, or Luis Caron of Colombia Precious Metals in Cartegena mean anything to you? And Carlos Quintaro or QUIMEX?"

"Hold on, PJ! Slow down! Quintaro I know," Barney answered. "He's an exporter. Owns QUIMEX. He's got a lock on anything that leaves from the ports of Barranquilla or Santa Marta. Coffee, cement, textiles. Bananas to carnations, you name it, he ships it. It's a big operation. They have an office across from me at the Santa Marta airport, and a huge docking facility there and at Barranquilla."

"Any drug connections?" PJ asked.

"Well, PJ, this is Colombia and there is a fine line between exporting and smuggling," Barney answered with a laugh. "I'm sure some contraband has found it's way through the company, but hell, they love him down here. He's a respected businessman. He's dumped a bunch of money into the towns between Cartegena and Riohacha, and even donated to Presidente Gomez's election campaign."

There was silence on the line for a moment.

"He's high profile, PJ," Barney added for emphasis.

" Did Jester have any direct dealings with him?" PJ asked.

"Not that I am aware of," Barney answered.

"Have you been to the mine recently?"

"Last week. Two days before you say Jester was shot. Jeez, I still can't believe that! Shot on a sailboat, you said. Oh, man!"

"I have to contact them and talk to the mine superintendent, Eduardo Nevita," PJ said.

"I know Eduardo well. I'll try to reach him."

There was a pause.

"Barney, the mine is the only connection I can make," PJ said. "I appreciate anything you can do."

"I'll do what I can, PJ," Barney pledged. "Look, I'll make a few calls, ask around. It's the least I can do for old Jester. You know, he said I'd be the one to go first. Damn, I wish he had been right!"

Raising the mine by radio proved to be unsuccessful. PJ's sense of urgency and Barney's own concern for Eduardo and the Indians made the decision to make this special trip an easy one.

Besides, they always loved his visits, Barney thought, as he pushed forward on the control wheel and began his descent toward the clouds. Barney's arrivals were a highlight in the Indians' routine.

* * *

Two miles below, Rex Simka felt the sweat building under his clothes despite the cooling breeze that swirled off the rock walls on the western side of the Valley of Codazzi. He bent over a water pump, a portable old machine with valves, levers, and rubber belts built around a motorcycle motor. He stared at the rusty nut that held the piston arm to the engine crankshaft. He knew very little about pumps, but he stared nonetheless. The swirling wind, however, occupied most of his thoughts.

Little tornadoes of dust touched down across the plateau as he stared. The wind seemed to blow from every direction. One moment he felt it coming up the plateau from the lake about a mile away. The next it seemed to come from directly above, pushed by unseen forces off the high canyon walls behind him.

The wind was a nuisance, thought Simka. It seemed to blow steady enough right down the runway from the north, funneled by the river and canyon walls. But, once it reached beyond the ridge at the north end of the valley, it spilled every which way. It made every take off and landing a guessing game. He was surprised that none of the aircraft had yet been damaged.

The usually deserted airstrip had seen a steady stream of air traffic since the takeover. The small parking area in front of the operations building overflowed with a new four engine De Havilland DHC-7, the old C-123 Provider, a Cessna Caravan, a dark Beechcraft twin, Simka's own Aerospatiale and Quintaro's private helicopter. Two mechanics worked full time to service the different craft.

A dozen other men concentrated on unloading the planes as they arrived with their various cargoes of foodstuffs, cocaine paste, and barrels of petrol and chemicals.

The barracks area, where the miners had once slept, remained unchanged, home now to four-dozen workers and security men. A new electric wire was strung from the barracks to a large diesel generator that was running just outside the mine entrance, the wire slung between a series of poles rigged in tripod fashion to keep the wire off the ground.

The generator thumped away a few feet from Simka under a quickly erected shelter, which also housed the broken water pump. Several thousand feet of two-inch fire hose ran side by side along the base of the rocky ridge that extended from the mine passed the operations building to the river. One hose supplied the hundreds of gallons of water needed during the cocaine production process and the other carried the wastewater back to the river.

Simka looked up at the men standing near by debating the problems with the pump, although no one had lifted a wrench to fix it.

"Pedro, the socket wrench!" he said, pointing to the toolbox while not hiding his frustration. Pedro did as he was told, and rejoined the group. A familiar taste developed in the back of Simka's mouth and he felt a desire to reach for the brown vial of cocaine he kept in his pocket.

"Simka!" came a shout from the mine entrance.

A second later the white haired figure of Carlos Quintaro strode briskly out of the tunnel's mouth, followed by a smaller man dressed in all white.

Quintaro himself wore a tan shirt under a suede waist jacket. Creased chino pants and pointed boots gave Quintaro a gentleman cowboy look, but the face mask with special breathing filters around his neck seemed oddly out of place. The hard set of his face coupled with the obvious irritation in his voice warned Rex his boss was on the warpath again.

"My friend, Rex," his voice seethed, "can we expect that water flow to resume sometime this week?"

The small crowd of workers snickered at the comment, only to fall silent as Simka glared up at them from the pump.

"Hell, Carlos, I don't know squat about water pumps," Simka spat in anger as he spun a socket wrench on the rusted nut on the piston arm. The nut sheared off under the socket's pressure, much to Simka's disgust.

"Son of a bitch!" he shouted, looking at the nut.

He turned to Pedro.

"Get the back up pump from the storage shed, we'll have to set it up here." The worker nodded and quickly headed for the shed with two companions.

Simka stood up and walked over to Carlos and the smaller man. He was annoyed at the breakdown, but also annoyed at his boss. He of all people should have known better than to embarrass him in front of the men.

"Carlos, we have been pushing very hard the last three days. Not everything can be expected to work perfectly."

"I don't want excuses, Rex," Quintaro said firmly. "We must keep the water flowing or we will lose this batch of coca."

"The coca paste must be cleansed of acetone at the precise moment or its potency will deteriorate," spoke the man dressed in white, his voice a raspy whisper.

Simka knew him as Julio, Quintaro's *cocinero*, or cocaine cook. A good foot shorter than Simka, he was a frail man with a thin, pasty-white face, and a few strands of reddish hair growing from his mostly baldhead. Nearly every time Simka saw Julio a cigarette dangled from his lips. The exception came when Julio's body was quaked with coughing fits, which were frequent. Then he would carefully clasp the cigarette between his thumb and index finger, holding it away from his body until the fit subsided, upon which he promptly stuck it back in his mouth.

The white suit he wore was immaculate, but it was old and frayed around the collar and wrists. His fingers had the telltale green stains of a coca cook and he didn't bother wearing a facemask in the lab, where the stench of cooking chemicals would gag even the strongest men. Julio seemed to enjoy the smell. In general, he gave off an unhealthy air and

Simka did not particularly like him.

However, Julio convinced Quintaro he could produce a very pure cocaine in mass quantities in less time than normal and Simka was not about to say or do anything that would disrupt that arrangement. Operation Snowmine was, after all, the reason they were in this forsaken mountain valley and he was not going to let his dislike of the frail cook ruin his own chance to earn a $100 million share of the billion dollar plan.

"I know about the water, Julio," Simka returned, glaring at the small man, who took a half step backward. Then Simka turned to Quintaro.

"I already sent a truckload of men to the river to hand carry water cans to the lab," he said. He pointed down the dirt roadway to the truck on the other side of the airstrip, where four men were busy at the river's edge.

"It will be slow, but at least we will not lose the batch."

"Good, Rex. Let's put more men on that task while you get the new pump set up." Quintaro's green eyes almost softened.

Quintaro watched the men at the river for a moment then allowed his eyes to drift, taking in the long valley and it's glacial lake that stretched north and south. This was only the second time he had been to there, the first since the takeover.

"It is remarkable sight, yes?" he said to the men standing next to him, who both turned and looked. "It looks like a valley there and a canyon here. Remarkable. I've never seen anything like it."

The mountain slopes around the lake at the southern end were not very steep as they rose into the cloud layer, although a steep transverse ridge did run abruptly across the end of the lake. In contrast, at the northern end, where the mine was situated, shear cliffs as high as 300 feet rose into the sky.

He admired the stark beauty of their isolation and the mixture of deep blue water, brown earth, and green shrubs. He then chuckled at the number of airplanes parked near the main building, their silver and white, sleek metal bodies a stark contrast to the upheavals of the earth that had created the valley millions of years ago.

"If only the sun would shine a little more, yes?"

"But that is why we are here, jefe. No sun, no photos," Simka reminded his boss. Although it made it tough on the pilots, the clouds hid the valley from the airborne reconnaissance of the *Rapidero Fuego*. It was the main reasons they moved the lab operations out of the jungle.

"Of course, Rex," Quintaro said softly.

"We must remain hidden from the fire dragon!" Julio rasped darkly.

The look of terror filled his face. "I have seen the dragon from the sky and the heartless men who burn the dead. We must not let them find us!"

"It appears the bomberderos have shaken Julio," Quintaro said with a thin smile. He respected the small man's fear, though he did not feel it himself.

"If we follow the planned air routes in and out, stay close and low, they will not find us, Carlos," Simka said.

"Good. We have fine pilots, Rex. I have trained them well. There will be no problems."

Even as they stood there, Simka noticed the breeze had shifted again, blowing right into their faces out of the east. So much of this plan depends on our pilots, Simka thought, but who can control the wind?

Quintaro had a look of satisfaction on his face as he breathed in the cool air blowing in his face.

"You are right, my friend, we have worked hard this week. But, we can not slow down just yet! In forty-eight hours, we embark on our great enterprise. We will have 4000 kilos ready to deliver to our wholesalers in America. And another 4000 for Europe. 8000 kilos of the purest cocaine the world has ever seen, right, Julio?"

"Ya, jefe. Very pure."

"And a pure $200 million, yes," said Simka. The thought brought a smile to his face. At $25,000 a kilo, one's week payoff would be a nice start to the twelve week billion dollar plan. Quintaro and Julio smiled also. Then Quintaro turned to Simka.

"There has been no problem moving the chemicals?" he asked.

"Well, Ulf has not had much sleep this past week, but there has been no problem, yet." replied Simka, thinking of his haggard transportation chief, Ulf Rodenborg. "We have been lucky there have been no accidents. He's been making three flights a day from Riohacha."

Quintaro nodded.

Julio's new cooking formula had sharply cut back on the amount of ether, acetone and hydrochloric acid needed to extract the cocaine alkaloid from the coca paste. Still, a steady supply of nearly 10,000 gallons of these volatile chemicals was required each week to keep up with the aggressive production schedule. Every drop had to be airlifted into the valley in fifty-five gallon drums, each drum weighing 330 pounds. It was the biggest hurdle Simka faced in planning Operation Snowmine.

The chemicals were imported from Madagascar and India by QUIMEX through Barranquilla. Six shipments, each one consisting of sixty tons of chemicals sealed inside large shipping containers, had already been ordered and were either in port or on ships enroute to Colombia.

On paper, the chemicals were destined for several paint manufacturers in Colombia. In reality, the containers were trucked from the Barranquilla docks to Quintaro's airstrip in Riohacha where they were opened and the drums loaded on planes for delivery to the Valley of Codazzi.

Simka knew the DEA kept a close eye on the movement of large amounts of chemicals worldwide, looking for a trail to the drug makers. Ether was especially easy to trace since there were less than a dozen producers of ether in the world. However, Simka had found a new supplier. Any drug agents would have to get very close to the operation to notice anything unusual.

"Our man in Barranquilla reports the unloading went smoothly with not a hint of interest on the part of the authorities," Simka continued.

"Good, good. We pay enough money in that port. We should expect no problems," Quintaro said. "Now come, I want to show you something." He walked back into the mine, adjusting his breathing filter. Simka grabbed one from a box near the entrance and followed him. The mask-less Julio trailed behind.

The greatest transformation in the valley had taken place two hundred feet inside the mine where a dimly lit tunnel led to a large cavern in the rock. Only a week before, the Indian miners had used picks, probes and dynamite to extract Goshenite crystals in their mother rock. Today, the cavern was a fully operating cocaine lab.

Floodlights illuminated stainless steel tanks of acetone, ether and hydrochloric acid that sat on wooden frames along the back wall. The tanks rose twenty feet in the air, their tops lost in the darkness. A network of plastic hoses ran from chemical drums in a corner to the tanks and then down to shallow vats where the cooking took place.

Underneath the vats a series of gas burners heated the smelly concoction of acid, solvents and cocaine paste. A bubbling brown scum floated on top of the rancid liquid. Metal hoods, suspended from scaffolds over each vat, vented the fumes through a fat hose that snaked through the mine tunnel carrying the foul-smelling gases outside. However, the smell was still strong in the mine and brought tears to the eyes of the uninitiated. To profit from cocaine one had to survive the evil smell of production.

A second series of vats stood near the cookers, ready for the filtering and rinsing cycles. There were hoses everywhere to bring fresh water in and the used chemicals out of the mine.

Six drying tables, each five feet wide and 30 feet long stood on one side of the cavern, filled with white powder, baking under high intensity lights.

Two dozen men and women were at work, most dressed in white and red coveralls, others in blue lab coats, all wearing facemasks.

Quintaro, Simka and Julio stopped along the right-hand wall just inside the cavern and watched half a dozen workers in front of mechanical packing machines. Each worker carefully laid a heavy-duty plastic wrap over a circular shaped mold, filling the mold with cocaine powder taken from a large bin. When the built in scale measured the exact amount, the worker stepped on a foot pedal that removed the mold, tightly folded the plastic around the cocaine, and compressed it into a six-inch ball of coke.

Twenty five sealed balls, each weighing one kilo, were carefully placed in a duffel bag and a dozen duffel bags loaded on a wooden skid that sat on a small railway flatbed once used to carry rock from the mine. The skid was wheeled to the mine entrance and its contents loaded on a pickup truck for the short trip to a storage shed behind the ops buildings where it awaited the next scheduled delivery.

Quintaro picked up a ball six inches across wrapped in plastic. He playfully tossed it toward Simka.

"A Q ball, yes," Quintaro said with a robust laugh that echoed in the cavern, even through his facemask.

Simka caught the ball and felt its weight. He picked up other balls, checking the weight of each against the other. He could not discern any difference among them.

"No mark?" Simka asked Quintaro, looking at the plain wrapper. It was customary for smugglers to identify their product with a distinctive trademark.

"No mark, Rex," Quintaro answered. "Its purity will be it's own trademark. Besides, I do not wish to raise any red flags with the authorities if they should seize balls with a big Q on them."

He reached for a small beaker and filled it with some bleach from a nearby bottle. He then took out a pocketknife with a pearl handle, reached into a large tub, scooped a small amount of the cocaine with the blade and sprinkled it into the beaker. The white powder fell through the liquid and quickly dissolved before it reached the bottom. In a few seconds, the only evidence of the powder was a yellowish film floating on top of the bleach. Any impurities would have fallen to the bottom, but there were none.

Even Simka was impressed. The powder dissolved quicker than in any other tests he had seen. He looked at Quintaro's wide-open eyes and imagined he was smiling under his facemask. Simka himself was grinning, the taste in the back of his mouth stronger.

"We are averaging about a duffel an hour for each worker, so we can pack 4000 kilos in just over a day," Julio said in his raspy voice. "We already have 2000 kilos we moved from the jungle labs, 3000 kilos packed here and the rest should be ready by Saturday, in two days."

"Yes, but the packers are getting ahead because the powder is not drying fast enough," Quintaro said and walked toward the long drying tables under the intense heat lamps.

"Rex, we need five more men to work on the tables and turn the powder gently every hour." He grabbed a wooden spatula from one of the tables and demonstrated with a careful digging and sprinkling motion. "Like this Julio, yes?" Quintaro turned toward his cook for approval. Julio nodded enthusiastically.

"But they must be clean, Rex. This is the final stage and we don't want any foreign matter in it," Quintaro laughed again.

"I'll see who I can spare, Carlos. Maybe from security. We are tight on manpower."

"Double shift some of the men, pay them a few more dollars, do what you have to do. We must meet our timetable." Quintaro just looked at him after he had finished.

"I'll take care of it, Carlos."

"Good, I know you will. Let's get into the fresh air." Quintaro moved off quickly and Simka followed. Julio stayed behind and dug into the drying cocaine powder with his fingers, bringing a small amount to his tongue.

Outside, Simka and Quintaro discarded their masks and started down the dirt road that led to the main operations building and the airstrip. Quintaro was in high spirits and walked with a jaunty step.

"Rex, we are on the verge of making the world sit up and notice Carlos Quintaro!"

"My friend, Carlos, I share your excitement, but I will not rest easy until the next phase of our plan goes smoothly," Simka replied.

"I am glad, Rex, you are still worried. That is what you are paid to do, look after the details, yes?"

"Yes, jefe."

They arrived at the operations building and Quintaro gave a circling motion to the pilot standing near his helicopter to get ready to leave.

"My friend," he said, turning toward Simka. "I will see you upon your

---

return from the Bahamas on Sunday night, yes? I trust there are no loose ends?"

The blades of the helicopter began to turn as the starter whined and the engine caught with a belch of grey smoke.

Simka thought of Brett Lesco and anticipated a call from him Friday night as scheduled.

"No loose ends, Carlos. The plan will work," Simka said as they shook hands.

Quintaro was just about to turn to the helicopter when Luis Caron came running from the operations building.

"Rex, Henri on the south ridge reports an aircraft is approaching!" Caron shouted, his walkie-talkie up to his ear.

Simka's eyes went wide, a look of disbelief on his face. All his planes were accounted for. No one was expected. He looked at Quintaro, who also had a look of disbelief.

"Rex, what is this?" he shouted, trying to be heard over the increasing sound of the helicopter rotors that were reaching full speed.

Simka shook his head. "I don't know, Carlos." He turned to Caron and shouted.

"Get some men, Luis. We can not let this plane land!"

* * *

Barney Devlin was back in the clouds and his eyes were back inside the cockpit. He watched the numbers click off on his instruments, especially conscious of the Rate of Descent meter. It indicated the plane was dropping at 1500 feet per minute, or 25 feet a second. Not quite free falling, but the unseen rocks were quickly closing on his metal machine and his decision point was just seconds away. Either he broke out of the clouds or he would pull up for a safe escape.

This was the hairiest part of his approach to the Valley of Codazzi and the bumpy air didn't make it any easier. Only the experience gained from dozens of previous runs and, trust in the numbers displayed on the instruments kept him descending. The GPS position indicator had him right on his planned glide slope. He dared a quick glance outside the windows, and silently prayed for the bottom of the clouds to appear.

Then, in a flash, he broke through into grey light.

"Yes!" he shouted with boyish glee, happy he had overcome the odds once again. "God, I hate this route," he moaned, his voice bouncing through the near empty plane.

One thousand feet under his nose a rocky ledge slid by, dropping several thousand feet away on the other side. He could see the river at the bottom of the ravine, the walls of the mountains on both sides sloping outward until they formed a valley less than a mile wide at his altitude.

He was four miles from the airstrip and felt comfortable about the rest of the approach. He slowed his descent, lowered his landing gear and focused on the last ridge clearly visible two miles ahead. He marveled at the view, one he called his *Window to Codazzi.*

The ridge formed the lower sill, with the cloud layer across the top and the mountains on each side. Through this natural frame he could see right down the valley. The airstrip and the valley floor were still obscured by the ridge, but he could see the climbing slopes of Pico Codazzi at the northern end and the twisted canyon walls that marked the path of the river at the far end of the runway.

A moment later, he flew into the window, passing 200 feet above the ridge. The lake and airstrip came into view and he quickly descended, setting up for the final mile and a half approach. To his left, he spotted the colorful sails of the five small sailboats along the shore that the Indians used for recreation. In the next instant he realized something was not right.

"What the hell?" he muttered. "It's a damn airplane convention!" He saw the planes parked near the airstrip and he reached for his microphone.

"Codazzi, this is Barney One, do your read?

No answer.

The runway was coming up very quickly. He was committed to touchdown and kept his eyes on the orange cone at the end. He twisted the controls, fighting the wind gusts.

"Damn aircraft carrier," he muttered to himself as he looked at the tiny strip of dirt waiting for him.

Out of the corner of his eyes, he saw a cloud of dust near the parked planes. It was a jeep bouncing across the plateau toward the runway. In the next instant, pinpoints of light came from the jeep. Someone was shooting at him!

The plane's wheels touched down at the end of the runway, but Devlin had already slammed the throttles back to full power. Bullets pinged off the metal skin and he saw other men on foot running and firing at him as he bounced once, then twice on the hard dirt surface. The plane jumped back into the air. He calmly pulled back on the control wheel, trying to gain altitude quickly without stalling. There was no room to maneuver and his only way out was straight ahead.

Thankful the plane was nearly empty, Barney felt it start to gain altitude. He passed the halfway point of the runway and glanced at the parked aircraft. He counted six all together, including the helicopter. He first thought a half dozen men were shooting at him, then upped the number to ten as the pings of bullets hitting the metal skin of the old C-47 multiplied. The helicopter elicited a deeply seated flicker of recognition, but that thought was quickly replaced by a bullet crashing through the side window of the cockpit, missing him, but spraying the compartment with glass.

Black smoke began to stream from his left engine and the oil gauge indicated a sudden drop in pressure. Black oil soon followed the smoke from the top of the engine and he shut it down.

"You bastards!" he shouted.

He was only sixty feet off the ground when the end of the runway passed under him and he flew into the safety of the river canyon. The gunfire stopped as abruptly as it had started. He tried to climb, and slowly the plane responded, the lone engine clawing for altitude.

The cold air rushed in through the broken window and he saw that his navigation instruments were not working. That didn't bother him as much as knowing he would have to fly out of the mountains with only one engine.

His heart began to settle down and he continued to slowly climb as he followed the river to the familiar point where it turned 90 degrees west. He banked left and climbed into the clouds knowing he had clear sailing back home to Santa Marta, if the lone working engine held on.

As the clouds closed in around him, his mind was filled with questions and worries. Something bad had happened at the mine. Where were Eduardo and the Indian miners? Where had all those planes come from? Why the hell were they firing at him?

He realized the planes he saw on the ground were all designed for one thing - cargo. The DHC-7 surprised him. It was a four-engine hauler that carried a five-ton payload and landed on runways as short as 2000 feet with a range of nearly 1000 miles.

"These guys are into hauling some heavy stuff," he said aloud. He set his course for home wondering why anyone would want to haul away tons of rocks.

Then it hit him. The helicopter. He remembered where he had seen it before, parked right outside his own offices at the Santa Marta airport.

"Oh, my Azulmora! PJ McDonough's gonna be real interested in today's adventure," he said to the picture of the dark haired woman taped on his instrument panel. He fell silent again, and his mind worried about the fate of Eduardo as the mountains rolled by unseen under his cockpit.

On the ground, Carlos Quintaro stood quietly, his face set in a firm line, his green eyes piercing straight into Rex Simka. He was thinking very hard about Simka's past with the DEA. Simka stared back, their silent face-off speaking volumes.

"Rex," Quintaro finally said quietly, "Operation Snowmine continues as planned. We will not stop now." He pointed to the ground where he had hastily scraped numbers in the dirt as the intruding plane flew through the valley.

Simka read "H K 3 4 7". They were the numbers on the plane's fuselage.

"Find out who belongs to this registration number," he said. "I'm sure you will find him at ALSA. Take care of him."

Simka looked up at Quintaro and nodded. He too, had seen the obvious logo on the side of the plane. He knew who owned the plane.

"It is done, Carlos. I will personally see to it."

Quintaro nodded and turned away, walking quickly to the helicopter. It took off as soon as he had closed the door, climbing straight up 200 feet before it banked toward the lake and continued climbing. Simka watched the chopper disappear into the clouds above the valley.

He cursed the intrusion of the ALSA cargo plane. They had known the schedule. It hadn't been expected until the following week. Simka silently blamed Quintaro for rushing the mine conversion. It had required all his attention and had forced a delay in his plans to keep ALSA out of the valley. Too many things to take care of. It was a costly mistake, he realized.

He turned toward Caron, who stood next to him reloading his MAC-10 machine pistol. Caron was angry that its firepower had proven ineffectual against the plane.

"Luis, we have a few loose ends to tie up," Simka said grimly. Caron nodded.

* * *

Later that night, two thousand miles to the north in Worcester, Massachusetts, the old man looked at his watch. It was 10:25. He sat in his car near a three-story walk up at 34 Spencer Street. Someone named Mario Terrazi lived in the apartment at that address. He was the man who owned the blacked out BMW that frequented the drug house on Boylston Street.

An old friend at Motor Vehicles...all his friends were old, he thought...had traced the "SNOWGO" license plate to here.

He was parked a half block away from the house, his blue Chevy melted among the cars parked on both sides of the street. He hoped the fact he had found a good parking spot was a sign of good things to come. From his position, he had a clear view in his mirror of the front porch and the driveway. If anyone came or went, he would see them.

The old man checked the camera settings on his beat up Nikon once again and got comfortable. He had been on stakeout many times as a cop and private investigator. He knew the secret was patience. He unscrewed a thermos of soup and poured a cup. He was going to find out who Mr. Terrazi was and what he did with his life. And where he got the drugs.

He sat there for less than an hour before a blue van pulled out of the driveway and passed him with two men in front. He started his car and slowly pulled out into the street just as the van turned right two blocks ahead. He sped up to keep them in sight and turned right to follow. It felt good to be out on the streets again.

~~~

CHAPTER ELEVEN

J ester Miller was buried next to his parents and his wife in a plot along the Mystic River six days after his murder. The names of Denison, Spicer, Wolfe, Mallory and Lathrop adorned the headstones around him. They were the sailors, shipwrights, merchants and millers, who helped create the history of Mystic seaport in the 18th and 19th century. Jester Miller's accomplishments were no less significant in the 20th Century.

Harold Miller, his son, and the McDonoughs were the only living souls close enough to Jester to be considered family, but his friends in auto racing and sailing were worldwide. Many came to pay their respects.

There were a dozen drivers from Formula One, NASCAR and IMSA racing circuits, several racecar owners, a dozen more mechanics and crew chiefs, even two executives from Ford, all beneficiaries of Jester's winning designs. Most of the Fabulous Fifties owners were there and many of their crews. The fifteen technicians, chemists and mechanics at Fast Car Caravan, the men and women who actually built and tested Jester's ideas, were also there. Town officials and just folk who knew Jester as a lifelong resident of Mystic also showed up. As did TV crews from CNN and three Connecticut stations.

A contingent of Mudheads carried his casket through the assembled crowd to the hole dug on the small bluff overlooking the river. Jester and PJ were both past commodores of the sailing group that was born on the Mystic River. Known for their love of racing and partying, the members were among the most intense club racers on the East Coast and had always held a special place in Jester's life.

Among the guests was a tall blonde woman with a camera crew never far from her side. It was PJ's ex, Cindy Brownstone-Miller, a TV reporter and the wife of Harold Miller.

PJ gave the eulogy. His voice mixed with the trickle of water placidly flowing behind him and the rustle of hundred-year-old elms and maples overhead, just beginning to turn toward their fall brilliance.

He spoke of happier times when Jester's quick laugh touched all around him, when his perseverance outlasted his doubters and the power of his belief in new technologies kept those working alongside energized. PJ asked the mourners not to give tears, but to take strength from the memories of the man and how he lived his life.

Then he invited everyone to his home for one last party in honor of Jester Miller.

They all came, ferried across the water to Ram Island in PJ's own boat and two other launches commandeered for the day. Dutch brought in his best people to cater the gathering, serving drinks and food. Quiet pockets of conversation formed on the grounds surrounding PJ's lighthouse home and the volume slowly grew as Jester's old friends renewed their friendships and tried to put the sadness behind them.

"Do you know everyone here?" Stoney Bullard asked PJ, as they walked on the thick grass near the dock. PJ stopped and took a sip from his rum and tonic. He squinted at the dozens of people spread around his property. He picked Kathryn out of the crowd near the food table in front of the house. She was talking with Ray and Crash. He caught the eye of a man several yards away who looked vaguely familiar. They nodded to each other.

"Just about everyone," he said to Stoney. "Most of them are from the race world, a part of my life that seems so long ago. A few town folks. The FFA guys. The crew, of course. Maybe half a dozen I don't remember seeing before. Probably mechanics or marketing guys with some of the race teams."

The sun was bright and the wind light. Three motorboats were at anchor several hundred yards off shore in the island cove. PJ saw a man fishing from the transom of one, bobbing near the shallows off the south end of the island. The cove was nestled in the crook of the elbow shaped island and was a popular anchorage for fishermen and boaters who enjoyed a quiet moment on a lunch hook protected from the predominate southwesterly breezes that blew in the afternoon. PJ was used to seeing boats there.

"I know only the crew, and a few sailors. That makes me nervous," Stoney said.

"You're an obsessive paranoid, Stone Man," PJ smiled. "If you're trying to scare me, it's not working. I don't think any of our enemies are here today."

"Stoney!" came a voice behind them and they both turned to see Harold Miller approaching with Cindy by his side, the camera crew several yards behind.

"Oh, I know him, too," Stoney smiled, walking up and shaking Harold's hand. Cindy gave him a hug and the three of them turned to PJ.

PJ had anticipated this moment, but his one time dread had been replaced by a need to embrace it.

He and Harold had spent some time on the phone two days prior and PJ had provided a detailed account of what happened on the waters of San Francisco Bay in the last moments of Jester's life. Their mutual love of Jester had easily melted the resentment PJ harbored and he apologized for being an idiot for three years.

"So, the government is good?" PJ asked half way through their conversation.

"Sure, it's good. Something new everyday. I get to use my language skills and the travel is, shall I say, educational," answered Harold. "Even got a little promotion last month...I'm now the second assistant to the Undersecretary."

"Second?" PJ laughed. "How many assistants are there?"

"Two," Harold laughed back. "It gives me a little more latitude and that's what counts on my end."

"Black bag stuff?"

"PJ, I'm not a doctor!"

"So, Harold, I'm sorry I didn't make the wedding," PJ said after a moment. There was a pause on the other end.

"PJ, I swear to you, she came to me as a friend," Harold said in earnest.

"And stayed as a lover," PJ couldn't resist retorting.

"She did and I'm glad she did. Not one regret, friend. I'm sorry for you, but no apologies from here. I love her and she loves me. She loved you, too, you idiot, but you were too busy building toy cars to really notice."

"I know, H., I know," PJ said with a sigh. "I've always known, but until recently, I couldn't let it go. Jester's death woke me up."

"And, you've met someone, right?" Harold taunted him, feeling a bit like the old days when the two of them used to pal around in high school.

"Yes, I have and it's like, we've missed three years over a woman who doesn't matter now," PJ said.

"Love holds the master key to the doors that jealousy closes," Harold quoted. "Lope de Vargas, a Spainard."

"I guess all that reading paid off," PJ laughed.

"But, she does matter, PJ," Harold said through his own laughter. "To me."

"I got it, H. I got it."

"Okay, so tell me what you know about this Colombia Precious Metals," Harold asked, getting down to business. "I think it's time to make a few phone calls."

PJ spent the next 15 minutes revealing the facts and speculation as he knew it surrounding the investigation into Jester's murder. Harold promised PJ he would gather what information he could from his sources in South America.

"And, PJ, Cindy is coming to the funeral," Harold told him before hanging up.

"I know," PJ nodded.

And here she stood now in front of him, a vision of beauty, a 6 foot tall blonde memory of a passionate, albeit much traveled relationship between Mystic and DC.

"You look good, Cindy," he said, smiling at her. They shared a brief hug and she whispered in his ear, "I'm so sorry for your loss. I know how important Jester was to you...is to you."

"Thanks," was all he said. He gestured to the camera crew and gave her a big smile. "I see you are still the center of attention."

"Yea, but not today, PJ." She looked at him and they both understood what was once there had gone away. "I'm going to say hi to your Mom," and she walked away with the camera crew following, ready for the cue to start rolling.

He nodded and watched her walk away and was aware of Harold and Stoney suddenly standing next to him.

"You have got yourself in a bee hive this time, Mr. McDonough." It was Harold. He handed PJ a disc in a plastic jewel case.

"I think you have a problem," Harold said matter of factly.

"We have a problem," corrected Stoney.

PJ looked at both of them. "You guys know each other? Since when?"

Stoney laughed and looked at Harold.

"Since a not too distant past," Stoney laughed.

PJ just shook his head and decided not to pursue it further. He looked at the disc instead. "What kind of a problem?"

"Lesco is bad news, PJ" Harold said. "He's definitely hooked into the drug network. DEA suspects a renegade agent named Rex Simka might be his contact. Simka spent a lot of time logged into Lesco's file before he disappeared into the drug underworld. It's only a thread, but Lesco might be working for Simka."

"Simka? And who is Simka working for?" PJ asked absently. He had a far away look in his eyes, trying to remember the last time he was truly afraid. He thought of the open ocean and a fragile shell of a sailboat in twenty-foot waves. Out beyond the southern end of the island, the Stonington police boat filled his vision, out on patrol. There were no waves out there.

"Maybe no one," Stoney was saying. "More likely, Simka's hooked up with one of the cartels, although he hasn't shown up in surveillance reports."

"Might they have missed him in the reports?" PJ asked.

"No. They're looking for him," Stoney answered firmly.

Harold continued. "Then again, he may have nothing to do with this. It really doesn't matter. Whoever it is, if they want you dead...and that's why they hired Lesco...they'll be back."

"You're right," he said, returning his gaze to his two friends. "Dave has convinced me the Starship explosion was definitely a bomb. Someone planted it in San Francisco or Wichita. He believes it was a double barometric fuse so it would blow when we were far away."

"Lesco's *modus operandi*," Stoney said. "He's had two misses now."

"Was their any hint of drug connections when you made the permit deal for the mine, H.?" PJ asked.

"Hell, no. Nothing. That was an easy phone call, one guy at INDIRENA and the papers were in place." Harold pulled out a copy of the deed and handed it to PJ. It looked official enough with a signature and seal embossed in the corner.

"So, we have Lesco's bad news reputation," PJ continued. "Jester's murder. A photo connecting Lesco and Esteban, phone records connecting Esteban and Precious Metals. Precious Metals and Caron. Caron and the mine."

"And Carlos Quintaro? Quintaro happens to be on the board of directors of Precious Metals," said Stoney with a smile.

"You know that?" PJ asked excitedly.

"It's all on the disc. But, does that connect Lesco with Quintaro? We're still not sure it was even Lesco who killed Jester."

"Even if we assume he did, it's still a stretch to connect him to Quintaro. But it certainly muddies Quintaro's name," Harold answered.

"Barney Devlin, the mine supply pilot says Quintaro's connections run all the way to the Colombian president. He's a respected businessman down there," PJ added.

"Respected, maybe," Harold nodded. "But in Colombia, you can buy respect. Quintaro bought a bank in Cartegena last year, with his brother, Bernardo Luis. They call it Sunrise International. Wire transfers between the bank and a variety of firms in the Netherlands, Malaysia and Spain increased 300 percent in the last year. Loans to companies that pay back within weeks."

"You think money laundering?" PJ asked.

"I think that, yes. My source suggested the amounts reported are only a fraction of what's actually moving. And cash assets at the bank have tripled in that time."

"So, the guy's a banker," PJ said, shrugging his shoulders, playing devil's advocate.

"And a major shipper who controls two ports in Northern Colombia. He moves five million tons of goods each year. Good cover for a smuggler, don't you think?" Harold smiled. He and Stoney looked at him, arms folded.

"Banker, launderer, shipper, smuggler," PJ smiled. "You say po-tay-toe, I say po-taa-toe."

"How do you say murder and kidnapping?" Stoney asked.

"Murder and kidnapping?"

"Kidnapping charges were brought and then dropped against Carlos Quintaro about thirty years ago."

"Kidnapping?"

"Kidnapping a kid."

PJ looked at Stoney. This was more than he expected.

"Where did you get that?"

"It's actually all in the public record. You just have to know who to ask to look it up," Stoney said with a grin.

"Okay, what about murder?"

"The brother, Bernardo Luis, was charged with murder for killing a judge who was investigating the kidnapping of an Indian child," Harold answered.

"Connection?"

"Murder happened two weeks after Quintaro's arrest. In Colombia, the judge is the investigator and prosecutor and jury. Poof went the judge, poof went the proof. Quintaro was set free almost immediately."

"Hmmm, nasty people," PJ said. "Had to be connected. Did the brother do time?"

"Don't know," Stoney said. "Not enough to prevent him from getting a banking permit."

"Interesting. But, we still can't link Quintaro to Brett Lesco, can we?" PJ said.

"Not directly, but you can link him to interest in the mine through Precious Metals. Unless this guy Caron is working on his own."

"Not likely," PJ said.

"Make sure you look at that thing tonight," Harold said firmly tappiing the disc in PJ's hand.

PJ slipped the disk into his pocket and nodded. He saw his mother walking toward them. She looked elegant in black, all the more so because she was smiling. She came up next to them and gave Stoney and Harold a hug, then took PJ's arm.

Stoney and Harold took their leave and wandered away deep in conversation. PJ walked with his mother toward the dock.

"I'm glad you and Harold are talking again," she smiled. PJ just nodded.

"I think everyone I called showed up," she laughed, gesturing to the crowd. PJ saw she was happy. "I liked what you said at the cemetery."

"Thanks. Jester believed in life, Mom. You know that. He didn't like dilly-dallying around. Let's get it done and get on!"

"Yes, let's get on," she echoed. "Still, it will be hard not seeing him around," she said without sadness or regret.

A waiter carrying a tray of hors d'oeuvres approached them and PJ reached for a cracker.

"PJ!" someone called from the house. He looked up to see Dutch at the front door, pantomiming a phone in hand.

"Excuse me," he said to his mother and started to walk. A flash of light caught his eye to the left, out on the water. He thought it might be the reflection of the sun on a boat windshield. But when the tray in the waiter's hands went flying, PJ knew immediately what had happened. He saw the frozen look on the young man's face as his knees collapsed, throwing the

---

cheese, crackers and dip in the air as if part of a juggling act. But the waiter was dead by the time he hit the ground at Ann's feet and the food landed on top of him, uncaught.

"Gunfire!" PJ screamed and tackled his mother, pushing her down to the ground and laying on top of her. "Get down, everyone!"

"From the water, there, in the boat!" It was Stoney yelling as he came running toward them. A bullet hit a tree with a snap and bark went flying above PJ's head.

He heard Dave's voice too, then screams and shouts from the guests as they tried to understand what was happening.

"Get down, everyone! Someone's shooting at us! Get down!" Dave was yelling. PJ was nose to nose with his mother and he looked right into her frightened eyes.

"Oh, PJ, what is happening?" she asked in pure terror.

"Don't move!" he hissed to her.

Suddenly, loud gunshots were heard nearby. PJ looked toward the sound and saw Stoney moving to his left in a crouch with a pistol in his hand, shooting at the motorboat where PJ had seen the fisherman earlier.

"Mother, time to move! Now! On your hands and knees to the shed!" PJ shouted, pushing her toward the small dockhouse twenty feet away.

Dirt sprayed up in front of them and his mother screamed, covered her head and stumbled. They were only ten feet from shelter. PJ grabbed her under the arms and pulled her the rest of the way and propped her safely against the dock house door. Three other guests were already there.

"Are you okay?" he asked her, looking at the dirt on her face.

"I think so," she said, somewhat dazed.

"Just dirt, you're not hit. Now stay here! Don't move!" PJ said firmly. "Don't any of you move!" he said to the others.

"Peter, be careful!" she pleaded.

He moved to the edge of the shed and looked around the corner. Guests were sprawled across the lawn. Several were running toward the house. There were many screams and shouts, punctuated by Stoney's gunshots. Stoney had re-positioned himself on the dock, using *Water Wheels* for cover.

The motorboat, where PJ had seen the first flash, started moving.

"Stoney!" PJ yelled and sprinted toward the dock. "He's moving! The white boat with blue bimini!"

PJ covered the fifteen yards to the dock in seconds and jumped into *Water Wheels*. Stoney realized immediately what PJ was thinking and untied the lines. Lenny and Mickey appeared from nowhere, running on the dock, and leaped onto the boat just as it began to move.

"He's heading East, PJ!" Lenny yelled, pointing toward Latimer Light.

"I got him!" PJ said as he gave full throttle to the twin engines. The bow rose up and the chase was on.

"Mickey, get on the radio. Channel 16. Notify the Coast Guard. Tell them we're chasing a man with a gun. He's in a white-hulled motorboat with a blue bimini. Looks like a Boston Whaler. Probably a 25-footer." He thought of the dead waiter lying back on his lawn.

"Tell them he has already killed at least one person!"

"I'm on it!" Mickey shouted back over the roar of the engines. He ducked into the cabin. Stoney joined PJ on the bridge deck, pointing toward the fleeing boat over half a mile away.

"Stoney, when did you start packing, man?" PJ said in amazement.

"Yesterday, my friend, after reading about Brett Lesco. Smith & Wesson .9 mm Parabellum." He held up the weapon with a wooden grip and square barrel. "He was too far away for it to do any damage."

"I think you scared him off."

"He got one. One of Dutch's people," Lenny said quietly. "Must have used a rifle."

"The son of a bitch almost hit my Mom!" PJ shouted angrily. He could feel the adrenalin coursing through him.

"You're starting to move on him, PJ," Stoney said.

"Do you think it's Lesco, Stoney?" PJ asked.

"Who knows?"

"That son of a bitch!" PJ shouted again. The wheel moved slightly in his hand as he gauged the boat's track and adjusted his course to intercept it. The last time he had been involved in a high-speed boat chase was in the Navy nearly a dozen years ago.

"He's turning south. Looks like he's heading toward Wicopesset," Stoney said. Wicopesset was a narrow cut between the rock-strewn waters that separated Fishers Island and Watch Hill. It led to Block Island Sound and open ocean.

"PJ, Coast Guard is notified," Mickey shouted up from the cabin doorway just below PJ. "They have a boat coming out of New London. There's a chopper already airborne on patrol over Block Island, but it's five or ten minutes away."

"Good, Mickey. Len, grab the flare guns. There's two of them behind the port bunk. Load them up and arm yourself."

"Let's not get *too* close, PJ," Lenny said as he moved below into the cabin.

"He's right," Stoney said. "This guy's got to make land somewhere. We just have to keep him in sight until the calvary arrives."

"I know. I don't intend on getting too close," PJ nodded. "But, make sure that gun of yours is ready, Stoney."

PJ had just finished talking when the white and blue boat suddenly slowed and then turned around, reversing its course and heading right for them.

"Jeez, Stoney, he's coming back!" PJ shook his head. "Everyone take cover! Lenny, we'll be needing those flare guns pretty quick!"

The boat with the unknown gunman on board was now heading right for *Water Wheels*, and had already cut the half-mile distance by a third. PJ adjusted his course to the left and the gunman mirrored him. PJ turned right with the same result.

"He's coming right for us!" PJ yelled. Stoney had already re-loaded his .9 mm and Lenny appeared on deck with two flare guns.

"These aren't going to do much, except at close range," Lenny said as he gave one of the small plastic distress pistols to Mickey by the radio. Lenny then crouched behind the windshield.

PJ started a gradual turn to the right, forcing the white and blue boat to adjust his course slightly left to maintain a collision course.

"You're exposing our flank to him!" Stoney yelled.

"Hey, I'm trying to stay away from him!" PJ returned.

The distance was now two hundred yards and *Water Wheels* was in front. The Black Watch had superior speed and they began to pull away. PJ could clearly see the man in sunglasses behind the open cockpit.

"God damn! The man's got a beard, Stoney! It's got to be Lesco!" he shouted.

Stoney didn't get a chance to answer because flashes began to come at them in rapid succession.

"Automatic weapon! Get down!" It was Mickey.

PJ spun the wheel hard to the left and then back to the right, juking like a broken field runner. The water behind them kicked up in small spouts as the bullets fell short. PJ continued his zigzag pattern, turning one way as soon as the gunman turned the other. After several maneuvers, the two boats were out of synch and the gunshots stopped. However, their maneuvers had taken them to the entrance of East Harbor on Fishers Island, a wide cove that turned into a narrow horseshoe shaped anchorage. PJ knew they would be trapped if they got inside the cove.

He drove blind, his head turned over his shoulder, watching the lighter Boston Whaler bouncing on *Water Wheels* twisting wake. PJ made another quick right and as soon as the Whaler turned right, PJ made a hard left and headed away from East Harbor along the northeastern shore. The Whaler was soon back on their tail.

PJ reached for the twin throttles and slowed down.

"What the hell are you doing!" Lenny yelled.

"I want to end this now," he said. He watched behind as the Whaler approached at full speed, the distance one hundred yards and closing.

"Stoney, give him something to think about!" PJ shouted and Stoney opened fire. The range was too far for his .9 mm to be effective, but they could see the man behind the center console duck.

PJ opened the throttles full again and accelerated toward a green can, a navigational marker in front of them. He zigged and zagged his way toward the can as more gunshots kicked up water behind them.

"This is totally bad, man!" Lenny was yelling. The transom on *Water Wheels* took several hits, sending fiberglass chips flying. The Whaler was now closer. Stoney fired two shots at a time, emptying his clip of twelve, then reloaded.

Then Lenny fired his flare gun, the orange glob of fire giving off a loud "*whoosh!*" as it flew in a lazy arch eighty yards and crashed into the cockpit shield in front of the gunman. It bounced crazily around the boat for several seconds, before falling harmlessly overboard.

"Nice shot!" PJ yelled.

The flare did no damage, but it distracted the gunman for a moment. PJ drove *Water Wheels* within a foot of the green buoy, keeping it to his left. Ten yards past the buoy, he turned hard right.

"Fire another flare! Mickey!" PJ yelled.

A second orange flare shot from behind PJ, this one missing the Whaler completely. The gunman ignored it and turned right to follow *Water Wheels*, which continued in a sharp right hand turn. He tried to cut inside *Water*

Wheels' turn and in doing so, passed about thirty feet to the right of the green can.

Suddenly, there was a loud crunch and the Whaler stopped as if it had hit a wall. The stern lifted completely out of the water and the gunman was thrown over the windshield, landing in the bow.

"Whoa! Did you see that!" Mickey yelled.

"Wow!" Stoney shouted.

"He hit a rock!" Lenny said.

"Young's Rock," PJ yelled, all smiles. "Son of a bitch! Yes!"

Young's Rock was more like a ledge, 100 yards around, that sat only a few inches under the surface at high tide and a boat length south of the green can. In the gunman's efforts to cut off PJ, he had driven right over the rock.

"I think he's down, Peej. Let's move in close," Stoney suggested. PJ slowed and they moved toward the damaged white and blue boat, which was sitting low in the water, its bottom hard on the rock.

"Stonington's finest coming!" Mickey shouted, pointing at another boat approaching from the north.

Stoney was on the bow, his .9 mm pointed at the prone body in the bow of the grounded Whaler still ten yards away.

"Can't get any closer, Stoney," PJ yelled down to him. The black shadow of the rock was visible below the surface. "Any movement?"

"Nothing, yet!" Stoney yelled.

The Stonington Police boat pulled up alongside, two men on the bridge and one in the stern, all with drawn guns. One on the bridge held a double barrel shotgun.

"Heave to, *Water Wheels*! You on the bow, lower your weapon!" The voice boomed through a deck speaker on the police boat. "I want everyone's hands in view!" the mechanical voice continued.

"There's a killer in the blue boat," PJ yelled to the man with the microphone in his hand. "He's got a gun!"

PJ also raised one hand, keeping the other on the steering wheel. Mickey and Lenny stood up and put their hands in view also.

Stoney was slow to respond, keeping his weapon trained on the bow of the blue boat. He did not look at the police, but kept his eyes on his target.

"Drop your weapon, mister!" the loud speaker hailed.

Stoney raised his left hand, but the pistol didn't move.

"Last warning, mister!"

Stoney wavered and looked at the police boat twenty yards away. He saw three guns pointed at him.

"I'm not the guy you want," he said, and lowered his weapon. "Keep your eyes right there." He pointed at the grounded boat.

Just then, the sound of the Coast Guard helicopter reached everyone and all eyes instinctively turned to the southeast to see the familiar orange and white HH-65A Dolphin flying in just a hundred feet off the water.

All eyes except Stoney's.

Which ruined the day of the gunman in the Whaler.

He chose that moment to leap up and fire his MAC-10 machine pistol in the direction of PJ. PJ, Lenny and Mickey all dove for cover and ten shots landed harmlessly in the hull of *Water Wheels*. Stoney fired two shots from his .9 mm, hitting the man in the arm and knocking him down.

Detective James Heslin, a ten-year veteran on the Stonington police force, fired twice with his shotgun. The second blast struck the man in the side of the head, killing him.

Immediately, the noise of the Coast Guard chopper overwhelmed everyone as it settled into a hover, the edge of it's downdraft rippling the waters just yards from the three boats.

PJ looked over the windshield at Stoney.

"Are you all right!?" he shouted, his voice lost in the din.

Stoney just nodded and slide his gun back into the holster hidden in the small of his back, under his suit jacket.

Then PJ saw the body in the Boston Whaler, slumped backward over the bow seat, the right side of the head a bloody, pulpy mess. But PJ saw the beard and the nose and the same sunglasses and recognized the man he had seen in the photo shown him by Wingate and Russo in San Francisco.

It was definitely Brett Lesco.

* * *

Thirty minutes later, PJ walked to the office in his home, sat down and dialed the number Dutch had written on a pad for him. He was surprised how calm he felt after the chase of Brett Lesco.

"ALSA, this is Devlin," came the voice on the other end.

"Barney, this is PJ," he spoke into the mouthpiece.

"McDonough, what happened?" Devlin sounded worried. "Your man there said you couldn't talk."

"Jeezus, Barney, all hell broke loose! Some madman shot up a little gathering we had in honor of Jester," PJ said. "A waiter took a bullet I think was meant for me. But, we got him. The local police shot him on the water. Barney, we think it was the same guy who killed Jester."

There was a pause,

"Did you find out anything at the mine?"

"You bet I did! I found out that someone doesn't want me to land there. Christ, PJ, I don't know what you and Jester got yourself into, but it's some deep ka-ka."

"Deep and deadly," PJ nodded in agreement.

"I don't know where to begin, but I'm lucky to be talking to you right now, I can tell you that. I don't like getting shot at! I got bad memories of being shot at," Barney continued.

"You were shot at, too, Barney?" PJ said. He looked up and saw Dutch and Kathryn standing by the open door. PJ couldn't help but notice the blood on Dutch's hands. The waiter's, he thought. He waved them inside and they shut the door behind.

"You're damn straight! Busted up my number one engine and the cockpit. Nearly crashed the plane in the mountains."

"Who, Barney? Who shot at you?"

"Well, I didn't stop to ask their names, PJ, but I did recognize one of the planes parked at the mine. It was an Italian job, an Agusta helicopter. Not too many of them around, but I've seen one at the airport here."

"You know whose helicopter it was?"

"You're gonna love this, PJ. I'm sure it's the same helicopter used by Carlos Quintaro. I've seen the guy come to QUIMEX, his company here, a dozen times. Hell, they land about a hundred yards outside my office window."

PJ felt a chill run up and down his spine. Quintaro!

"Now here's more bad news," Devlin continued. "I made a few inquiries at INDERENA, the department of the interior, you know, to see if they knew anything about the mine. Well, they didn't know what the hell I was talking about. They have no record of the Miller Mine."

"Impossible!" cried PJ. "I have a copy of the deed myself, right here!

We've been getting the Goshenite for five years!"

"All they have is a deed assigned to Colombia Precious Metals of Cartegena. Luis Caron is listed as the owner," Devlin paused. "I guess your hunches were right on."

"Barney, they kill Jester and move in and take over the mine, like it was nothing!" PJ couldn't believe it. "What the hell kinds of people are we dealing with here?"

PJ remembered Russo's worlds about bodies and kilos going together.

"Ruthless, greedy...it can be a shitstorm down here, PJ. Hell, murder and bribery are a way of life for some of these people. They must have pulled a switch and cover up, I don't know. The guy at INDERENA was not very forthcoming."

He paused to catch his breath.

"When I first saw all the planes at the mine and then the bullets started flying...I thought it might be the guerrillas, maybe Delta 7 or FARC, but they don't have a whole fleet of planes. They certainly don't have the power to pull strings in government."

"They're moving something, man. The fleet of planes I saw...they got an old C-123, a new DHC-7 and a hot new turbo prop, the TBM 700. Except for the TBM, the planes I saw carry cargo. That DHC-7 is one of the latest...big load, short takeoff...I bet it's got a four million dollar price tag. There are only two reasons to be in the middle of nowhere with that kind of high priced hardware. Rocks or drugs. I don't think it's Goshenite," Barney said.

"No, it can't be," PJ agreed. "We'd know if someone else was trying to sell to our own customers."

"Nobody discovered real emeralds, did they?" asked Barney. "Maybe old Klaus Luki wasn't so crazy after all, you just had to dig deep enough."

"Wouldn't that be something," PJ laughed grimly, "but Eduardo would have said something, I'm sure."

"Unless he never got the chance," Devlin said, anger in his voice. PJ thought of the fifteen Indians working the mine, all employed by Jester.

"Barney, what about Eduardo, and the Indians?" PJ asked quietly.

There was a pause and the static of the phone line filled PJ's ear before Devlin answered, his voice subdued and full of frustration.

"Not a sign of them, PJ, but I must tell you I was flying low and fast with bullets popping all around me. They could be anywhere."

"Quintaro's name shows up again, Barney. He has to behind whatever is going on here," PJ said.

"I agree. Drugs would certainly explain why they laid out a lead welcome mat," Barney answered. "Maybe they are using the mine and the airfield for some kind of transshipment point or storage."

"From the pictures I've seen, the mine has a large cavern that could be used for storage," PJ said. "Damn! Drugs!"

"I can tell you one thing, PJ, we won't get far with the local police. First of all, Quintaro owns the police down here, especially along the coast. They think he is a god. A real citizen of the community. Frankly, no one goes into the mountains, except the Indians."

"Are you sure it was Quintaro's helicopter?" PJ asked.

"As sure as I can be. I didn't see any numbers, but his is the only one I've seen around here. Same colors, blue and white," Barney answered. There was quiet again for a full fifteen seconds before Barney continued.

"You know, PJ, without the deed, there is going to be some trouble convincing officials here that anything is wrong."

"Barney, did they identify you?" PJ asked suddenly worried.

"Well, ALSA is a pretty small company, PJ. Just me and my plane," he said. "My schedule is not a secret and I'm sure they at least saw the reg numbers."

"You had better lay low for a while until we sort this out," PJ ordered.

"I know the drill, already made some plans," Barney answered, "But, I think we need a little recon in the valley to see what's really going on there."

"No way, Barney," PJ answered quickly. "You've already been put in enough danger. Do you have a safe place to stay?"

"Hey, danger's my middle name," Barney joked. "Don't worry, PJ. I'll keep my hairy face low for a while. I got some friends to help me."

He gave PJ a phone number and an address of an apartment in Santa Marta. He said he would be safe there and they promised to talk tomorrow.

PJ hung up and felt elated, angry and sickened at the same time.

"Well, what happened?" Dutch asked.

"Did you find out anything?" Kathryn asked.

"I think we found the ballpark," PJ answered, looking at his two friends.

~~~

CHAPTER TWELVE

L ate Friday night, quiet descended on Ram Island. The police had taken statements from the guests, goodbyes were said and everyone was ferried back to the mainland to go their separate ways, most still unsure of what they had seen. Water Wheels sat tied to the dock, the bullet holes in her hull the only evidence of the day's deadly events. PJ did not get a chance to say goodbye to Harold and Cindy, but his mother did and said Harold would be in touch.

The body of the dead waiter, Josh Bellows, had been removed to the morgue. Dutch went to nearby Groton to be with the boy's family. Lenny and Dave returned to their homes with Stoney, Mickey, Ray and Christina in tow. The full crew planned to lunch at Dutch's Mystic restaurant Saturday.

PJ sat in his darkened study, curled in a leather chair, the only light coming from his computer screen. His fingers tapped the keyboard in his lap, his right hand doing most of the work, his left encased in a sailing glove, the bullet wound still tender and the pinky and ring finger still without feeling. His eyes moved with the text on the screen, pausing frequently to absorb details about Carlos Quintaro, Colombian geography and its government, and other information left by Stoney on the computer disc.

PJ was just beginning to appreciate the help Harold provided. He had tapped into some sensitive areas in Washington to obtain the dossier information, foreign newspaper articles, embassy cables, recon photos, maps and charts. Some of the documents bore the mark of Naval Intelligence, but there was also information from the Drug Enforcement Agency, the State Department and the Coast Guard.

There was plenty of information on the drug wars, Colombian police efforts, and the violence that had torn that country apart. Several articles translated from Colombian newspapers were about Carlos Quintaro. However, PJ could not find anything to tie drugs and Quintaro together. Apparently, he had only recently attracted the attention of DEA, who were focusing most of their efforts on the big cartels in Medellin and Cali.

PJ came across a photo of Quintaro, with his brother, Bernardo, presiding at the opening of new docking facilities in Santa Marta. He stared at the computer screen.

"He's a handsome enough devil, isn't he," he said to himself. The man's piercing eyes set in the long, narrow face, framed by white hair and mustache, stared back at him. The smile of white teeth sent a chill down PJ's spine. It was not the innocent smile of joy, but a cold smile of superiority that dominated the scene of several men cutting a ribbon.

So intent was his focus, he did not acknowledge Kathryn when she set a cup of black coffee on the desktop. She looked at the screen over his shoulder.

"Who is that man?" she asked.

"Carlos Octavio Quintaro," PJ said, pointing to the white hair man. "His brother, Bernardo Luis Quintaro, is the dark haired man next to him."

"Oh," she said quietly, and sat down in a nearby chair in front of a smaller table where her own laptop computer sat unopened. "Carlos has a dangerous smile," she added. "I'll bet he can be very charming, too."

A full minute passed before PJ looked at her and smiled.

"Thanks for the coffee," he said quietly.

"I'm starting to get used to the routine," she answered.

Since the first night they had talked in the lighthouse, they had made it a habit to share a nightcap, be it rum, wine or coffee. She found herself looking forward to sitting down with him each night and discussing the day's events.

In the confusion caused by Jester's death and her new job at Fast Car Caravan, she had not begun the search for a place to live. PJ had not pushed her to do so. Her clothes had been recovered and in the cozy surroundings of his island home, she admitted she was not in any hurry to change the arrangement.

"You made the news at eleven," she said.

"Did they connect Lesco and Jester?"

"No, but the investigation was continuing, they said. They had you sandwiched between bloody shots of Lesco's boat and that poor waiter." She shook her head. "Just another news story. They interviewed Cindy. I guess she was the only real celeb who would talk on camera. TV is so desensitizing."

"That's why I stopped watching it," he said.

"Your mother is sleeping in your bed. She took two sleeping pills," Kathryn said. "I can sleep on the couch tonight, so you can have the guest room."

"Nonsense," PJ said. "The couch is for me. I want to sleep down here tonight."

"Do you think someone else will come after you?" she asked after a moment. He looked at her, his face expressionless. Or was he just tired?

"I don't think anyone will be coming tonight," he said, fully aware of his old Navy M15 pistol sitting in his desk drawer. He had pulled the .45 from its storage box earlier in the evening. It was cleaned and loaded.

He put the computer keyboard on the desk and spun the chair around to face her, swinging his legs to the floor. She felt a certain intimacy as she watched him yawn, then stretch his arms and legs. She was unsure if his sighs and groans signaled pain or pleasure.

He laughed.

"Been sitting much too long," he said sheepishly and stood up, arching his back before turning back to the keyboard and screen.

"You remind me of a cat," she said. "A couch potato ready to jump through a window."

Text replaced the photo and scrolled on his computer screen, the words flashing by too fast to read. He stopped tapping the keys when the screen displayed an aeronautical chart. Kathryn recognized it immediately.

"You're going to Colombia, aren't you?" she said simply.

"Yes," he answered, studying the chart, which showed the air, approaches to South America.

"I want to go with you."

"I don't think so!"

"Don't dismiss me so lightly!" she said with some annoyance. "You're not going alone, are you?"

He looked at her carefully.

"You're going to ask the crew for help, right?" she pressed him.

He sighed and nodded his head, reaching for his coffee.

"I'm sorry, Kathryn. I didn't mean to dismiss you. It's just...Colombia is not a very safe place to be."

"And how safe has it been around you for the last week?" she asked quietly. A small smile creased her lips.

"You're right, of course," he sighed, returning her knowing smile. "Someone wants me dead. Whether it's about the mine or something else, it doesn't matter. I'm a target and as long as I'm a target, my friends, you, my mother, for God's sakes, my whole existence, is in danger!"

"And it's a company matter," he continued. "I don't know the situation with the Indians at the mine. They work for me now and I can't just sit by and do nothing."

"What about the police?" Kathryn asked.

"They aren't interested in much beyond Brett Lesco and they got him," PJ said with a wave. "DEA doesn't seem to have much interest in Quintaro yet and I haven't been able to get through to Russo. Barney says the Colombian police aren't going to be much help either. At least not without some kind of rock hard proof."

"So, what's the plan?"

"To go see Carlos Quintaro."

"Quintaro....And?"

"And...find out what he knows about the mine."

"You're just going to knock on his door and say, 'hey, Carlos, my man, how's the export business? Heard any good mine jokes lately?'"

"That's a start," PJ said, smiling at her. "If he doesn't have any answers, we'll go to the mine."

"We? The crew, you mean?" she asked.

"I'm going to ask them to join me tomorrow," he said steadily.

"Am I a member of the crew?" she asked.

"Of course you are...I guess, ah..well, you're different, Kathryn," he said. She could see he was uncomfortable.

"I may be new but, I am a part of this, PJ. As much as Stoney or Dutch or..."

"I know that. It's just ...the danger...I wouldn't want anything to happen to you.... Look, you've been here and I'm...what I really mean,...ah," he moved closer to her in the chair, gently touched her cheek with his hand and bent down to eye level.

She responded to his warm touch with a mixture of surprise and pleasure. She covered his hand with her own. His eyes were locked on hers.

"I'm having trouble keeping an unbiased, cool eye here," he said with a smile. "My instinct is to be protective...protect the woman I care for. And I'm caring for you right now more than ever."

She was touched. She felt the warmth of his hands. But, she was determined not to let his feelings smother her.

"I know you care for me, PJ," she said softly. "I see how you pay attention to me at work. I like it...a lot. You're been wonderful. I like being with you. But, look, it works both ways. Today was scary. Somebody wants you dead."

She touched his lips with her fingers.

"That upsets me as much as being in danger myself."

She traced the outline of his cheek with her finger, following it to his ears.

"I don't want anything to happen to you, either. But, you're not a wallflower. And neither am I. I'll face the danger. Especially if avoiding it means staying away from you."

"You're very brave, Kathryn Byrnie."

"Baloney! I'm no braver than you. Or the rest of the crew. But, I know when something is worth fighting for. So do they."

She leaned forward and kissed him softly on the lips. He responded in kind and they savored the closeness for a long moment.

"Besides, I can help you," she said when they parted.

"Hmmmm," he said, still thinking of her warm mouth.

"You'll need an interpreter, at your side," she smiled.

"You speak Spanish?"

"Fluently. Studied it in high school and college. I even spent a year in Madrid."

She spoke a sentence, the words spilling from her lips like leaves falling on a windy autumn day. If translated, it would have sounded like this:

"You will need a lovely woman by your side to add to your stature as a world famous race car driver and yachtsman, entrepreneur and all around man of the history books!"

PJ laughed.

"That sounded good, though I have no idea what you said!"

"I said, basically, I'm the best person to accompany you on this trip."

He laughed again.

"You are quite wonderful, Kathryn Byrnie," he smiled, then grew serious again. "Going to Colombia will not be a vacation trip. I'm talking about taking back the mine by force, if necessary. Once I get there, I don't plan on leaving until the threats to my life are put to bed, whatever it takes."

She looked at him for a moment.

"What do you know about fighting?" she asked.

"I spent three years in the Navy, with the Riverine Forces. I was mostly a boat driver, but I trained with the Navy Seals. I can handle myself."

"What about the rest of the crew?"

"Most of them did their time. Stoney can help train them. Lenny was an officer in the Air Force. We're a resourceful group, especially when angry."

"Then it's settled. Let me be the first crew member to volunteer," she said, a full smile on her face. "If not for you, or for Jester, then for myself. Because I want to work for you. To stay with Caravan. And that puts *me* in danger, too."

PJ shook his head and looked at her carefully. She was a delicate, dark beauty with a determined, confident look. She had touched him in a way no woman had in many years.

"You're right, Kathryn. I do need you with me," he said. "It will not be easy."

"I'm not afraid," she said.

They kissed again, a soft, sweet kiss, connected not only by their growing desire for each other, but by their desire to move past the danger and get on with their lives.

PJ backed away and stood up. He wanted her, but knew the time was not right.

"I've got to get back to work here," he said. She nodded and stood up herself.

"Can I help tonight?"

"Tell you what, let me finish alone tonight and then you can look through the files in the morning," he said. "Then we can trade ideas before we talk to the crew at lunch tomorrow."

"Sounds good. Goodnight." She kissed him on the cheek, pressing herself against his chest for a moment and then turned and walked to the door. PJ watched her leaving, admiring her athletic grace.

At the door, she turned and looked back with a smile, her eyes and teeth catching the light in the semi-darkness. He thought she looked beautiful.

"Thanks for caring about me, PJ."

"I do," he said and turned back to the computer screen.

* * *

Kathryn left PJ in the study and walked through the kitchen, dropping her coffee cup in the sink. She enjoyed the room in the base of the lighthouse, and felt a genuine warmth despite the stone walls. She wandered outside onto the deck and found the noise of the waters of the Mystic River flowing along the rocks as soothing as music.

She could still feel PJ on her cheek and the softness of his kiss. Their brief closeness had awakened a glow in her. What was it? Love, desire, passion, lust...friendship? The feelings swam together. She knew they had simmered below the surface since they had first met, cooled by the tragic events of the last week. It would be hard to suppress them again, she thought.

He made her feel so damn comfortable! Their relationship seemed to foster an openness that she had never experienced with the other men in her life. At the same time, she had inadvertently come into his life at a dangerous time and that was unsettling.

It had been a tough decision to leave home and switch coasts, but the lure of new technology was very strong. She enjoyed the excitement of creating things. The pay was certainly better, nearly twice what she had been making at Oakland Software. She was only thirty-five, still young. If it didn't work out, she could always go home and start over. But, not if she were dead.

She smiled sadly as she remembered how Jester had sweetened his job offer by including the Great Bay Sailing Series as the first week of work. That helped cinch her decision. She loved to race sailboats and liked the idea of working for people with a similar obsession. She was pleasantly surprised how well she had fit into the crew.

Standing at the deck railing, she idly watched the water patterns reflected in the light from the house. After a moment, she sensed a change in the water's movement. A large rock a few feet off the porch split the water flow in several directions, spinning off tiny, sparkling whirlpools that spiraled in the light. The tidal current was switching direction, she thought.

She stood still and stared for several moments, allowing the aura of the water's energy to envelop her. The events of nature had always fascinated her and she felt the power of the rushing liquid. It was strong. She felt it drawing her closer, as if it was alive. The water patterns rippled and changed, breaking the glare into shards of light.

As she watched, different shapes appeared and disappeared, reforming and dissipating farther away, like cloud images, but at high speed. Then for an instant a distinct shape appeared. It was a face, she thought, the eyes pinpoints of black surrounded by white. A golden glow seemed to hover under its chin.

The image hung there, suspended just under the surface, even as the rushing water spilled around the rocks and under the porch. A gurgling, hissing sound filled her consciousness and seemed to take on a rhythm different than the normal flow of water. The more she listened, the more distinct was the pattern of noise. Was she hearing a voice? The mouth on the face moved, as if forming words. Then a voice reached her, but its tone was so deep she felt it more than heard it.

It was a confident voice, not a plaintive cry, she thought. But, try as she might, she couldn't understand the words. She thought she saw it smile and just as suddenly as it had appeared, the image was gone, its reflections spiraling out of sight, forming new shapes as they joined the flow of water to the Atlantic Ocean.

She stirred as if broken from a trance, shivering in the warm night, the sound of the swirling water in her ears, the shards of light dancing across the surface reflecting in her eyes.

Had she imagined it? No! The face and the voice were firmly etched on her brain. She had seen it, heard it and felt it. But she didn't understand what the voice said, nor recognized its tone. The face, however, was vaguely familiar; as if her memory had been jostled by forces she did not comprehend.

* * *

"You guys are crazy!" Dave was saying. "Look at my lips, PJ. Real guns, real bullets, like the ones that ripped through your hand, through Jester, Dutch's waiter. Real bombs. There are probably another dozen guys just like Brett Lesco. This isn't just another sailboat race."

"You've been shot at twice on your turf, PJ," Lenny said. "What the hell do you think will happen when you go to their home town?"

"I read somewhere that 150 Colombian cops were killed last year by the drug cartels," Christina added.

PJ sat at the end of the long table, leaning on his elbows. Above his head a poster sized duplicate of the same photo of *Camp Hobo* that hung in his mother's living room dominated the back room at Dutch's Mystic restaurant.

He looked at each of his friends sitting around the table. Except for Kathryn and Ray, they had all been on board in that moment of triumph. He held the gaze of each one. He was their friend, their mate, their leader.

He thought about the major storm they had survived during that Bermuda race. They had relied on each other in that crisis. Courage. Trust. Skill. Danger. The words bounced through his memory. This was another crisis, one he could handle, with their help.

"You're absolutely right, Dave," PJ said. "There are a dozen guys like Brett Lesco, maybe twenty. If they want me dead, they will keep coming. I don't want to live in fear for my life, or the life of my mother, or anyone else I care for."

He looked at Kathryn, then his gaze moved around the room.

"I have to go to the source of this trouble and stop it there. I have to go to Colombia and I need your help."

"I'm ready, PJ. When do we leave?" Dutch said immediately. PJ silently thanked his friend with a slight nod.

"I'm in, too," Kathryn said.

PJ looked at her. She returned his gaze and smiled. A few murmurs swept around the table.

"I've been put in danger, too. We all have," she said easily. "I can speak fluent Spanish." She started speaking Spanish, surprising some of the crew.

"Only my beauty at your side can match your world famous reputation as a race car driver, yachtsman and all around man of the history books," she said grandly.

Only Dutch laughed. PJ thought he heard some of the same words she had spoken to him the night before.

"Dutch, what did she say?" Lenny asked.

Dutch had studied some Spanish in high school.

"Something about a beauty on the side, a famous sailor and an historian, I think," he answered.

"History books, a man of the history books!" Kathryn corrected.

"Yeah, man of the history books." He laughed again.

PJ smiled. He bowed politely toward Kathryn.

"You're right, of course." That seemed to crack the tension in the room as the others broke up laughing.

"Do we have a plan yet?" Stoney asked as the crew settled down. "Snoop or attack? Is Quintaro our target?"

"I like a frontal assault," Dutch said with a trace of anger in his voice.

The loss of one of his employees had stung him badly and brought the situation into clear focus in his mind. "These bastards need a taste of their own medicine."

"I think we explore this through official channels first, Stoney," PJ said. "I also think I have to meet Carlos Quintaro. A peaceful meeting. Snoop, if you will, find out more about him before we try something else."

"And if he stonewalls you?" Dave asked.

"Well, we have to get to the mine, somehow. That might mean a frontal assault." PJ had already told the crew about Barney Devlin's attempt to land there.

"With what?" Mickey asked. "Winch handles? PJ, we're sailors, not soldiers."

"Weapons are not a big problem," Stoney said quietly. "As long as you have the money."

"Money I have," PJ said. "Does that mean you are in, Stone Man?"

"You bet I'm in," he grinned. "Who the hell else you got to whip these boy scouts into shape!" PJ smiled and nodded thanks.

"Lenny, what about you?"

Lenny held PJ's eyes. He remembered the fear when the bullets snapped around him in San Francisco Bay and during the boat chase the day before. He didn't enjoy feeling so vulnerable.

"Kathryn's right," he said. "They may be after PJ but, we are all exposed. Next time I come under fire, I want a gun in my hands. I'm in, Peej. We'll kick some butt!" Lenny said, sitting back, relieved he had made the decision.

"Thanks, Lenny." PJ next looked at Dave Bender, the big guy sitting with his head resting on his clasped hands.

He was the classic gentle giant, playful, but quiet, with legendary strength. PJ remembered one situation in a rough race two years ago on his old 44-footer. Crash was out on the end of the spinnaker pole during a spinnaker change when the boat slammed off a rogue wave. The shackle on her safety harness opened and she fell from the pole into the water with the boat doing ten knots. Dave was crouched in the cockpit watching and jumped to the rail before anyone could move, reached down into the water, grabbed her by the jacket as she went past the speeding hull and deposited all of her ninety pounds on the deck. Crash, soaking wet, her eyes wide, gasping for breath, hardly hesitated and ran back to the bow to finish the sail change with a simple, "Damn! I slipped. Thanks, Dave!"

It was a once in a lifetime feat. What struck PJ the most was the incredibly primal scream that came from somewhere deep inside Dave's huge and powerful body as he lifted Crash on board. He was someone PJ needed by his side.

"Damn, PJ, I hate you. And, I love you, mate. You're gonna need someone to take care of your ass. I'm in, but if I get hurt, my mother is gonna be pissed at you, big time," Dave said with a grin.

"My mother, too," PJ laughed.

Dave looked at Crash, sitting next to him.

"You gonna come, too?" Dave asked.

"Yeah," she said, nodding her head slowly. "I'm in. You need me to watch *your* back, Dave." He put his arm around her.

"I'm in, too," Mickey sighed. "It was crazy out there yesterday, but someone's got to make a stand. It will make a good story, too."

"I hope you take this a little more seriously than one of your stories, Mick," Stoney said grimly.

"Kiss off, Stoney! I take my stories very seriously," he retorted.

"Good anger, Mickey. Save it for the bad guys!" Stoney said smiling.

Everyone now looked at Ray.

"Look, guys," Ray said, shifting uncomfortable in his chair. He put up his hands. "I appreciate the situation here, but I'm just a lawnmower man. You guys all did your time in the service, probably had weapons training or at least went through the obstacle course. I missed all that. I'm not sure how I'd be under fire. I'm not sure I want to find out."

"This is strictly volunteer, Ray" PJ said.

"Of course, if you say no," Lenny suggested, leaning forward with a sly look on his face, "We'll never talk to you again, pour sugar in all your gas tanks, drown your cat and basically make your life so miserable, you'll wish you'd never heard of us."

"Lenny, you're a shit!" PJ said, shaking his head, while the rest of the crew chuckled.

"Hey, I already wish I never had heard of you, Lenny," Ray said smiling. They all quieted down and Ray sat there saying nothing, looking down at his hands.

"I can't promise any heroics," he said finally, "But, I'm in."

"Are you sure, Ray?" PJ asked, giving Lenny a dirty look.

"I'm sure," Ray nodded.

"Great. Thank you. All of you."

"This one's for Jester, okay?" Dutch said, raising his beer glass.

"And for PJ," Kathryn suggested.

"Hey, friends. This one is for all of us," PJ said.

"Yeah," said Stoney, "But I'm not sure any of us know what we've got ourselves into."

"Hey, it's just a fight, Stoney. A fight between the good guys and the bad guys," Dutch said.

"Very bad guys," Stoney said carefully.

"Anyone got any ideas on what the hell we can do?" Lenny asked to no one in particular.

PJ reached for a cold beer. "I think I have an idea," he said and for the next two hours, they all sat sipping beer and formulated a rough outline of the plan, which was destined to change their lives forever.

~~~

CHAPTER THIRTEEN

R ex Simka squinted behind his dark glasses. He saw nothing but sand, water and sky, but felt much too close to his past. For the first time in three years he was outside of Colombia. Several federal agents he knew personally would be happy to put a bullet through his head without as much as a hello. If they found him.

He knew the U.S. Coast Guard and the Royal Bahamian Police Forces had increased their drug patrols nearby. Airborne radar planes were likely sweeping the skies overhead. And the Cubans, co-operative, but unpredictable, were only sixty miles to the west. Florida, his former home, was three hundred miles to the north. He was tense.

Tension wasn't all bad, he thought. He was alert and that was good. It was Sunday, the last day of September, only five days since he had led the takeover of the Miller mine in the Valley of Codazzi. The first three thousand kilos of pure cocaine processed at the new mountain lab would soon arrive at this remote island in the Bahamas, called Marib Cay.

Named for an Indian goddess who protected white sands, Marib Cay was the last in a broken line of more than thirty small islands called the Jumento Cays. They stretched south from Great Exuma toward Cuba, some less than 100 yards across, others nearly a mile. On a map the Jumentos appeared like skeletal remains of some animal's tail from another age. At least on the maps that actually showed the tiny islands for many did not.

Its quiet reputation was precisely why it was chosen as a transfer point. Shortly after arriving from Colombia, the drugs would be on their way to Chicago, New York and Boston, the first of twelve weekly shipments that would establish Carlos Quintaro as a major player in the cocaine game.

Simka congratulated himself on his plan and savored thoughts of his $100 million share of the take. He wasn't interested in empire building. He would leave that for Carlos. He wanted the power to be free of Carlos, to answer to no one, to lead a life where he was the king and greed was a virtue. He wanted the money.

He let his mind wonder into the daydream that had become a part of his daily routine. He was on an island in the Mediterranean, surrounded by women of fine features, golden brown in the sun, willing and ready to satisfy his every need. Then he was hop scotching from one international locale to another, on fancy planes and fancy boats with more fancy women.

He dreamed of being one of the high rollers in the casinos of Europe, not unlike James Bond. He dreamed of a constant high, the excitement to be had from fast living and good drugs.

He didn't care about respect from others. He wouldn't need them. He wanted only to be his own master, to set his own rules and to live his own life, surrounded by the luxuries of the world.

Deep down, he wondered if he would ever be able to leave the drug business. Death was often the only way out and he already had thought about faking his own. He liked Quintaro, but knew their relationship was destined for an explosive ending.

He looked at his watch. The plane carrying Lesco was late. Lesco was a loose end that worried him. They had missed a scheduled phone contact on Friday night, which was very unlike the professional's past behavior. He knew Lesco was a cowboy, but he got results. Still, Simka did not like loose ends.

"Nothing like a steady breeze," he said out loud, feeling the easterly on his face. The water caught the early afternoon sun and was a bit easier on his eyes. He marveled at the turquoise hues that turned deep blue only a few hundred yards off the east end of the island. The Crooked Island Passage to the Atlantic Ocean began there and the sandy bottom ran down quickly to 5000 feet. There was great fishing in these waters he had heard, though he had no interest in fish.

The previous owner of Marib Cay, an elderly millionaire from Buffalo who had made his fortune baking cookies, had built a runway and three buildings. Simka was pleasantly surprised when he landed on the island for the first time earlier in the day. It had taken only two days to convert it into a smuggler's pit stop.

A camouflage net was erected next to a wooden hangar and several rows of fifty-five gallon fuel drums sat in the shade, connected to a small pump, run by a diesel generator. The 1500-gallon system had been installed just the day before. A second building, with six rooms and a large kitchen sat a few hundred yards to the south.

He watched two men work on his plane, a white Aerospatiale TBM 700. The sleek, single engine turbo prop, was capable of 300 knots, making the two and a half hour flight from Colombia a breeze. He smiled at the innocent bulge under the cockpit where he had made a minor modification, adding a special piece of equipment. He wondered if he would ever get to use it.

He walked back inside the room. It was airy and empty except for a wooden desk, two wicker chairs and a VHF radio on a shelf. The VHF was his, but the other contents came with the island. The hardwood floor creaked as he moved to the desk and looked at the charts scattered about and the four envelopes that lay on top of them. The windows were open on all four sides, and the light blue walls provided a pleasing mix with the bright sky and the colorful water. However, Simka was not in a sightseeing mood.

He withdrew a small brown vial from his pants pocket and unscrewed the cap, gingerly spilling a small amount of white powder onto his fingertip. He held it up to his nose and inhaled lustily. The pure cocaine shot through his mucous membranes directly into his blood stream. In seconds he could feel the rush as the drug reached his heart and quickened his pulse. He repeated the act for his other nostril.

God, he loved the feel! He remembered his first hit with a small amount seized in a drug bust several years ago. He had used it on stake-out, hoping it would keep him awake. It did, and more, gave him a feeling of strength and readiness. He began to rely on the drug and it helped him forget his immediate concerns. It left him alert and anxious to get on with it.

He thought of the mounds of the pure white powder in the Valley of Codazzi mine where he had stood only days before. Quintaro frowned on drug use among the men, but the hunger was there and Simka was happy to be in the Bahamas.

"Bring on your demons!" he sang to himself. The rush continued for several minutes, then backed off slightly and settled into a steady sensation, his brain waves crackling with the charge.

He thought of the U.S. mainland and Lesco. He reassured himself the loose ends would all be tied up and walked back to the balcony to scan the sky once again.

At that moment, 140 miles to the east on Great Inagua Island, Raymond Fitz-Osborne worked on a cranky fuel filter on engine number one of his ancient DC-3 cargo plane. The work was hot and Fitz-Osborne's normally reserved British demeanor was beginning to fray thin. It was a regular ritual that was mostly bluster.

"Bloody piece of American trash," he mumbled as a wrench slipped off a stubborn nut and his knuckles smacked against hard metal. The jolt was enough to shake the half filled bottle of stout that was carefully balanced on the engine cowling.

Fitz-Osborne was an honest to goodness Duke, a member of royalty through ancestry. His father, descended from a 3rd cousin of King Henry VIII, on his mother's side, had owned a title and an estate, complete with castle and moat in the English countryside. As a young lord, Raymond had not had to work a day in his life and enjoyed the daily ritual of riding horses, hunting and chatting, proudly wearing the crest of his ancestors.

It came to an end when his parents died. He was twenty-five and broke. There was no cash inheritance and insurmountable back taxes forced him to sell off the family's estate, leaving him with a few dollars and no visible means of support.

That was twenty years ago. Since then, he had grown quite rough around the edges. He knocked about the globe a bit and learned to fly. Six years ago he bought a DC-3 and established Fitz Air Inc., flying freight and passengers from island to island in the Greater Antilles, mainly in the Bahamas. The job kept his belly full of food and stout, and left him enough to spend on the ladies during his frequent trips to the mainland. And plenty of time to lay in the sun.

His main customer was the National Salt Company for whom he made weekly trips to the U.S. for supplies, occasionally ferrying visiting company executives to the casinos of Nassau and Freeport. His bright blue plane, with the yellow stripe around the fuselage and the British jack on the tail were a common sight in the out-islands. A week ago, he had signed up another customer who paid well for very little work.

He had not asked a lot of questions when the man named Luis flashed a big money roll and peeled off half of it. He knew drugs were involved, or maybe weapons, or some other nasty business. He needed the money and he didn't want to know more than what he was to do.

"Key-ryst!" he shouted. His knuckles were smashed again.

He pushed on, loosened the nut and in twenty minutes had replaced the filter, fired up the engine and pronounced it one hundred percent ready.

"You're a bloody wanker, ain't ya'?" he said to the plane as the even drone of the engine satisfied his hearing. "But in the end, baby, it's me you 'ave to answer to, idn't it?" He laughed and shut down the engine, picked up his tools and wandered over to the Salt Bar in the one story building that passed as the main terminal at the Great Inagua airport.

"Elmo, 'ow about a pint," Fitz-Osborne said as he entered the shadowy tavern and slipped onto the familiar corner stool. The sunlight poured through the open wooden shutters, slashed across the floor, up over the counter, and reflected off the mirror on the back wall up to the ceiling, filling the room with the impression of prison bars.

"Coming right up, Fitzi," the bartender answered, reaching into the cooler for the distinctive brown bottle. "How's she doing?"

"Bloody bitch is cantankerous as they come, but I got her purring right now," Raymond answered. He took a long pull from the bottle.

"Seen the latest from Nassau?" Elmo asked, pushing a day old newspaper in front of him. The article on the front page announced the U.S. Coast Guard would install a radar balloon on Great Inagua in their expanding effort to locate drug smugglers. Construction of the facility was to begin in six months.

"Hell, they been yakking about that for least a year!" Raymond snorted, taking another pull on his bottle.

"I could use the business," Elmo said with a sigh, absently wiping down the mahogany bar. "You heading out today?"

Raymond nodded as he finished off the contents of the bottle. His big hands wiped the foam from his handlebar mustache.

"About two hours, me boy, heading north to the land of palm trees, blue hair and $200 hookers. Need anything while I'm gone?" he asked, gesturing for another beer.

"We'll be needing more stout if you keep this up," Elmo laughed and slide another in front of him.

"Two cases it'll be, then," Fitzi said and took another long pull, downing the second bottle. He flipped a twenty-dollar bill on the counter and left for the dispatch office to file his flight plan.

"Keep it, Elmo. I'm feeling pretty good today!"

* * *

Ulf Rodenborg wasn't feeling so good. Rex Simka's ground transportation chief was having a rough time of it in the C-123 cargo plane that was enroute to Marib Cay flying at 12,000 feet. In the pilot's seat, Luis Caron's hands were in constant motion as he tried to keep the plane steady in the bumpy air. He ignored the erratic compass needle, concentrating instead on the GPS read outs that indicated they were doing 220 knots and would reach Marib Cay in about forty minutes.

"It's the devil, eh, Ulf. Strange forces have a hold of our lives," smiled Caron as the air rocked the wings. "Look at that compass needle."

Distinct aberrations in the earth's magnetic field were concentrated in an area between Crooked Island and Great Inagua. They played havoc with the C-123's magnetic compass. Caron knew it was one bit of truth amidst the myths that surrounded the Bermuda Triangle.

"I will be happy when we are on the ground," Ulf answered shakily. He had volunteered to be Caron's co-pilot to get a first hand look at the Marib Cay operation. He was regretting the late breakfast he had gulped down just before they left.

Caron didn't help matters. He suddenly turned the airplane to the west and began a rapid descent for the protection of Cuban airspace. Any U.S. planes watching on radar would see a blip that would appear to be landing on the Cuban mainland. Once over the northeastern tip of Cuba, Caron would turn directly for Marib Cay, flying the last 100 miles about 100 feet above the water.

Back in the cargo bay, ten pallets were strapped to the deck, each pallet holding a dozen duffel bags, each bag holding twenty-five kilos of pure cocaine, each kilo sealed in a clear plastic ball. The 3,000 kilos of cargo, over three tons, had been loaded in the Valley of Codazzi that morning.

At that moment, from different airstrips scattered throughout the Bahamas, three planes, the corporate passenger seats removed and external fuel tanks attached to the wing tips, lifted off their respective runways. The young Colombian pilots, dedicated to their leader, Carlos Quintaro, stayed low, and set their GPS receivers for a direct course to Marib Cay.

* * *

The sound of a single engine interrupted Simka's pacing on the balcony. A few seconds later, it appeared riding in on the wind from the east. Simka recognized the Green Trinidad TB21, a smaller version of his own plane.

"Jesus, they got lost!" he said out loud.

The Trinidad flew over the island at about 500 feet and then smoothly executed a 180-degree left hand turn into the wind and touched down softly on the runway. Simka immediately knew something was wrong. There was no passenger. The good feeling of his cocaine rush began to take on a rough edge as he moved to the tarmac to await the plane.

"Where's your passenger?" he shouted at the pilot before the engine had been shut off. The young man just shrugged his shoulders and handed Simka a copy of USA Today dated Saturday, September 29.

"What's this?" he asked. His annoyance was clear.

"The man was a no show," the pilot said. "I think the reason is right there." He pointed to a small article on the NATIONLINE page that read:

MURDER SUSPECT KILLED AFTER CHASE

STONINGTON - An ex-marine wanted by the FBI killed a man and was then shot by local police after a high-speed boat chase on Fishers Island Sound. Brett Lesco, 46, a decorated Vietnam veteran, killed Josh Bellows, 23, of Groton. Police say Lesco used a high-powered rifle to kill Bellows while he waited on guests at an outdoor gathering in honor of slain automobile designer, Jester Miller.

Peter McDonough, Miller's business partner, reportedly chased Lesco by boat and forced him to run aground. When police approached Lesco's disabled boat, he shot at police and was killed by a Stonington detective.

Lesco had been the subject of a nationwide search by the FBI and other federal agencies in connection with several murders, including Miller's, who was shot while sailing a week ago in San Francisco Bay.

"Stupid, son of a bitch, asshole cowboy!" Simka cried in disbelief after reading the story. He was livid that a man he had trusted to do a job could screw it up so badly. His anger was at first directed at Lesco, then he shifted the blame to himself. He should never had listened to Lesco's suggestion to eliminate McDonough as well as Miller.

Suddenly, he felt powerless and feared the anger of Carlos Quintaro. First the cargo pilot and now, Lesco's failure. He was losing control of his plan. He smashed the newspaper in frustration against the wing of the aircraft.

His mind buzzed with options as he frantically sought to regain control. Quintaro did not know about McDonough, that he was sure. His orders had been to eliminate Jester Miller, the man whose name appeared on the mine lease. That had been accomplished.

Lesco was dead, according to the newspaper. That solved one loose end that Simka had planned to tie up himself. Could Simka be traced to Lesco? He doubted it. Their original contact had come through an associate in the Medellin cartel. Since then, they had communicated over public phones. Lesco had told Simka he never wrote anything down. He believed him.

Simka walked back inside the main building, up the stairs to the second floor and sat down in a chair. The quiet was deafening, and he didn't move for a moment, as if in a spell, soldered to the chair, smothered by the peacefulness of the island. He thought about the brown vial in his pocket, but decided not to reach for it just then.

McDonough was apparently still alive and there was nothing he could do about that, at least not right away. And maybe he didn't have to. McDonough couldn't possibly know who had sent Lesco. Besides, the operation was already underway. No one could stop them now. He convinced himself there was no need to concern Quintaro about Brett Lesco. Nor was there reason to be concerned with PJ McDonough just yet.

Five minutes passed with Simka unmoved when the deep sounds of a large aircraft's engines reached his ears. He recognized it immediately as the C-123 from Colombia and was snapped into action, moving quickly to the balcony.

Caron was about a mile out, low and slow on final approach. The C-123 touched down easily at the very end of the runway and Caron rolled her right up to the hangar.

For the next thirty minutes, Simka supervised a four man ground crew, glad to be active. Working with a small fork-lift, they unloaded the duffel bags. Ulf, feeling much better with his feet on solid ground, supervised the refueling.

Forty-five minutes later, Caron and Rodenborg were back in the cockpit and the empty C-123 lifted off the coral runway and turned west at an altitude of 100 feet for the sixty mile flight to the Cuban border before climbing to 15,000 feet and setting course back to Colombia.

Simka checked his watch. 3:25 in the afternoon. Like clockwork, the first of the three corporate twins, a Piper Cheyenne, appeared to the north. From a distance it appeared to be on the water. It landed, followed within minutes by the other two, a pair of Beech King Airs.

The passenger-turned-cargo planes were loaded with thirty-three duffel bags each, King Air One taking the extra bag. One thousand kilos per plane, just over a ton. The fuel tanks were topped off and Simka met alone with each pilot in the second floor room, briefing them on their individual routes.

It was the first time the pilots learned of their destinations. Simka was careful to make sure each of them was aware only of the route they were to travel once they reached the United States.

When the Cheyenne touched down at Marib Cay, precisely at 3:30, Raymond Fitz-Osborne and his DC-3 rattled down the runway at Great Inagua, lifted off and climbed to 3000 feet on a course to Florida. Upon reaching 3000 feet, he turned on his radio, switching to the Unicom frequency of 128.00.

"Nassau Control, this is Victor-Romeo 7-8. I'm at 3000 feet, heading 3-1-5, speed 180 knots."

There was no reply, as Fitz-Osborne expected. He was nearly 400 miles from the controllers in Nassau and there was no way they could hear him. Although pilots were required to notify Nassau when airborne, sharp eyes were still the main navigational tools. Fitz-Osborne did turn on his transponder, setting it on the VFR code 1200. Any radar sweeps from airborne or coastal radars would easily pick up this signal.

On Marib Cay, Simka had brought all three pilots together to review their flight maneuvers before they reached the U.S. He paused to listen to a weak transmission on the VHF radio, then looked at his watch.

"You have about a half hour to grab something to eat," he smiled at the young pilots. None of them are a day over twenty, Simka thought.

"Sure thing, Señor Simka," one of the young men answered, and all three picked up their flight bags and headed for the small barracks building.

Simka sat alone for a second and allowed himself to enjoy the scenery that flowed in through the open windows on the gentle breeze.

~~~

CHAPTER FOURTEEN

D eep in the bowels of a windowless building in Oklahoma City, U.S. Customs agent Stanley Krups stared intently at the twenty-six inch radar monitor. A small yellow blip had appeared in the lower right hand corner, just north of the Cuban coastline outlined on his screen. He spun the cursor ball at his fingertips and typed in a few commands.

Seconds later the screen displayed "TRK 4" over the blip. "Too weak, too far," Stanley mumbled to himself. He wasn't surprised. The blip was at least 350 miles away from the Coast Guard E-2 Hawkeye radar plane circling just east of Key West. The accuracy of their radar system was limited beyond 200 miles.

He typed in a few more commands, changing the weak signal designation to "UNK 1", and ordered the system to track it. Then he switched to another blip of an aircraft about sixty miles south of Miami heading north. It was a fast mover, speed about 450 knots, altitude 21,500 feet and dead on the airway toward Miami. The plane was displayed on the screen as a small data box with numbers indicating altitude and speed, transmitted from the plane's transponder.

He hit a key and the plane's course appeared on the display. The transponder code indicated it was a scheduled airliner. Probably bringing some tanned folks back from the Virgin Islands, he thought.

"Coffee?" asked Janet Peck, the operator sitting next to Krups. She took off her headsets and pushed back from the console. He watched her push the blonde curls back from her face and stand up, his eyes following her ample breasts not easily concealed by her blue uniform blouse.

"Black would be fine, Janet. Thanks," he smiled at her. She returned it with a warm smile of her own, revealing a white, but gaped, row of teeth.

"Cover sector 270 for me," she said and was gone.

Her teeth were such a small imperfection on an otherwise perfect sample of the female species, he thought as he watched her walk away.

Peck and Krups were the only two operators on duty at the moment. Several consoles were empty, their screens displaying the logo of the U.S. Customs Agency and a large C3I in the middle. C3I stood for Command,

Control, Communication and Intelligence, a sophisticated $50 million command post built for the sole purpose of detecting and tracking drug smugglers trying to enter the country illegally. The biggest task was to co-ordinate the seven federal agencies involved in the Anti-Drug Network, including similar radar tracking centers in Miami and Houston.

In Oklahoma City, the focus of America's technology was on the southern borders of Florida and the Gulf of Mexico. It was a monumental task. An impossible task. There were nearly 2,000,000 square miles of airspace and ocean to watch.

Radar signals from military and civilian sources were channeled by fiber optic landlines to the consoles in the dimly lit room. Operators could select the source of input, track planes and boats that fit smuggler profiles and then co-ordinate intercepts by U.S. Custom agents in Blackhawk helicopters and H-25U pursuit jets, the Coast Guard in patrol boats or state and local police on the ground.

Increased flights by private pilots and commercial airlines to the popular sunny islands in the Greater and Lesser Antilles, plus the frequent helicopter ferry flights to revived off shore drilling platforms in the Gulf of Mexico, only served to complicate the nightmarish job of picking out a smuggler and his load, flying low over the water in a lone plane or speeding across the waves in an ocean racer, heading for the thousands of coves and inlets that dotted the southern coastline.

The results were far less impressive than the technology. The border protectors were simply outnumbered. A few helicopters and jets, even 100 Coast Guard patrol boats were not enough to cover the territory. America had lost control of her borders.

Under pressure from the White House, the Department of Defense had reluctantly agreed to provide some help, but it did not carry the full weight of the Pentagon, where officials privately admitted they did not want to be associated with a losing effort.

Although the present administration proudly talked about doubling drug seizures and arrests in the last year, they admitted only a quarter of the drugs smuggled into the U.S. were actually confiscated. Still, an additional two billion dollars had recently been appropriated to help the drug interdiction efforts. The technology, when it worked, was an obstacle a drug smuggler could not afford to ignore.

"Stanley, my boy, are you having fun today!"

Les Victors sauntered over to Krups and slapped Stanley hard on the back, almost knocking his glasses off. "Catch any bad guys?"

"Les, knock it off," Stanley whined. He could do without Victors' loud

---

and boorish personality, but he put up with it with little protest. At least Victors was here to help with the always-hectic Sunday afternoon traffic returning to the states from a weekend in the Caribbean.

Janet came back with the coffee and her ever-present smile. "Anything going on?" she asked, slipping her headsets over her blonde locks.

"All quiet on the southern front, Janet," Stanley replied, taking a sideways glance at her blouse. She caught him looking, and rolled her eyes in a hopeless look.

"Drink your coffee, Stan," she said, returning to her screen.

Stanley took a sip, went back to his screen, smiling as he spun the cursor ball to select another random target for surveillance.

* * *

In the cockpit of the DC-3, Raymond Fitz-Osborne checked his watch and the GPS read-out. He was twenty miles southeast of Marib Cay, still at 3,000 feet. It was time for another radio message.

"Nassau Control, this is Victor-Romeo 7-8. Maintaining 3,000," he reported. Again, no answer, as expected.

The transmission was heard in the headsets of the three young pilots sitting in their planes at the end of the runway at Marib Cay. Together they started up their engines, completed their pre- flight checks and in minutes were ready to roll, their planes loaded to the windowsills with duffel bags of cocaine.

Simka watched them from the balcony, the VHF radio in his hands. He looked at his watch, did a quick calculation and then spoke into the mouthpiece.

"Go with the wind, my friends."

King Air One pilot pushed the throttles forward and accelerated down the runway. The King Air Two rolled when the first plane was about 100 yards down the runway, followed by the Cheyenne. The three planes lifted off within seconds of each other, and quickly closed up into a tight group, maintaining an altitude of 100 feet. Two miles from Marib Cay the formation began a slow left hand climb to 3100 feet.

King Air Two was tucked just above and behind King Air One, while the Cheyenne did the same above and behind King Air Two. They completed a full circle before they reached altitude and rolled out of the turn onto a course of 315, setting their speed to 175 knots.

Fitz-Osborne in the DC-3 had a grandstand seat to watch the three planes climbing under him, their flight path timed perfectly to intercept his course. He was impressed by the precision flying.

"Just like the man said, sweetie!" he said to his plane. "Bloody marvelous, chaps. Now, how about a fourth?" The three plane formation reached 3100 feet less than half a mile in front of Fitz-Osborne. In just fifteen seconds, without changing position, he slid his DC-3 underneath the stacked formation, wagging his wings once in place.

The three pilots above him, moving as one, increased their speed to match the 180 knots of the DC-3. Fitz-Osborne looked through the small skylight above his head. He could just see the pilot's face in the King Air above him and gave a wave.

"Key-ryst, he's young," he shook his head. "I hope they know what they are doing, 'cause if they scratch you one little bit, you lovely wanker, I'll be tearing out some flesh!"

Fitz-Osborne had been ordered not to communicate with the three plane formation by radio, but he was expected to maintain all proper communications with Nassau and Miami, including proper transponder codes.

"Fly your normal route, Raymond," the man named Luis had told him. Simple enough for $15,000, he thought, about three months pay. Luis had given him half that day and the other half was to be delivered upon landing in Palm Beach, provided everything went well.

"Nassau Radio, this is Victor-Romeo 7-8. Climbing to 12,500 feet," he radioed. He checked his transponder, still set to 1200 and gently added power, giving the nose a little nudge skyward. The three twins above reacted, too, and the stack of four planes began an easy climb.

* * *

In Oklahoma City, Stanley Krups spun his cursor to the blip he had designated "UNK 1", switched to the Nassau aerostat radar blimp that was tethered on the southern side of the island and waited for the screen to reconfigure. "TRK 1" came back on the screen, indicated a reliable contact. The blip was clearly visible, squawking 1200 VFR and Mode C, just south of Andros Island, about 165 miles south east of Miami, moving northwest at 12,500 feet on the normal air corridor designated A315. The computer clocked his speed at 180 knots.

He checked the printout of the flight plans for the day and saw a DC-3, call sign Victor-Romeo 7-8 was scheduled to be there. That must be him, he thought. Right on schedule. Expected ADIZ penetration in thirty-one minutes.

The Air Defense Identification Zone surrounded the coast of the United

States and presented a twenty-mile wide national security buffer. FAA regulations required all aircraft entering the ADIZ from foreign shores, regardless of altitude or speed, to notify aviation authorities of their plans and the time they expected to enter the ADIZ. Any planes without a flight plan or those that deviated dramatically from their filed plan, would be treated as intruders, which meant an Air Force fighter or a Coast Guard jet could be scrambled to investigate.

Though the Soviet Air Force was the main threat envisioned when the ADIZ was created, smugglers were the primary suspects in the post Cold War era.

Krups typed in more commands and the target designated "UNK 1" was changed to "VR-78". Krups moved on to other targets, while the tiny blip that was the DC-3 continued along it's flight plan among the dozens of other blips on the screen that showed all of southern Florida and the northern Bahamas in Sector 180.

In the cockpit of "VR-78", the late afternoon sun backlit the coastline creating a painting of hazy blue-grey forms horizontally spread across the windshield.

At a distance of 150 miles off the coast, Fitz-Osborne had switched from Nassau Control to South Atlantic Control and reported his estimated time of penetration of the ADIZ as required. Now just over Bimini, only fifty miles out, he turned his DC-3 toward Palm Beach International. So far, the flight was only two minutes behind the schedule he had laid out in his flight plans.

"South Atlantic Control, Good afternoon, this is Victor-Romeo 7-8," Fitz-Osborne intoned cheerfully into his microphone. "ADIZ penetration west of Bimini at this time. Speed 180 knots. Course 345. 20 miles to BONDI intersect for PBI."

"Victor-Romeo,7-8, this is South Atlantic Control. Squawk 2-9-0-4."

Fitz-Osborne switched his transponder to the requested number, keeping the Mode C altitude activated. The DC-3 would show up on the controller's screen in a data box with the proper code to clearly identify him as they crossed into the busy traffic patterns along the coast.

"Victor-Romeo squawking 2904," Fitz-Osborne replied.

There was a pause. Then the controller's voice again, "Confirm 2904, Victor-Romeo. Cleared to BONDI, descend to 5-5. You may contact Palm Beach Approach on 124.6."

"Victor-Romeo 7-8, roger, cleared to 5-5. Thank you, gents!"

So far, so good, Fitz-Osborne thought, switching to the Palm Beach Control frequency. He cut back the throttles and the nose of the old DC-3 dipped. He could see the pinpoint flash of the rotating beacon at the Palm Beach Airport about thirty-five miles ahead, and down the coast to the left the other beacons of Fort Lauderdale, Opa Locka and Miami airports.

He looked through the skylight porthole above his head, and noticed that the three planes had changed formation. The two King Airs were now tucked in side-by-side only 25 feet above him with the Cheyenne riding above and between the other two.

The ninety-foot wingspan of the DC-3 was still the largest object in the formation and provided the target from which radar beams were bounced back to the coastal radar network. The tighter formation helped reduce the profile as they descended to lower altitudes. Fitz-Osborne didn't think it would make much difference, especially with his transponder glowing on the controller's radar screens. He turned back to his instruments to watch his rate of descent, holding it steady at 1200 feet per minute.

In Oklahoma City, Stanley Krups switched to a twenty square mile scan of the area just east of Fort Lauderdale. He had been watching "VR-78" on and off during it's penetration of the ADIZ and now zoomed in for a closer look. The readings had been fluctuating just a bit, as if the signal strength varied with each scan of the radar. He punched in both the Key West and Miami Control radars, waited for the computer to reconfigure the display and then looked at the little square designated "VR-78".

He saw that the pilot was descending and the last reading had him at 8,000 feet. The read-outs were strong with good reliability, the transponder was functioning properly and the flight was still on schedule. He adjusted the monitor contrast slightly and "VR-78" remained strong on the screen. Then he noticed something odd. The symbol showing "VR-78" position seemed to jump slightly to the right, indicating a "TRK 4" target in the data box. A few seconds later, the data box of "VR-78" returned to its original position.

"What's this?" he asked himself. It happened again a moment later, switching for only a couple of seconds and then held steady on "VR-78" for a full two minutes.

Krups ran his cursor over the blip and reconfirmed the information, which showed "VR-78" was on course.

"Hmmm, computer brain cramp," he said to himself.

"What's that, Stanley?" came Janet Peck's voice.

He turned to see her smiling at him, leaning over her own screen, her breasts resting on the console table.

"Oh, nothing, just a computer hiccup or something in Sector 90," he smiled back. "Coffee? I'll run this time," he asked. She leaned back in her chair and nodded, rubbing her eyes. Stanley took advantage of her closed eyes to feast his eyes as long as he dared, then went for coffee with a smile on his face.

* * *

In King Air One, Gabriel Castro Ortiz's eyes were constantly on alert. His friends called him *Aguila* because he moved like an eagle and didn't miss much.

He looked left at Gerardo at the controls of King Air Two and nodded to him. Gerardo was at the same altitude, tucked twenty-five feet behind Gabriel's left wing tip and twenty-five feet above the DC- 3. Gerardo smiled back and gave a small wave.

Gabriel could see the Cheyenne tucked in behind the two King Airs, about twenty-five feet above. The Cheyenne's wings blocked Stephane, the third pilot,, but he was there, holding formation.

Gabriel complimented Fitz-Osborne for his steady hand at the controls of the DC-3. The movements he made were small ones through occasional turbulence and the three pilots had been able to maintain their distance fairly comfortably.

The formation flying had been just as they had practiced it two weeks ago over the deserts of the Guajira Peninsula north of Quintaro's ranch in Riohacha, even without the DC-3. The fifty-foot separation early in the flight had been a breeze. They halved the distance close to the coastline and all three pilots were being extra careful now. It was six o'clock in the evening. They would be out of the ADIZ in two minutes and then continue descending to about 2,000 feet.

"Palm Beach Approach, this is Victor-Romeo 7-8. Passing 7 for 5, at BONDI intersect, requesting 9 left."

Gabriel couldn't help but smile. That old bloke sure sounded cheery. Gabriel had spoken English for ten of his twenty years, and hearing a proper Englishman speaking made him laugh.

"Victor-Romeo 7-8, this is West Palm Approach. State type of aircraft."

There was just a moment's pause. Then Fitz-Osborne came on again. "West Palm, Victor-Romeo 7-8 is a DC-3, sir. She's a damn fine one at that!"

There was a thirty-second pause before the controller answered.

"Victor-Romeo 7-8. Cleared to RUBIN, hold there left turns. Descend to 2,000. P.B.I. Altimeter 29.92, winds 10 at 095. Runway 9 left. Report RUBIN."

"Roger that, Palm Beach. Cleared to RUBIN."

RUBIN was the outer marker west of the Palm Beach active runway. Fitz-Osborne would have to fly in circles there in a holding pattern. Gabriel wondered for a moment if there was a problem. Had the controllers suspected something as they viewed their screens? He doubted it. Probably traffic already in the landing pattern. Anyway, they were committed and once they reached RUBIN, it wouldn't matter.

He checked the list of co-ordinates taped to his control wheel and punched in the next two sets in the GPS receiver. The formation continued to descend, passing through 4,000 feet.

In six minutes they crossed over the sandy beaches of Florida and a minute later reached the RUBIN beacon. The DC-3 began a slow left hand turn.

"P.B. Approach, Victor-Romeo 7-8 at RUBIN, and holding."

"Roger, Victor-Romeo. You are now cleared to land runway 9 left," answered Palm Beach.

As the DC-3 rolled left, Ortiz in King Air One smoothly broke off from the formation to the right and pushed the nose of his King Air into a shallow dive.

The other two followed, holding in a tight formation flying directly west. The DC-3 continued it's turn in the opposite direction, no longer providing cover from the radar. On the Palm Beach Approach controller's screen, a second target suddenly appeared, moving away from the DC-3.

"Victor-Romeo 7-8, this is Palm Beach. I have traffic to your right and below. Do you see him?"

"Negative, Palm Beach, don't have anyone," Fitz-Osborne replied honestly. He was turning in the opposite direction, and could not see the three planes even if he wanted.

"Victor-Romeo, you are cleared to land. Break. Unidentified traffic one mile west of RUBIN, please state your intentions," the controller asked.

In the King Air One, Gabriel ignored the request and concentrated on controlling his fully loaded plane as it dove toward the ground. He leveled out at 100 feet above the marshes near the airport. Gerardo and Stephane mimicked his actions and spread out behind him, carefully staying out of his prop wash.

"Sportaire 2-8-9, Palm Beach, immediate turn right, course 180. Traffic two miles on nose, course 2-7-0," the controller called to a small plane lined up to land behind the DC-3.

"Roger, Palm Beach. Sportaire 2-8-9 right turn, 1-8-0. Negative contact," came the female voice of the small plane's pilot. She looked out her window to the east, saw nothing but the flatness of Florida.

The three drug planes held formation and increased speed to 250 knots, covering about a mile every fifteen seconds. They followed the Palm Beach Canal, turning northwesterly toward Lake Okeechobee. Over the lake, they followed Gabriel's lead altering course to due north. Each pilot was critically focused on the horizon ahead and except for two minor course corrections to avoid some high-tension towers, they stayed at 100 feet on the northerly heading toward Blue Cypress Lake.

At Palm Beach International, the sudden appearance of the second target caused a momentary stir with the controller, whose responsibility is to see that planes don't get that close to each other. However, shortly after he cleared the small Sportaire from the crowded airspace, the target disappeared from the screen as abruptly as it had appeared. He mentioned it to his supervisor, who told him to fill out a report. That was as far as the incident went. There were other planes stacking up to land that required his attention.

Fitz-Osborne landed without incident, taxied directly to U.S. Customs where the official quickly looked at his empty cargo bay and signed him in to the country.

Fitz-Osborne parked the plane, filed a flight plan to return to Great Inagua Island the next day with his load of supplies for the National Salt Company and the two cases of stout. Once the paper work was finished he went into the busy airport lounge. A young woman came over and sat next to him, impressed with his handlebar mustache and accent. She left after one drink, discreetly leaving behind an envelope containing $7500. Fitz-Osborne ordered another and happily contemplated his entertainment plans for the evening.

Meanwhile, the cocaine laden planes zoomed low over the marshes for fifty miles until reaching Mace Ranch, a small dirt airfield about thirty miles south of Orlando. Gabriel checked his GPS readings, gently pulled back on the control wheel and allowed his King Air to climb. As it did, he switched on his transponder set to 1200.

Four minutes later, Gerardo did the same in his King Air, altering his course 25 degrees to the east, and four minutes after that, Stephane began to climb in the Cheyenne, altering his course to the west. The first part of their deception was over.

As each of the planes climbed, their VFR 1200 transponder codes showed up on the radar screens at Jacksonville Air Traffic Control. The controller's job there was to guide aircraft through Northern Florida and there was nothing unusual about new targets showing up suddenly. It was also not unusual for pilots to file a flight plan in the air if they took off from small, uncontrolled airports. That is exactly what the pilots of the three drug planes had in mind.

When Gabriel reached 6,000 feet he hesitated only for a moment before opening his mike and calling Jacksonville.

"JAXS Departure, King Air November 9-7-2-8."

"Roger, King Air 9-7-2-8, JAXS," answered the voice of a controller.

"November 2-8 out of River Ranch at 6,000. Requesting IFR to Newport at flight level 2-5-0." Gabriel spoke clearly, with hardly a trace of an accent. He was proud of his English.

"Roger, November 2-8. Go ahead with flight plan."

"Roger. IFR, November 9-7-2-8, King Air with F at 235 true from River Ranch at 6:20 pm. Flight level 2-5-0, request direct to JAXS via preferred to Baltimore. Direct SEAISLE Victor 139 to HTO, Victor 268 to Block Island, AVONN intersect direct to Newport." Gabriel read from the typewritten list Simka had provided. He continued, "Time enroute 3 hours 47 minutes, 5 hours fuel. Pilot Hanscomb, on file at Miami. Three souls, white aircraft. Did you copy, JAXS?"

To the air controller, it sounded just like another corporate plane leaving a small airpark and flying home from a weekend business trip. Gabriel had broadcast the truth except for the number of people on board, and the amount of fuel. He actually had enough to climb to 25,000 feet, fly to Newport with maybe ten minutes of reserve. It was well below FAA safety regulations, but the plan by Rex Simka was designed to use FAA regs only when they suited his purpose.

If anyone should look up the name Hanscomb, there was a pilot John Hanscomb on file at the Miami FAA offices, employed by Randall Enterprises, a front company created and owned by Carlos Quintaro.

"November 2-8, JAXS. Stand by for clearance. Turn right 0-3-0 for JAXS. Squawk 5-1-2-4."

"Roger, 0-3-0."

Gabriel switched his transponder to the proper code, which would label his data block on all radarscopes during the flight to Newport, Rhode Island. About three minutes later, the Jacksonville Center controller returned.

"November 2-8, JAXS. Cleared to Newport as filed. Flight level 2-5-0. 5-1-2-4. Switch to JAXS Center on 118.0."

"Roger, JAXS. Switching to 118.0."

Gabriel smiled. He was in the air traffic control system and it would carefully guide him the next 865 nautical miles to his destination just outside of Newport, Rhode Island.

Within minutes, Gerardo and Stephane had also successfully come up on the air traffic control system and requested IFR flight clearances to their respective destinations of Cyclone, Indiana, 910 nautical miles and Kutztown, Pennsylvania, 700 nautical miles.

With good weather each plane would be able to make it to the carefully selected airstrips, arriving between 10 and 11 pm that night. At each airstrip a four man ground crew awaited, ready to unload the cocaine cargo. In 24 hours, it would be in Quintaro's distribution network in New England, New York City and Chicago.

* * *

Mario Terrazi, the leader of the ground unit waiting for Gabriel's plane at Newport State Airport, just north of the famous sailing harbor, was telling jokes when he heard the sound of Gabriel's plane overhead. It was 11:10 pm and the airport was deserted. The landing lights suddenly came on, switched on with a few clicks from Gabriel's radio transmitter on the published frequency. Terrazi crushed out his cigarette and the three men with him opened up the doors of the two vans and waited for the plane to land.

Unknown to the four, an old man crouched well hidden along the airport fence with a video camera outfitted with a night lens. The old man had tailed Terrazi's van all the way from Worcester.

He hadn't used the camera in several years, but the machine worked fine, and silently recorded the unloading of the plane in the dim light of the headlights from the vans parked on the tarmac. He then followed both vans to a house near Fitchburg, north of Worcester, where the duffel bags were unloaded.

It was an exciting night for the old man who returned to his Boylston Street apartment just before dawn, tired, but satisfied he had enough information to bring to the police. He smiled as his head hit the pillow. They would listen to this old crank now, he thought.

~~~

CHAPTER FIFTEEN

Kathryn looked up from the aeronautical chart of Northern Colombia and looked over at PJ in the left hand seat of the Starship. "Peter, you don't think we are underestimating Quintaro, do you?" she asked, "What if he knows about you?"

PJ turned his head and gave her a serious look. She had asked him the same question at least a dozen times in the last two days.

"Well, Kathryn, I'm hoping your beauty will distract him, blind him to the truth, just as you have done to me!"

She laughed and shook her head. She was not yet convinced, but his confidence was beginning to grow on her.

"It's not funny!" she said seriously. "He must know who you are and what you look like!"

"If he's a racing fan, maybe he'll recognize me from the circuit," he admitted. He knew she was worried and tried again to allay her fears. "But, I don't think so. Besides, he has an image to protect. Too many people will know where we are, including air traffic control. This guy has people believing he's a banker. And I'm just a playboy on vacation with his beautiful girl friend, remember?"

"I don't think his backyard is public enough."

"The aerocivil authorities will know," PJ answered. He placed his hand on hers. "Just play our roles and we should be all right."

"I hope he's home," Kathryn added, glancing sideways at PJ.

"Ha! So do I," PJ laughed at the thought that part of their plan could simply be foiled by poor timing. "We'll know inside the hour."

It was midweek, early in October, eleven days since the shooting on San Francisco Bay. PJ and Kathryn were cruising at 31,000 feet above the Caribbean Sea, doing 350 knots, northeast of the Aruba VOR navigational beacon. Princess Juliana airport on St. Maarten was ninety minutes behind them.

Tuesday night they had played the role of carefree vacationers from Connecticut in a Philipsburg hotel. For a few hours, the strain of recent events had been eased. An open-air dinner, some rum punches, and their laughter, floating easily on the tropical breezes of the evening, gave them both a sense of escape. They walked on the beach, held hands and talked of sailing, flying and childhood memories.

Her hand was warm in his, and their growing desire for each other was heavy in the air. Several times they embraced, their lips touching softly, his strong hands on her back, pulling her close. They walked slowly back to the hotel, lovemaking the next logical step, only to fall soundly asleep, tired and comfortable in each other's arms.

They woke fully dressed and an hour later than planned Wednesday morning and any thoughts of lovemaking were replaced by the anticipation of getting their trip to Colombia underway. At the airport, they ran into a three-hour delay caused by Colombian officials who were slow to approve their flight plan from St. Maarten to Cartegena. PJ had expected the delay, and was pleased it hadn't taken longer.

He realized international travel was on a different timetable south of Florida. And why the hell not! The sky was perfectly blue, the sun was warm. He and Kathryn had put the wait to good use, spending the morning on the beach next to the airport. Noisy, but nice. The sun felt good on his body and it sure looked good on Kathryn's brown skinned figure. They both doubted another night would pass without their passion fully revealing itself.

PJ checked the distance to the next checkpoint and the fuel gauges. He knew his calculations were correct. They would run out of fuel about thirty miles east of Riohacha.

PJ knew that dropping in on Carlos Quintaro's ranch uninvited, was a major risk, but he had insisted on it. He hoped to gain some sense of the man and his world before going to the Colombian authorities with his story. There was also a little voice inside him that hoped Quintaro would recognize him and create an immediate confrontation. He was ready for that, too.

The rest of the crew was on their own schedule. Dutch, Lenny and Dave had flown direct from Groton to Miami 24 hours ago in one of Lenny's Citations. The plan was to refuel there, pick up Crash, and head for Cartegena.

Crash had gone ahead to Miami to rejoin *Poly Rocket* after the cross-country trek by truck. She supervised the loading of the sailboat on a freighter for the trip to Tortola. The final regatta of the sailing season was only three weeks away and PJ found himself wishing it were sooner. He knew what to expect from sailing. He didn't know what to expect from the next few days in Colombia.

Stoney took Ray and Mickey with him and said they would be in

Cartegena before Thursday. He gave no specifics.

PJ was gratified by the enthusiasm of the crew. Whether they understood the danger or not, they were with him. It felt good to have friends like that. The would all be in Colombia tonight.

"I imagine the four musketeers are sunning themselves in Cartegena right now," Kathryn said, guessing his thoughts.

"Rum and tonics in their hands, oil on their bodies," he smiled, "Lenny is probably telling stories, while Dutch translates his own version."

She laughed at the picture. "I hope they know when to get serious," she said.

"They do. Guaranteed."

"November Oscar 3-7-9 Sierra. This is Curacao control."

The European filled his headsets. "Cleared to flight level 1-5-0. Switch to Colombia Cerrejon after passing ABA VOR. 119.3. Good day."

"Roger, Curacao. Flight level 1-5-0. 3-7-9 Sierra," answered PJ. He cut power to the twin turbo pusher engines and settling the Starship into a rate of descent of 750 feet a minute. The mechanics had installed the new engine in record time, patched the holes in the fuselage and she had performed flawlessly on the trip so far.

The lack of scenery toyed with PJ's concentration and he was happy to see the island of Aruba appear on the water's horizon. Beyond Aruba was the Guajira Peninsula, the northeastern tip of Colombia. Though brown and plain looking on the horizon, he always felt better with land in sight.

Kathryn punched in several numbers on the cockpit computer and pointed at the results of the calculations.

"Forty minutes of fuel."

PJ nodded, "That should be enough. Switch to Correjon and double check the freqs for Barranquilla FIR, Riohacha and Valledupar, just in case."

"They're ready," she answered, scrolling through the preselected radio frequencies displayed on the instrument panel.

Colombia had declared a state of siege to help fight the drug traffic. There was a special interest in private planes entering the country. If the amount of preliminary paperwork didn't put you off, the warnings about Air Force jets shooting down suspicious planes might. It all sounded very ominous.

"With all the forms that I filled out, I half expected we would have a military escort," PJ said to Kathryn.

"They can only hassle us on the ground," she smiled. "Up here, we can go anywhere, if we really wanted." She pointed out the window to the mountains just coming into view on the horizon.

"The Sierra Nevada de Santa Marta," he said. "The mine is somewhere in the middle of those babies."

"I have goose bumps, PJ!"

She stared at the distant mountains as they crossed over the coastline. "Colombia. The emerald country. The land of El Dorado, the land of myths. Good things will happen here, PJ. I just feel it."

He looked at her, her face serene, her eyes transfixed on the snowcapped peaks visible at eighty miles.

"I certainly hope so, Kathryn, because in the last two weeks Colombia hasn't been much more than the Land From Which Bad Things Happen," he said.

They were now over the Guajira Desert, covering nearly six miles every minute. The land was flat, a mixture of white salt and brown sand, infrequently etched with a blue line where a river snaked through the dryness.

Aerocivil Bogota' had approved their route westerly on the normal airway, designated A574, with checkpoints over Riohacha, Santa Marta and Barranquilla before turning southerly to the resort city of Cartegena, about forty-five minutes away. However, fifteen minutes after crossing the coast, still thirty miles east of Riohacha, with the mountains now filling their view on the left and the Caribbean Sea on the right, PJ looked at Kathryn.

"Are you ready to rock and roll, girl?"

"I'm ready," she answered, returning his look.

"God, I love your black eyes," he said and reached for the throttles, moving them back slowly to decrease power. The fuel gauge showed less than fifty gallons in the tanks and PJ knew that was enough to fly for maybe ten minutes, in an emergency. However, their plan was to shut down the engines completely and glide the Starship onto Quintaro's backyard landing strip. Their arrival had to appear totally accidental.

"Cerrejon, Cerrejon, this is November Oscar 3-7-9 Sierra," PJ spoke, a touch of tension in his voice. "Ah, we have a fuel emergency here. I repeat. We have a fuel emergency! We have to land at the nearest field. Do you copy, Cerrejon?"

"3-7-9. Please confirm. You have a fuel emergency. Is that correct?" came the response from the ATC.

"Roger, Cerrejon. We are declaring a fuel emergency. November Oscar 3-7-9 Sierra. Flight level 1-5-0. Course 257. We are losing power. We must land as soon as possible. Request immediate clearance to Riohacha. Request clearance to land at *Almarante Padilla* airport."

"3-7-9 Sierra, Cerrejon. Understand. You are cleared direct to *Almarante Padilla* Riohacha and may descend at your discretion. Contact Riohacha control on 122.2. Good day."

PJ brought the throttles back to idle, then he shut them down. The engines went quiet, the props feathered and the Starship slowed dramatically. PJ pushed the nose down slightly to keep up the speed. The Starship was now a six-ton plastic glider.

PJ focused on the airspeed, keeping it at 130 knots to get the best distance from the powerless plane. If speed dropped, he pushed the nose down to accelerate. If speed increased too much, he pulled the nose up, playing with gravity and lift to stretch the momentum necessary for a safe landing now twenty-five miles away.

The flight computers, running on battery, already had the approach to Quintaro's ranch on screen and PJ estimated he would make the airfield with altitude to spare.

"I'll call Riohacha, Kathryn, and you contact Barranquilla FIR. Tell them we have lost power and are attempting to land near Riohacha," PJ ordered. Barranquilla was the Flight Information Region authority and would handle any rescue efforts in an emergency. PJ wanted to make sure the FIR knew where they were heading.

In the lookout post that doubled as a control tower at Quintaro's private airfield, the guard on duty was tuned to the Riohacha control frequency and he heard PJ's call.

"Riohacha control, this is November Oscar 379 Sierra. We have declared a fuel emergency. Our position is twenty-five miles east passing through flight level 1-2-0. Request clearance to land. We have lost power in both engines. Do you copy, Riohacha?"

On the second channel, Kathryn was conversing in Spanish with the Barranquilla controller, advising him of their situation. Riohacha was not responding.

"Riohacha, Almarante Padilla airfield, this is November Oscar 379 Sierra. We request immediate clearance to land. We have lost power. Flight level 1-0-0," PJ's voice was a couple of octaves higher now.

He banked the Starship to the right toward the Caribbean, planning to approach from the sea. He dropped the nose down a touch holding speed at 135 knots. Then he spotted Quintaro's airstrip hugging the water.

"There it is! Wonderful! We have some airspace to play with," PJ said out loud to Kathryn.

Two minutes passed and two more radio attempts by PJ before the airfield responded.

"November Oscar 379 Sierra, this is Riohacha. Understand emergency. You are cleared to land. Active runway 27, wind from 2-1-5 at 5 knots."

"Riohacha, I have visual on airfield. Roger, ah...Please repeat. Did you say runway 27?" PJ smiled as he waited for the answer.

"Correct, 379 Sierra. Runway 27, wind 5 knots," came Riohacha's reply.

"Riohacha, I have visual on airfield, however I see only one runway ..ah, it appears to be 18. North-south."

"379 Sierra, negative. Runway 27 or 09 active runway. Only runway!"

"Roger, Riohacha. I understand. You have runway 27 active. I repeat. I see only runway 18. That's one hundred eighty degrees, course south. *Sud*. Do you copy?"

"379 Sierra, what is your location?"

"Riohacha, 379 Sierra is over water, 10 miles north east of Riohacha beacon. Flight level now 5000. I am committing to approach runway 180."

There was a pause from the ground control. PJ clearly saw the Quintaro ranch ahead and the spread of land around a large house. The runway was on a bump in the coastline, surrounded on three sides by water. He saw two hangars and other smaller buildings along the black ribbon. The commercial airfield was visible to the west with the city in between, but they were not going there.

"November Oscar 379 Sierra. You have wrong airport. Runway 18 is at private airfield. You cannot land there. *Prohibir!* Can you land runway 27, Almarante Padilla?"

"Negative, Riohacha. Flight level 2500. I have no power. Unable to make Almarante Padilla. November Oscar 379 Sierra. I am landing runway 18 at airfield east of Riohacha."

The guard at Quintaro's ranch was at first amused by the twenty questions game between Riohacha control and the unseen airplane. However, when he realized the plane was talking about landing at the ranch, his smile disappeared. He reached for his walkie-talkie, looking out the tower window toward the blue green Caribbean. He nearly dropped his radio.

Five hundred feet above the ground and 300 yards away was the strangest looking airplane he had ever seen. The engines were on backwards and the propellers weren't turning! The plane's body was black as night, and diving right at him!

The guard ducked as the Starship buzzed the tower with a whooshing sound that rattled the water glasses and sent the newspapers on the table flying.

"Son of a bitch!" he yelled and made the sign of the cross as he watched the plane zoom low across the airfield, just clearing the hangars on the other side.

"Garcia, Garcia, this is Roqua," the guard called on the radio, contacting the security chief on duty. "We have an intruder trying to make an emergency landing. Do you see it? It's turning north!"

"I see it, Roqua. We are coming," came Garcia's voice over the radio. The Starship at that moment was flying over Garcia's head just above the treetops.

PJ's dive built speed to over 200 knots and provided enough momentum to allow the Starship to climb back to 750 feet. At the top of the climb, just before all lift in the wings was exhausted, he banked left and lowered the nose to increase airspeed.

Kathryn was enjoying the ride and the view. She could see two vehicles coming toward the airfield from near the large mansion with the salmon tile roof that seemed to be balancing on the edge of the ocean cliffs about half a mile away beyond an orange grove.

"I'm impressed, PJ," she said.

"Just getting into my role, Kathryn," he answered, a smile on his face. He was enjoying his aerobatics and never felt close to losing control of the big bird.

"No, not with you, Peter! I'm impressed with this spread we are landing on. Mr. Quintaro has a nice estate here," she said dryly. "He even has a golf course!" PJ didn't say anything, just smiled and shook his head as he concentrated on the landing.

"Watch out for that radio tower," she said, pointing to the red and white frame tower to their right. It looked to be about 150 feet tall.

"I see it," he said calmly.

PJ expertly balanced the nose angle to keep the plane flying. He maneuvered back over the water then turned south again onto the final approach to the runway. At 500 feet he moved the canard wing forward, and lowered the flaps. A moment later the landing gear locked into place. The speed dropped from 130 to 125 and continued to decrease, but the Starship was floating toward the ground. PJ nudged back on the controls

---

Crew

and flared out just thirty feet above the seawall at the end of the runway.

Seconds later, the main wheels touched down together, leaving a short, double skid mark right on the big white numbers that designated the strip's 180 degree compass orientation. The nose wheel touched next and PJ gently applied pressure to the brakes to slow the roll out.

"Nicely done, PJ," Kathryn said quietly. "I'll let Barranquilla know where we are." She called the regional controller and advised they had landed safely on an airfield just to the east of the city. She asked and they confirmed the field was Carlos Quintaro's private property.

"Damn, he only has one turnoff here, we're going to be stuck at the end of the runway," PJ said to himself as they rolled past the hangar taxiway. Three-quarters of the way down the runway he slowed the plane enough to attempt a U-turn on the narrow strip, but the momentum that had begun thirty miles away at 15,000 feet was finally all used up and the Starship came to a stop sitting across the runway.

"Well, I once read a book that said, 'Go to the heart of danger, there you will find safety'," PJ intoned as he shut down all the plane's instruments, except for the radio. "I guess we find out right now."

"Here's our welcoming party," she said, pointing at the trail of dust coming from beyond the trees. A jeep and a pickup proved to be the source as they appeared and raced toward them. They stopped directly in front of the plane, blocking any escape. PJ and Kathryn sat there with no intentions of leaving.

PJ counted five men, all with automatic weapons. He identified them as Kalashnikov AKM's, the modern version of the legendary Russian AK-47. The distinctive curved clip held thirty rounds, he remembered. Three of the men also had side arms.

They fanned out in front and to the side of the plane, more intrigued with the strangely shaped winged intruder than with any danger it might present. However, their weapons were at the ready.

"Let's go meet our new friends, dear. Remember, this is the vacation of your lifetime," he said, slipping out of the pilot's seat, "but they may not understand that." He reached behind his seat and pulled out a beat-up yellow baseball cap with the Penzoil logo across the front.

"It's cool," she said, following him into the cabin. "You look like Roger Penske with that hat," Kathryn cracked, her nerves tensing.

"How about a lost sailor?" he joked holding up his left hand with the fingerless sailing glove covering his wound. He released the cabin door, lowering the built-in stairs to the tarmac. The Starship cabin was still cool from their air-conditioned flight and the heat of the tropical day rushed in like a burst from a furnace.

"Let me go first!" she said suddenly and pushed passed him and bounded down the stairs.

"*Hola!*" she waved, smiling broadly. She quickly scanned the five men around the plane. They had the look of pros, four of them wearing grey shirts without any visible insignia and all with brown fatigue pants, a uniform of sorts. They held their rifles in a disciplined manner, pointed directly at her.

She didn't hesitate, but walked up to the fifth man, stocky, and well built with a colorful shirt open to his chest, his rifle pointed at her and a pearl handled .9 mm pistol hanging low on his hip. He looked mean and in charge. She offered her hand in greeting.

Garcia hesitated before this friendly, black-haired beauty, dressed in a white blouse and khaki pants, who had just dropped into their midst. But, he quickly regained his hard composure and gestured with his rifle to keep her back.

She stepped back, her palms up, but continued to speak, apologizing for their intrusion.

"It's okay. Excuse us. Please. We mean no harm. We ran out of gas and had to make an emergency landing. This airstrip was the closest one. It was an emergency," she said in Spanish.

She turned and introduced PJ as the race car driver, PJ McDonough, and herself as his companion, Kathryn Byrnie. One of the guards gave the hint of a smile at the mention of PJ's name, but Garcia was stone faced. Kathryn was all smiles and fluent and PJ just stood by the stairs wondering what she was saying.

"I am Garcia Ramones, head of security. Where are you from?" asked Garcia in Spanish, cutting her off.

"United States, through St. Maarten," she answered. "*Vacaciones.* We've come to see Colombia. The Emerald Festival?"

"Ask them if they have any aviation gasoline, Kathryn," PJ interjected. "Or if they speak English," he added.

"We need gasoline. Then we will leave. We will pay for it," Kathryn repeated her request.

"Turn around, hands on the plane," Garcia commanded in Spanish. "Both of you!"

"Hey! Easy with the lady!" PJ shouted, as Garcia pushed Kathryn against the fuselage. He walked up to PJ and gestured for him to turn

---

around also.

"It's okay, PJ," Kathryn said grimly as Garcia ran his hands quickly over her body, patting her everywhere in search of a hidden weapon. His hands moved quickly and professionally, PJ thought. Garcia did the same to PJ, close enough for PJ to smell the man's cologne, a type he could not identify.

Finding nothing, Garcia motioned PJ away from the doorway and stuck his head inside the cabin. He ordered a second guard to check inside.

"Look for their papers and weapons!" Garcia commanded as the guard disappeared inside. "Search everything!"

"Do you speak Spanish?" he asked PJ sternly.

"No, I don't," he said. He jerked his thumb toward Kathryn. "She's the brains."

Garcia laughed, the first sign of civility since the landing.

"She's the brains," he repeated to the other men. They also laughed.

"She's the brains and the beauty," one shouted back and the others all hooted and hollered their agreement.

Garcia walked up to Kathryn, who tried to maintain a friendly grin, although the guards' lusty cackles worried her as did the way Garcia looked at her. During the frisk, his hands had not lingered on her, but they had not missed much.

"Are you the pilot?" Garcia asked Kathryn, still in Spanish.

"No, he's the pilot," Kathryn answered, pointing to PJ.

Garcia looked back at PJ and PJ returned his gaze with steady eyes. Garcia nodded his head.

"Gasolina?" PJ asked Garcia, pointing to the plane. "Check the engines? Then we will take off again and leave."

"*Silencio!*" Garcia gruffly shouted with a menacing move of his AKM. Then he turned and walked away, circling the plane. He felt along the wings and stopped momentarily to look inside both engines. He completed his tour as the guard appeared in the cabin doorway with PJ's flight bag, Kathryn's small shoulder bag, two suitcases and a garment bag.

"This is all there is," the man said placing the bags on the ground.

"Hey, that's our luggage!" PJ shouted and made a move toward it. However, the guard stepped in front of him with his rifle, pushing him back.

"Stand there and don't move!" Garcia ordered in English. He coldly watched PJ take a step back next to Kathryn before reaching into the flight bag. He sifted through some charts and papers and come out with PJ's travel wallet, which included his passport, $5000 in traveler's checks and $1500 in US currency. PJ was surprised when Garcia ignored the cash, but pulled out only his passport and tourist card, dropping the wallet back into the case. He also pulled out the plane's documents, which were sealed in a plastic pouch. He rummaged through Kathryn's bag and pulled out her passport and tourist card also.

The guard bent down and opened the suitcases, feeling around as if searching for a weapon or other documents. He shook his head to Garcia when finished.

"*Nada.*" He closed the cases with the clothes in disarray.

"Hey, I've got some dresses in there. Be careful!" Kathryn protested from a distance.

"*Señorita, Silencio!* Please!" Garcia shouted at her, his exasperated voice booming around the airstrip. She nodded and stood quietly.

"*Gracias,*" he grunted, turning away with a command to the guard, who stepped forward and, motioning with his rifle, directed PJ and Kathryn to sit on the runway under the Starship's wing on the runway.

"Are we under arrest?" PJ asked.

"We just need gasoline for the plane," Kathryn said to Garcia's back. Garcia just waved his hand without turning and the guard repeated his motion with the rifle. They sat down in the shadow of the wing and the guard stood about fifteen feet away and kept an eye on them, standing comfortably in the hot sun. The other three guards held their positions. Garcia went to the jeep and spoke out of earshot on the radio.

"I think the master is home," PJ whispered to Kathryn. She nodded, trying to hear Garcia on the radio but could not.

"Ruiz! Back on patrol," Garcia yelled after a moment and the three guards near the front of the plane jumped into the pick up truck and drove off toward the hangars and disappeared through the trees from which they had first appeared. Garcia just sat back in his jeep, lit up a cigarette, and looked through the documents, obviously waiting for someone.

The departure of most of the guards eased PJ's mind somewhat. He looked around the airfield. The Caribbean Sea was only fifty yards away, Quintaro's wooden guard tower spoiling an otherwise magnificent view. He could see the lone guard in the tower watching them, his rifle at the ready, hanging across his chest from its harness. From that vantage point, the guard could see the entire airstrip and the hangars. Probably a heavy caliber machine gun up there, too, he thought.

PJ counted three other men, also armed with Kalashnikovs - two patrolling near the hangars and the third standing outside a smaller shack at the airfield gate. A fence extended in both directions behind the buildings as far as he could see. He thought it odd there were no vehicles visible except for the jeep where Garcia smoked and read through their documents. There was no sign of a helicopter.

"Nice place for a vacation," said Kathryn. "The colors in the water sparkle!"

PJ nodded. "Is the fishing good here?" he asked the guard, who appeared to be about twenty years old. The guard just looked over at the two of them under the wing and smiled in answer.

It was peacefully quiet for several minutes and PJ was sure he could hear the afternoon sun as it rose up from the black tarmac in searing heat waves that distorted his view of each end of the runway. He was thankful they were in the shadow of the wing. He looked at Kathryn, with her head propped up on her hand. She looked cool in the heat. She smiled at him.

The sound of approaching vehicles brought him back to the immediate problem at hand. A man in a wide brimmed sun hat, with white hair and a mustache drove the first jeep. PJ recognized him immediately. It was Carlos Quintaro.

~~~

CHAPTER SIXTEEN

T he two jeeps jerked to a halt next to Garcia. The second carried two men, bodyguards PJ guessed, judging by the short, nasty looking machine pistols they carried. They jumped quickly to the side of the white haired man wearing the sun hat in the first jeep. He acted as if they were invisible, taking the documents from Garcia and leafing through them as he walked casually toward PJ and Kathryn. He paused for a moment to look at the Starship and then, with a wave, commanded the guard standing near PJ to back away.

"It is all right, friends. Please, get up," he spoke in perfect English. "Señorita, let me help you." He reached down and gave a hand to Kathryn, pulling her to her feet.

"Gracias," she said, smiling at him. "We apologize for intruding on your lovely ranch."

Quintaro seemed lost in thought for a moment as he gazed at her. The gaze turned into a stare and then he laughed, realizing he was in fact staring.

"Forgive me, but it is all that much more lovely with you standing here," he said with a slight nod.

Kathryn smiled back, embarrassed by his compliment.

"Muchas gracias, ah, Señor...?"

"I am Carlos Octavio Quintaro. This is my home, my airfield. You are Señorita Byrnie, yes?" he said, waving the passports in his hand. His eyes remained fixed on her face. A spark of memory had been ignited, but too dim to recognize yet. He turned to PJ.

"I'm PJ McDonough, Mr. Quintaro, nice to meet you!" PJ said cheerfully, shaking his hand. The grip was a strong one, PJ thought.

"Yes, Mr. McDonough," he said. "Pleased to meet you." He seemed genuinely interested. "Forgive my men, but they are paid to protect me. It is only their job they are doing and, you must admit, they do it well."

"They were very polite, actually," PJ suggested to Quintaro, looking him in the eye. How green they are, PJ thought. "But why do you need so many soldiers?"

Quintaro looked carefully at PJ, smiling and raising his hands. "It is a part of doing business in Colombia, I'm afraid. You see, some would call me a wealthy man and that makes me a target for blackmailers and kidnapers."

There was an obvious moment of silence before PJ spoke.

"I'm kind of embarrassed by this whole thing," he half laughed, "but we had a fuel problem and had to land here. Hope it didn't interrupt your day too much."

"Nonsense, Mr. McDonough! Nothing much happens on this ranch anyway," Quintaro laughed, turning back to Kathryn. "My friends at Barranquilla already called to advise me of your *unexpected* arrival."

"This is a remarkable plane you have here, Señor McDonough. It is the Starship, yes? I have read about it in magazines, but I have never seen one. Please, tell me about it," Quintaro asked and walked over to the cabin door to look in. "Is it true it is made out of plastics?"

"Yes, it is. Even the engines," PJ pointed. "The seats, however, are leather."

Quintaro laughed lightly. "It must be hard to see on radar," he said, feeling the leading edge of the wing.

"Yes, it's the corporate stealth model," PJ laughed again. "This one is the first without the aluminum lightning arrestor rig in the fuselage and is pretty much invisible on radar if the transponder is off."

Quintaro nodded, feeling the joint of the wing and tip sail and the trailing edge rudder.

"Carries a ton about 1300 miles in four hours," Kathryn added.

"Do you also fly?" he asked with interest.

"I do," she answered.

"I see. We do not have many lady pilots in Colombia," he smiled. "It is a nice plane," he continued, ducking under the wing to look at the landing gear. "A plane like this could be very valuable in Colombia."

"Well, not so valuable without gas," PJ said.

"Yes, I suspect not," Quintaro answered, coming out from under the wing. "But, why such a hurry, Mr. McDonough? Please, show me the cockpit. I am a pilot myself. New technologies interest me."

"What do you fly?" PJ asked him as they climbed into the cabin.

"Oh, a little bit of everything, from helicopters to four engine beasts. I have a Beech twin I especially like," he said lightly.

The three of them crowded into the Starship cockpit. Quintaro took the pilot's seat at PJ's insistence. PJ flipped switches and the instrument panel came to life. He was thankful he had cleared the screens of the approach vectors to the airfield. Quintaro seemed duly impressed as the multicolor displays filled the TV monitors.

"With all this gadgetry, it is a wonder you ran out of fuel!" Quintaro said to PJ with a thin-lipped grin, looking at the fuel read-out. PJ looked at him for a moment then broke into a wide grin.

"Well, a series of little foul-ups, I guess. We hit severe head winds north of Aruba," PJ said, trying his best to look embarrassed. "Damn weatherman! I hadn't topped off the tanks in St. Maarten because I figured we had plenty to get to Cartegena. Then when the engines started to run uneven, well, I shut them down just to be on the safe side. Thought there might be some contaminants in the tanks. Then, we saw your airfield and landed."

"You should be more careful in the future," Quintaro said, wagging his finger. "A prudent pilot always has enough fuel. So, let's see about doing just that so you continue your trip. I think we can sell you some."

They exited the plane and Quintaro directed Garcia to back up the jeep to the front wheel. PJ lashed the strut to the jeep with a length of rope from the back seat.

"Señor McDonough, why don't you go with Garcia and refuel the plane. I will take Señorita Byrnie to the main house to relax, maybe have a cool drink. How does that sound?" Quintaro gestured to Kathryn with a slight bow.

Kathryn looked at PJ, trying to read his eyes.

"That would be fine, I guess, Señor Quintaro," Kathryn nodded. "Okay with you, dear?" Kathryn asked PJ.

"Yeah, sure, I'll join you when we finish, shouldn't take thirty minutes to check everything out," PJ agreed.

"Please, call me Carlos," Quintaro said, taking her hand and leading her to his jeep.

"I'm Kathryn," she smiled.

"Garcia tells me you speak our language very well," Quintaro continued as they walked out of earshot.

PJ's eyes locked on Kathryn's as they drove by and he watched them cross the grassy field toward the small guard shack at the airfield entrance. He felt a twinge of concern, and tried to put it behind him. Kathryn could take care of herself, he reminded himself. And the authorities knew they were here. Quintaro seemed deep in conversation with her, his arm waving to the scenery around them as they disappeared through the orange orchard.

PJ loaded the bags back on the plane and climbed into the cockpit. Garcia drove the jeep with the Starship in tow to the large gas tank next to the far hangar. PJ estimated the tank was capable of holding several thousand gallons. The pump couplings were standard and in a matter of minutes, a hose was carrying fuel to the Starship's right tank.

Garcia walked to the front of the plane for a smoke, while PJ stayed at the hose, scanning the hangar area, searching for some plan to get a look inside one of the hangars. Nothing looked out of the ordinary, though he could hear noises from the nearest hangar. A guard stood by the pump thirty feet away. The narrow windows around the top of the hangars were well beyond his reach.

"Hey, Garcia, is there a place to take a leak?" PJ yelled, unable to come up with a better plan. "Toilet?"

Garcia turned with annoyance, then crushed his cigarette on the pavement and walked over to PJ, the AKM on his shoulder.

PJ grinned sheepishly, "Gotta go," he said.

Garcia pointed him toward the hangar. PJ walked calmly with Garcia following about ten feet behind.

"To the left over here," Garcia said in English.

"Over here?" PJ asked and took a step toward his right and purposely opened the side door to the hangar.

"No, not there, behind the tank!" shouted Garcia, but it was too late. PJ opened the door for a brief moment and caught a flash of activity. The large T tail of a four-engine prop plane seemed to fill the hangar and dwarfed the two men in front of the fuselage. One was driving a fork-lift loaded with blue and yellow barrels.

PJ could see white letters stenciled on the barrels, which were stacked everywhere, including four high near the door. The labels read "Ether". He did not have enough time to make out the other writing on the barrel as the hanger door slammed shut with the weight of Garcia's boot. In an instant, the stocky man had knocked PJ to the ground and stood over him with the rifle only inches from his nose.

PJ smiled a goofy grin and apologized. "Hey, sorry. I'm a little confused today, hangover, you know, last night...." He grinned weakly up at the glaring face of Garcia.

"Get up!" he seethed, pulling the rifle away. "Now, over here."

PJ dusted himself off and backed away grinning to where Garcia gestured, relieving himself behind the gas pumps. Garcia stood a few feet away watching his every move.

PJ was elated. Ether was one of the chemical precursors essential to processing cocaine, as essential as coca paste itself. Any large stockpile in Colombia would raise a red flag with police who would immediately suspect a drug operation. There were at least fifty barrels of ether in that hangar, probably more.

The plane fit Barney's description of what he had seen at the mine. There was no sign of Quintaro's helicopter, but in that instant, PJ was firmly convinced Quintaro was his man. He felt a twinge of concern about Kathryn.

* * *

At the house, Quintaro had gone out of his way to make Kathryn feel comfortable. They were chatting in Spanish on the second story porch, a pitcher of lemonade, a bottle of Arguardiente and a bowl of fruit on a table. A sea breeze began to take the searing edge off the day.

Quintaro asked her about their trip to Colombia. His distinguished, almost fatherly tone, charmed her.

"It seems an odd time to vacation in our country," he was saying. "We are going through a difficult period. Things are very unstable. Only a few miles away from us, the Guajira Indians have taken to terrorists acts in protest of the government's new mine in Cerrejon. Americans run the mine for a big multi national corporation and I'm afraid Americans are not very popular in this area." He smiled, shook his head and spread his hands as if to say he didn't feel the same, but it was a fact of life.

"I guess it was the lure of adventure, Señor Quintaro..ah, Carlos, that made us decide to come to Colombia," she said, sipping her lemonade. "The instability makes it kind of dangerous and, well, PJ and I enjoy adventures. The danger makes it exotic, don't you think? Maybe only to an outsider, but Colombia is somewhat mysterious. I feel drawn to it, as if a force was pulling me here for a reason."

"There is no mystery about danger, my dear. The moth burns quickly when it flies close to the flame," he said seriously. "Colombia is a land that reacts badly to nosey adventurers."

"Well, we just want to enjoy Cartegena, maybe travel into the mountains for a day or two and enjoy the sun and sand. And PJ promised me an emerald before we left!" she said with a giggle. She found it easy to act girlish around him. "That's not nosey is it?"

"Ah, esmarelda, the magical green, the mythical madness," Quintaro said with great enthusiasm. "You would be surprised, my child, at the evil that surrounds the beauty of that precious gem." He leaned in close to her, as if sharing a great secret.

"They are pulled from the muck of the earth by amoral men who will kill you to protect their stake and will steal yours in a minute if you turn your back. Adventure, ha! Lunacy!"

"But I will tell you, Muzo emeralds are the only true emeralds," he continued. "It is the chromium that makes them green. In Brazil, they sell emeralds green from vanadium, and in your United States they are growing emeralds in microwaves!" he shook his head in disbelief, "but it is the Muzo gems that are the pure gem of the earth. They garner the glances...and the big money. But, watch out for the scoundrels, they are everywhere."

"Carlos, you speak in such dark tones. Surely, this country has some good in it?" Kathryn laughed, intrigued by this man. She wondered for a moment if they were wrong about him. Never let your enemy see you as you are, PJ had told her. It worked both ways, she thought.

"Good? Yes, there is good. Our land is one of the most beautiful in the world," he gestured to the blue green Caribbean lapping at the rocks on one side of the porch and the snowcapped peaks in the distance to the south. "You will enjoy Cartegena. One of our poets, Luis Carlos Lopez said it inspires affection and comfort as a pair of old shoes." Kathryn laughed.

"The people are good, too. They are gentle, they are loyal to family. Most believe in our democracy, but most struggle hard to make a living," he said looking at the sea. "Most of them are in old shoes," he laughed quietly at the irony of the poet's words. "Caught in the crossfire of violence and poverty, many are desperate."

"Some less than others," Kathryn teased him.

"Yes, I have been most fortunate," he smiled, re-filling her glass. "What is your background, Kathryn Byrnie. Byrnie is British? Scottish? You certainly don't look Irish! You look...well, like *'Indio de montanas'*...."

He suddenly stopped as a long lost image appeared in his mind, one that had been lingering in his subconscious from the moment he helped her off the runway. It suddenly boiled to the surface with his last words, as fleeting and hot as a meteor slashing across a clear night sky.

In a millisecond, he replayed a chapter of his life. There was brief pleasure followed by intense pain and an explosion of violence. The flash of his knife, the spurt of red and the desperate rush into the woods with the Indians in chase.

He looked at Kathryn sitting across from him. Her long dark hair over one shoulder, her high cheek bones and full mouth gave her an exotic look. Her black eyes seemed to pierce him and he felt a tightness in his chest. This woman was the reincarnate image of the Indian woman he had raped in lust and murdered in anger thirty years ago on the slopes of the Sierra Nevada de Santa Marta!

"Señor Quintaro, are you all right?" Kathryn asked. She had seen his eyes open wide even as his face drained to the color of his mustache and hair.

It was impossible, he thought, standing up abruptly. It is the drink again! He walked to the railing and looked out at the sea. He turned toward the mountains and rubbed his shoulder. His heart pounded in his ears, his mind on fire from the unearthed memories. A flash of guilt tore at his consciousness, quickly replaced by anger. The sudden intrusion of a moment of passion and violence from his past was like a deep gouge in his veneer of respectability.

He looked up slowly, afraid to meet her eyes again. He forced himself to look at this woman ghost. Those eyes! The same, deep black color! She was looking at him with a half smile, unsure of what had suddenly caused him to react in such a manner.

"Is everything all right?" she asked again.

"Yes, my dear," he struggled for control, keeping his voice strong. "A sudden business problem, a bit of unfinished business came to mind, nothing serious..." he never finished for his brother, Bernardo, appeared on the porch.

"Carlos, an important message...," Bernardo also stopped in mid-sentence when he saw the unexpected visitor sitting at the table. "Oh, I am sorry...," his apology quickly turned into recognition. He looked at Carlos and back at the woman.

"Excuse us, please, Señorita. Business calls. I will be right back. Enjoy the sunshine, please," Carlos Quintaro said, as if it were his own.

He grabbed his brother and pushed him back into the room. Bernardo stared dumbfounded at Kathryn. They went into a small side room and Carlos closed the door and sat on a chair.

"Carlos, it is her!" cried Bernardo. "How can that be?"

"It is a cruel joke, brother, a twist of chance, a coincidence, that is all," Quintaro said, not at all convinced. Bernardo saw great pain and worry etched on his brother's face.

"But how...the child!" Bernardo was stunned. "Is it possible?" He curled up on a couch, and grabbed his ankles with crossed arms, trying hard to sink into the pillows. He had lived with the terrible secret for thirty years and had pushed the memory deep into his own subconscious. As with his brother moments before, that bloody episode in their lives was alive again.

They were young and were ferrying bales of marijuana down from the mountain fields when they stopped for lunch near the woman's hut. There were five of them and she fed them, forced at gunpoint to some bread, beans and water. A beautifully dark Indian, with long dark hair, high cheekbones, deep, black eyes and a forced smile that surely hid the fear she felt for herself and her three children.

Bernardo knew trouble was coming because Carlos had tried to approach her, but she rebuffed him, wanting no part. He stroked the hair of the two younger girls, both no more than four years old. Then, as the other men watched, Quintaro forced himself on the woman, raping her in the small hut. The children heard their mother's cries and cried in response, unsure what was happening.

Carlos finished and the other men stood laughing, lined up for their turns. They were stopped by the sounds of approaching Indians who also heard her screams while working in the nearby field. Three of the men grabbed their marijuana bundles and scrambled into the jungle.

Bernardo waited for his brother. In the confusion, the woman, dazed, battered and filled with rage, grabbed a hoe from behind Quintaro and swung at him, catching the flesh of his right arm, tearing into the shoulder muscle.

He cried out in pain, and turned, the blade of his unsheathed knife flashing. It zipped across her throat, opening a fatal wound. He cursed her loudly. Bernardo stood in amazement at the sight of the bloodied woman and then saw the wound in Quintaro's arm and the bloodied knife in his hand.

"The *puta* hoed me!" Carlos cried in pain and amazement. "She won't do that again!"

As Bernardo helped Carlos get up, his brother said. "We will tear her family apart!" He pointed toward the children, even as the sounds of the Indians grew nearer. They were only a few seconds away.

"Take this one, she will bring good money on the black market," Quintaro seethed. Bernardo, dumbfounded by the events, grabbed one of the little girls. He pushed aside the young boy, who was pounding on Bernardo's legs fruitlessly with his tiny fists, and they both slipped away into the jungle just as the Indians came into the clearing.

"The child had black eyes, Carlos," Bernardo said quietly, a look of great pain on his face.

Carlos had regained color in his face and stood up. Denial was escape for the moment. He chose to pace around the room.

"Pure coincidence, Bernardo Luis. She looks like a lot of Indian women. Our memories have fuzzed the edges, our hearts have carried this for years and our emotions are distorted," he spoke steadily. Each word was resealing the tear that had appeared in the fabric of his story.

"Yes, it is only a cruel joke, Carlos," Bernardo repeated, but he sat scrunched in a ball on the couch, not moving.

"What is the message?" Carlos asked.

"What? Oh, yes. Terrible news! Luis radioed on the HF. The Provider crashed in the valley. It hit the ridge trying to land and exploded."

"Was it carrying any paste?" Carlos asked quickly.

"No, only chemicals. 750 gallons of ether, 750 gallons of acetone."

"Who was the pilot?" Carlos asked.

"Ulf. He didn't make it."

"Where's Simka?"

"Barranquilla this afternoon, then Santa Marta tomorrow. I already left a message for him."

Carlos did not like it when he couldn't reach his people immediately. He had to keep things moving in Operation Snowmine. The lost chemicals would have to be replaced within twenty-four hours to avoid shutting down the production line.

"The runway is not blocked? Good! The de Havilland is being loaded right now. Radio Luis, tell him Rafael will take the flight when it is ready. He should be able to make a run before sunset."

Carlos was energized. The bad news had acted as a stimulus. He embraced the death of Ulf, the loss of the chemicals and the plane. Crisis required action and he took it. Ghostly images had vanished.

"One more thing. Get another message to Simka to check out this PJ McDonough and Kathryn Byrnie. Here are their passport numbers. Use our source at the tourist bureau. Tell him it is important."

Bernardo took the piece of paper and looked at his brother. He saw those piercing green eyes moving quickly as Carlos walked around the room, thinking and giving orders. Carlos was under control again. Seeing Carlos act this way made Bernardo feel better. Carlos himself felt better as he walked back to the porch to rejoin Kathryn.

"Forgive me, Señorita Byrnie, but I am called away on business. Such is the cross I must bear for all this," he said gesturing to their surroundings.

"Oh, I am so sorry to hear that. I hope it isn't anything serious." Kathryn said with concern in her voice. "I did enjoy our little talk. And your hospitality."

"I also enjoyed meeting you, Kathryn Byrnie," he said grandly. He caught himself actually meaning it. "I have an idea. I am giving a little *parranda* tomorrow night in Santa Marta, as part of the festival. Many of my friends will be coming, I would be delighted if you would come with your friend. I promise I will introduce you to an honest emerald dealer."

He wondered if he had over stepped good sense by inviting her to the party. However, she intrigued him, and, at that moment, he felt no danger, even from his past. He found strength in taking charge.

"Oh, a party! Why Carlos, that is sweet of you. I do love parties. Thank you!" She hoped she didn't sound too excited.

"Let us say nine tomorrow night at the new Tourist Office on Avenida Bastidas. On the beach! It is a wonderful old mansion away from the glare of el Rodadareo. I look forward to hearing more about you at that time," and with that he politely shook her hand and walked back inside his home.

One of the bodyguards led Kathryn to a jeep and drove her back to the airfield. As they approached through the trees, she heard one of the Starship engines start followed shortly by the second. The guard handed Kathryn the plane's documents and passports, his smile more than a little friendly. It gave Kathryn the creeps.

"Barranquilla FIR as okayed resumption of our flight plan. Everything okay with you?" PJ asked as Kathryn closed the door and slipped into the right hand seat.

"Yes, we have been invited to a party! He seemed a nice man. I met his brother, too, but I'll tell you all about it on the way."

"This nice man has a hangar full of chemicals, Kathryn. And a four engine plane like Barney described," PJ said as he taxied the plane to the end of the runway. "Dozens of barrels labeled Ether," he said. "I only got a quick look."

"Did you see any cocaine?" she asked.

"No, but I'm sure we're on the right trail," PJ answered as he spun the plane into the wind.

"Riohacha control, this is November Oscar 3 7 9 Sierra, request permission to depart from airstrip east of city."

"Roger, 379 Sierra. Cleared to take off. Climb to flight level 9000. Cleared to Barranquilla."

PJ pushed the throttles forward for full power and the Starship responded with its unique throaty roar. The plane rose into the sky and out over the Caribbean. PJ made a sharp turn back toward the airfield and made a low pass, rocking his wings as he flew over the heads of Garcia and three of the guards.

"Try to take a mental picture of the grounds in case we have to visit these guys again," he told her. She nodded, looking out the window. There was no sign of activity, but she caught a glimpse of Carlos Quintaro standing inside the doorway of his house, watching them fly off.

She wondered about his sudden mood swing when he asked about her nationality. The question troubled her, too, because as American as she felt, she wasn't so sure that was the answer.

PJ, on the other hand, felt as though he had gotten away with the crown jewels. His gamble had worked! Quintaro had given no indication he recognized PJ. The elation was tempered by the fear he felt just before take off. It was as if the danger to Kathryn and him was greatest the closer they came to escape.

Escape from what? Quintaro had let them go, with his blessing, and his fuel. Was he no more than the newspapers portrayed him, a wealthy shipping magnate? And what had he really learned? The ether in the hanger was a strong indictment. It was used in cocaine processing. It was also a widely used commercial solvent and anesthetic. PJ thought the secrecy surrounding the loading of the plane was unusual for a legitimate shipment.

But, was Quintaro the man responsible for Jester's murder? And the mine takeover? There was plenty of circumstantial evidence, he thought. PJ wished he had seen the helicopter. And so he continued, searching for rock solid proof to justify the path he had set out on. A path he knew would lead to violence.

~~~

CHAPTER SEVENTEEN

K athryn sat quietly in the Starship's right hand seat, staring at the green water below them. She had not spoken since they took off from Quintaro's ranch.

"Anything wrong?" PJ asked.

"No. Well, yes. It was something Carlos said." She turned, but looked past PJ at the Sierra Nevada de Santa Marta Mountains still visible to their left.

"Carlos?" PJ asked, surprised by the informality.

"It was the way he asked me about my background. He said I looked like *'Indio de montanas'*. Indian from the mountains. Then he got all weird, like I had grown antlers or something. His brother came out and looked at me funny, too. They both disappeared and five minutes later I was ushered off the porch."

"You don't have antlers," he said seriously.

"He made me feel real comfortable, PJ. He was a gentleman, almost fatherly," she said, surprised at the effect Quintaro had on her. "I really wanted to tell him the truth about my nationality, but, I didn't know what to tell him. I mean, I'm American, but it was as if he knew I was something else."

He could hear the confusion in her voice.

"Maybe you are an Indian," PJ suggested. "Then again, maybe you're the offspring of a great pirate and a brave woman warrior who had to leave you because of their insatiable desire to plunder."

"In 1957?" she laughed.

"Well, maybe a Cuban gun runner and a mercenary cook," he laughed. Then he grew serious.

"Look, your real parents could be anyone," he said. "Why worry about it? Estelle and Tom did a fine job raising you. They're your parents. Let it go."

"You know, I dreamt about the mountains again last night," she said. "I don't know. All that's happened...he got me thinking."

"Hey, now is the time to look ahead," PJ said soothingly, trying to shift her focus. "Prepare yourself for the magic of 16th century Cartegena, the only city you will ever visit where the local hero is a one eyed, one armed, one legged soldier." he said. "Want to take her in?"

She nodded and put her hands on the control wheel of the Starship, willing to think about something else. The heavily accented voice of a ground controller came on the radio.

"379 Sierra, Barranquilla Control. You may switch to Cartegena approach on 120.3. Good day."

"Roger, Barranquilla. 120.3. Thank you," PJ responded.

As they approached Rafael Nunez Airport, named for the man who penned the Colombian national anthem, the landing pattern took them directly over Cartegena's walled city. A pilot's eye view at two thousand feet was a perfect first time look at the ancient gateway to South America.

Located along the Caribbean Sea, with a well-protected harbor and access to the navigable Magdelena River, Cartegena was an ideal starting point for the Spanish efforts to conquer South America in 1533. From the busy seaport supplies were distributed to the colonies inland and Spanish plunder was stored for shipment back to the mother country.

This abundance of wealth attracted the British Navy and Caribbean pirates. Many bloody battles were fought to control the city. In the mid-17th century, seven miles of stonewalls, sixty feet wide and forty feet high, were erected around the city for protection. The fight for Colombian independence ended when Simon Bolivar drove out the Spanish in 1819, naming Cartegena *La Heroica*, the Heroic City. It remained a busy port and the old city inside the walls was virtually unchanged.

However, instead of pirates, 20th century tourists came to Cartegena and helped it grow outside the walls. The Starship's landing gear lowered on their final approach over the Bocagrande sandbar, where the likes of Don Blas de Lezo, the city's legendary protector who had lost his leg, eye and arm fighting for Spain, once did battle. A string of resort hotels now guarded the harbor.

"I hope we get a chance to take a moonlit walk along the walls," PJ said. "National Geographic says the locals call the walls 'stone beds'."

"Shhh, I'm trying to land, PJ," she smiled. She manipulated the Starship controls with confidence, her right hand on the wheel, her left on the throttles, and the plastic bird touched down at the end of runway 36.

"It's a lot easier with two engines," she remarked as they slowed on the roll out.

"Hey, there's Lenny's jet! And what the hell!" PJ said as the Starship landed. Passing over the end of the runway, he saw the flashing lights of police cars in front of one of the hangars. A cluster of people stood nearby as if waiting. Lenny's white jet, with its distinctive orange and blue trim, was parked in front of the same hangar, an old corrugated steel Quonset hut that looked somewhat neglected next to the newer, larger hangars on that side of the runway.

"I wonder what's going on there?" he said to himself. He switched the radio to ground control. PJ had a sinking feeling the police were in front of the same hangar Barney Devlin had arranged for their use as a base of operations.

"Where are we going?" Kathryn asked PJ. She had the Starship rolling slowly along the taxiway toward the main terminal.

"I think toward that end," PJ said, pointing back toward the flashing blue lights at the far end of the runway. He pressed the mike switch.

"Cartegena Ground, 379 Sierra."

"Go ahead 379," came back a female voice.

"Can you direct us to the ALSA hangar. Air Lift South America. We are scheduled to park there."

"Roger, 379. Cross 36 to the first hangar at south end. Be advised Customs Police are waiting there for inspection. You are cleared to cross now."

"Roger, Cartegena. Thank you. 379 Sierra."

As they crossed over the main runway, PJ could see two police cars, an army jeep, and a station wagon. He recognized Dave and Christina immediately. Dutch and Lenny were leaning against one of the police cars.

"Look's like the four musketeers are here. Wonder if they had problems getting into the country?" he said allowed.

"Oh, great," Kathryn said, "More guns."

She saw two helmeted Colombian soldiers in jungle camouflage uniforms. They carried M-16's over their shoulders and stood with three uniformed policemen. A man in a brown suit was talking with the soldiers.

"Well, let's find out what's going on here," PJ said as she maneuvered the Starship next to Lenny's Citation. PJ had the door open and was down the steps before the engines were shut down.

"Dutch, what the hell is going on here?" he yelled.

"PJ, it's great to see you!" Dutch said, shaking his hand.

"Stoney's nuts!" yelled Lenny.

"Stoney?" PJ asked. "Where's Stoney? Are they here already?"

"Yeah, big time!" Dutch said. "We should've known that half baked midget would want a special reception!"

"He's gonna get us all fried, PJ. I'm surprised they haven't bombed the hangar yet!" Lenny said, chewing on a toothpick.

"Reinforcements are probably on the way. I hate this place already!" Dave said, tossing in his two cents.

"Me, too," Dutch snorted.

"At least the weather's nice," Lenny laughed.

"Hi, Kathryn!" Christina waved, seeing her coming up to the group.

"Hi, Crash. Guys. What's going on?" she asked, looking at the soldiers.

"I think Stoney's had a melt down!" Christina said to Kathryn.

"Not again?" Kathryn said in dismay. "What happened?"

PJ was standing in the middle of his friends who were all talking over each other, offering their assessments of the current situation. No one had actually told him what had happened.

"Would someone mind telling me what the hell is going on?" PJ yelled.

"Stoney landed without a flight plan," Dutch started.

"Man, he picked the wrong country to do that in," added Lenny. "He doesn't like flight plans."

"When Customs arrived, he was already holed up in the hangar here," said Dutch. "Then the police were called in."

"With guns!" said Christina.

"Stoney wouldn't let them in," Lenny chimed in, "Said they had to contact you at the hotel. We came rushing out and found a standoff.

"Stoney's in there with Mickey and Ray and they have weapons, too. It's a Mexican standoff. Or Colombian. We got here just before they planned to raid the hangar!" Dutch finished.

"He's a nut case, PJ!" Lenny added.

"Damn!" PJ cursed. He immediately understood the problem. Stoney wasn't the only one who did not want Customs looking inside the plane.

"I thought Barney had greased the skids on this one," PJ said. "Who's the customs guy, the one in the brown suit?"

"Señor Jose Ruiz Herrara. No hablo English," Dutch said.

"A customs guy who doesn't speak English?" PJ muttered in disbelief.

"I think he's more the middle level bureaucrat customs type, Peej, rather than customer relations," Lenny laughed.

"He's kept this thing local, so far, PJ," Dutch added. "I think he just wants the paperwork. Maybe some scratch."

PJ walked over to Señor Herrara and introduced himself. The man was not very happy with the situation, but he calmed down, especially when Kathryn started translating in her soothing voice. PJ smiled at her knack of turning men into polite pussycats with a few smiles and her flawless Spanish.

"He says he's spoken with Barney Devlin, but can not let the plane into the country without a flight plan," Kathryn interpreted. "For his records," she added. "He has to answer to his superiors."

"Ask him if we can file a flight plan now so he will have a record. Tell him we apologize. Perhaps we can compensate him for his troubles? Maybe $200 American," PJ said.

Damn, PJ thought, he's been in this country less than one afternoon and already he's bribing government officials and breaking international aviation laws!

Kathryn relayed the message, PJ watching the man's reaction when the dollars came up. He didn't flinch, but gave her an immediate answer.

"He says he has to take care of the police and the soldiers also," Kathryn smiled at PJ. "And he wants to see passports."

"$500?" PJ asked the man directly. He shook his head no and held up one finger.

"One Thousand?" PJ said. Herrara smiled and nodded. He understood enough English, PJ thought.

"It's a deal," PJ shook his hand. Herrara spoke with the soldiers and they all followed Kathryn to the Starship for their payment. PJ walked toward the hangar.

"Stoney, dammit! Open the door!" PJ yelled, pounding on the side entrance. A sign over the rusty door read *Prohibido en paso*. He looked off behind the building and saw the city limits with homes and businesses

---

backed right up to the end of the runway. The Caribbean wasn't far beyond. Looking the other way he could see a large stone fortress on a hill overlooking the city about a mile away, its impenetrable walls warmed by the reflection of the late afternoon sun.

"PJ! Is that you?" came a voice inside.

It was Mickey.

"Mickey, open the damn door!"

The door opened a crack and Mickey stuck the barrel of a rifle out, then his face slowly appeared.

"PJ! Oh, man, am I glad to see you. Stoney's nuts!" Mickey was all smiles when he saw PJ, pushed the door open wide and they stepped inside the old hangar.

"What the hell you got there, Mickey? Is that a new computer attachment?" PJ asked sarcastically, with a touch of amazement as he shook Mickey's hand. Mickey was holding a rifle that looked a lot like the rifles PJ had seen at Quintaro's ranch.

Mickey just grinned sheepishly. "Russian, PJ. What's going' on out there? Did you straighten this thing out?" he asked nervously.

"Yes. They just need to see your passport, but they won't be coming in here," PJ answered.

"No passports!"

The voice came from up above, from the cockpit of the plane that sat right in front of them. He recognized the standard U.S. Navy paint scheme, grey fuselage, white on top and bottom. PJ looked up to see Stoney's face appear in the cockpit window.

"Hi, PJ!" he waved, his .9 mm in his hand. "Where the hell you been?"

"Stoney, do you have to create an international incident everywhere you go?" PJ laughed.

"What international incident! I knew you would take care of it." Stoney stopped. "You did take care of it, right?"

"Stoney, you could have filed a flight plan," PJ said.

"Hey, I thought it was all arranged through Devlin. Besides, PJ, I haven't filed a flight plan...."

"...in the last twenty years," PJ finished for him. "Yeah, I've heard it before. No passport either?"

"Not for the Colombians, PJ," Stoney grinned.

Stoney Bullard was one guy PJ trusted implicitly, on a sailboat, in a plane or anywhere else, but there was a whole portion of his life that he had stopped asking about.

"So, what have you brought, Stoney? What is this thing?" PJ asked, looking at the rather large plane with its wings folded back along the fuselage like some gigantic insect.

PJ realized Stoney's arrival would make the crew aware of what they had gotten themselves into. In a hurry.

"This is a Greyhound, PJ, a Grumman C-2A. Don't you recognize it from the brochure?" he laughed. "It was designed to deliver pizza to aircraft carriers!"

The U.S. Navy had PJ for three years, but he never got close to a carrier, spending most of his time in riverboats on the Chesapeake and surrounding rivers.

The C-2 was a high winged, twin-engine turboprop with a blunt nose built specifically to resupply aircraft carriers. Even with it's eighty-foot wingspan folded, the plane filled the old hangar. The oddly shaped tail section with four vertical fins nearly touched the roof. It looked like the fat brother of the Navy's sleek E-2 Hawkeye radar plane upon which the C-2 design was based. This one came complete with a tail hook for a carrier landing.

"Should I even ask where you got this thing?" Dutch said.

"Sure. Buddy of mine at NAS Key West. Grumman had it scheduled for some tests, so, who better to test it than me," he smiled. "He thinks I'm in the Bahamas. No problem. I left him my T-46 Eaglet."

"Stoney, you are dangerous," Lenny said. "You are working for our side, right?"

"Lenny, my boy, you are right. I am dangerous and I am working. Now, come in, everyone, and see what Ray's playing with."

The Greyhound was built to carry troops and cargo, but in a minimum amount of space. The headroom in the cargo cabin was only five feet, five inches. Like a racing sailboat, PJ thought. They found Ray sitting on the floor trying to untangle a nest of wires coming from headset mikes attached to a dozen walkie-talkies sitting in a bank of battery chargers. Boxes and crates of all sizes were stacked along both walls of the cabin.

"Hello, PJ. Hi, guys! Glad you could make it," Ray said cheerfully. A rifle, like the one Mickey carried, was lying on the deck next to Ray. "He's nuts, PJ," Ray laughed pointing toward Stoney who had climbed down from the cockpit.

Stoney shot a universal gesture at Ray and greeted his friends with a lot of hand shaking and shoulder slapping. Nothing like a little covert action to pump Stoney up, PJ thought. Everyone turned at the same time as the side door to the hangar opened again, but it was Kathryn and Christina. PJ could see them both stop for a second to adjust to their first look at the big plane right in front of them.

"Welcome to Stoney World, girls!" Lenny called out as they climbed into the cabin.

"The officials have left, PJ," Kathryn reported. PJ nodded and watched carefully as the crew swapped good-natured greetings and verbal jabs. It made him feel good that they were together again.

Kathryn, Christina and Stoney moved around at will, but everyone else was forced into a crouch until they found a seat on the floor or on a box. PJ perched himself on the cockpit ladder and looked at his assembled team.

"I never had any doubt you would come, but I still want to say thanks," PJ started. He looked at each of them. Their faces had turned serious, grim almost, and they were all looking at him.

"You know why we are here, PJ," Mickey said, followed by a chorus of agreement from the rest of the team.

"I know, Mickey. Unfortunately, this is not another sailboat race. This is a deadly serious game and we are facing some people who play for keeps. We have to play for keeps also."

He briefly told them about their encounter with Quintaro and his guards. He mentioned the chemicals in the hangar, and he explained the general layout of the ranch and the security set up they saw. He couldn't remember them ever being as attentive.

"Is that our target?" Christina asked when he finished.

"I came here thinking the mine would be our target, Christina. If we go after Quintaro. If," he emphasized, " ...the ranch may come into play. I haven't given up on a peaceful settlement with the government's help, but I want us to be ready in case that doesn't happen."

He nodded toward Stoney. "Ready to do your thing?"

"You bet, PJ," Stoney said with enthusiasm. He was sitting on a long crate at the other end of the cabin. "When PJ and I spoke on Saturday, he didn't know what the hell he wanted. He just said I had to outfit the crew to go fighting in the mountains. And to be ready in four days. No problem!"

He laughed, then stopped, his face getting serious.

"Are you people ready to do that?" he asked loudly, standing up, his head an inch shorter than the cabin ceiling.

"I know you're ready, Dutch. You're always ready for a fight," Stoney laughed. "But, damn it, people, you had better be ready for *this* fight. Are you ready, Crash?"

She didn't say anything.

He opened the crate he had been sitting on and pulled out another rifle like Mickey's. He tossed it to Lenny, who caught it in mid air.

"All you guys did your time in the military, except Ray, but he and I already did a one on one. Anyway, you should know which end you're supposed to point," he continued as he handed out the weapons to each crewmember. "Ladies, I think you know also, but listen." He handed out the weapons until everyone had one.

"This is the Kalashnikov AK-74, the latest in Russian assault rifles, and the most recent modification to the AK-47. It handles like the M-16, but fires a smaller bullet, the 5.45 mm. However, it's more accurate up to 400 yards and the bullet tends to tumble when it hits a medium heavier than air, like a human body. It will wreck havoc on anyone's lifestyle."

He paused for effect. The crew were examining the weapons, but looked up at Stoney's last comment. Stoney looked back with a serious face, grunted and continued.

"It's quieter than the M-16. Semi-automatic or full auto. Thirty rounds in the clip. PJ, I saved you a bundle on this stuff! The Russians are in a serious money crunch and they are having a fire sale on weapons. Can you believe the independent states are selling and buying from each other!"

He opened a smaller box and pulled two more weapons out. He handed one to Dutch. It looked like the others, but there was a folding bipod under the barrel and a larger magazine.

"Dutch, this is for you. I'll take the other. The RPKS-74 light machine gun," Stoney said. "Same as the AK-74, but a bit more firepower. Now, here's how these deadly toys work!"

He went through a quick class on gun operations. Kathryn and Christina were the only two who had not handled a weapon before and he paid special attention to them. For the next hour, the nine of them, with Stoney's guidance, handled the AK-74 and also went through the other boxes.

They found a carefully selected inventory of military and civilian equipment from camouflage uniforms to GPS portable receivers, tacpacks to Israelis commando boots, ammo to first-aid kits.

"Where the hell did you get all this stuff?" Dutch asked.

"The soft goods came right out of a catalog," Stoney said. "Big Army Navy store in Texas."

"Here, Lenny, for our resident gourmand," Stoney said, tossing a foot long plastic pouch labeled MRE. Lenny held it up and read out loud, "Diced beef in gravy. Made in USA."

"Meals-Ready-to-Eat," Stoney explained. "Complete with beans and cake. Just heat it up by holding it against your body."

"Dutch, maybe you can serve this stuff at your restaurant," Lenny suggested.

"You'd be my best customer, I bet. Isn't your motto, if it isn't moving, eat it," Dutch came back.

PJ pulled out a seven-inch knife from its olive green sheath and held it up to Mickey. "In 1975 my friend, I could throw this thing thirty feet and it would stick in a six inch fence post."

"You probably can't throw it thirty feet today, much less make it stick," Mickey answered with a serious look on his face.

PJ looked at his friend, their eyes connected for a second.

"Sure I can. Here, put this against that crate."

He handed him a package of the MRE, it was a Chicken al la King, and pointed to a nearby wooden box filled with Israeli commando boots next to the cockpit ladder.

Mickey walked the fifteen feet to the box and held it up for a second. PJ took aim, feeling the balance of the knife. Everyone in the plane's cabin shifted their attention to the pending scene. Dave was buckling an equipment harness to his chest and he looked at Christina. "Watch this, C."

PJ shifted his feet and Mickey held the bag low, then moved it right, then left, then up. "Here?" he asked.

PJ nodded and cocked his arm. Mickey reached for the knife on his belt and stabbed the pouch, pinning the bag of food to the box. He moved his hand and two seconds later, PJ's knife went flying through the air. All eyes were on the blade as it flew in a lazy arc toward the pinned package. No one saw it better than Stoney Bullard, standing next to the cockpit ladder.

Like a frog grabbing a fly, Stoney's hand shot out and grabbed the knife out of mid-air, catching it on the handle two feet short of its target.

"This is not a dart, man!" he said with a smile. "So stop playing with it!" He jammed the blade into the top of the box.

"Oh, Stoney, it was right on line!" PJ cried out.

"You're the only guy I know who can catch arrows, Stoney!" Lenny laughed, shaking his head in amazement.

"How do you do that, Bullard?" Dutch asked seriously.

"Eyes, my son," Stoney said, a big grin on his face. "It's all in the eyes."

Kathryn just stood there amazed at PJ. She had not known he could throw a knife. She suddenly felt very different. In fact, seeing the rest of the crew apparently comfortable with weapons was a side of them she had not imagined before this moment.

"Stoney, what are these for?" Christina asked holding up a box of sausage-sized bullets.

"Ah, the *coup de gras* of this load, Crash," Stoney said, moving to the back of the cabin to another crate. From it he pulled a squat looking gun and tripod. It resembled a machine gun except the barrel was wide and short. Ray helped him set it up.

"The Russian AGS-17 30 millimeter grenade launcher. It will toss one of those babies about 900 yards, Crash, " Stoney said with pride, "and blow up a jeep or a tank. Rate of fire is one a second."

"Man, oh man," Christina said holding up a belt of the grenades all ready to be fed into the launcher. "I guess we are going to war." She put down the belt and looked at Dave. "Pretty scary stuff, huh?"

"Yeah, this is real, Crash," Dave said. "It gives us firepower."

"Hey, anyone hungry?" PJ asked and immediately ducked three MRE packs that came flying at him from various parts of the cabin. "No, I'm talking crew dinner."

"Yeah, crew dinner!" shouted Dutch

"Tomorrow, we get a chance to fire the weapons," PJ told them. "Barney Devlin has made arrangements for some target practice in the jungle. Let's break, get something to eat and get in a good night's sleep."

It was another twenty minutes before they sorted all the uniforms and personal gear into piles in the back of the C-2A.

"We'll check in at the hotel first and then meet you for dinner," PJ suggested. "Where?"

"Dutch, how about that seafood place we saw, Nautilus. You know where it is, at the end of the main drag along the wall," Lenny said.

"Okay, thirty minutes," Dutch answered.

The wagon held only six, with luggage, so PJ, Kathryn and Dutch walked across the airstrip, stopped at Señor Herrara's office, filed the proper

---

paperwork, showed everyone's passport, except Stoney's, and then caught a cab from the airport's main terminal.

Riding along Avenida Santander with the last rays of the sun striking the Caribbean Sea on their right and the high walls of the city on their left, Kathryn didn't pay much attention to the sights that Dutch was pointing out to them. She was thinking about the AK-74 she had just held. She knew before they left the states that weapons would likely be involved in this adventure. Still, handling a weapon for the first time had been unsettling. She didn't know if she could kill another human.

They turned around a traffic circle, left the walls behind and were suddenly in the plush surroundings of the modern tourist resorts on Bocagrande, with high-rise hotels sharing the evening with restaurants and nightclubs highlighted in neon. At the very end of the strip, on a small spit of sand called El Laguito, the cab pulled up in front of the low buildings of their luxury hotel.

PJ went right to his room for a shower and let the cold-water splash on his body. His head wound was uncovered, the stitches removed and only a small scar remained that his doctor had promised would heal completely.

His left hand, however, was still severely scarred, though he felt little pain. He accepted the fact he would have a permanent indentation in the base of his hand behind the pinkie. He tried to wiggle his fingers, but only the first three responded. He felt nothing in the other two.

He dressed quickly and decided to wear the fingerless sailing glove on his left hand to hide the discoloration. He walked down the hall to Kathryn's room and stood in the open doorway watching her unpack.

She smiled at him and waved him to a chair by the balcony. He sat watching the waves of the Caribbean for a moment and the lights of the city coming on in the dusk. Then he turned to watch her.

"What did you think of the weapons?" he asked. He could sense her deep in thought.

"It was certainly different," she said, sitting on the bed. "I'm kind of surprised how the guys seemed to, well, enjoy it."

He came over and sat next to her.

"Guys know how to play soldier," he laughed. "It's part of growing up in America. You learn how to throw a ball and point a gun before you're eight. Of course, no one was shooting at us today."

"That would make it different," she smiled thinly.

"Five of us did military time, went on maneuvers and training missions and such. Stoney did two Vietnam tours."

"Have you ever shot anyone?" she asked, her eyes searching his, trying to learn more about him. He looked back and smiled.

"No. I've never had to fire a weapon in anger. I would have if I had a weapon the other day," he admitted. "For defense." He thought of Lesco's dead body lying in the boat on Fishers Island Sound.

"In the Navy they trained us how to kill, but we never had to," he continued. "Hey, I was mostly a river chauffeur. The worst it ever got for me was dropping a SEAL team into the New London Sub Base on a security check. No one told the base it was an exercise and some young guard started firing at us. It was at night, fortunately, and he didn't hit anything." He laughed.

"Maybe we can solve this tomorrow, diplomatically?" she said hopefully.

"I want to," he nodded. "Harold and I will be meeting in the city. Maybe he can help us make some headway with the Colombian government. But, I can't leave Colombia without the mine back in our control. If that means a fight, we have the firepower to fight."

She sighed heavily and smiled at him. "I like Harold. I'm glad he's helping. I'm glad you two have patched things up," she said. "I still believe something good will come from this trip."

He kissed her and agreed. "I'm famished. Let's start making something good happen, like supper! If nothing else, at least we can always say we had Cartegena!"

Two hours later, the crew spilled out of the Nautilus restaurant after a satisfying repast that included lobsters, seafood stew, rice cooked in coconut milk, and fried sliced bananas. Plenty of Arguardiente and Colombian beer helped lift the group's spirits after a somewhat somber start to the meal. Despite Kathryn's accurate assessment of the apparent ease with which the crew took to the weapons, it was clear they knew they were not in Colombia on vacation.

As they walked along the Avenida Venezuela, PJ grabbed Kathryn's hand, feeling refreshed in the clean night air.

"Let's check out this monument. There's one on every corner is seems," he said pulling her into the middle of the square where the main road enters the old town. They were both surprised by what they found.

It was a bronze of a young Indian girl, *Monumento a la India Catalina*. The plaque at its base said Eladio Gil, a Spanish sculptor living in Cartegena, had created it in 1974. The young girl was looking into the middle distance with round, sad eyes, and a small smile on her innocent face.

PJ stared at the face, intrigued. When he looked over at Kathryn, he saw a similarity in their profiles. He also saw the transfixed look on her face that he had seen earlier when they first spotted the Sierra Nevada de Santa Marta mountains.

Tonight, her stare seemed more hypnotic, her black pupils glistening in the middle of the pure whiteness of her eyes. He realized the street lamps around the statue were reflecting tears spilling down her brown cheeks. He didn't know what to say. They stood there for a long time, it seemed.

Kathryn thought the statue was alive, that the little girl was flesh and blood, and her dark eyes were looking right into Kathryn's soul. Then the statue began to speak to her, in a deep tone, like the tone she heard the night she saw the face in the water off Ram Island.

"Zarzamora," the voice repeated.

This time she heard the words clearly. And, again, felt them. She was mystified, then skeptical. It had to be the Arguardiente, she thought, but it seemed so clear! She wasn't drunk. She looked at PJ who seemed unaware of any voices and then back at the statue, now a cast of bronze again. Was she going crazy? She was unsettled by the whole event.

The laughter of the rest of the crew had long drifted off down the avenue when PJ put his arm around Kathryn and she dropped her head on his shoulder. They started walking and were soon under the high walls at the east end of the city, holding each other against the stones. She knew it would be hard to resist him when he was this close and she didn't want to. She was quietly crying, her tears running freely onto his shirt.

"I'm scared, PJ," she whispered. "Please hold me."

He didn't ask why, just pulled her to him. She held on, and they gently rocked together.

"Don't be scared, Kathryn," he whispered.

Time was lost to them. They walked back to the hotel later that night. They passed ancient church steeples, wrought-iron balconies of 16th century homes and stone archways, but did not really see them. The rhythm of *cumbias* drifted from the late night cafes, but were a dim background to the growing turmoil in Kathryn's mind.

She needed him near her and silently led him into her room.

"Don't leave me tonight," she whispered.

"I'm not going anywhere," he answered.

He stood behind her on the balcony, his arms over her shoulders, his face buried in her hair. He wanted her, but his passion was subdued as he gentle caressed her body. His lust grew from a deep-seated feeling of warmth, of connecting, as if their friendship and their desire would meld naturally together. It felt right.

Later in her bed, they lay naked together, her head resting in the crook of his right arm, his hand tenderly caressing her breasts, his front spooned to her back. She took his left hand, gently pressed it to her flat stomach and shifted her legs to allow his growing hardness to slip between her thighs. She tenderly guided him into her, both of them moving slowly to savor each hot touch of flesh. Their juices mingled together, their union so complete neither could tell where their own skin ended and the other's began.

She loved this man, his love for life, his tenderness, his quiet passion. She opened herself for him completely, and he had done the same for her. In their mutual openness, she had found strength and protection. As their passion built, she quickened her movements, pushing back and forth on him, needing him more than ever to give her the security that was fraying at the edges. He responded in concert, his hands on her nerve centers, his lips whispering passionate thoughts in her ear and his desire filling her completely.

They came together, a shuddering climax, their moans breaking the silence of the night, flying off the terrace to become lost in the pinpoints of light that outlined Cartegena in the window.

They lay together for several moments, their breath and their pulses vibrating through each other. Then Kathryn pulled away from PJ, bringing a small moan from his lips, but turned to look at him. His blue eyes were visible in the glow of the night. She drew close to him, their noses touching, their eyes wide, their lips gently caressing each other.

"I love you," she said in a whisper.

"I love you," he whispered back. He pulled her to him and they snuggled there in the damp warmth of their love until sleep overtook them both.

In the moments before Kathryn drifted into a deep sleep, she thought of the statue of the little girl. She was convinced the statue had spoken to her. She whispered the word "Zarzamora", letting it role off her lips.

She dreamed of the mountains again, saw herself playing along a river and under the broad leaves of the forest. She heard the name many times and dreamt that she was not alone.

PJ also had a dream.

He felt weightless, suspended in pitch black. The wind blew hard on his face, yet, his eyes were wide open, unaffected by the wind's force. A pinpoint of light appeared far away and he suddenly realized rather than being weightless he was, in fact, moving rapidly toward the light.

Their closing speed increased and he became confused. He couldn't tell if he was rising to meet the light, or falling toward it, or standing still, the light moving toward him. Suddenly the light was upon him and it enveloped him for a split second before he found himself underwater, still moving rapidly, unable to breath and close to drowning.

He awoke gasping for breath, Kathryn shaking him and calling his name. "PJ! PJ! Wake up! It's only a dream!" He saw her in the half-light of the clear night, a look of fear on her face. "It's all right, it's all right," she repeated. "It was only dream, it was only a dream."

"What was it, PJ?" she asked, settling her head back to the pillow. PJ pulled her close to him, returning to the much nicer reality of the fragrance of her skin.

"I don't know, Kathryn. Just the wind, moving fast, wet..." his voice trailed off and he kissed her gently, pulling her closer still, and they touched each other tenderly driving their passions in a satisfying spiral that ended in a deep sleep.

* * *

As they slept, up the coast in Santa Marta, others also slept, but not all. A flatbed trailer truck drove slowly through the stacks of cargo containers along a quiet Pier 12 and parked under a cargo crane next to a freighter named *Alma de Maria Vargas* preparing to depart for the Netherlands. She was a new breed of ship, with modern engines capable of speeds approaching twenty-five knots.

The crane came to life even as the driver methodically released a series of pins and chains holding a container in place on the flatbed. With a minimum of maneuvering, the crane operator gripped the 10,000-pound container and lifted it on board the ship, placing it gently next to several rows of other containers stacked three high on the deck just forward of the large pilothouse.

"Henri, that's not right. They left the container perpendicular to the others," the first mate said, watching the procedure.

"Leave it. That is how it should be," his captain replied. The mate and shrugged his shoulders.

As soon as the container was secured on deck, the captain gave the order to cast off and the 850 foot long *Alma de Maria Vargas*, with assistance from a tugboat, left the harbor for its 4500-mile journey and a midnight rendezvous at sea in eight days.

~~~

CHAPTER EIGHTEEN

Santa Marta was locked in its usual midday stupor, the cooling sea breezes of the afternoon still hours away. The air under the display tents and around the sidewalk food vendors along *Avenida Rodrigo de Bastidas* was as thick as a furnace. The *jugo* vendors plied a steady trade selling cool fruit juices of all colors, but the hot snack vendors, the *fritanguera*, were mostly left watching. It was just too hot to eat.

What was unusual about the day was the emerald dealers who had gathered in Colombia's oldest city for the *Festival Internacional Esmeralda*. They baked under the colorful canvas, their handkerchiefs mopped their damp brows, and their eyes scanned the crowd around them. Many sat with revolvers boldly strapped to their sides. Others kept their weapons out of sight, but within easy reach. They were wary, protecting the precious green gems sitting on the tables in front of him, yet ready to offer them to a buyer with interest and cash.

The international clientele, all men, drifted among the tables and tents, frequently stopping to inspect the rows of green stones, some cut, but most in their natural state. English, German, Spanish, Japanese and other languages filled the hot air, but the emeralds spoke one language.

Each buyer eyed the piece that sparked their interest, looked deeply inside its green world and searched for imperfections, inclusions that formed when the stone crystallized in the earth's crust. Too many inclusions were undesirable. It was, however, extremely rare to find a stone perfectly formed without some signature from its moment of creation.

Some crystals were bathed in oil to mask inclusions, raising the price for the unsuspecting buyer who would not find out he had overpaid until a year or two later when the oil evaporated. Each stone seemed to have a life of its own and it was said that good buyers could identify stones they had viewed in the past, readily remembering the size and pattern.

Tourists moved along the avenue, too, some venturing among the tents and tables, but most on the periphery, curious about the bargaining taking place, too timid to participate. Or too poor.

The cash and emeralds on the city streets were a tempting feast and the police were also out in force, patrolling in pairs, their M-16's and German made G3 rifles slung on their shoulders. Used to dealing with marijuana smugglers, they were prepared for the worst. The first day of the event, however, had been quiet and the police provided both a sense of security to the hundreds who shared in the festive atmosphere, and a reminder that it could turn ugly at any moment.

An angry Rex Simka was stuck in the unusually heavy traffic, his jeep crawling through the throngs that choked the main avenue along the Caribbean. The traffic did not help his state of mind, already agitated by a variety of loose ends that threatened to unravel Operation Snowmine.

The first shipments from the Valley of Codazzi to the U.S.A., through Marib Cay, had been a stunning success. However, he had little time to celebrate. He had been shuttling between Cartegena and Barranquilla, making cash payments to a variety of key government contacts. He also made a one million dollar deposit at the Sunrise International Bank in Cartegena, carrying a briefcase of $100 dollar bills through the lobby.

Rex disliked being polite to the greedy men who were on the payroll because of their position in government. They saw to it the police and other officials looked the other way. He knew they were important to the operation, but he did not like playing errand boy. He felt that was a job for Bernardo.

When he awoke in Santa Marta that morning, he had received the messages about the plane crash, Ulf's death and Carlos' inquiry concerning PJ McDonough. The last annoyed him the most.

How the hell did Carlos find out about McDonough? He worried that he had made a serious miscalculation and knew he would have to answer to Quintaro soon. May that cowboy Brett Lesco rot in hell! And that cargo pilot at the Santa Marta airport. He had yet to take care of that loose end!

Simka leaned on his horn and cursed himself for not cutting across the other side of town to get to the Santa Marta seaport terminal and the QUIMEX offices. The jeep edged forward a few feet before it was blocked by a heated discussion between several people and two policemen. Frustrated by the delay, Simka pulled to the side of the avenue, and parked on the sidewalk in front of a building he recognized.

It was the new tourism office, an old white mansion of three stories with balconies overlooking the Caribbean. Carlos Quintaro was deeply involved with the tourism board and had an office reserved for him on the third floor. It would be a good place to phone him.

Simka walked through the large colonial archway that led to a sunny courtyard where flowers and trees bloomed. The building was scheduled to

---

open for the public after Quintaro's party that night and workmen were busy with preparations for the festivities and the arrival of Presidente Gomez. They were hanging lights and putting the final touches on the deeply varnished wooden trim around the doorways and on the banisters. The workmen didn't give him a second glance as he quickly climbed the three flights of stairs and found the empty office.

Bernardo's voice answered on Carlos' private line after the third ring, "Yes?"

"Bernardo, the money has been deposited as you requested," Simka started, trying to be polite to Carlos's brother.

"Ah, Rex. That is good. Did you get the messages?" he asked with concern.

"I did. Bad news, Bernardo. I must speak to Carlos immediately."

"Yes, he wants to speak to you."

In a moment Quintaro came on the line. He was not happy.

"Rex, where the hell are you?!" Carlos rarely raised his voice.

"Santa Marta, Carlos. Bad news about Ulf," Rex started.

"Yes, but Rafael has taken over. We are back on schedule. Where are you?" he asked again.

"Santa Marta, at the tourist office. I'm alone. It is safe to talk," Simka said.

"Did you find out about those two names?" Carlos asked.

Simka paused for a moment before answering.

"McDonough is a friend and business partner of Jester Miller. He had an interest in the mine, but no direct ownership. I don't think he'll be a problem. How did you hear about him?"

"He's what? A partner? Simka, this is unacceptable!"

Carlos yelled into the receiver loud enough that Simka had to hold it away from his ear.

"Carlos, what is the problem?"

"You idiot! McDonough and a woman were here yesterday, at the ranch!" Carlos continued.

"At the ranch?" Simka was dumbfounded. "How in the world...?" He didn't get to finish.

"I thought I told you to take care of this problem weeks ago. Didn't I say I wanted the American mine connection taken out of play? Didn't I?" Carlos yelled.

"Yes, Carlos and it was done. Jester Miller is out of play. I did not expect McDonough to become involved. I did not expect him to come here."

"Well, Rex, McDonough is here! Now what?"

"Carlos, calm yourself! Do you think this McDonough suspects you of anything?"

"Why the hell else would he come to Colombia! And come to see me? You idiot!" Carlos was still yelling and Simka was starting to get irritated.

"Carlos, please. Be calm. Nothing has been compromised."

"You're right, Rex, my friend. I should calm myself, but you have put our whole operation in jeopardy with carelessness!"

"Yes, Carlos, I have let you down," Simka said after a moment. He had to check his words, least he anger Quintaro further. "Let me make it up to you. I can take care of this today. McDonough is a small problem and I will personally take him out of play."

There was silence on the line. Simka realized his was sweating profusely, not just from the heat of the room.

"Rex, my friend, you have angered me, but we are too far along to change our plans. I have an idea. Do nothing about McDonough just yet," Carlos' voice came soothingly through the line. Simka knew from past experience Quintaro had a plan.

"We must be careful. If he does suspect something, I am sure there are others who have knowledge of his presence in Colombia and will be watching. We must move cautiously," Carlos continued. "McDonough will be at the *parranda* tonight. I want you and six men there. Take the usual security precautions."

"Do you think it wise that I be there, Carlos? After all, with Presidente Gomez in attendance, there will be international attention from the Americans." Simka had avoided functions where official U.S. representatives were present.

"I need you there tonight, Rex," Carlos said firmly.

"Then I will be there, Don Carlos," Simka answered, unhappy with the decision.

"Good. What about the woman, Kathryn Byrnie? Did you find out anything about her?" Quintaro asked, calmer, but still exasperated.

"Not much. Her tourist card lists her birthplace as Texas and her current address is San Jose, California."

"Yes, that was on her passport," Carlos said disappointed.

There was another long pause.

"Rex, you have been a trusted friend, but I am greatly disappointed," Carlos spoke in almost fatherly tones. Simka was glad he had at least stopped yelling.

"Our operation must not be compromised," Carlos repeated. "Have you taken care of that unexpected visitor to the mine?"

"I am attending to that matter right now, as soon as we are finished here," he said.

"Good. Make sure, Rex. I think it best if we increase security at the mine. Do you agree?"

"That is a good idea, Carlos."

"Rex, I want your personal guarantee that there will be no more mistakes," Carlos said.

"You have it, Don Carlos. I will see to it myself immediately!" he pledged. He knew what would happen to him if he failed this time.

"Good. Then tonight we will take care of Señor McDonough," Carlos said and hung up.

Simka felt like a scolded child and sat deflated for a few moments staring at the phone. He was angry with Carlos, but knew his anger should be directed at himself. Things had slipped some, he admitted, but he was determined to stop the slide. He did not want to lose his chance to break free from Carlos.

He reached into his pocket and pulled out the brown vial with the white powder inside. Two small spoonfuls quickly made their way into his bloodstream through his nostrils. The rush was immediate. His ego cast off the sting of the scolding and took on a new confidence.

He left the small office on the third floor and made a quick inspection of the building. He thought of the usual security measures to insure Quintaro's own safety. He decided he would bring in more men, enough to handle any eventuality, especially if Carlos had special plans for McDonough and the woman.

Then it was outside to his jeep. He drove aggressively through the crowded streets, forcing people to move. In a couple of blocks he was past the crowds and soon arrived at the offices of QUIMEX on Point Betin at the north end of town. The two-story wooden building sat at the end of Pier 12. He rarely showed his face in this world of Carlos Quintaro, but decided the delivery entrance on the side was not for him today.

The receptionist working alone at a large desk in the main office looked up when he came in and smiled, but Simka ignored her and climbed the stairs to a back room filled with computers and communications equipment. The wide windows on one side offered a panoramic view of the docks. The door simply said Operations.

There he spoke quietly with a young man who led him down a back stairway into a storage room. Less than ten minutes after his arrival, Simka departed through the front lobby, carrying a small leather satchel.

"It is time to tie up one loose end, Mr. Barney Devlin," he said to himself. He turned left at the railroad station and headed away from the water to avoid the festival. In a few minutes he was on the main road heading south toward the Simon Bolivar Airport ten miles outside of town.

After he had walked out of the front door, the young woman at the front desk took a small card out of her purse and dialed the number scrawled on it.

"Hello," a male voice answered.

"He's been here. The one whose picture you showed me," she said quietly.

"Where is he going?" the voice asked.

"I don't know. He just left in a white jeep carrying a leather bag."

"Thank you."

The man hung up and the woman went back to her work sorting bills of lading.

* * *

The heat of the day beat down on PJ's crew, six men and two women spread out in a ragged line on the edge of a deserted jungle clearing about ten miles outside of Cartegena. Dressed in camouflage uniforms and commando boots, armed with Russian weapons and surrounded by boxes of ammunition, a wildly painted wooden bus parked nearby, they looked like a cross between a squad of mercenaries and a circus troupe.

"Okay, couch warriors. Watch the kick. Commence firing!"

The quiet heat was shattered by the staccato burst of semi- automatic gunfire as the line of weapons came alive at the command of Stoney Bullard.

Christina "Crash" Clarke and Kathryn Byrnie had never fired a weapon before and the sudden bursts of power created by the force of the 5.45 mm bullets exploding inside the AK-74's sent both their weapons climbing skyward, the bullets tracing paths up the tall trees about 100 yards in front of them.

"Wow!" shouted Christina, taking her finger off the trigger.

"Use that front grip and hold tight, keep the barrel horizontal!" Stoney shouted above the roar of the other guns. He stood between the two women. He had anticipated the natural effect of the weapon taking control of the inexperienced shooters.

"Tuck the stock in here and pivot it on your side," he demonstrated. His right hand firmly held the pistol grip, and his left hand grabbed under the barrel, then he braced the wooden shoulder stock tight against his side, held in place by his locked right elbow, and he squeezed off a dozen rounds. In his experienced hands, the weapon sprayed a line of lead traveling at 1000 yards a second, cutting a swath through the air at about the height of an average man's navel.

Kathryn mimicked his position and squeezed the trigger. The sounds and feel of the gun were powerful. She concentrated on holding the molded barrel grip and the arc of bullets leveled off as they cut into the trees.

"Don't forget, sports fans," Stoney shouted down the line, "The AK-74 can shoot 600 rounds per minute, but, you only have thirty rounds in your magazine! Shoot from the hip for cover fire. Put the weapon on your shoulder for specific targets. And *squeeze* off only a few at a time."

A deeper sound, different from the pops that jumped from the assault rifles, came from the far end of the line. It was distinctive enough that everyone noticed. A few seconds later the practice firing was brought to a halt by a sudden explosion deep in the jungle behind the line of trees they had been peppering. It was a grenade launched by the AGS-17 manned by Dave.

Parts of trees and leaves went flying into the air above the tree line and came raining down in front of everyone.

"Did you see that?" exclaimed Ray.

Lenny and Dutch just looked at each other in disbelief. Lenny rolled his eyes skyward.

"What have we gotten ourselves into here?" Lenny asked. His own military experience in the U.S. Air Force was limited to flying cargo planes. Clean and without weapons.

"War," Dutch answered quietly and slapped another 70 round magazine into his light machine gun. He flipped the bipod legs into position, flopped on his stomach and squeezed off the full clip in a matter of seconds, focusing his shots on a large tree stump 100 yards away. All the bullets ripped into the target. His combat shirt hid the blue cast over his broken left arm and it did not affect his aim.

Dutch looked up at his buddy after the last shots rang out.

"Deadly accurate, my friend. That's the only answer. Kill or be killed!"

"Whoa, it's Sergeant Rock and Easy Company!" laughed Lenny. "Where have you been hiding this killer instinct?" He brought the AK-74 to his shoulder, sighted a tree and squeezed off six single shots into the distant foliage. It was hard to tell where they all ended up, but leaves moved around and Lenny seemed satisfied with the results.

"Killed a few trees, I suspect," he said seriously.

The sound of Mickey's clicking camera made him turn.

"Well, looks like word is out! Maybe the cover of Soldier of Fortune magazine for me. Drug dealers beware! The Cain Killer is here!" Lenny posed with his weapon, looking off into the distance as if the enemy was out there, somewhere.

"I hope you don't plan shooting with only your camera when all hell breaks loose, Mickey-Man," Dutch said from his prone position, even as he smiled for the camera.

"I'm ready. I just hope you two know what to do when the trees start shooting back," Mickey answered, clicking away.

"I'm not afraid of trees," Lenny said, but they both quieted down a bit and Dutch turned back to his machine gun, inserted a new magazine and sprayed the woods. Lenny finished out his clip with a few shots from the kneeling position and Ray moved along side and tried the same. Mickey, too, picked up his weapon and began peppering the trees.

Kathryn and Christina listened to Stoney explain the use of the metal sights on top of the rifle and how to shift from semi- auto to automatic fire.

"They call these things assault rifles because they lay down a wall of lead," he was saying. "But, a bullet can kill up to 400 yards away, so make the most of whatever cover you find. Fire off two or three shot groups at your target. Stay out of the line of oncoming fire. Conserve your ammo. Without it, this thing is just a metal and plastic club, range about one meter."

Kathryn tried a few single shots, ruffling the trees near where she had been aiming. The weapon made her feel vulnerable. She realized that using it meant she was opening the door to the possibility of her own death. She had already done that by coming to Colombia with PJ, but the weapon drove the point home.

The kick of the AK-74 was manageable once the shooter was prepared for it and she found herself able to control the weapon. Next to her, Christina seemed to be enjoying it, expressing herself with enthusiasm with each shot grouping.

"Wow! Did you see that? Man! I like this! Whoa!" came out of her in a steady stream. Her five-foot body seemed smaller still with the meter long rifle in her hands and her uniform, a size too big, drooping on her body. However, she handled the eight-pound weapon with ease. Kathryn couldn't help but smile.

"I guess you're doing all right with that thing," she said to her female companion.

"Most fun I've had in a long time, Kath," Christina answered as if she were playing with a new toy.

"I don't know if I could kill someone," Kathryn said seriously. Christina lowered her weapon and looked at her.

"Cross that bridge when you come to it," Christina said. "At least you'll know what to do." She brought the rifle up to her shoulder again and fired off three shots.

"It's a little like playing God," Kathryn said.

Christina laughed. "Hey, what's wrong with that?"

Stoney watched her and smiled, pleased with her quick success. She was regularly hitting the makeshift cardboard targets they had hung among the trees. He moved next to Kathryn and watched her closely, realizing she was still having some problems adjusting to the world of small arms.

"I killed a few soldiers in Vietnam," he said to her reflectively, loud enough for only her to hear. "I think it was '65. I didn't ask to go out there, but I went and I shot anyone who was the enemy. It was strictly survival, Kathryn, and believe me the only way to get back alive was to stay alert and be ready to kill."

He looked up at her and she returned his look, their eyes connecting for a moment. She liked Stoney, but knew he was cut from different cloth. He seemed to live easily with his lifestyle and the hardware of war. This was new to her.

"I want to protect my friends," she said. "And myself. That's why I'm here. I won't let you down."

"I know you won't," Stoney said and walked away, turning his attention to the other crewmembers, offering hints as each fired off the 200 rounds of allotted practice ammo.

He walked a few yards behind the firing line and stood near the bus that had brought them to this remote spot. In a few minutes, Dutch came over, carrying his RPKS machine gun, smoke still coming from the barrel.

"Quite the weapon, Stoney," he said. Stoney just nodded, his concentration focused on Ray and Lenny taking single shots from the standing position.

"Keep your right elbow up, Ray!" he shouted.

Dutch sat down on the bumper of the bus and had an image of the crew going into battle in the colorfully painted *chiva*. He laughed out loud.

"What's so funny, Dutch?" Stoney asked.

"This thing. It's kind of surreal, don't you think?" he said, pointing at the wooden vehicle with its wildly psychedelic swirls of yellow, blue, pink and green on a red background.

"Hey, there used to be thousands of these works of art on wheels. It's how the *campesinos* got to work everyday, the backbone of Colombian mass transit!" Stoney explained. "Now, you got your basic modern, air-conditioned metal buses with no style. This has style! Even when it's sitting in a yard and rotting, it's rotting with style."

"I was thinking of us going into battle with it," Dutch laughed. "Weird about the scene on the back, eh?"

It had been disquieting earlier that morning when the crew came out of the hotel for the trip to the airport hanger to change into their battle fatigues and pick up the weapons. The sight of the old bus alone was enough to make them pause. In the tradition of all *chives*, there was a painted scene on the back. This bus had a full color painting of the Golden Gate Bridge, another reminder that they were not on vacation.

"Yeah, I wondered if Barney Devlin didn't pick it on purpose," Stoney said.

"So, what do you think, Stoney?" Dutch asked after awhile.

"About what?" the older man answered.

"The weather!" Dutch answered sarcastically. "What are you starting to forget things, old man? About us, about this!" he said pointing to the scene in front of them. "I want to know what you think about our chances if we have to get into a fire fight, take over the mine, or whatever we're here for?"

"Dutch, you know these people as well as I do," Stoney answered after a pause. "In a drinking contest or a sailboat race, there are few crews better. In a fire fight, well, let's say we would be the heavy underdog."

"Not a chance in hell, right?" Dutch said.

"I didn't say that, my friend. I said underdog. We need a tricky plan, some smoke and mirrors and lots of luck. That's to even things up. At least everyone is pointing the rifles in the same direction."

The two of them watched the crew firing into the woods. Dave's launcher lobbed another grenade, this one deeper into the jungle and they all watched as it sent more trees flying.

"We do have some firepower, though," Dutch said, amazed at the ability of the AGS-17 to lob grenades nearly half a mile.

"That we do," Stoney said confidently. "We can get around in the C-2, even land it in the valley on that small strip, provided of course, we can get into there without finding the rocks first."

"Or getting shot up like sardines in a can before the plane stops rolling," Dutch added.

"Right now, I think the best plan is to pray that PJ gets this thing settled diplomatically without a shot being fired," Stoney said looking at his friend.

"That would be nice," Dutch said shaking his head. He didn't believe that was going to happen and neither did Stoney.

* * *

In fact, PJ was standing in front of a multi-columned building made of granite that would fit comfortable on the mall in Washington, DC. This one was inside the walled city of Cartegena at the *Plaza de la Aduana*. The sign embossed in metal on the corner of the stone stairway read *Instituto Nacional de los Recursos Naturales Renovables y del Ambiente*. PJ had been told it was called INDERENA, the Colombian version of the parks department and the administrative branch responsible for handing out mining permits in the Sierra Nevada de Santa Marta mountains.

He was scheduled to meet a US State Department official named Vic and was mildly surprised to see Harold Miller pull up in a small car. He had not seen or heard from him since the funeral shootout.

"What the hell are you doing here?" PJ asked, happy to see his old friend.

"I've got a personal stake in this, PJ," Harold said grimly as they shook hands.

"Of course you do, but I thought…"

"Stop thinking and just come listen. I've got a 24 hour window before I have to be….some place else. Let me run this meeting," Harold ordered and went up the stairs and into the building with PJ following, wondering what Harold was into.

In less than two minutes, they were seated on a couch across from Jorge Orlando Meli, the assistant director general of the Magdalena region of INDERENA.

"Where's Guillermo?" Harold asked, comfortable with his Spanish.

"He is gone," Meli said without looking up.

"Shit," muttered Harold. He looked over at PJ shaking his head. "Not good."

PJ didn't like the feeling in the pit of his stomach.

Mr. Meli appeared to be studying several papers on his desk and gave no hint of interest in the two men in front of him.

In fact, Meli, a small, wiry man with a thin black mustache and sharp facial features, proved to be most uncooperative and the meeting quickly began to disintegrate, frustrating PJ and Harold. Meli seemed unaffected by Harold's name dropping, waving off the three bureaucrats Harold was close to and had been directly involved in the original mine deed.

PJ showed off all the documents from Jester's files, including the original deed to the mine with an INDERENA seal embossed in the corner and signed in an officially undecipherable handwriting four years ago. Señor Meli did not consider it a legitimate document.

Neither the photos of the Indians working at the mine and views of the surrounding valley persuaded him, nor did receipts of paid license fees. When questioned by Harold, Meli admitted he had been in office only five months and was not completely aware of the past history of the department. However, he did show a copy of a deed he brought from the main office in Santa Marta, and the one his department considered the legitimate deed to the mine in question. It was issued in the name of Colombia Precious Metals.

Meli admitted when pressed by PJ that he was not aware of the minerals being mined in the Valley of Codazzi. He said that wasn't his concern. The deed merely permitted mining activities of an unspecified nature. He denied knowing the owner of Colombia Precious Metals, and said he assumed it was Luis Caron, the name on the deed.

When PJ suggested men shot at a supply plane flying into the valley, he brushed off the idea as ridiculous. He had heard no such report. Meli sat fidgeting with a paperweight on the desk, his eyes nervously shifting between the two Americans. Beads of sweat formed above his thin mustache and he frequently glanced at his watch as if he had already wasted enough time on this interview.

PJ did not like Meli's manner at all. Each piece of evidence PJ presented

---

was swept aside as irrelevant, untrue or unconvincing. Meli's smile might denote ignorance, but PJ felt it was closer to arrogance. After only twenty minutes, PJ broke off the meeting, standing up quickly, gathering his papers and walking out, leaving Harold to offer goodbyes.

"I told him we were not satisfied with his answers," Harold said to PJ outside in the sunshine of the square. "That will let him know we are not dropping our queries. Sometimes you have to keep pressure on the government to make them move."

"I just can't believe how he stonewalled us!" PJ was mad and frustrated.

"Well, that's Colombia. I'm not sure he knows anymore than he told us," Harold suggested.

PJ stood for a second and looked around. He nodded at Harold and allowed Meli the benefit of the doubt. But he was still angry. PJ pulled out a small map of Cartegena to get his bearings. They were in a triangle surrounded by buildings with red tiled roofs. Across the plaza, built against the inner walls was the *Museo de Arte Moderne*.

"What a dummy I am!" he exclaimed, slapped the map and started walking along the wall toward the *Plaza de los Coches*.

"Colombia Precious Metals," he said excitedly to Harold. "It's only three blocks away in the next square! We've walked passed it twice since last night!"

Harold hurried to keep up, his long strides easily catching PJ and falling in step. PJ looked over at him and had to smile. He hated him only a few days ago, but here they were, friends again on a mission. Harold looked good, he thought with his blonde hair, sun glasses and a dark blue suit that seemed out of place in the old world atmosphere inside the walls of the city.

"Is that how most of Inter-American Affairs goes?" PJ asked as they walked along.

"In my ten years at State, we have learned that most countries do things their own way, especially the Colombians. I doubt he would have met with you without me setting up the invite. Certainly, not this quickly. Now, if the tables were reversed and his government needed a few million dollars to tie them over, then we would be the best of friends," Harold laughed.

"Is this what you do all the time? Grease the skids?" PJ asked.

"I've acquired a bit of a rep," he laughed. "I think it has more to do with the six languages I speak. Besides, this is personal, so whatever it takes, I'm here to help."

"Six! Shheettt!" PJ laughed. "I remember you took French and Spanish in high school. We thought you kind of a nerd. No offense."

"None taken. I do love to read. I wish I had taken more time to play. Or learn to race. It's too bad."

"What's too bad?"

"I couldn't keep up with my father like you could," Harold said, almost to himself. "I wished I could do half the things you did...do."

"Hey, Harold!" PJ said sharply, grabbing his friend and stopping in the middle of the plaza. "You look at me. He loved you."

"Sure, I know he did, but he spent most of my play time with you."

"Okay, we spent a lot of time together. We shared the same interests, but, Harold, he never replaced my father. And I never replaced you."

PJ looked steadily at Harold until he returned his gaze.

"It felt like it sometimes," Harold said.

PJ held his gaze and then nodded slightly.

"Yea, it did. Sometimes. I understand. But, not often! He will always be your father and he always loved you unconditionally. And if you need me to tell you that, then wake the fuck up!"

PJ gave Harold a slight slap on the cheek. Harold reacted instinctually grabbing PJ's wrist. It was a surprisingly strong grip. He looked hurt, but not so much from the slap as from the truth that his father was dead, his father that he had loved so dearly.

"Thanks, PJ. Let's get this done."

The strong grip relaxed and evolved into a solid handshake. PJ felt the past slip away at that moment and their next steps the first of a new beginning. After a moment, they turned and took those steps toward the address of Colombia Precious Metals.

The *Plaza de los Coches* was behind the main entrance to the old city. Tourists and locals entered through three archways cut through the fifty - foot thick walls under a tall clock tower. After a search around the plaza they found the right building number. It was three stories, with a white washed front. An old man on a chair out front directed them to the top floor. They found only an unmarked, locked door, which went unanswered when they knocked. The old man told Harold that a young girl used to come there everyday but not for several days.

"Dead ends!" PJ exclaimed as the two Americans walked through the archway and stopped for a cool juice drink next to the convention center. They walked along the old harbor, taking in the sights of the easygoing life style. Fishing boats rocked gently along the quay. A few fishermen worked on their nets. One appeared to be fixing a radar antenna on his cabin roof.

A boatload of tourists headed out from the dock for a tour of the new commercial harbor near Manga Island to the south.

"So, Harold, tell me. Where to next?" PJ asked, sipping the refreshing yellow mango drink. "We've got ether at Quintaro's ranch, a four-engine cargo plane, what appears to be his helicopter at the mine and gunshots at Barney Devlin. And we can connect Brett Lesco to Colombia Precious Metals. Isn't that enough to get some kind of an investigation going with the police?"

"At home it might be, PJ, but here, it is kind of iffy," Harold spoke slowly. "Don't forget, Colombian judges are also investigator and prosecutor. They're not going to move until something happens here. We need pretty concrete 'somethings' besides a couple of quick looks at airplanes to get a judge to start investigating a prominent person like Carlos Quintaro. And if drugs are involved, there are not many judges who want to put their lives and their family's on the line."

"Any suggestions?" PJ asked. "What about DEA?"

"Maybe, but frankly, they're in the process of breaking in a new section chief and their agenda is full."

"What about Colonel Jesus Cesar? I understand he's in charge of Colombia's special anti-narcotics unit?" PJ asked.

Harold looked at PJ carefully.

"Where did you hear that?" he asked. He knew it to be a closely guarded secret in the South American section.

"I have a few sources," PJ said.

Harold shrugged his shoulders. "This goes no further, understand?"

"What goes no further?" PJ asked. "You know Cesar?" PJ smiled and shook his head in amazement. Harold looked around and leaned closer to PJ.

"Let's say I do know him, I don't know if I can get in touch with him Last report we had at the embassy his outfit was in the jungle.. He has his own agenda, but he might take an interest in your information."

"Well, screw, Harold! That's not good enough, is it? We need to do something," PJ said loudly.

He thought about the crew at target practice outside of town. He wondered how they were taking to the weapons. Kathryn especially. The thought of using force left him very depressed.

"Why not go to the top?" Harold interjected after a few moments.

"You mean tonight? Of course, the Presidente will be at Quintaro's party, right?"

"Yes he will," Harold nodded with a big smile. He actually liked the idea. "He's big on tourism and I think it is part payback for Quintaro's support. Most of the foreign delegation will be there." He eyed PJ carefully, trying to read his mind.

"You don't have any official standing here," Harold continued. "You're just a tourist. I'm sure Presidente Gomez isn't ready to have you nosing around in his country's drug problems. But, you can probably get a minute or two with him."

"It doesn't have to be drugs," PJ said. "Don't forget, Fast Car Caravan is doing business here, at least we were. He's concerned about exports, right? And Indians. The miners are missing, H. I'm sure Presidente Gomez would be interested in that fact."

"He'll probably hand it off to one of his department heads."

"That's a start. Then we'll talk about Quintaro's involvement in drugs. That kind of info should catch his attention. He is anti-drug, isn't he?"

"Yes, but he's pro-Quintaro," Harold shot back. "Quintaro helped the man get elected."

"Well, it's time someone straightened him out about Quintaro!" PJ said.

"We still need proof, damn it!"

"I've got enough!"

PJ was frustrated and wondered if he indeed had enough proof. He shoved the doubt out of his head.

"What about the media?" PJ asked after a few moments. "I'll bet there's a paper who would take an interest in this story. An American reporter even? Doesn't the *Times* have someone down here?"

"Hey, PJ, come on!" Harold said. "The US Government doesn't need you creating an international incident. Gomez is trying to make things work."

Harold was wary of the press. Part of his job was to protect the relationship between the United States and Colombia. This was often accomplished by controlling when, where and how much pressure could and should be exerted on the host government to meet foreign policy goals. It was part of the *quid pro quo* game of politics. He also was not interested in any publicity about him being in Colombia. Harold knew any press would take a lot of control out of his hands.

He smiled at PJ. "Look, let's give it a shot," he said. "Even if it's 'bad diplomatic form' to be accusing one of the most influential men in this region of drug smuggling, especially when the Presidente is his honored guest."

"Bad diplomatic form is your concern, not mine," PJ said.

"Okay, PJ, fine. You talk to the Presidente tonight, but be careful it doesn't blow up in your face."

"Oh, I don't know, Harold. An international incident might be just the right thing to wake up some people in this country."

~~~

CHAPTER NINETEEN

K illing Barney Devlin was going to be more complicated than Rex Simka first thought. The problem began when he scouted the ALSA office at Simon Bolivar Airport only to find the hangar locked and Barney Devlin not there. Simka felt the need to do something. He decided he didn't have to kill Devlin.

Instead, he would plant a bomb. A bomb would be enough of an explosive message and would put ALSA out of action. Fear had worked before as a deterrent, and Simka believed it would work with Devlin. The small frame office on the side of the hangar was barely more than a shack, in contrast to the modern QUIMEX airfreight facilities across the tarmac. He decided to put his plan into action at sunset, three hours away.

With time on his hands, he made the thirty-minute flight into the Valley of Codazzi in his TBM 700 to check on the preparations for the second weekly shipment scheduled in two days on Saturday morning.

The valley was only sixty-five miles from Santa Marta as the crow flies, although not too many crows could make the flight over and between the 18,000-foot peaks of the mountains. Simka had already made half a dozen flights to the cloud-shrouded valley and was feeling more comfortable with the approach. He did triple check the GPS bearings entered into his flight computer before he left. He did have one moment of doubt while descending inside the clouds, but he eventually broke through the bottom layer five miles from the valley with 1000 feet of air still between him and the rocks below.

The charred wreckage of the C-123 was visible on the south ridge. Ulf had been too low on his approach and crashed nose first a good 100 feet below the crest of the ridge. The chemical laden plane had exploded on impact. The tail section and wing tips were the only parts of the plane still identifiable. Simka guessed Ulf had developed an engine problem or was hit by wind shear as the wind tumbled over the ridge from the valley. There was little room for error. Simka had liked the carefree Dane who had always been willing to do any job he was asked.

He crossed the ridge himself and set up for landing, noticing immediately Luis had beefed up security. Two men waved to him from their lookout positions atop the south ridge and two more could be seen in the middle of the plateau beyond the barracks, where they had a full 360 degree view of the valley and the surrounding mountains from a freshly built wooden watch tower.

The oversized tires on the TBM 700's landing gear absorbed the shock of touchdown on the hard dirt, and Simka again felt the relief of another successful landing. The mountain winds had not been very strong this time.

He taxied to the parking area in front of the Ops Building and saw two more men positioned in a bunker guarding the river approach into the valley. All the guards had their weapons at the ready and he could see that their MAC-10 submachine guns had been replaced with the more powerful Spanish CETME rifle.

Rafael was supervising a six-man crew unloading barrels of ether and acetone from the DHC-7. Another crew could be seen stacking bags of cocaine behind the Ops Building. Luis was waiting out front as Simka climbed from his plane.

"What do you think?" Luis asked, gesturing to the new watchtower. It looked odd standing twenty feet high, isolated in the middle of the plateau.

"I like it!" Rex answered. "Did the new Uirapuru arrive?"

Luis smiled and spoke into his ever-present walkie-talkie.

"Anton, show Señor Simka the Uirapuru."

The loud sound of a heavy caliber machine gun burst from the guard tower half a mile away. The Brazilian weapon fired 7.62 mm bullets, had a range of 1200 yards, and could fire 600 rounds a minute. Simka could see the trail of dust kicked up along the plateau and up the far walls of the mountain face. He was impressed.

"Excellent! Carlos will be pleased," he said. "I must tell you he is on the rampage of late and will not tolerate any screw ups!" Simka didn't tell him why.

"Everyone has been put on extra alert, Rex. There will be no screw ups," Luis said proudly.

"Good, Luis. And I have good news. The weapons we requested from Barranquilla will be here Saturday."

"Excellent! That will complete our security," Luis beamed.

"Now, let's get with Rafael and sort out the schedule changes for this weekend," Simka said.

Rafael joined them inside the Ops Building. A chart of the U.S. and the Caribbean hung on one wall. Several charts were scattered on a table, alongside a lap top computer.

The death of Ulf and the loss of the C-123, had forced some changes. It was decided Rafael would take the DHC-7 to supply the transfer point at Marib Cay for the East Coast deliveries. Rafael would supervise the loading of the smaller planes there, while Simka and Luis remained in the valley.

"We have added a fourth plane this week. Our British decoy will be landing in Jacksonville," Simka said, pointing to the chart. "Once the formation is inside the ADIZ, three planes will be going to Alabama. They are to fly VFR."

"In broad daylight?" Rafael asked.

"Yes," Simka smiled. "There is no need to conserve fuel for these three. They can stay below 14,000 feet in uncontrolled airspace and won't have to contact ATC. No one will bother with them once inside the U.S. The planes will land in daylight, but will be unloaded after dark. All the product will go out west by truck. The fourth plane will follow standard ATC procedures and fly to Massachusetts."

He smiled at his own brilliance. He had set up twelve different flight plans for each week of Operation Snowmine. He handed Rafael four envelopes of flight instructions.

"Remember, Rafael, each pilot must not know the destinations of the others," Simka warned.

"It will be done, Señor Simka," Rafael answered.

Luis then updated Simka on cocaine production. There had been no interruption by the loss of the chemicals in the crash. In fact, the workers had already turned out half of the third week's shipments.

"At this rate, we should be two weeks ahead by the end of next week," Luis said proudly. He also reported three of the workers had taken ill from the fumes and been sent home.

"Where's Julio?" Simka asked.

"He's in the lab right now, want me to call him?" Luis answered reaching for his radio.

"No! Let him stay there," Simka said, not wishing to see the sickly looking man.

"Carlos will be very pleased," Simka said after Luis' report and then repeated his comment about Carlos' mood and the need to be extra vigilant. "Now, we must prepare for tonight."

The meeting broke up shortly and Simka left the valley in the rapidly dwindling daylight with four additional passengers, including Luis.

They landed at Santa Marta at sunset and he parked near the main terminal far from the QUIMEX and ALSA offices. He failed to notice the odd looking black plane with the tip sails and reverse mounted engines parked among the other private planes.

Luis and the extra men took Simka's jeep into town with specific instructions for the party security. Simka walked across the airport grounds and used his own key to enter the QUIMEX offices. The workers had already left for the day. He strode alone through the darkened freight area where pallets of cargo awaited early flights the next day. He retrieved a leather satchel he had hidden among the boxes earlier in the afternoon.

From the lobby, he could see the naked light bulb shining over the front door of the ALSA office. Slipping out the back, he crossed the tarmac in the dusk, using parked aircraft and their shadows as cover, and ended up behind the ALSA hangar.

He popped the simple hasp lock on the rear door, prying the pad eye from its two screws with a screwdriver he had drawn from the leather satchel. A dog barked in the distance and he paused to listen, then pushed the door open, satisfied the animal was not concerned with him.

The hangar was unlit, but he could make out the dark outline of a large plane. He pulled out a flashlight and shined it on the tail section and the registration "HK347". It was the same plane that had flown into the Valley of Codazzi.

Climbing through the double cargo door, he moved into the plane's cockpit. He pulled out a small block of C-4 explosive, smuggled two days ago out of the Colombian Army arsenal in Barranquilla, and a detonator, the size of a woman's compact. He taped the explosive charge directly on the GPS receiver mounted in the middle of the instrument panel. The wire dangling from the detonator had a metal plug on the end and he inserted this plug into the clay like explosive. Small numbers above the thumb dial lit up as he slide back the detonator's front cover. He set the timer for thirty-five minutes.

When the clock reached zero it would send a small electric charge from a tiny battery through the wire to the metal plug which was actually a fuse. The heat from the electricity would vaporize the thin fuse wire, ignite the detonating powder packed around it and create a miniature but intense shockwave that would cause the half pound of C-4 to explode in a violent white hot flash, completely destroying the GPS receiver and along with it the stored numbers that Devlin used to navigate into the Valley of Codazzi.

Simka was sure that Devlin could recreate the numbers, but not in this plane because the blast would destroy the entire cockpit as well. And to insure the message was made clear, Simka placed explosive charges twice the size under both fuel tanks near the wing roots. He set the timers to coincide with the first explosion.

He had one more charge in the satchel and moved into the office. His light flashed over a large map of South America and the Caribbean on one wall and a montage of photos, posters, flyers, notes and calendars hung in many layers on the other two. It settled on a four-drawer file cabinet next to the desk and he taped the final charge there. Simka had a grim smile on his face as he bent to his task, checking his watch before setting the last timer for twenty minutes to detonate with the others. That gave him plenty of time to be far from the airport when Air Lift South America went up in smoke.

He rubbed his hands on his pants, removing the oily residue from the C-4 plastique, grabbed the now lighter satchel and stood up to leave. A noise near the door stopped him cold and he reached into the satchel for his handgun, but he never got to use it. The door suddenly burst open and a dark figure leaped on him, knocking the gun and flashlight out of his hand, both bodies tumbling to the floor.

Something hard hit him squarely on the face and everything went white as pain shot through his head. He grappled in the dark, rolling on the floor, trying to hit his unseen attacker, but he was overwhelmed. He took two more hits to the face and then a third, hard hit on the back of the neck, and everything went black.

When he awoke, the lights had been turned on in the office. He tried to get up, but his hands were tied behind his back. He thought it might be tape around his wrists. His eyes had trouble focusing, but they started to come around as he raised himself to his knees.

"How long have I been out?" he practically shouted, his mind filled with images of little batteries, no larger than thumbnails, sitting in four detonators ready to turn everything into ash.

"Not long enough, you bastard," came the deep voice behind him. He turned to look at the man sitting on the desk, and another hard crash from the man's fist fell against Simka's face, knocking him back to the floor. He tasted blood, but his eyes were focused sharply. The small cube of plastique set against the file cabinet was in the left hand of a man dressed in khaki. The black shoes he wore rang a distant bell in Simka's foggy brain.

U.S. Government issue!

"I should just shoot you between the eyes and leave you for the maggots, Rex Simka," the man said nonchalantly, tossing the plastique up and down. "Or stick this up your ass!"

"Who the hell are you?" Simka asked, his eyes finding a wall clock that read 7:10. Five minutes! Did this guy know about the other charges?

The man slipped off the desk, moving very casually, and placed the plastique in the leather satchel on the desk. He picked up Simka by the shirt, pushing him roughly onto a chair, his pinned arms taking the full force of the fall.

"You don't recognize me, you cop-killing traitor?" The man stuck his face up close to Simka's. In need of a shave, blue eyes, black hair, pug nose, Simka didn't know him. The man reached in his back pocket and pulled out a wallet, letting it fall open three inches in front of Simka's eyes. It was the gold shield of a DEA agent. The ID card under the badge read Deke Hamilton and the picture showed a different face, a young man with dark hair, a square jaw and a slight grin.

Simka closed his eyes and saw that same grin on the face of the man who had been his partner three years ago in Miami, moments after Simka had shot him.

"Deke's dead!" Simka whispered, trying to recognize the man in front of him, even as he wondered why he hadn't been shot yet. Then he remembered a name and put it with the pug nosed face.

"Russo. Frank Russo," he muttered. Hamilton's partner before he had been paired with Simka.

"Good, Rex. You remember me. I'm pleased," Russo said with sarcasm.

"How did you find me?" Simka asked quietly.

Russo sat back on the desk, his arms crossed, a .45 caliber pistol in his hand.

"We figured you were in Colombia, Rex, we just didn't know where," Russo started to explain. "But the whole agency knew you would do something stupid and we would catch up to you eventually."

Simka's mind was abuzz. There wasn't much time before the other charges exploded, but he found himself trying to think of where he had left a trail for DEA to follow.

"Our snitch network in Colombia got a good workout. One of our friends spied a gas receipt at Nunez airport last month with your signature on it. That was dumb, Rex! It matched you with QUIMEX and that sweet ass plane of yours. We just waited for you and the TBM to show up again. Yesterday, I got the tip you were in Santa Marta."

The clock read 7:12 and Rex started looking for a way out. The office's front door was solid wood, but there was a window next to it.

"Thought I had lost you this afternoon when your plane was gone," Russo continued, "but I played a hunch tonight, and low and behold there you were, Rex, sneaking like a slug across the airport. And here I am. So, what's your beef with this guy at ALSA. Competition?"

"Yeah. It's just business," Simka answered, calculating the distance between him and the window. It was less than 10 feet. "You came alone? Isn't that against agency regs?" Simka asked seriously, tensing his muscles to move.

"I'm not alone anymore, Rexy boy, I got you!" Russo smiled.

The minute hand click to 7:14 on the wall clock.

"Okay, weasel breath, time to go!" Russo said and grabbed Simka by his shirt, pulling him out of the chair and pushing him toward the hangar door. With his .45 in one hand and the satchel in the other, he gave Rex a nudge with the gun.

"No! Not through the hangar, Frank. Let's go out the front door!" Simka suggested, trying to be nonchalant.

"Relax, Rex, are you worried about something in the hangar?" Russo smiled and poked Simka harder in the back with the barrel of his pistol. "Now, move!"

"You'll get us both killed," Simka turned as they went into the hangar, lit only by the office light spilling through the doorway. He yelled at Russo, any attempt at calm forgotten.

"There's no time!"

Russo smiled at Simka and opened the satchel, revealing the blocks of explosives and their disconnected detonators. Simka counted only three and looked up at Russo's smiling face. Simka smiled right back at him.

"You hot dog!" Simka said, shaking his head in disgust. At that instant, the detonator of the explosive charge taped to the cockpit instrument panel clicked to zero and the half-pound of C-4 exploded.

The short blast completely destroyed the GPS receiver and created a gaping hole in the instrument panel, driving the instruments toward the nose of the aircraft. But, much of the explosive energy moved toward the line of least resistance, the open space of the cockpit. It was absorbed by the seats and the rear cockpit wall and dissipated back through the empty cargo bay, the tough metal frame and skin of the rebuilt plane flexing for an instant, but holding intact.

It was the cockpit windows that were no match for the explosive force. They instantly blew out and showered Simka and Russo, standing in front of the right wing thirty feet away, with shards of flying Plexiglas and pieces of tattered aluminum.

Simka expected it, but Russo was caught completely by surprise. He obviously thought he had found all the explosives. The sound and the white flash diverted his attention for a second and he looked up, raising his arms to protect his face, even as Simka swung with all his might, landing his foot in Russo's groin. In the same instant, the shrapnel peppered Russo's face, one piece from the side window catching him in the eye before his arms could block it, and he fell in a heap.

Simka fell too, the flying debris hitting him in the back. He lay on his side and swiftly kicked at the DEA agent's slumped body, connected with the handgun and sent it skittering back through the doorway into the office.

Simka knew he had to move fast and rolled to his feet with some difficulty. His knees felt broken Plexiglas around him. He stood and delivered several more kicks to Russo' face and crotch. Fighting for his life, with nothing but his shoes for a weapon, he kicked like a man possessed. Russo was overmatched and soon stopped struggling, his face a bloody mess, and soft moans coming from his bruised lips.

Satisfied that Russo was not going anywhere for the moment, Simka stumbled around looking for something to cut the tape on his hands. He scanned the tool bench in the dimness without success. He headed toward the office when he saw the large propeller under the right engine. The blades were streamlined enough to cut tape, but it was six inches too high. He kicked a toolbox under the right engine and carefully balanced himself on it. It was rather awkward as he leaned backward, rubbing the tape against the blade. It took thirty seconds before the tape finally split and Simka lost his balance and fell backward onto the floor. He cried out in pain as he landed on sharp debris from the explosion.

But, his hands were now free and he gathered up the leather satchel with his gun and found Russo's gun in the office. Shutting off the lights, he looked through the window. Nothing moved on the tarmac out front. The airport terminal lights glowed on the other side of the runway. The Customs Office next to the QUIMEX office was dark.

Back in the hanger he shined the flashlight on Russo's crumpled body. It looked like the DEA agent was trying to say something, but the words weren't coming out.

"You should have shot me without saying a word, Frank Russo," Simka spoke softly, tauntingly. "Say hi to Deke for me," he finished coldly and squeezed the trigger of Russo's .45, killing the DEA agent instantly with a shot in the head. The report from the gun was loud, the kick a bit more than Simka's own .9 mm. He wiped the gun clean with his shirt and dropped it onto the lifeless body.

He looked around, his mind working hard to anticipate all the possibilities. There was nothing that could place him here. He started to leave, but returned once again to Russo' body and removed the brown vial with the white powder from his own pocket and placed it in one of Russo's pockets. He smiled as he thought about the police reaction. Just a small clue to confuse the issue, he thought. He certainly didn't need a high right now. His heart already raced like a high-speed motor.

He flashed the light around one last time and realized he still had explosives in his bag. Quickly, he set two of the bombs under the fuselage and reset the timer for an hour. Then, carefully wiping his fingerprints off the back door, he walked in the shadows along the airport fence to his plane and changed his clothes.

The back of his shirt was pockmarked with small bloodstains from the shrapnel of the explosion and he grimaced as he buttoned the new shirt and donned a lightweight sports jacket. He didn't have time to worry about the pain right then. He stashed the remaining explosives in his plane, tucked his own .9 mm pistol into the holster on the back of his belt then calmly walked over to the main airport terminal and caught the last bus for the twenty minute ride into Santa Marta.

It was 7:30 and he had to get to the party. He tried to control his nerves as the bus made its way along the highway. He looked at the five others riding with him, satisfied they were airport workers. Nothing seemed out of the ordinary. He wished the bus had been full so he would not be noticed.

He knew his next actions would have to be very cautious. The primary concern was Quintaro's security, but he knew he dared not show his face at the party, at least when any Americans were around. Luis could front for him while he ran things from upstairs.

He shook his head at his schizoid predicament. Here he was rushing to insure Quintaro's security even as he put his own life and his $100 million future of freedom in dire risk. Once they discovered Frank Russo's body, DAS and DEA would be all over town. Damn, he thought, he should have moved the body closer to the plane. Maybe it would be destroyed in the explosion. He cursed himself. Was he losing his touch? He would have to lay low after this week's shipment went out, probably hole up in the valley until things settled down.

Yes, he needed Quintaro, but for only three more months, he reminded himself. Then he could afford to be his own man.

~~~

CHAPTER TWENTY

It was a moonless night, but no one was looking at the sky in Santa Marta. The refreshing sea breeze had cooled the city to perfection and the action was on the ground, in the streets, in the cafes. The wheeling and dealing over gems under the tent had ended and the night was reserved for celebration, festival style.

There were no parades, no costumes, no fireworks, but the city was alive with festival noise. *Cumbias*, the reggae-calypso-jazz combination of sound unique to the Colombian coast, drifted from open-air cafes. Celebrants crowded in the streets, on balconies and in dark alleys, laughing, talking, shouting, dancing and drinking.

A group from different nations shared beers in front of an old Spanish church, a family enjoyed Arguardiente in a dark doorway, a smuggler and an off duty policeman got high from a *bazuko* cigarette, filled with cocaine paste. Occasionally, a car filled with revelers punctuated their shouts with gunshots and horn beeping. Were everyone not so carefree, one might think the city bordered on a riot.

PJ and Kathryn flew from Cartegena in the Starship late that afternoon for Quintaro's party. Harold hitched a ride with them and was scheduled to fly back to Washington in the morning. He had no plans to attend the party, only saying he was going to work some contacts later tonight.

All three checked into the Hotel Yuldama and PJ spent some time on the phone updating Barney Devlin. Barney said he was laying low with a friend nearby. Hearing about the chemicals in Quintaro's hanger, he agreed they should be prepared for a fight.

PJ hung up the phone and felt a nervous shiver. The decision had been made. They had to go to the mine and that would mean a direct confrontation with weapons. He set his resolve to see it through for Jester, and the Indians.

He joined Kathryn and Harold in the hotel lobby, and they stepped into the festive atmosphere of the street. The trio immediately turned a few heads.

Kathryn wore a white, double-breasted sports coat-style dress that came to mid-thigh. The white contrasted with her brown skin and her long, black hair and eyes. A pair of gold earrings completed the striking image. PJ was also turned out in all white. He wore a tropical suit with open necked shirt. His sun-tanned face, reddish brown hair and piercing blue eyes, the scar above his left eye and the fingerless sailing glove on his left hand gave him a dramatic look. Harold looked very diplomatic, his tall figure neatly clothed in his ever-present blue suit.

PJ and Kathryn had spent little time alone since they woke up in each other's arms that morning. Their lovemaking had seemed so natural to PJ, and he took Kathryn's hand as they walked along. She felt warmed by his touch.

Harold proved to be a good guide and entertained them through supper with a history of the region. He admitted he had become a sort of Colombiaphile since obtaining the permits for the mine. The many indigenous Indian tribes had especially earned his interest.

"The Samarios are probably the best smugglers in the world," Harold was saying as they dug into plates of *arroz con chipichipi*, rice with shellfish, one of the mainstays of the coastal diet.

"Marijuana, cocaine, gold, emeralds, treasures from Indian graves, it's all come through here at some point or another from the mountains," he said between mouthfuls. "The police are paid off, the customs people are paid off, and other smugglers are paid off. It's a way of life. Can you believe the grave robbers even tried to form a union a few years back!" he laughed. "They wanted some respect!"

"Whose graves were they robbing?" Kathryn asked innocently.

"The Tairona Indians in the Sierra Nevadas. They are the ancestors of the Kogi tribe. Made their mark as goldsmiths long before the Incas and Aztecs," he answered.

"Since the 16th century, the treasures of Colombia have been treated as plunder by pirates of all types. Finders, keepers. In the last twenty years or so, it has been Indian artifacts," Harold said, enjoying Kathryn's fine facial features. He thought PJ a lucky man to be with her. "Like those earrings of yours. Where did you get them?" he asked her.

"San Francisco. I found them in a little shop in the Marina district," she grinned. She took one off and handed it to him

"Hmmm. This is very old," he said, studying it in his open palm. It was only an inch high, but the detail was extraordinary. It depicted a human body with an alligator head wearing a plumed, ribbon like crest.

"The Indians consider animals sacred, almost godlike," Harold said. "This looks authentic. I've seen similar ones in the Gold Museum in Bogota'. I'm pretty sure it's Taironian. They did amazing things with gold. Did the shop owner know he was selling artifacts?"

"No, actually, she didn't act out of the ordinary that I can remember," Kathryn said. "It was just a trinket. They are certainly unique, aren't they? I think I paid twenty dollars."

She picked the earring from Harold's hand and looked at it very closely. She remembered passing the shop three years ago and for some reason had looked in the window, her eye going immediately to these earrings.

"A bargain, Kathryn! That shopkeeper should be more aware of what she's selling," Harold smiled. "People have been killed over trinkets like this."

"Violence seems a way of life in Colombia," PJ said sadly. He couldn't help but admit that Harold was a talker and a charmer. More gunshots came from the street as another carload of revelers drove past. Harold nodded.

Kathryn was preoccupied with the alligator head, staring at it as if in a trance. PJ had seen that look before, when she looked at the photos of the mine.

"Something wrong, Kathryn?" PJ asked.

"Hmmm, no, PJ. I just had a strong memory of the day I bought these. Odd. As if this piece of gold had its own energy." She closed her hand on the earring and squeezed it tight. There was something happening to her.

"PJ, do you remember those dreams I told you about?" she asked him.

"Mountains of the mind," he smiled.

"Exactly. Something clicked when I saw those photos of Jester and Eduardo at the mine. It happened again last night when we looked at the statue of the little girl in Cartegena. And it just happened again. Each time, I get this strong feeling inside me, a memory, or deja vu or something...." her voice trailed off, and she looked down at the earring again. She took the other one off and held them both. There were no voices.

"Deja vu'? You've been here before?" Harold asked. He was intrigued by Kathryn's sudden revelations.

"Not so much that I've been here before. It's more like I remembered something that I never knew I had known," she smiled weakly. She realized she couldn't explain something to them without first understanding it herself. "That doesn't sound possible, does it?"

"Sometimes I'll meet someone for the first time, but they do something or say something that makes me think I've met them before," PJ offered. "But, of course, I haven't."

"Yeah," Kathryn said excitedly. "Maybe the memory is trapped deep in the sub-conscious and pops out unexpectedly. But there's no frame of reference. It feels like a memory, but it means nothing."

"A memory out of context," PJ said.

"Yes," she said, but she was still troubled. "Do you think a memory could be so strong that you actually hear it speaking to you?"

PJ pursed his lips and raised his eyebrow at her.

"Are you hearing voices?" he asked, almost as a joke.

She looked at him, then at Harold sitting across the table. She had not told him about the voices. The noise in the tiny restaurant in which they were sitting seemed much louder. Horns blew outside.

"Yes. The statute of Catalina spoke to me last night," she said.

"Really?" PJ said. "What did it, she, say?"

"Zarzamora. I think it means blackberry."

"Zarzamora?"

"Yes. I heard it clearly. Then I heard it again in a dream later, after we...," she smiled and blushed. PJ smiled back and took her hand.

No one said anything for a moment. Harold had been listening and broke the silence. He reached over and took the earring from Kathryn's hand, holding it up between his fingers.

"Maybe it's Kogi magic," he said seriously.

"Magic?" she said, wanting to believe.

"Yes, magic," Harold said matter of factly.

"There are thirty-eight different Indian tribes in this country," he started to explain. "Many of them have been Colombianized, if you will. They have pretty much discontinued the rituals of their ancestors. But, not the Kogi. They are different. Isolated in the mountains, they live pretty much the way they did four hundred years ago. Only a few have come out of the mountains, and even they aren't really a part of mainstream Colombia. The few who know them, well, they suggest they possess powers beyond normal men."

He held Kathryn's earring up high. Its golden glow seemed to catch all available light from the dimly lit restaurant.

"There's an aura of mystery surrounding them," Harold continued. Kathryn stared at the small figure, hanging on his every word.

"What kind of powers?" PJ asked.

"Shape shifting, telepathy, divination," Harold said. "They believe the spiritual and real worlds are together, no separation, no boundaries. They call it *aluna*."

"*Aluna!*" Kathryn said with surprise. She knew she had heard that word before, but could not remember when.

PJ looked at her.

"Another memory?" he asked.

She just looked at him with wide eyes and nodded.

"As I understand it," Harold continued, "the high chiefs, called Mamas, are the ones who possess these powers. They are separated from the tribe and trained from the moment they are born."

"Are you saying they learn these powers?" PJ asked in disbelief. Harold smiled and shook his head.

"I don't know, PJ. I do know the Mamas devote their entire lives to *aluna*. Even then, only those with the purest of thoughts ever attain all seven levels of the spiritual and natural worlds."

"Do you believe in it?" PJ asked him.

"Hey, I'm not one to judge. I've never seen one change shapes in front of my eyes, but I've talked to Kogi who very much believe." He paused for a moment. "My dad believed it."

"He never spoke of it to me," PJ said.

"Dad learned a bit about them. Got me going on it,' he smiled remembering one very animated conversation they had after his first trip to the mine. "They hold themselves as "The Elders", sort of guardians of the world. It's very strong medicine in the mountains," Harold finished.

Kathryn just sat silently and nodded. She didn't know if she was prepared to believe. She suddenly realized the face she had seen shimmering in the waters around Ram Island was the same face she had seen in the photo of Jester Miller at the mine.

"Eduardo is a Kogi," she said. Harold nodded.

"The mine superintendent," she went on. "All the Indians are Kogis."

"I'll speak to the office of Indian Affairs, PJ," Harold suggested. "Fifteen missing Indians is exactly what they are empowered to investigate. They have an office in town here."

"PJ, let me talk to the Presidente about the Indians tonight," Kathryn said with a trace of excitement in her voice. She had an idea and wanted to make it happen. She smiled at him. "How could he refuse to talk to me?

Maybe I'll even dance with him."

"That would be a positive step rather than throwing Quintaro's possible drug involvement in his face," Harold said earnestly. He was still worried about creating an incident.

"You know what, Kathryn. That is exactly what you can do," PJ said seriously, leaning over to touch her hair.

After dinner, Harold bid them farewell. He pulled PJ to the side.

"This is as far as I can go," he said. "Keep your wits about you tonight. Both of you. I wish I could hang longer, but ... well, I can't"

"Where are you heading?" PJ asked. "Let me guess. You can't say."

"Good guess." Harold smiled and shook PJ's hand. "Good luck." With that, he turned and walked back toward the hotel.

PJ and Kathryn went the other way, strolling leisurely toward the party, both lost in thought about the Kogi Indians. PJ couldn't help but think that Harold was involved in more than just mid-level bureaucratic negotiations.

They arrived at the new tourist center and entered under the mansion's colonial arch and were stopped by two security people who passed portable metal detectors over them. There was a collective turning of heads by the two dozen or so guests already in attendance.

PJ counted four soldiers complete with white helmets, shoulder braids and M-16s, standing just inside the entrance. As they entered the flower filled courtyard, lit by spotlights of white, blue and red, he saw other soldiers placed throughout the floor and on the balconies. There was even one positioned behind the two guitar players and the percussionist who were playing a fast paced *cumbia* in one corner.

"The Presidente is not here yet," Kathryn suggested as they walked toward the bar. PJ nodded.

"His security is," he said.

PJ felt everyone staring at them, but when his eyes met the guests individually, smiles and congenial nods were returned. He recognized no one. Carlos Quintaro was nowhere to be seen.

A tall, thin man, dressed immaculately in a black tuxedo with colorful ribbons above his breast pocket, introduced himself to the couple.

"Hello, strangers. Welcome. I am Huervo Mutea, Director General of the Colombia Tourism Board."

Mutea made an elaborate scene of taking Kathryn's hand, and bowing to kiss it, keeping his lips a respectful two inches away.

"Are you American, my dear, like your friend?" Mutea asked.

Kathryn remembered the statue of Catalina for an instant. She had never thought as much about her background as she had since leaving the United States two days ago!

"Why yes, Señor Mutea, of course I am American. Born in Texas, raised in California," she said, imitating a southern drawl for the first part. "Living in Connecticut now, on the East Coast."

"Señora, I thought you were a native. Still, your beauty brings life to a rather dull gathering of bureaucrats and pirates," he said graciously.

"You are most kind, Señor Mutea. Pirates, you say?" she laughed.

"Everyone's here to steal something from our Presidente, no?" he smiled. "There are many problems in Colombia, and each politician wants his piece of the small pie."

"It's a little like the Wild West, eh, Huervo?" came a voice behind them. It belonged to a short, rotund, bearded man with a baldhead, a napkin under his chin, already stained from a red sauce that also filled his plate along with what appeared to be shrimp.

"It is more like Santa Marta herself, Jefe, no?" Mutea responded, "Untamed. Unchallenged. On the verge of a new age. Or extinction!"

"Very good, my friend! But do not write us off yet," he laughed loudly. "We are only on the verge of the sea, and I see no danger of us falling in."

"My new friends, please let me introduce Señor Juan Javier Jacinto, the distinguished mayor of Santa Marta," Mutea said. "It is he who donated this lovely mansion for our tourism purposes."

"Forgive me if I do not shake your hands," he said, giving a small bow with his head and plate. "This house has special significance to our city. It is said that Bolivar himself kept two mistresses right here," Jacinto laughed.

"Señor Jacinto!" Mutea protested. "The lady, please!"

"Forgive me, Señora, a joke only. I could not resist."

"No harm done, Señor Jacinto," Kathryn smiled. "Bolivar was a great man. I'm sure his mistresses were worthy of this lovely home."

The two men looked at each other, then her and laughed loudly. PJ joined in the laughter. She was charming them all, PJ thought. Presidente beware!

"Would you like a drink, Kathryn?" PJ asked. She nodded yes and PJ left her talking with the two men and wandered to the bar under a tree in the corner.

"Two rum and tonics, please," PJ ordered. He surveyed the courtyard. There were three stories, the second and third with wrap around balconies leading to the black sky overhead. The tri-color of Colombia, gold, black and red, hung from a wire strung across the second floor, centered over the courtyard. He counted four soldiers on the first balcony and another man who stood on the third floor looking down. The glare from the spotlights made it hard for PJ to make out his features. He was tall, dressed in a sport coat and stared directly at PJ.

He was about to give the man a playful wave, but his attention was diverted by a well endowed, red haired woman who came up to the bar and ordered a Polar beer, then turned to PJ and looked up, too.

"One of the Presidente's spies, maybe?" she said in English.

"Probably. The first one I've seen without a uniform," he smiled at her, his eyes working hard not to stare at her ample cleavage.

"Maybe private security for Señor Quintaro, eh?" she smiled again, then changed the subject. "I have seen your face before, haven't I? A few years ago, maybe." She eyed him carefully.

PJ smiled back at her. She was carefully made up, with high cheekbones and a thin, Grecian nose. She was maybe fifty, but her looks had yet to fade.

"I don't think so, this is my first trip to Colombia."

"The Brazil Grand Prix! You're PJ McDonough, aren't you?" she said excitedly. PJ was surprised and embarrassed.

"Yes, I am," he said simply. "That was a long time ago."

Their drinks came.

"I am Gabriela Alvarez," she offered her hand. "I think you drove wonderfully that day. It is such a shame what happened. You were not treated fairly."

She said it matter of factly. PJ smiled weakly.

"Life isn't fair sometimes," he said. "I have no regrets."

"My husband is that white haired man over there, Marcello. He's the Brazilian attaché'. He would love to meet you!" she said, grabbed his arm and started to drag him across the floor.

Over the next half hour, PJ found himself moving around the room, Gabriela Alvarez his newly found sponsor. He met representatives of various governments, a few emerald dealers, two members of the Santa

Marta city council, plus the Police Chief. He used his dozen or so words of Spanish, the guests' better command of English, and Gabriela's translations to smooth over the language differences to carry out the social graces of a cocktail party. He told everyone he built engines and was in Colombia on vacation. PJ was not surprised that most of the guests thought the world of Carlos Quintaro.

Two nicely dressed men he did not meet caught his attention by their odd behavior. They moved casually, but steadily, back and forth along the sides of the room. At one point he noticed one of them on the first balcony. The man who he had seen on the upper balcony had disappeared. More security, he assumed.

Kathryn, in turn, held her ground in the middle of the courtyard. It was the group of men that changed, shifting in and out of the circle, amidst her fluent Spanish and much laughter. A few women also came to her side to whisper things in her ear.

A flourish from the guitars caught everyone's attention and one of the players invited the guests into the main room of the mansion where the Presidente would speak.

PJ moved to Kathryn's side and they slowly filed in. The room, once a large dining area, had been turned into a small theater, ideal for a press conference. Two TV cameras were set up at the back of the room and spotlights lit up a podium, with a large map of Colombia on the wall behind and two national flags on each side. A banner read *Corporacion Nacional de Turismo* above the map.

PJ heard the sound of a helicopter, then a second one. He looked up through the courtyard and caught a quick glance as one passed overhead. He recognized the extended nose and the streamlined tail section of an Agusta.

His heart skipped a beat. Quintaro, he thought! He had anticipated it, but actually seeing the helicopter had surprised him. He suddenly felt another cold shiver. The helicopter landed on the beach directly in front of the mansion. He never saw the second one and assumed it was for security, circling nearby.

In a moment, a group appeared at the front entrance. Two soldiers led the way through the courtyard, followed by Carlos Quintaro himself, dressed in a white cape coat with brown pants and a white panama on his head. Next to him was a smaller man in a brown suit with dark, short hair who PJ thought must be the Colombian Presidente.

Two more men, also in dark suits, brought up the rear of the entourage. As they passed through the courtyard, Quintaro stopped for a moment in front of Kathryn and PJ who were standing in the doorway.

"Señor McDonough, Señora Byrnie. How good of you to come!" Quintaro greeted them graciously in Spanish. His green eyes pierced PJ's. "May I present the honorable Presidente of the Republic of Colombia, Ferdinand Barranqui Gomez! Ferdinand, these are two Americans whom I had the pleasure of making their acquaintance just yesterday. They are here to enjoy our country...as tourists."

PJ thought Quintaro's smile was as evil a smile as he had ever seen and his voice dripped sarcasm as he pronounced the word "tourist". PJ's muscles tightened slightly. He found himself staring right back at those powerful green eyes.

Quintaro broke it off first to hold the hand of Kathryn in greeting. He bowed to her slightly and looked into her eyes. He said nothing for a moment, Kathryn's smile changing from polite to inquisitive as he continued to stare.

"Again you have struck me dumb with your beauty," Quintaro finally broke the awkward silence and PJ thought he actually saw Kathryn blush.

"You are too kind, Carlos," she answered, clearly embarrassed. There was something about him that intrigued her and kept her off balance.

"But he speaks the truth," added Presidente Gomez. "I, too, am struck by your radiance. If our tourism campaign can attract Americans like you, we will have to call it a success."

Kathryn responded to the Presidente's greeting, holding his hand for several seconds. She spoke to him in Spanish.

"I am truly honored, Mr. Presidente. It has been a distinct pleasure visiting your gracious country. You have done wonderful things for your people and it is evident to us as outsiders. Perhaps we can speak later?"

Presidente Gomez smiled broadly at Kathryn, thanked her and said he would look forward to talking, even as Quintaro pushed him gently on the arm toward the guests waiting in the other room. PJ and Kathryn followed the entourage and stood against the back wall.

The Presidente made his way through the crowd, shaking hands with many of the men, taking hugs from the women, a few shouts of "Viva Gomez!" helped him on the way. These were obviously people who supported their Presidente or as Mutea had said, wanted to steal something from him. PJ thought probably a little of both.

Quintaro himself took the podium to begin the proceedings and the crowd quieted down and the TV camera crews bent to their task of videotaping the event.

Quintaro was an experienced and articulate speaker, but after a few moments, PJ got fidgety. He didn't understand a word and never liked lectures, especially from politicians and Quintaro sounded ever bit like the ones PJ had heard, even though his comments were in Spanish.

"Listen for both of us," he whispered to Kathryn. "I'm going outside for some air."

She squeezed his hand and he slipped out the door and walked through the courtyard, passed the two armed soldiers at the door and stepped into the street.

The partying was going strong and a small crowd had gathered around the blue and white helicopter on a small strip of grass between the roadway and the beach. The second chopper was circling somewhere upwind over the water, but PJ could only hear it. He worked his way among the crowd and saw one man standing by the machine. He carried a gun of some kind, slung over his shoulder with a long magazine clip. PJ guessed it was a TEC-9 or a MAC-10, the weapon de jour among drug smugglers.

"She's a beauty!" he said to the man he presumed was the pilot. "Is that the MKII model or the 109K?" PJ had done some reading on the Agusta before coming to Colombia.

"Who wants to know?" came the reply in English. PJ smiled. Most pilots speak the international language of aviation.

"I'm just a fellow pilot. I like planes and helicopters," he said, strolling closer with a friendly face. He looked under the fuselage and at the sweeping tail section. "Looks like the military version, the MKII. Allison or Turbomeca engine?"

The man smiled, keeping an eye on PJ as he moved to the tail rotor section. "You know your helicopters, Señor," the man said.

"I've read a little, flown a few," he lied. He had flown in a few, maybe, but was not checked out as a rotary pilot. He stopped and faced the man. "So, which is it?"

"Turbomeca, Arriel 1 K. It's the export military model. We've adopted it for private use," the man spoke English well.

"It is not the Presidente's transport?" PJ inquired.

"No, owned by QUIMEX, Carlos Quintaro, the shipping boss," the man said, pointing to the small QUIMEX logo just forward of the door. It was a bold "Q" with a long tail that drooped, forming an "I" then finished with an upward sweep with a cross hatch through it, creating an "X".

"Quintaro Import Export. Clever," PJ said. "Can't be too many of these birds around."

"A couple of the oil companies in Venezuela use them, but this one's the only one in this part of the world," the pilot bragged. "Ideal for mountain travel, easy to maintain, works in the jungle. All around basic transport for Colombia."

"GPS?" PJ asked.

"One must have GPS to fly in the mountains," the pilot smiled. "Clouds come out of nowhere!"

"I guess so!" PJ smiled. He glanced inside the cockpit at the pilot's invitation and was impressed with the avionics. It was top shelf.

"Well, thanks for the chat. Got to get back to the party. Got a lady waiting," PJ smiled knowingly at the pilot.

"Lucky you. This is my lady tonight," he said pointing at the Agusta.

"Well, treat her well." PJ waved and waded back through the crowd and into the mansion. He felt a familiar calm. The helicopter was the final piece of the puzzle that convinced him Quintaro was the man who had taken the mine. Certainty brought with it a confidence that showed itself in the bounce of PJ's step. He returned to the party ready for a man-to-man talk with Señor Quintaro.

~~~

CHAPTER TWENTY-ONE

The speeches had ended and the courtyard was again filled with guests and their drinks. Presidente Gomez was the center of attention and a small crowd had formed around him. PJ smiled at Kathryn standing to the Presidente's left. He seemed to be listening intently to her. She gave PJ a wave.

Carlos Quintaro was on the other side of the room, surrounded by three men and the redhead, Gabriela Alvarez. Quintaro listened to Gabriela's chatter, but his eyes were on Kathryn and the Presidente. As PJ watched, Quintaro excused himself from his group and started across the floor toward Kathryn. PJ moved quickly and intercepted him at the center of the courtyard.

"Señor Quintaro, a splendid evening! Thank you for inviting us," PJ said loudly. He shook Quintaro's hand. "You and I should talk. There is some business I believe is of mutual interest to us," he continued, more quietly, grasping Quintaro's hand firmly.

"Yes, Señor McDonough, I had hoped that we could talk tonight. But, would you excuse me for just a moment," and he turned to go. PJ did not let go of his hand, forcing Quintaro to turn back to face him.

"I don't think we can wait any longer, Señor. We should talk right now," PJ said firmly, his eyes challenging Quintaro. PJ was still holding his grip tightly. Quintaro's expression changed.

"Very well, Señor McDonough. If you insist. If you will let go of my hand, I will happily lead you upstairs to my office where we can have some privacy," Quintaro said slowly. PJ released his hand immediately. Quintaro nodded and pointed toward the stairs.

PJ fired a glance at Kathryn, pointed up and she nodded. PJ did not feel any imminent danger, but was glad she knew where he was heading. Then it was up the two flights of stairs to the third floor office of Carlos Quintaro.

At the top of the stairs PJ came face to face with a tall man in a sport coat. PJ recognized him immediately as the one surveying the party from the third floor earlier in the evening.

"It's all right, Rex," Quintaro said from behind. "Mr. McDonough and I are going to have a small chat."

Hearing the name Rex was like a whip cracking in PJ's brain. He remembered the information from Stoney about the renegade DEA agent. At the same time, Simka was equally surprised at hearing PJ's name, realizing one of the loose ends of his plan was standing right in front of him.

Each man scrutinized the other before Simka stepped back with a nod, allowing PJ to enter the office. PJ gave him a small smile. The man called Rex had a stare that suggested any violence this evening would come from him first. PJ suddenly felt less secure than he had at the bottom of the stairs.

It was not much of an office - small, a large desk took up nearly half the space, along with a phone, two chairs and a lamp. There was no window, but PJ took note of a second entrance at the back. Quintaro entered behind him, closing the door, leaving Simka in the hallway.

"You seem to have as many guards as the Presidente," PJ suggested. "Even Americans watch over you."

"I employ many people, Mr. McDonough, of many nationalities. As I told you yesterday, security is required to protect my many interests. Please sit down," Quintaro offered coolly.

"I'd rather stand," PJ answered.

"Suit yourself," Quintaro shrugged and sat down behind the desk. He reached into a drawer and pulled out a bottle of Arguardiente and two glasses.

"Perhaps a drink?" he asked, filling one glass.

"No."

The two of them were silent for a moment. Quintaro took a sip, sat back and looked at PJ, waiting.

"Your guests speak highly of you," PJ smiled. "Yet, all this security seems a bit paranoid for a man with such a respected reputation."

"Call it what you wish, I have the respect of many people. Many powerful friends," he gestured toward the courtyard. "And the envy of many others. Desperate people who want what I have."

"People you have angered by your business practices?" PJ asked, seizing the opportunity. "Angered by *Plata y plomo?*"

"I don't know what you are talking about."

"Oh, come, Carlos. Sure you do. Silver or lead. Do as I say or take a bullet. How about the Miller Mine? Colombia Precious Metals? Murder. Does any of this strike a bell?"

Good, PJ, he thought. Jump in with both feet!

Crew   **249**

"Ha! Mr. McDonough, please!"

"I fail to see the humor, Carlos," PJ pushed on, standing in front of the desk, his gaze holding Quintaro's. "There is no humor in the Valley of Codazzi. In San Francisco Bay. At my home! There is only blood on your hands. I have come to stop you."

"Did you bring an army?" Quintaro laughed. He seemed genuinely amused.

"Two people are dead, Carlos, including my dear friend. I believe you are responsible. There are fifteen Indians missing from the mine. Are you not aware of this?

Quintaro didn't move.

"I'm sure the authorities would be most interested in this darker side of the life of the great citizen Carlos Quintaro!"

Quintaro now stood up behind the desk. He looked at PJ for a long time and smiled, his fists resting on the desktop. A phone rang three times from an office below them before it was answered.

"Is that all? Nothing more?" Quintaro's mocking tone broke the silence.

"Well, I would think murder is pretty serious, Carlos," PJ said, mimicking the mocking tone. He threw his arms wide. "How about kidnapping?"

Quintaro's smile went cold and he stood up abruptly. PJ thought he struck a nerve.

"Who do you think you are, McDonough, coming here, as my guest, and accusing me of heinous crimes?" Quintaro's tone was now indignant. "The authorities, you say? That's very funny! *I* am the authority here, Mr. McDonough."

Quintaro walked out from behind the desk and stood tall, face to face with PJ. "Who would believe such nonsense?"

"I have proof," PJ said defiantly. "Witnesses, documents, I've seen enough myself. The U.S. Government is interested."

He knew he was stretching the truth, but now wasn't the time to be shy.

"Really?" Quintaro was curious. He looked at PJ carefully, then returned to his earlier indignant tone.

"Do you think the U.S. Government concerns me?" he spat. "I am one of the untouchables in Colombia. Your American laws mean little."

"Colombian law also seems unimportant to you," PJ said.

Quintaro took another drink of his Arguardiente. He held his glass, eyeing PJ again, then laughed.

"Do you know what Presidente Gomez said to me tonight? He asked me if I wanted to run for the Senate. 'I would be an easy winner,' he said."

"It appears you have him fooled, too."

"He is a fool. A politician, McDonough. I collect politicians! That is what I told him tonight. And you walk in here with your pitiful threats about the authorities! Ha!"

"Do not underestimate me, Carlos. You may believe you are above the laws of this country, but you are not above me."

"Oh?"

"You may not understand the concept, but justice must be served here. You must pay for your crimes."

"You are either very brave or very stupid, McDonough."

"I admit to being desperate, Carlos. Desperate men can be very stupid and very brave."

PJ raised one eyebrow. He felt very vulnerable; his cards on the table face up. Quintaro held his look for a moment then turned away. He knew at another time, another place, this meeting would have ended in bloodshed. But their meeting was much too public. He realized that is exactly how McDonough had planned it.

He walked behind the desk and refilled his drink. "I am afraid I cannot help, Señor McDonough. I have already wasted too much time with you."

"It is you, isn't it?" PJ asked quietly. PJ realized no respected community leader would turn his back on a foreigner's plight.

"I admit nothing, Señor!" he shouted, slapping the desk again.

"Then you leave me no choice but to pursue this matter until you have been brought to justice."

"Señor McDonough, you have a lot to learn about justice and Carlos Quintaro!"

Three sharp knocks at the door interrupted their standoff.

"Carlos!" came the voice of Rex Simka through the door.

Before Carlos could reach the door, the whine from the starter motor on his helicopter reached their ears. Quintaro look surprised.

"What is that?" he said, knowing full well the sound. He opened the door and stepped to the balcony railing. PJ followed.

"The Presidente is leaving, Carlos," Simka explained, even as Quintaro looked over the balcony.

The party was still going strong, but Presidente Gomez was indeed moving toward the door in the middle of his entourage. PJ could see four helmeted soldiers around him. He could not find Kathryn in the crowd.

"Presidente!" Carlos called down grandly. "Are you leaving so soon?" Aside to PJ he said, "The fool. Doesn't he know it's my helicopter!"

He took to the stairs, bounding down them two at a time, looking much younger than his fifty years. He reached Presidente Gomez's entourage in the street. Great clouds of sand and dirt from the spinning rotors of the Agusta helicopter had scattered the crowd and the swirling air made it difficult to breathe. Quintaro had to shout over the roar.

"Ferdinand! Why are you leaving? We have much to discuss yet!" Quintaro yelled in Gomez's ear.

"Carlos, I have just received a disturbing phone call," Presidente Gomez shouted back. "I must return to Bogota' immediately!" He paused a moment to look at Quintaro, the Presidente's small round face sizing up the taller, white haired man with the distinguished look. Dare he violate a confidence?

He thought of the great help Quintaro had been to him during the last year, especially with his campaign contributions and his seemingly genuine efforts to help the people in the north. He knew of the rumors about this community leader, but he had discounted them. However, tonight he had been given information from two sources that brought the wisdom of his association with Quintaro into question. Still, the man had helped him attain his present office.

He leaned close to Quintaro so his shout would be as confidential as possible under the circumstances. "I received a call tonight from Colonel Cesar. Do not go home, Carlos! I will send the copter back after it drops me at the airport." Before Quintaro could respond, the Presidente stepped into the noisy helicopter with his entourage.

"What do you mean, don't go home?" Quintaro shouted.

The Presidente's face was unmoved as he looked at Quintaro through the cabin window as the copter slowly rose into the sky and turned toward the airport. The second helicopter suddenly appeared, made a low pass over the street and followed the first one. The two quickly disappeared over the buildings and their noise was replaced by the sound of music and Samarios enjoying the all night party.

"Cesar," Quintaro said to himself, understanding slowly coming to him.

"Son of a bitch!" he shouted after the winking red lights. "Cesar," he repeated.

For all the power and control Quintaro and the other self-proclaimed drug lords wielded, the name of Colonel Jesus Cesar brought them to a cold stop.

A No Corromper. The Incorruptible.

Quintaro had never dealt directly with the Colonel, but knew well of Cesar's deeds. As head of the Anti-Narcotics Force, Cesar had been given great powers by the Presidente, even beyond those of DAS. Many thought it was a public relations gesture, but Cesar had created a powerful force that even the Presidente might not control. Julio, the cocaine cook, had told Quintaro of a fiery attack on a jungle lab and the bodies Cesar had ordered burned.

The irony did not escape Quintaro. It was the *Rapidero Fuego* attacks on the jungle labs that had opened the opportunity for Quintaro. Was the cure now the curse? Did Gomez mean that Cesar now suspected Quintaro? Impossible! Quintaro refused to believe it.

"Political problems, Carlos?" came a voice from behind. He turned and looked at PJ leaning against the front entrance to the mansion.

"My problems are small compared to yours, McDonough," Quintaro said calmly with that evil smile that PJ had seen earlier in the evening. "Go home, forget about Colombia and live your life. Live is the key word, Señor."

"I'm not leaving until the Indians have been accounted for and the mine returned," PJ said calmly, his arms folded across his chest. "Justice?"

"You will die first!" Quintaro hissed and poked his finger into PJ's chest with surprising strength. Quintaro's green eyes smoldered in their sockets, and then he strode away into the mansion. PJ followed.

Quintaro went directly to the stairs, motioning to the two men in dark suits. One of them spoke into his radio. Quintaro turned on the stairway and faced PJ one more time. "Go home or die, McDonough!" He turned quickly and climbed the stairs.

PJ watched him for a moment and then scanned the room for Kathryn. She was nowhere to be seen. He spotted Gabriel Alvarez talking with some people and walked over to her.

"Have you seen Kathryn?" PJ interrupted, smiling at the woman.

"Not in five minutes, PJ. I think she went off toward the ladies room," pointing toward the back. "She's a real sweetie, there, PJ. Don't let her get away."

PJ moved quickly to the back rooms of the mansion. No one was in the press conference room. He went down a hallway to the right that led to a side door and a dark alley. He peered into the darkness and saw a dim figure silhouetted in a light at the back of the house, the end of his cigarette glowing amidst a cloud of blue smoke.

PJ tried the other side of the mansion. A hall went to other rooms that had been turned into offices. The hall turned left. As he followed it around the corner, PJ bumped into another guest.

"Oh, excuse me!" the woman laughed.

"Sorry, I wasn't watching!" PJ smiled.

"Please, don't apologize. It was fun," she smiled wickedly.

"Ah, I'm looking for the ladies room?" he said. She gave him a funny look. "For my companion. Dark hair, white dress, ah, coat thing. Have you seen her?"

"Oh, what a lovely girl! You are a lucky one! And so is she!" the woman gushed. "I saw her in there a minute ago, but she left just before me."

"Oh. Thanks. I'll just look around," PJ smiled and wandered deeper into the mansion, walking through a large pantry and then into the well-lit kitchen where four servers were busy talking and preparing food for the guests.

PJ was about to ask if anyone had seen a black haired woman when the sound of Kathryn's voice came through the window.

"PJ!" he heard, followed by a blood-curdling scream.

The four women, looked up, momentarily startled, then began jabbering again with great excitement.

PJ bolted toward the back door of the kitchen, ignoring the shout of one of the women. He pushed open the door and tripped over a garbage can that had been set just outside. He went sprawling down three steps, landing on the gravel and stones in the backyard. His left hand cushioned the fall, but his glove did not protect him from the pain. He scrambled to his feet and heard Kathryn scream again.

"Peee Ja..!"

He felt her terror as the cry was cut short.

He chased the sound along the side of the house, squeezing past a black car parked in the alley. Three men, carrying a white bundle on their shoulders, were running across the street onto the beach. It was Kathryn! Her long black hair and white dress were clearly recognizable. Gunshots rang out and PJ jumped out of the way of another car of revelers. He sprinted across the street and onto the beach. His feet churned in the heavy sand, but he was gaining on the three men.

"Kathryn!" he yelled.

One of the men turned and opened fire with a sub machine gun. PJ saw the movement an instant before the trigger was squeezed and dove onto the sand, rolling to his right. The burst from the gun set off screams on the street as the bullets bounced off trees and the tourist mansion. People hit the ground or ran inside. More screams answered a second burst.

"This is crazy!" PJ said to himself. He rolled farther to his right, then jumped up and resumed the chase. Fortunately, the man with the gun had more than enough to handle with Kathryn's kicking feet. PJ started to close on them again, coming in from the side this time.

The street lights didn't reach to the water's edge, but he could see the three men struggling with Kathryn in silhouette against the distant lights of the Santa Marta docks to the north. They ran into the water with their human package and PJ realized there was a boat just off the beach. He reached the water even as the engine came to life and the men with Kathryn in her white sports coat dress sped away, heading for the lighted docks.

A last burst of the submachine gun sent PJ diving into the shallow water. When he surfaced he could see the dark shape of the speedboat as it made a sweeping turn to the south, away from the docks.

"Kathryn!" PJ screamed in vain. His heart was pounding. And sinking. This was exactly what he feared the most! Soaking wet, he started running back up the beach, cursing himself for confronting Quintaro tonight. A distant siren could be heard. Good, someone called the police, he thought.

As he approached the street, people were picking themselves up. Suddenly, a black Mercedes, the one he had seen on the side of the house, came roaring out into the street. The crowd scattered again as it wheeled away. PJ saw the white-cloaked shoulder of a man in the back seat. He started running after the car and the man turned and looked at him. It was Quintaro.

The Mercedes driver, in his haste to get down the street, didn't see the police motorcycle making the turn a block from the mansion. The white helmeted rider was forced to swerve to avoid the speeding black car and the cycle and rider went flying across the street onto the beach. PJ kept running and came upon the officer, who was stunned, but stirring. PJ made an impulsive decision, but the obvious one.

He righted the bike, a Norton 650, and it started right up. He kicked it down into first gear and let off on the clutch, but it stalled.

"Damn!" he shouted, starting it again. He hadn't been on a motorcycle since he had taken Christina's for a spin. That was two years ago! This time he got it moving, spinning and squirming in the sand until it hit the grass strip and bounded over the curb onto the street. He skidded and swerved as the tires grabbed the pavement, but he kept it under control and concentrated on the red taillights of the Mercedes, a good five blocks ahead of him, but he was quickly gaining ground.

He tried to remember the layout of the streets he had seen during the taxi ride from the airport that afternoon, but came up with nothing. The Mercedes turned left. He was just three blocks behind now and kept the throttle open. He braked hard and made a left also, the taillights still visible ahead.

They came to a merge and PJ remembered the intersection. The airport was to the right, but the Mercedes turned left again, staying on the main street. He accelerated faster out of the turns, and soon he was only two blocks behind, thankful traffic was light away from the beach.

The Mercedes taillights went bright red and turned hard right onto a secondary street. PJ did likewise, just missing another car coming the other way. The Mercedes zigged and zagged down side streets, making a quick left followed by a quick right. Two blocks, then a right, one block, a left, three blocks and another right. PJ stayed right behind. The Mercedes driver could not shake him. At one point, PJ was close enough to clearly see Quintaro in the back seat.

"Quintaro, I'm going to hang you!" he shouted into the wind. The chase continued for several minutes and a familiar calm possessed him. He felt in tune with the gearbox. The throttle became a part of his hand, the power readily at his command. He could feel the tires gripping the roughly paved roads. He knew he was not going to lose the Mercedes, unless they started shooting at him.

Which, of course, they did.

At the first salvo, a long burst from the left hand window, he jammed on the brakes and took a hard left turn, sliding down a side street, then a hard right at the next short block. He accelerated, catching up to them as they passed in front of him on the cross street.

He followed, staying back and staying calm. Four blocks was a safe distance he felt, until they started zigging and zagging again. Then he moved in closer, anticipating their turns, but holding back enough to keep the shooter from getting a good bead on him.

However, after a series of quick lefts and rights, he lost them. They had just gone left and he was only a block behind. He turned left and saw nothing. There were no side streets to turn off, but they were gone! He noticed a stadium of some sort on his right and suddenly headlights appeared directly behind him. He realized, too late, they had pulled into a driveway.

He accelerated, but the Mercedes came roaring up from behind. He thought he heard the sound of gunfire, but the motorcycle's engine was revving at top end and things got very confusing. There was an explosion under him, and a bump.

The motorcycle was suddenly flying through the air, as was he, his right hand still on the throttle. For a moment everything was peaceful. Then the lights went out as he and the bike came down in the street and skittered across rough cobblestones, crashing up on the curb and landing against the wall of a café called Sport.

PJ saw the wall coming and somehow got his legs in front of him so they hit first and took the shock. He remembered feeling the same compression once before. He had been mogul skiing. He had taken a big bump a bit too hard. Like that time, his knees came up, hit his jaw and knocked him out.

Blackness surrounded him. He felt like he was drowning in sand. His brain was awake, but his body was lifeless, a shell, the nerve endings short-circuited by the crash. Maybe he was dreaming. He wondered if he would become a permanent part of the dream if he didn't wake up his body.

"Kathryn!"

He cried out for Kathryn to hit him, to jog him awake, to crack the shell of sleep, to snap his nerves to work. He felt the first grains of blackness reaching his mouth. Soon, he wouldn't be able to yell and that would be the end!

"Kathryn!" he shouted and his eyes opened.

There were several faces around, all of them brown and jabbering in Spanish. He looked up into the eyes of an older gentleman, his face browner than the rest, with white hair cropped short, like moss, on his chin and ears.

"Careful, my friend. Slowly. Don't move yet," the old man said.

"Put this rag on him!" a woman's excited voice called.

PJ felt dampness on his forehead. He started to feel pain in his legs. He was happy to feel anything. He looked at his hands and was surprised they were still working. His glove had protected his left hand and his right hand still held the rubber shield that had covered the motorcycle's throttle.

There was a great deal of pain in his jaw, his legs and back. He tried to get up with the help of the old man and found he could stand, although balance was difficult.

"Where am I?" he asked. About a dozen people had gathered.

"The Mercedes? Did you see the auto?" he started talking fast. "Black car? Which way did it go?"

One teenager pointed toward the stadium, the front gates open across the street. Several people were standing around the motorcycle, which had fared worse than PJ. The front wheel had been dislodged and the rear tire blown out, the rim mangled.

"Where am I?" he asked again and looked at a street sign on the side of the building. *Avenida del Libertador*, it read. He recognized that name. He took a few tentative steps, isolating the worst pain as coming from his backside. It had taken the brunt of his skittering across the street. His pants and jacket were torn.

"I guess I won't be wearing this to any important functions again," he said to himself, looking at the ragged cloth. He was surprised that two people apparently understood and laughed with him.

He walked around in circles and remembered that Barney Devlin was staying at an address on this street. What was the number? Barney had explained Colombian city streets are set in a grid and the address is comprised of two sets of numbers. The first set indicated the nearest cross street and the second set the number of meters the house was actually located from the cross street.

PJ had memorized the address as a year of significance in his life. 19 something. 1981, the last year he was in the Navy! He smiled because his brain was still working.

"19? he asked in Spanish. "Carrera 19?"

One of the young boys pointed along the main boulevard. PJ thanked him and started walking.

"Hey, what about the bike?" the young boy asked.

"Give it to the police," PJ said absently as we walked slowly up the street, his legs still wobbly. He was dazed, but suddenly the anguish hit him. Kathryn's been kidnapped! He cried out, his voice echoing off the stone buildings.

"Kathryn!"

He felt a wave of depression descending and focused on walking, putting one step in front of the other. He had gone only two blocks when he reached Carrera 19. The houses were three-story buildings and he counted 81 steps, which took him to the entrance of the third building.

His head began swimming as he stood in the street. He had no idea which apartment he was looking for. There were no mailboxes or nameplates at the entrance, and no buzzers. Three of the six apartments in front had lights shining in their windows.

An open door led into a tiled hallway to narrow stairs. The placed smelled of dead air and sour milk. He had no choice but to knock on each door. The bottom two did not answer.

He slowly climbed to the second floor and knocked on the back apartments first. A man came to the door of the first one wearing only shorts. A smell of boiled chicken came with him, adding to the other smells in the building.

"*Que?*" the man said, looking suspiciously at PJ's torn clothes.

"Barney Devlin?" PJ asked. The man looked at him blankly, shook his head and closed the door. He tried the second door and no one answered his knocks. A tiny sounding dog yapped with each knock and continued for several seconds.

In front, he remembered the apartment on the left had its light on. He suddenly felt a wave of nausea. The aromas of the building were getting to him. He reached out to support himself. His vision was blurring. He took several deep breaths and then stood upright and knocked on the door of apartment number five.

He knocked a second time and the door opened slowly, revealing a small woman dressed in a white *ruanao*, a Colombian poncho, over white pants, both made from rough cotton weave. Her long black hair spilled onto her shoulders. Her eyes were as black as coal in milk. Her high cheekbones and finely chiseled nose, with full, flared nostrils, slightly upturned, created an exotic look to her face. Her full lips moved toward a smile when she looked at PJ standing there, his white suit dirty and tattered, as if he had been on an all night binge. The flash of her white teeth formed a crooked smile favoring the left side of her beautiful, brown face.

PJ stood aghast, staring at her.

"Yes? Can I help you," she asked in Spanish.

"Kathryn? Kathryn!" PJ could barely get the words out. He could not believe his eyes. It was Kathryn!

"No, Azulmora Nevita. Who are you?" she asked, but never got an answer. PJ fainted onto his knees and fell into her doorway.

~~~

CHAPTER TWENTY-TWO

PJ was in black sand again, but this time he floated effortlessly with Kathryn Byrnie by his side. They were touching, whispering and nuzzling each other, safe in a dark world, their closeness giving them light and warmth. He felt her hands on his back, gently swabbing his pain with a damp cloth. He knew everything was going to be all right.

Then he regained consciousness.

A pillow was stuffed in his face, his nostrils aware of the sweetness of fruit. He still felt the gentle touch of someone cleaning his wounds, but he was definitely awake, his clothes half off. He craned his neck and looked at the woman who had greeted him at the door.

"Kathryn, is that you?" he asked, trying to sit up. It was the woman from his dreams. How could it be Kathryn? Something was not right. Her hair and her clothes were different, but the face!

"Lay still!" she commanded in English, "You're a bloody mess!" Her voice was deep and strong like Kathryn's, but accented.

"Who are you?" he asked.

Her hand held a bloody cloth, and she smiled at his insistence. The identical smile, he thought!

"My name is Azulmora Nevita, Mr. McDonough. I am not this Kathryn you keep calling," she said calmly.

"But, you look..." he started, but didn't finish, dropping his face back to the pillow in confusion.

"PJ, you're awake! Excellent!" boomed a man's voice from the other room. PJ immediately recognized it.

"Barney! Thank God!" PJ exclaimed. "Ouch!"

Azulmora continued to work on the cuts on his back and he gave himself up to her competent hands. His adrenalin was wearing off and pain was replacing it.

"PJ, what the hell happened?" Barney asked, as he set a bowl of hot water and packages of bandages next to Azulmora.

"Kathryn's been kidnapped by Quintaro!" he blurted, trying to remember what had happened in the last hour. He was haunted by Kathryn's muffled cries and the vision of her struggle with the three men.

"You were right, Barney! It was his helicopter you saw at the mine. Quintaro's the one. Now he's taken Kathryn and I chased them, but they took her in a boat, and then they shot up the bike and somehow I found this apartment...and I thought she was Kathryn. Damn it! We've got to get going, Barney! I've got to call Cartegena and the crew!"

Barney and Azulmora just looked at each other, confused by the rush of words.

"Slow down, fellow, take it easy. Azulmora's almost finished," Barney said. "Let's start at the beginning. Who's Kathryn?"

Barney moved to the couch and knelt down, his head at eye level to PJ. They had never met face to face and PJ looked at Barney's distinctive white hair fringing his baldhead, his alert eyes, and his kindly smile. The smile reminded him of Jester.

"Hi, Barney Devlin. Nice to see the face behind the voice. I'm PJ McDonough."

"Hello, PJ. Nice to meet you in the flesh," Barney laughed looking at PJ's exposed derriere. They shook hands.

"Azulmora is my friend. This is her apartment, as you might have guessed. She's an internist, so I can assure you she knows what she is doing."

PJ laughed, craning his neck again to watch Azulmora bandage a deep abrasion on his right buttock.

"Yes, she does," he said.

"We've got a lot to talk about. I've got some interesting news, but you start. What happened? How did you get here?" Barney asked.

"Barney, I confronted Quintaro tonight and everything went to hell! I accused him of Jester's murder and the take over of the mine. I demanded to know the fate of the Indians and..."

"What did he say?" Azulmora interrupted him.

"...he didn't admit to anything," PJ answered. She looked at Barney and then she looked down. Her hands stopped working for a moment and her lip began to tremble. PJ again thought he was looking at Kathryn.

"Azulmora's brother, Eduardo, is the mine super, PJ," Barney explained. "We both know many of the Indians working there. She's been very worried since my experience with Quintaro's marksmen last week."

"You're Eduardo's sister!? That means you're a Kogi Indian!"

"Yes. I am a Kogi," she said through the tears. She slapped a last piece of tape on PJ's bandages. "There, I'm done. You may get dressed now."

"I thought Kogis did not leave the mountains," PJ said, gingerly pulling up his torn pants and pulling down his shirt. He remembered Harold's stories at dinner.

"Blame Barney," Azulmora smiled, wiping the tears. "He opened up our curiosity about the outside world many years ago. Eduardo was the first in our tribe to leave. I followed after my father died. But, I still spend time with my people."

"Azulmora is one of the few sources of medical care in the Sierra Nevadas. The Indian Affairs office supports her trips," Barney added.

"Her family and I go back a long time, PJ," Barney continued. "Azulmora's father saved my life back in the sixties. He nursed me back to health and then showed me the ways of the Kogi, taught me the language and traditions."

"Barney showed me the good of his world, too," she said. "We kind of share everything."

PJ listened, but didn't really hear. He couldn't get over how Azulmora looked like Kathryn.

"Barney, I think I'm dreaming!" He reached for a table lamp and tilted it toward Azulmora.

"You asked who Kathryn is?" he said to them both. "She is Kathryn Byrnie, my friend. She works for Fast Car Caravan. We met about three weeks ago in California. She came to Colombia with the crew. Raised in California, speaks fluent Spanish. She's a pilot, a sailor, resourceful, courageous, stunning..." he laughed.

"I guess I'm kind of in love with her, " he smiled at the revelation.

"Azulmora, Kathryn looks exactly like you! I don't mean she looks a little like you. I mean she looks exactly like you! Long black hair, a little curlier, but the same beautifully black eyes, the same nose, the same lips and the same smile. She looks like your twin! I'm amazed! And very confused."

Azulmora's eyes grew wide as PJ spoke, her mouth opened and she began to shake her head slowly.

"My twin?" she said. "Oh, Barney, can it be?" she spoke the last with intensity, but so softly, PJ didn't understand at first. "I have felt it! I have known the presence in my heart this week, but, it was so distant I could not believe it was real. My dear sister, Zarzamora! My twin! Can it be true?"

She buried her head in Barney's chest and arms.

"Twin?" PJ said. "You have a twin!?" PJ was astonished.

She nodded, the tears renewed in her eyes. "We were separated when we were young. Zarzamora was kidnapped by *marimberos* and I never saw her again."

"Azulmora's mother, Maria, was murdered by a marijuana smuggler," Barney explained. "Zarzamora was snatched away right in front of her sister and brother. They never caught the murderer or the kidnappers. Colombian justice doesn't come to the mountains, or the Kogis."

PJ was unable to think. It was so improbable, but Azulmora's look was identical.

"Kathryn told me that she felt a force drawing her to Colombia," PJ said quietly. "She reacted strongly to a photo of Eduardo and the mountains. Last night, she said she heard the statue of Indio de Catalina in Cartegena speaking to her. I heard nothing, but she was clearly moved by something. What did you say your sister's name was?"

"Zarzamora Nevita," she smiled.

"Zarzamora," PJ repeated. "Oh, my God! That's what Kathryn heard! Oh, man, this is too crazy!"

"My father and brother spoke many times about our sister. I have such little memory of her, but sometimes I feel a part of me is far away, like I am not completely whole." She looked confused, and a little lost.

"When was the last time you spoke to Eduardo?" PJ asked.

"Maybe a month ago. I went with Barney on one of the re-supply missions to check up on the miners," she said. "They were all very healthy. Eduardo took me out on one of those little sailboats." She smiled at the memory.

"There is no sign of the Indians at the mine, PJ," Barney said sadly. He went to a side table and brought back a crudely drawn map for PJ. "I just received this tonight. Two Kogis hiked into the valley right after I was shot at. They moved fast, taking only three days. They saw planes make many landings and takeoffs. They guess forty men or so are there. Maybe a half a dozen actively on guard, a dozen working in the mine at one time, around the clock shifts, plus a several who work on the planes."

The hand drawn map showed the valley and the defensive arrangements.

"It looks pretty secure. Do you think they took Kathryn there?" PJ asked.

"Are you sure it was Quintaro who kidnapped her?" Barney asked.

"Oh, I'm sure. It was his men who took her to the boat. He left by car and I chased him, that's how I ended up here."

"By boat? They could be anywhere, PJ," Barney said.

"But, someplace where Quintaro isn't known, right?" PJ said. "Someplace secure and hard to find, like the mine?"

"It would be suicidal to fly into the valley at night," Barney declared. "Hell, I'm the only pilot I know who has flown in there the last five years, and I sweat it out every time, in broad daylight. Of course, maybe..."

"Maybe what?" PJ urged.

"Well, maybe with night goggles you could land. The trucks at the mine have headlights to light up the runway. But, you'd better have the proper approach co-ordinates or you'll be eating rocks!"

"Could a helicopter do it?"

"Yeah, but it would still be a major risk. First light would be smarter."

"Barney, Quintaro kidnapped Kathryn to stop me from bringing in the authorities, right? He said I had become a nuisance. So, he's got to get a hold of me for the ransom, right?"

"Ransom?" Barney raised his eyebrow. "Maybe he just wants to show you his power. If the man is what we suspect he is, he doesn't need a ransom."

Suddenly, PJ felt very powerless. Barney was right. Quintaro didn't have to do anything. He had Kathryn. Pain shot through the back of PJ's legs as he stood up and started pacing.

"Barney, we've got to move," PJ said. "We've got to find Quintaro, and he'll lead us to Kathryn. And the Indians."

"Maybe he went to his ranch," Barney suggested. "To wait until dawn, then fly into the valley."

"Yes! His ranch. It's well guarded, fenced in. He would think that was safe for awhile," PJ agreed.

"But it may not be, PJ," Barney said slowly. He didn't look pleased. "Colonel Jesus Cesar is going to raid it."

"Cesar! What do you mean?" PJ asked.

"I spoke with him tonight, about an hour ago. That's my other news. I told him about the chemicals you saw," Barney explained. "He said he already knew about it."

"He what?"

"He received a tip earlier in the day. They've already planned a raid. Soon. The way he said 'soon', it wouldn't surprise me if he meant tonight."

"How do you know Cesar?" PJ asked.

"He's my friend in Bogota'. We've had contact over the years."

"I thought he was in the jungle?"

"He is."

"Barney, if Cesar's already on Quintaro's trail, Kathryn will be worthless to him. He'll kill her for sure. Is there any way to stop the attack. Maybe get to Cesar first?"

"I doubt it," Barney said. "When I spoke with him, they were ready to move. Once they plan an attack, they go dark. Even Bogota' doesn't know where he is until it's over.' Barney spread his hands. "PJ, I'm sorry."

"Look, we've got to get to Quintaro first!" PJ decided. "Where's the phone?"

"But, you're not even sure he's at his ranch!" Barney said.

"Damn it, Barney, it's the only place I can think of to start. If he's not there, we'll try the mine. I've got to try something!"

In a moment he had Dutch on the phone from the Cartegena Hilton.

"Dutch, get the crew, it's our turn at bat," PJ said simply.

"What's happened?" he asked.

"A lot. Kathryn's been kidnapped by Quintaro and we have to get her back. I need the crew ready for action at the Santa Marta airport as soon as possible."

"I guess this is what we signed up for," Dutch said.

"It is, Dutch. Tell everyone it will get hairy from here on in," PJ said, wishing there were a better way to do it. "Tell Stoney to bring the C-2 to the east side of the Santa Marta airport, at ALSA freight, and hurry!"

PJ hung up.

"We'll take Azulmora's wagon. She can drive," Barney said and ran into a back room, returning a moment later with a .45 handgun nestled in a shoulder holster under his cracked leather jacket. Azulmora grabbed a large mochila bag, "Medical supplies," she said, and the three of them hurried down the back stairs and piled into a four-wheel drive wagon.

They passed the scene of PJ's motorcycle crash. One police car was there and two officers were taking notes among the crowd.

"Stay down, PJ," Barney hissed as they drove past the flashing blue lights. Fifteen minutes later, they arrived at the Santa Marta Airport.

No one anticipated the scene they found there. A fire truck and a police car were parked in front of the charred remains of what had once been Air Lift South America. Four firemen were folding hoses back onto the truck. The smell of charred wood and gasoline hung in the air like a wet blanket. Barney sat stunned in the front seat of the car and stared.

"I guess they found me," he said softly. His whole life had been inside that building. Azulmora held his arm.

A uniformed policeman came up to the car and Barney stepped out and identified himself. The officer told Barney an explosion and fire had caused the damage shortly after the airport closed at nine. By the time the fire trucks arrived on the scene, the fire had burned through the roof and the adjoining office. Only a portion of the walls and the steel frame of the hanger were left standing.

"*Narcotrafficantes o guerrilleros,*" suggested the policeman.

Barney grabbed a flashlight from the car, and with Azulmora at his side, walked amid the rubble. They stopped next to his destroyed airplane. The right wing had collapsed at the wing root, the metal obviously torn by an explosion. The burned out shell of the fuselage lay at an angle on the concrete, the left wingtip still attached, pointing toward the sky.

"This has to be Quintaro's doing," PJ offered. He looked at Barney. "I'm sorry I got you into this, friend."

Barney said nothing. Only his eyes moved, following the light as it swept the debris.

"What the hell!"

Barney saw what looked like a shoe sticking out from under his rolling toolbox, which had been knocked over. He and PJ moved it.

"Oh, my God!" PJ shouted in disgust.

"I think it's a body," Barney said simply. It was a body, burned beyond recognition. Only the teeth in a partially exposed skull gave an indication it was human. Barney bent down and looked carefully at the remains. He found a charred wallet. Inside he found a badge. The ID card was burned away. "DEA," Barney said grimly, staring at the gold shield that was still intact. The policeman walked up behind them.

"What do you have there?" he asked in Spanish. "Is that evidence?"

Barney handed him the badge.

"This is from an American law enforcement agent," he said to the officer. "It looks like we have a situation here. You had better call your superior."

The policeman rolled his eyes.

"Look at this!" PJ called and held up a second wallet, this one had fared better and the identification card was still readable.

"Deke Hamilton," Barney read. "Also DEA."

"Only one body?" PJ asked.

"Best I can tell," Barney said.

"Do you know him?" PJ asked, trying hard not to get sick. He had never seen death so ugly.

"No, I don't," Barney said. "There are only six DEA in country and Hamilton isn't one of them." He looked at PJ.

"This complicates things, doesn't it?" PJ asked.

"You bet it does. This place will be crawling with U.S. officials, probably within the hour. The closest DEA office is thirty miles away in Barranquilla. If we can tie this to Quintaro, you might be able to get more official help."

"But, anything official is probably going to be at least a day away or more," PJ interjected. "Reports, decisions, bullshit, the government norm, you know."

"We don't have any time," Barney admitted softly. "And you know there is no government agency that is going to give you the okay to fly into a hornet's nest with your own commando squad," Barney smiled.

"So, we go as soon as the crew gets here," PJ said.

"I'm ready, PJ, more than ever," Barney said firmly. They walked out of the wreckage and back to Azulmora's car. In a few moments they agreed on the tactical plan PJ had been working on since the moment he decided to come to Colombia. He drew several maps of the Quintaro ranch from memory and made notes on each team member's assignment.

The C-2 Greyhound arrived half an hour later, just after midnight, Friday morning. Though the airport was officially closed, the blue runway lights were on and Stoney had no trouble landing. PJ and Barney intercepted the plane at the end of the runway, keeping them away from the activity around the ALSA hangar, where a police sergeant from Santa Marta had joined the lone policeman. The firemen had left, but more officials were on the way.

Barney was more than a little surprised when he saw the Navy plane.

He watched the crew as they filed out, dressed in Army camouflage fatigues, Israeli lightweight packs, Russian weapons slung on their shoulders, headsets and mikes for communication around their necks, and GPS receivers, no bigger than a paperback novel, strapped to their equipment vests. They had already blackened their faces.

"Who are these people?" he asked PJ.

"My sailboat crew," PJ answered matter of factly.

"That must be one hell of a sailboat!" Barney said, shaking his head in disbelief at the fearsome looking unit in battle dress.

"Is there a coffee shop open nearby?" Lenny asked as he stepped out of the plane and shook PJ's hand.

"Sorry, Len, it just closed," PJ said with a grim smile. That was the extent of the levity. The crew seemed nervous. The appearance of Azulmora surprised everyone and PJ did the introductions and a quick explanation. The mood stayed serious as PJ explained one man was already dead in the bombing of Barney's hangar.

"He was DEA," PJ told the assembled group under the wing of the Greyhound. "I don't know if he was fighting the same fight. But, this place is about to become a magnet for U.S. officials. We have to move quickly. There is no time to enlist help. Frankly, when word leaks out we are on the loose in Colombia, it isn't help they are going to give us. That means we have to do it ourselves."

"What else is new?" Dutch laughed. There were grunts of agreement. "Stoney, next stop is Riohacha."

In ten minutes both the G-2 and Starship were airborne, PJ falling in behind Stoney, flying 200 feet above the water, about 300 yards behind. It was a moonless night, but he could plainly see the lights on Stoney's wings. Inside both planes it was quiet as each crewmember went over their assignments and mentally prepared for what was to come.

~~~

CHAPTER TWENTY-THREE

PJ would rather have plotted wind and course for a sailboat race than make tactical decisions about a commando raid, but felt as comfortable as he could with their final plan. They certainly had the equipment to get the job done. He just didn't know how everyone would react under fire.

It was decided their main goal would be reconnaissance. A frontal assault on the Quintaro ranch was dismissed by PJ as too dangerous. That prompted a laugh from Lenny.

"Which part of this isn't going to be too dangerous?" he had said. PJ had just nodded.

By 2:05 in the morning, the two planes had landed at the deserted *Allmarante Padilla* airport on the outskirts of Riohacha and the crew had assembled in their combat gear. The camouflage paint seemed to emphasize the grim looks on their faces.

"I sure wouldn't want to be racing against you folks. You look pretty mean," PJ said.

"Hey, PJ, this is how I always look," Lenny snorted. "Mean, clean, fighting machine. 170 pounds of blood, guts and hate."

"More like 200 pounds," Dutch said with a grin and everyone laughed uneasily. Except Stoney. He seemed in a tense mood.

"Everyone knows their assignment. Be smart, cover your buddy, shoot defensively, and pray we can pull this off," Stoney spoke firmly..

"I know Kathryn is counting on us," PJ added. "No one else is going to get it done," he said, searching for the right words to say to the friends he was sending off to possible death

"What else is new?" Mickey said.

"Let's do it!" Dutch shouted, raising his rifle in the air. A chorus of guttural sounds followed and PJ smiled, hearing the same sounds he heard before the start of every sailboat race. He wished it were that simple. He watched Dave and Christina, then Barney and Azulmora share a hug and kiss. Dutch made a joke of it and gave Stoney a bear hug, too.

PJ split the crew into three ground teams and an airborne team. The ground teams planned to infiltrate the ranch from three different directions and search for Kathryn. Stoney would pilot the C-2, with Azulmora, Dave and the grenade launcher on board. They would provide aerial firepower and a quick escape route for the crew, if needed.

With a final wave, the ground teams climbed into a pickup truck that Stoney hot wired from the terminal maintenance garage and drove away.

The small, dusty town of Riohacha appeared deserted except for a few late-night drinkers still enjoying the music at a corner tavern. Three people huddled in front of the building barely glanced at the truck as it noisily rolled past. The main road was the only way to the ranch. It was also the only way to the Guajira Peninsula, a barren desert that few people traveled, making it a haven for smugglers and rogues of all types. PJ hoped a noisy pickup wouldn't arouse suspicions.

Soon they were out of town, Barney driving at a sensible speed. It was dark, only the dim headlights of the truck lighting the way. Just before a sharp right hand turn, he slowed and pulled to the side. Barney and PJ jumped out, and Lenny slid into the driver's seat.

"Don't forget, get to first positions and then wait for my signal," PJ whispered. "We should be in place in thirty minutes."

"Good luck," Lenny said seriously.

"You, too," PJ answered. "Boy, this is going to make some story, eh, Mickey?"

"Great pictures, too!" Mickey whispered from the back of the pickup. But PJ was already gone. He and Barney jogged across the paved roadway and into the bushes on the far side, heading for the shoreline just 200 yards from the road.

"Okay, everyone, down low, it's show time," Lenny called to the four in back and slipped the clutch, pulling back onto the roadway. As they made the right hand turn, Lenny could see a chain link fence start on the left side of the road. He estimated it was about eight feet high, with a barbed wire extension on top, well overgrown with vines and bushes and frequent trees planted just inside the metal barrier.

A half-mile farther the chain link fence turned into a stone wall and soon an archway appeared with two large metal gates at the main entrance to the Quintaro compound. Lenny snuck a glance as he drove by, spotting a guard standing in front of the gate smoking a cigarette, a machine pistol slung over his shoulder.

The hair on his neck prickled and moisture suddenly appeared on his upper lip, but he kept on driving, expected a fusillade of bullets to pepper the truck any second. Nothing happened and the fence angled away from the road, replaced by dense jungle overgrowth.

He drove another mile to a narrow dirt road on the left that disappeared in a grove of trees. He doused the lights and slowly turned, the truck immediately falling into deep ruts, the kind made by heavy truck traffic. He drove only fifty yards before pulling off the path, and coming to a halt in the deep underbrush.

"End of the line," he whispered to everyone in back and they jumped out. He pressed the radio transmit switch on his belt and whispered into the microphone suspended from his earpiece.

"Lenny radio check."

"Dutch check. Sound good," Dutch answered. The others followed suit.

"PJ check, hear you fine," came PJ's slightly out of breath voice over the headsets.

"Sky Blue team check, you all sound fine," came Stoney's voice. "We are airborne."

"Dutch and Lenny teams moving out," Lenny radioed.

Both teams moved swiftly along the rutted path, and had gone just over a mile when they realized the perimeter fence was again to their left.

Lenny held up his hand and the five huddled together. No one spoke. It was time to split up. It was dark, but they all exchanged glances and pats on the shoulder, silently wishing each other good luck.

Then Dutch, carrying the machine gun, and Mickey, with extra ammo, continued along the road to their designated position another mile ahead near the rear entrance.

Lenny, Ray and Christina bent down by the fence and examined it for hidden wires that would indicate some kind of an electric alarm system. They covered two twenty-foot sections and couldn't find anything to make them believe it was anything more than a chain link fence with barbed wire on top.

Lenny tapped Christina and she removed a poncho from her pack. Ray used his six-five height to throw the poncho over the top of the barbed wire. The fence was only eight feet high, but the barbed wire extended outward another two feet. Christina pulled a kevlar rope from her pack and this was thrown over the poncho and down the other side of the fence, then pulled taut through the fence, the two ends tied together and secured on the fence. It provided a handhold as the three climbed up the fence and over the barbed wire with little difficulty, the poncho helping protect their bodies from the barbs.

Lenny was last over and had trouble removing the poncho, which had become entangled in the sharp wire. He was balanced on the top of the fence struggling with the reluctant nylon when all three heard a motor coming their way from inside the fence.

Christina ran to the fence and untied the rope, pulling it through. Lenny was still struggling with the poncho when a pair of headlights appeared in the distance.

"Hurry up!" Ray hissed to Lenny, but it was too late. He and Christina jumped into the bushes just as the headlights reached their location. Lenny sat frozen on top of the fence as the vehicle approached.

He reached for the pistol on his hip, slipping it quietly from the holster. He fumbled for a moment for the safety, but found it and clicked it off, his whole body tensed while he balanced in his delicate position. He could hear voices above the sound of the motor. His upper lip was wet again.

The headlights bathed the ground below him and the vehicle, an open jeep, rolled past at about ten miles an hour, the two men inside talking earnestly, their words often overlapping. Lenny could see their hands moving as they talked, passing not four feet below him. So engrossed were they in their conversation, the two men never even looked at the fence.

He dared not move until they were out of sight. He counted an additional thirty seconds before he made one last attempt at freeing the poncho and succeeded by ripping it, leaving a two by two foot swatch on the wire. He dropped to the ground, his clothes damp with sweat, and crossed the road to join Ray and Christina. Christina rolled up the poncho, realized it was ripped, and showed it to Lenny.

"That was too close!" Lenny whispered excitedly to her. "I'm not going back for the rest!" Then he keyed his mike.

"Dutch, this is Len. Jeep patrol coming your way."

Two clicks were heard in answer. That was the agreed upon signal that meant, "Understand. Can't talk." Lenny figured the jeep might be right in front of Dutch and Mickey.

A few moments later, Dutch's voice came on the radio.

"Dutch here. Jeep is gone. Two men. We're still half a mile from position one."

Lenny gave him a double click and realized he still had his gun drawn. He put it away. He knew he had been ready to use it.

"I bet you never tried to get so small!" Christina joked with Lenny. For the first time since she had known Lenny, he didn't have a comeback.

"Let's go, we've got some ground to cover," was all he said and they moved off through the line of trees and brush in a westerly direction. After about 400 yards of dense undergrowth, they broke into a clearing. In the distance, above the sparsely planted trees, they could see the glow of lights.

Lenny pulled out his GPS receiver and punched in some numbers. The dim glow from the liquid crystal display went blank and then a series of new numbers appeared, displaying the distance and direction to their target, the guard's sleeping quarters in the middle of the ranch complex.

"Seven-tenths of a mile, sports fans. About fourteen football fields that way," he pointed westerly to the left of the lights. "Those lights must be coming from the airstrip and hangars."

"What's that?" Ray asked, looking off to their right where something long and narrow was silhouetted against the glow. They walked up to it and discovered a ball cleaner, like you might find on a golf course.

"Did you bring your clubs, Ray?" Lenny joked. PJ had told them there would be a golf course on the east end of the ranch. Christina giggled, glad Lenny was joking again and they moved on. The ground was clear and flat, and they move swiftly through the darkness.

They crossed the golf course and were back among the bushes and trees. They found good cover on the other side of a road and moved closer to lights visible through the foliage. Soon, they had a good view of the two buildings that PJ suspected housed the guards and workers on the ranch.

The lights came from over each entrance. The buildings were stone, two stories, tiled roofs and simple entrances. Lenny counted the windows and guessed there were eight rooms in each building. The biggest problem was the lighted area in front of the buildings, which would expose them as soon as they made their move.

"Looks like they can sleep lots of people," Ray suggested dryly.

"More than three," Lenny added. He felt that prickly feeling on his neck again. He looked at his watch. It was 2:45.

"Lenny team in place," he whispered into his mike. "Quiet here."

"Lenny, this Dutch. We're in place, too. One guard on the back gate. Also quiet."

There was a collective sigh of relief. Lenny, Ray and Christina fanned out like clock hands, each lying at an angle to the other so they could cover a 360 degree view from their location. Then they waited for PJ's signal.

PJ and Barney were having a rough time. The rocky coastline made for slow going as they climbed over slippery boulders and struggled through sand and surf to cover the mile to their position. PJ was numb, placing one foot in front of the other, his legs yelling at him to stop, his breath a steady pant.

Barney, fifteen years older than PJ, was doing worse and on more than one occasion, PJ had to stop and wait for his partner.

"You okay?" PJ gasped, looking behind him at Barney maneuvering over a wet boulder. He nodded yes, saving his breath. Both of them were soaked from the waist down from the steady pounding of the surf. The waves were small, but continuous. Their sound gave a rhythm to PJ's movement, their crashing as endless as the number of steps he seemed to be taking.

He thought about Kathryn, hoping each step would bring him closer to her. He knew he loved her and was ready to kill to get her back. He hoped it wouldn't come to that. He thought about Azulmora and the amazing possibility that the two were sisters. And about Quintaro. Was he the man who had torn their family apart?

He looked up the sharp slope that led from the water to ground level at the ranch, about 20 feet over their heads. He could see the glow of lights that came from the main house. The glow ahead he surmised came from the hangar area. His GPS showed 300 yards before they reached the agreed point where they would be able to scan the airstrip. Barney stopped next to him, breathing heavily, bending at the knees.

"Been a long time, my friend, since I had to pull a stunt like this," he said between gasps. "Too long, actually."

"I think I gave us the toughest assignment," PJ laughed quietly. He was also feeling the effects of the trek.

"300 more yards then we go up," he said and slipped the GPS back in his vest pocket. "Ready?"

Barney pushed him forward and they continued, the water up around their boots, sometimes to their knees, as they scrambled over rocks and tromped through sandy sections, eventually reaching their destination.

PJ started to climb upward, looking for handholds on the rocks. He guessed it was a sixty percent grade, steeper than San Francisco's Lombard Street he thought. The water had smoothed the rocks over the centuries, but grasses, weeds and small plants grew in-between and provided handholds. He stopped a few feet below the edge of the grassy field that separated the main house from the airstrip. Barney joined him a several moments later, happily flopping down next to PJ.

PJ pulled out the night binoculars from his pack and peered over the lip of the slope, half his head exposed. They were right at the end of the runway, the nearest blue light only sixty feet away. Suddenly, a pair of headlights turned right at PJ, only 100 yards away. He ducked back below the edge and hoped he hadn't been seen. The motor approached, but didn't stop and continued to the right toward the main house. He peered over the lip again, watching the red taillights moving into the grove of orange trees.

Beyond the trees, lights shone in two upstairs rooms of the house and a light came from another building immediately to the left. He focused the binoculars on the lighted windows but did not detect any movement. He could see clearly into the open second floor doorway. From his low angle, he could only see the walls of the room. They appeared to be covered with knives and swords.

PJ swung the binoculars to the airstrip and let out a soft whistle. A four engine jet cargo plane sat on the tarmac surrounded by activity. He watched as two forklifts removed pallets of boxes and carried them into the nearby hangar. PJ counted three armed men by the plane. Three others helped load the fork-lifts, at least one other appeared inside the plane and two rotund men stood off to the side.

One he recognized as Garcia, the chief security guard at the ranch. He didn't recognize the other, a man twice the size of Garcia. Closer to him was another guard, standing by the small shack near the road that led from the airfield to the main house.

Scanning the rest of the field he saw a dim light from the guard tower. Only one man there. He looked at the plane again, trying to read the insignia under the tail section. He slid back down under the edge where Barney was resting on his back.

"Red dot, white ring, red ring?" he asked Barney softly.

"Peruvian Air Force usually displays the white on red target," Barney answered immediately. "Where is it?"

"On a jet cargo plane a dozen men are unloading right now, looks like one of those British Aerospace jets, a 146," PJ said.

"We've caught them in the act!" Barney said excitedly, trying to hold his voice down. "Most of the cocaine paste in the world comes from Peru, or Bolivia. What exactly are they unloading."

"Boxes on pallets. I'm sure it's not carnations." PJ said. PJ looked at his watch. It was 2:55. He and Barney were ten minutes late reporting.

"Lenny, this is PJ, do you copy?" PJ spoke softly into the mike. He waited a few seconds then repeated the call.

"PJ, Lenny here. You okay?"

"Roger, Len. We're in position. Dutch, you copy?"

"Dutch here, reading you fine. Very quiet out back."

"Same here, PJ. Perimeter patrol with two guards only thing we've seen. In a jeep."

"Roger that, Lenny. I saw them also. They might be coming your way shortly. Everyone hold positions for a moment. We have a dozen men unloading a plane on airstrip."

PJ looked at Barney.

"No sign of Quintaro's chopper. I'd sure like to get a look in the house," PJ said.

"Is there something we can do about the jet? Maybe get closer to see what they're unloading," Barney asked.

"Barney, we're first concerned about Kathryn, right?" PJ said firmly.

"Right, I just thought we are so close, this is the kind of evidence that could bring down Quintaro's whole operation. Oh, man, if Peru is involved...." He let it trail off, realizing now wasn't the time.

"Lenny, this is PJ."

Two clicks answered.

"PJ, this is Lenny," crackled in everyone's ear about three minutes later. "Patrol just passed us."

"Good. Lenny, go to second positions. Lenny team only. Dutch hold."

"Roger, PJ. Second positions. Lenny out."

"Roger, Dutch holding."

"Barney, let's move up closer to the house. That orange grove will give us some cover," PJ whispered.

"OK, PJ. Lead the way."

"This is PJ, we are going into the main house," he announced over the radio.

Two clicks came from Dutch and Lenny's radios.

PJ unstrapped his AK-74 that had been secured across his back, and looked at the guard tower about three-tenths of a mile away. He couldn't see the guard. He crawled over the top of the slope anyway and started moving in a running crouch for the trees about fifty yards to his right. He moved inland first about twenty yards and then turned toward the trees. For someone watching from a distance, his silhouette would be harder to see against the grass rather than a moonless sky filled with stars.

Barney followed, angling inland about twenty steps behind PJ. His feet felt rejuvenated on the smooth grassy field after the struggle in the sand and rocks. They made cover in a matter of seconds and moved to within 100 feet of the stairs heading to the porch, just outside the throw of light from the spotlights that lit up the immediate grounds around the house.

They sat for a few minutes and then PJ gestured with his hand that he would go up the back stairs, and Barney should cover. He moved to the edge of the trees and then sprinted to the shadows under the porch. Barney moved to his left to get a clearer view of the stairs, his rifle at the ready.

PJ wasted no time and quickly ascended to the second floor porch where Quintaro and Kathryn had sat and talked just the other day. Pressed against the outer wall, he had a good view of the entire room and saw no one. He stood very still. His heartbeat pounded in his ears as he poised at the opening. Then he moved inside quickly, his rifle out in front. He saw a room to the right and went to the door. It was dark inside. He heard nothing but the distant hum, as if a generator were running somewhere outside.

He unclipped his flashlight, gripping it firmly in his hand. Counting to three, he ducked into the room, crouched low, the light held high in his left hand, pointed in front of him, the rifle in his right aimed at the circle of light. It was an office, with a desk and file cabinets, but there was no one in it.

Staying low, he moved back into the main room and to the far door. He paused for only a moment to look at the collection of knives and swords that he had seen through the binoculars earlier. He had to force himself away, it was so extensive and impressive. Crossing to the far door, he found himself in the hallway at the top of stairs. He searched two more rooms on the second floor and found only empty bedrooms.

One room was larger than the other with a view toward the water. A canopy hung over a king size bed and PJ thought it must be Quintaro's room. He moved his light over the furniture, and along the floor.

The phone was a complicated looking piece of electronics, with multicolored buttons and lights, but what looked like only one line. It was attached to a black box under the nightstand, probably a scrambler thought PJ.

He bent down under the bed and his light reflected on something shiny. He froze as he realized it was one of the gold earrings that Kathryn had worn at the party. So, they had come to the ranch! Were they still here? He grabbed it, inspecting it carefully. He noticed the slightest stain of blood on the alligator's head.

"PJ, this is Barney. We have company." Barney's whisper over the radio interrupted his thoughts.

A pair of headlights had appeared suddenly around the side of the house. Barney had not heard the vehicle coming. He crouched low among the trees as the lights swung over his position, and the jeep stopped at the bottom of the stairs.

"One male. PJ, he's heading right for you! Get out!"

"Roger, Barney. I'm on the second floor in Quintaro's bedroom. I've found an earring of Kathryn's. They were here, maybe still are!" PJ's heart was pounding. Barney answered with two clicks. PJ still had no idea where Kathryn could be. He snapped off his flashlight and decided to stay in the room near the door.

"PJ, Lenny here," came the call over the radio. 'Building One secure. A male and female are in custody, I think it's the maid and the cook." He sounded a little disappointed, PJ thought.

"We're going into Building Two," Lenny said.

Lenny's team had encountered no problems in the first building. They moved inside and had conducted a room-by-room search. Christina covered their backs while Lenny ducked into each room, Ray close behind, each one covering half the room.

The first two rooms had revealed only empty beds, but in the third room they found the man and woman. For an instant, their sleeping forms in the light of two flashlights startled Lenny, but Ray moved quickly to the bed as the man woke up to see a rifle barrel pointed six inches from his startled face.

"*Silencio si no muerte!*" Ray hissed to the man, pronouncing it as best he remembered after Barney's brief Spanish lesson. The man nodded his head, clearly believing silence was better than death. The woman awoke then and let out a cry. Ray repeated his threat and she also nodded, a terrified look on her face.

Ray bound their hands with plastic ties and taped their mouths. He finished the job by tying their legs to the bed.

"I don't think these are guards," Lenny said to Ray.

"But they're not with us," Ray answered.

The upper floor was living quarters for six people in open barracks style, the beds against the walls. They found no one there.

The second building was laid out slightly differently. The downstairs had a large kitchen, dinning room and sitting room, complete with television. Upstairs was another open sleeping area with eight bunks, but again there was no one there.

"Building Two secure, PJ. No one here," Lenny spoke into his mike.

Two clicks came back.

"Crash, watch the front, Ray, the back," Lenny ordered and pulled out his GPS to check the distance and direction to their next position.

Meanwhile, on the north end of the ranch, fifty yards from the rear entrance guard shack, Dutch and Mickey waited patiently in the dense undergrowth for their turn to move. Mickey was particularly nervous about snakes and had spread out his poncho under him, his knife drawn, anxiously listening for any rustling in the grass. Except for the passing of the patrol jeep, it had been quiet. Dutch timed the jeep at seventeen minutes to complete a full circuit of the grounds.

However, they now head a louder motor coming along the outside road and soon a tractor-trailer appeared, pulling a ship container. It rolled up to the guard shack and the driver leaned out and handed a piece of material to the guard. Dutch couldn't quite make it out at first through the binoculars, but in shifting for a better look, he put his hand down on Mickey's poncho. Then he knew.

"It's a piece of poncho!" he said softly to Mickey.

"What is?" Mickey asked.

"That piece of cloth the driver gave the guard. It's part of a poncho! Damn!"

"Dutch here. Anyone lost a poncho?" he radioed.

"Just a piece hung up on the fence," came back Lenny's reply after a pause.

"Well, we got a truck at the back gate and I think the driver found it. Stay alert. It may hit the fan," Dutch replied.

"PJ, you copy?" Dutch called.

PJ heard but dared not move, even to click his radio transmitter button. He had followed the man who entered the main house down to the first floor and then to a small basement where he now crouched just outside of a room.

He could hear voices, static, and computer noises. He knew he couldn't turn back now. He wished Barney was with him for backup, but there was no time. The man could leave the room any second and PJ would be exposed. He decided to make the first move.

His nervous fear was quickly replaced by a sense of confidence, strength and aggression, the way he felt when dicing it out on the starting line with a couple of fifty-foot sailboats in close quarters, confident he could make the reactions necessary to avoid a collision and take the advantage.

He had a sudden flashback to the wisps of clouds that had hovered over the Golden Gate Bridge the afternoon Jester had been killed and he wounded. A sudden vision appeared, a flying object just in front of his eye. Like a freeze frame, the moving pictures in his mind stopped with a bullet fragment squarely in front of his eye, its crushed form a crystal clear piece of art and then he knew he had moved, maybe only a centimeter, but enough for the bullet to graze his forehead. In a millisecond, these thoughts filled his head and were gone. He leaped into the room.

The man was packing stacks of money into a box on a long table. The sudden intrusion of a man dressed in combat gear with an assault rifle pointed squarely at his eyes completely startled him. He didn't even think about reaching for the pistol that was uselessly sitting on the other side of the table. He merely put up his hands, both filled with a thick packet of one hundred dollar bills.

"*Silencio si no muerte!*" PJ hissed in his meanest, deepest voice. The man nodded. PJ motioned him away from the table, still holding the money.

"*Dejar!*" he commanded, telling him to lay down. The man did so, falling to his stomach. PJ took the pistol, a .9 mm, from the table, and slid it across the floor to the back of the room.

He laid his rifle on the table and pulled his own .45 pistol from its belt holster. He moved behind the man, placing the barrel of the gun against the man's cheek, while placing his knee squarely and forcefully in the man's back.

"*Silencio si no muerte!*" he repeated then tucked his gun in his belt, secured the man's hands and feet with a plastic tie, rolled him over and sat him against the wall.

"Comfortable?" PJ asked, crouched down in front of the man so they were eye to eye. The man just looked at him.

"You speak English?" PJ asked. The man nodded.

"What is your name?" PJ asked, sizing him up. He was small, with a thin mustache. His shirt, pants and shoes looked expensive and he wore three rings, all with large stones.

"Bernardo," the man answered.

"Bernardo Quintaro?" PJ asked surprised.

The man nodded.

"Where is your brother, Carlos?" PJ asked calmly.

The man said nothing.

"Come on, Bernardo, where's Carlos and Kathryn?"

"Are you McDonough?" Bernardo asked.

"That's right, Bernardo, I'm PJ McDonough and your brother has really pissed me off. I am ready to knock the *chipchippi* out of you if you don't answer my questions!" PJ finished by grabbing Bernardo's expensive shirt by the collar and lifting him off the ground so their faces were only inches apart. PJ put on his steeliest face, his blue eyes opened wide and his mouth showing teeth. Bernardo said nothing and PJ let him fall back to the floor.

PJ stood up and looked around. He was in a command center of sorts, with tables of radio and computer equipment on one side, and the table full of money standing in front of a walk-in vault built into the wall.

He walked over to one of the computers and tapped a few keys. With a few keystrokes he found a list of directories and files that seemed to cover a wide range of activities, all sorted by country.

Next to the computer workspace were several radios stacked together, tuned to different frequencies. There were two fax machines, a single side band radio, a phone with a scrambler box like PJ had seen in Quintaro's bedroom and three more computer screens, each one displaying a map graphic. One of the United States, the second showed the Caribbean from Florida to Colombia and the third was of Colombia itself. Various numbers appeared over the maps. Sitting on a shelf above and connected to the three screens was a large black box with the name METOTRAK emblazoned on the side. PJ recognized the brand.

"More company, PJ," his headsets crackled. It was Barney.

"Go ahead, Barney," PJ answered. He looked at his watch. He had been inside almost five minutes.

"Jeep pulling up to side. I'm moving closer," Barney replied.

PJ looked at Bernardo and decided it was best to tape his mouth shut.

"Where's Carlos?" he asked once again. Again no answer. Bernardo just looked at PJ, his eyes wide in fear. PJ pulled a strip of gaffer's tape from the roll in his pack and slapped it roughly over Bernardo's mouth.

"You will talk, Bernardo, or you will die!" PJ threatened him, although he didn't believe it himself. He wasn't about to torture anyone for information.

He dragged Bernardo by the back of his shirt into the vault, momentarily amazed at the amount of cash around him. Boxes of it, all wrapped and stacked neatly. Several millions he thought. Two counting machines stood in the middle of the room.

He left Bernardo with the money and stepped back into the room. He only had time to pick up his rifle and look around for a hiding spot, thinking behind the computers might work, when Garcia stepped into the room.

For a split second, PJ thought about raising his rifle to fire, but then he thought better of it. Garcia didn't say a word, but his pistol was aimed right at PJ's head and he knew any move would mean instant death. He was surprised Garcia hadn't fired already.

"McDonough, drop the rifle!" Garcia commanded in English.

PJ complied, the AK-74 clattering noisily on the floor.

"Hands up!" Garcia ordered sharply, now only four feet away. PJ, his hands at his side, reached for his belt as he brought his hands up, pressing his radio mike button to transmit.

"Garcia, I see you found me. I was just looking for someplace to take a pee," PJ said, hoping everyone was listening and hoping they could still hear him despite standing in the doorway to the vault.

Garcia stepped forward and took a backhanded swipe at PJ with the pistol, the barrel coming right for PJ's head.

"You stupid American!" he spat, his face angered by PJ's mockery.

PJ blocked the gun with his right arm and kicked hard at Garcia's belly with his right foot. His left hand joined his right on Garcia's wrist and he slammed the gun as hard as he could against the open vault door. The pistol dropped to the floor and went off, sending a bullet into the vault.

Garcia recovered from the boot in the gut and landed a solid left on PJ's chin, the impact sending white flashes through PJ's brain and knocking him back, his radio headset torn from his head. Garcia pinned PJ against the wall, driving his shoulder into PJ's mid-section, knocking the wind from him. Garcia pressed the attack, with short punches from his meaty hands to PJ's stomach and groin.

PJ found a shred of energy and kneed Garcia in his own groin several times, causing him to fall backward over the table. It collapsed and the money Bernardo had been neatly packing went flying. PJ was stunned and gasping for air. Garcia's shoulder had taken its toll on him. Garcia was himself in pain, writhing on the busted up table and money.

Garcia rolled to his left, struggling to his hands and knees and found his gun where it had fallen near the vault door. A smile came to his face as he raised up to fire. PJ was bent over and saw the gun in Garcia's hand. He sprang toward Garcia, hoping to hit him low, when a shot rang out and Garcia's face froze in a wicked smile, the gun dropped from his hand and the burly man's body crumpled just as PJ tackled him.

Barney Devlin stood in the doorway to the room, his .45 propped against the doorjamb, the barrel smoking in the dim light.

"PJ, don't you know not to go into strange rooms without proper cover?" Barney said straight-faced.

PJ was stunned, his gut hurt, but he managed a smile for Barney as he rolled off the dead body of Garcia.

"I knew you'd be there. Thanks, Barney. I owe you one."

"Hell, you'll owe me a few more if we get out of here alive. Let's move! We got to get outta here now!" Barney bent down and unhooked Garcia's walkie-talkie and turned up the volume. The radio was alive with chatter in Spanish. Barney and PJ exchanged glances.

"Do we go with the Exit Plan?" PJ asked Barney.

"What else do we have. No Kathryn. This place will be crawling with Colombians in a minute," answered Barney.

PJ reached inside his vest and pulled out his radio. The headset was useless and he disconnected the belt switch, using the hand switch on the side to transmit.

"All teams, this is PJ. Go with the Exit Plan. Repeat. Go with the Exit Plan immediately. Be ready to take fire. It will probably center on the main house first. Barney and I are okay. Rendezvous at the south end of the airstrip. Do you copy?"

"Roger, PJ. This is Dutch. We're going to Exit Plan."

"PJ, this is Lenny. We already have company, two jeeps moving toward main house. We'll try and stop them. See you on the airstrip."

"Hey, guys, Sky Blue is on her way!" came Stoney's voice from the Greyhound. He sounded delighted to get into the action.

In the basement, PJ and Barney were deep in conversation.

"Barney, give me two minutes. This is the heart of Quintaro's operation, his records, a tracking system for his planes and ships!" PJ moved to the three computer screens, trying a few keystrokes to get information from it. "I know this METOTRAK system. It uses backscatter signals bounced off meteor showers to keep track of boats, planes, cars...his whole set up is right here!"

"PJ, you don't have two seconds. We're going to have to shoot our way out already. Forget that and think about saving yourself. You can't find Kathryn if you're dead!"

PJ looked at Barney and realized his friend was saying just what he had said a few moments ago. He grabbed his rifle. He took one last look at the screen with the map of Colombia. He was sure one of the numbers on the display was coming from a transmitter on Quintaro's helicopter. Barney slapped him on the arm and went into the hall. Already they could hear footsteps from above.

Bernardo! He had forgotten completely about Bernardo in the vault but the sound of Barney's rifle opening fire right outside the room refocused his attention. He moved to the door, where Barney was at the side of the stairs, two bodies at his feet. He started climbing, and PJ moved quickly into a covering position.

They got to the ground floor and quickly through the main hallway and out the front door. Headlights were coming from two different directions. PJ could hear gunshots from Lenny's location and from the far side of the ranch. He and Barney jumped off the front porch, turned right and ducked around the side of the house closest to the sea. They ran along the edge of the yard, passed the orange grove and onto the open field.

Barney was moving well, but PJ was having trouble, his ribs on fire from Garcia's beating. He looked behind and did not see the headlights of the jeeps, but knew they would be upon them soon. Gunfire continued around the ranch. He heard the distinctive sound of the RPKS machine gun from the far side and realized Dutch had joined the fight.

The sense of urgency in PJ's voice and the gunshots they heard from the other side of the ranch made it a bit easier for Dutch and Mickey when they opened fire on the guard. A short burst of six shots from Mickey found their mark and the guard fell dead in place.

"Nice shooting, Mickey Man," Dutch said as he let go a burst from the machine gun, spraying the area in case there were others in hiding. Then they both moved from their hiding spot, through the gate and along the road to the airstrip.

Their assignment was to take up a cover fire position at the north end of the runway. That was over half a mile away. They hadn't covered half of the distance when they heard vehicles coming their way from the airfield. Dutch waved Mickey off to the right and he went left, both setting up in firing position.

"Let them go through unless they see us," Dutch radioed to Mickey. Two clicks came back.

A jeep with four men appeared and went speeding by them, heading for the gate. A pick up with two men followed a moment later. They weren't 100 yards past when Dutch got up and started moving again, Mickey close behind.

"Stay on the right, same drill if more come," Dutch radioed between breaths. The RPKS weighed sixteen pounds, twice the weight of the AK-74, and used seventy round clips instead of the normal thirty rounds. With ten clips in his pack, Dutch was hauling an extra eighteen pounds compared to Mickey. As they saw the lights of the airfield hangar area, he was glad for those early morning runs that kept his lungs in shape. Still, he was tired when they stopped along the trees, behind the large white gas tank that housed the aviation fuel for Quintaro's fleet.

They moved right to the edge of the clearing and set up a firing position. They could see the end of the runway, but not much else. Mickey kept an eye behind them, expecting the men who had passed them would be back soon. Dutch didn't like the lack of anything substantial to stop bullets in front of them and he hoped Stoney would land soon.

Dutch could hear gunfire coming from the middle of the ranch and wondered how Lenny, Ray and Crash were doing. He hadn't heard much on the radio in a while.

"Dutch here. We're in position north of the gas tank. Seven men in two vehicles working this side. Anyone copy?"

Lenny heard but couldn't answer because he, Ray and Crash were pinned down inside Building Number Two by the gunfire. Just after the order from PJ to get out, the perimeter patrol jeep had turned back.

They must have seen Crash in the window because as they passed, the jeep braked and both men jumped out firing, sending bullets into the room. She ducked below the window just before they shot and started crawling toward the front hallway.

"Two guys out front!" she shouted, forgetting her radio. She crawled to the hall just as one of the men reached the front steps. His upper body was visible next to a flowerpot against the stair railing. Crash was angled the wrong way for her right hand shot. Without thinking, she rolled over once in the hall, swinging her legs around into position and let off a long burst at the door, burning up her 30 rounds. The guard died quickly.

The second man was right behind, but he went down in a hail of bullets, from above and behind her. Crash turned to see Ray.

"This is no good here!" Lenny yelled. "Move back!"

The three scrambled back into the kitchen. They were excited, breathing hard, adrenalin coursing through their bodies. Crash appeared the worst of the three.

"I'm scared!" she said even as she checked her weapon, slipped in another magazine of thirty rounds and made sure it was on semi-automatic. She kept feeling her vest to make sure she had more clips. She was near panic and Lenny knew it.

"No time for that, Crash!" Lenny said loudly. "I'm going up stairs to cover this side," he said, pointing toward the main house as he formulated a plan in his head. "Ray, you cover the back door, Crash back up front." He looked at her. She was pacing nervously and didn't move toward the front.

"Crash, damn it, go forward and hold them off!"

The words "go forward" worked. She was used to hearing that on a sailboat and it focused her.

"Can you do it, Crash?" Lenny asked her, his voice filled with a sense of urgency.

She looked at him directly, nodded yes and moved back into the hallway. She wished she were hanging on the pole doing a chute peel in a forty knot storm or racing her motorcycle from Sydney to Darwin rather than holding the AK-74 weapon she had in her hand, but she made her way to the front door. She ignored the two bloody bodies there and crouched in the doorway, peering out into the semi-darkness.

The next attack came from Ray's side. He guessed four men in the trees about 100 yards away on the other side of the house. Pinpoints of light came in rapid succession from the cover there, but the bullets smacked harmlessly into the building. Ray and Lenny returned the fire. The superior power and range of the AK-74 worked to their advantage.

Lenny picked off two of the men, firing at the flashes from his high vantage point. He never saw the men, but the flashes stopped. Ray knew he also hit one because the flashes made an arc skyward after he let go a string of eight shots.

The fourth shooter either retreated or was shot by a stray bullet, but just as suddenly as it had started, the shooting stopped. Lenny scanned the roadway toward the airfield and saw no lights. However, he heard the whine of a jet engine.

"Lenny here, radio check. Dutch?" he spoke into his radio.

"Go ahead, Lenny," Dutch answered, the whine of the jet clearly heard in the background of his transmission.

"Len, this is Barney," Barney Devlin's voice interrupted.

"Go ahead, Barney. Where's PJ?" Lenny asked with concern.

"He's okay, busted radio. What's your situation?"

"We've had contact with six or seven bad guys, two confirmed killed, three more probable. Ray and Crash are okay."

"Can you move out?" Barney asked.

"We'd love to try," came the response.

"Stay in the cover of the trees and head for the rendezvous."

"We're on our way. Lenny out."

He took one last look around and ran down the stairs.

"How's it look out there?" he asked Christina at the front door.

"Nothing moving," she said.

"We move! We're outta here through the back," Lenny helped her up and gave her a gentle push down the hallway.

They found Ray crouched in the dark by the corner window, dozens of spent shells around him on the kitchen floor.

"I go first, Crash you second. Don't move until I signal it's all right," Lenny commanded. "There may be someone hiding in ambush."

He opened the kitchen door slowly, and the first thing to catch his eye was the naked light bulb, which still was burning brightly above the door. He reached up with his rifle and smashed the bulb.

"You could've just turned off the light," Ray laughed nervously.

"I'm in a smashing mood, okay?" Lenny retorted. "See ya!" and out he went, running the 100 yards to the tree line from where the gunfire had just come. Halfway there, he wished he had joined Dutch on more of those early morning runs. His breath was coming fast, but he huffed and puffed and churned his legs, expecting bullets from every direction to rip into him any second. Just as he reached the tree line he tripped over a body lying in the undergrowth.

He went sprawling, hard, smashing his radio and back against a tree. His finger, tensed around the trigger of his rifle sent a burst of gunfire into the ground and toward the house.

"Jesus H.!" he cried out, and lay in agony, gasping for air. It was a full minute before he could speak, but there was no answer to his repeated tries on the radio. He felt the main body of the walkie-talkie and realized the casing was cracked.

He looked back over the open field he had just crossed. No sign of Crash or Ray. How long would they wait? He reached for his flashlight and was thankful it was still attached to his utility vest.

"Ray to Lenny, do you copy?" Ray repeated several times. Crouched at the window, he was waiting for Len's signal. The gunfire and no answer on the radio had him worried. The whine of the jets had increased and he suddenly felt very alone. Then he saw two blinks of light from the woods, each one about a second long.

"Look, Chris, two blinks of a light. Think that's Len?" Ray said to her. She was standing by the door, ready to make the run. She opened it a crack and saw the lights, too. Two flashes, each one a second long.

"What's it mean? Two? Two what? Should we go?" Ray asked. "Maybe it's a trick."

"Yes or no? What's he mean?" Christina pondered. "Hey, I know. Rules of the Road at sea. Oncoming traffic. Two flashes means I'm going to pass on your right side, starboard to starboard, right side to right side...all right, yeah, all right. It's all right!," she said excitedly.

"One if by land, two if by sea. *Si!* means yes in Spanish," Ray added, smiling.

"I'm outta here!" Crash said and opened the door and took off running as fast as her five-foot frame could move carrying ten pounds on her back and an eight-pound assault rifle.

She saw the signal again and changed her course slightly to aim right for it. Ray didn't wait for her to reach cover, but took off himself. All three regrouped in the darkness, catching their breath, happy to be out of the confines of the building.

"We follow the tree line right to the airstrip. I got point. Ray you have tail. Keep moving!" Lenny got up, but had trouble. The pain in his back was intense. He limped off slowly, but after fifty yards he was able to pick up the pace.

They made good time and reached the end of the trees along the road to the airstrip. All the jet's engines were running and Lenny expected that any minute it would be taking off. He stopped abruptly at the edge of the trees. Crash, following close behind, bumped into him.

"Shhh!" he said and punched up some numbers on his GPS. The display indicated the rendezvous point was to their left, a 400-yard run across open field. Lenny pointed toward the water, put away the GPS and held up three fingers. He counted down 3-2-1 and they moved out of cover and started running across the field.

They went across a gravel road, strung out in a staggered line, and hit smooth grass. Only 100 yards into their run, gunfire opened up on them from the guard tower to their right. A heavy caliber weapon was spitting up earth all around them. They dove to the ground. A bullet sent up sand, grass and dirt into Ray's eyes, blinding him momentarily. He kept crawling. They were in the middle of a deadly fire zone.

Lenny was scared. The ground around him was alive with bullets. It was 100 yards back to the trees. They would never make it. He thought they had bought it this time. Suddenly, he heard a low flying plane. It appeared out of nowhere directly overhead, banking to the right over the airfield.

A line of explosions began walking their way toward the guard tower and the fourth one scored a direct hit. The gunfire stopped and the three jumped up and started running again toward the sea.

"All right, Stoney!" Lenny shouted as they moved back onto the open field. Ray was still blinded by the debris in his eyes, but Crash grabbed his hand.

"Just run!" she shouted. "I've got you!"

They reached the end of the runway where PJ and Barney were hiding just below the crest of the shoreline slope. They watched as explosions rained down from Stoney and the Greyhound, more landing around the tower and then on the tarmac. The jet started moving toward the runway, when a series of small explosions walked their way to the gas storage tank. The last one scored a direct hit and a huge fireball lit up the night as the tank exploded at the far end of the runway.

"Mickey! Mickey! Move!" was all Dutch had time to say as they saw the first explosion near the gas tank. Mickey didn't need much more and he took off ahead of Dutch, running toward the water 100 feet away. As soon as they left cover, one of the guards near the jet opened fire. Dutch felt a bullet hit his left arm but his blue cast deflected it away. However, the force of the impact knocked Dutch down. It probably saved his life.

He went sprawling across the grass just as the gas tank erupted and a huge fireball rolled outward in every direction, consuming everything four feet above the ground within 150 feet.

Dutch watched in horror as it rolled right towards him. Burning was not the way to die, he thought. Then he remembered Boy Scout training. Roll! Roll! Roll! And he did. He felt the furnace like heat, and raised his arms in front of his face and kept rolling and rolling until he felt himself falling off the end of the earth, and then he landed in the water.

It wasn't very deep, only two feet, but it was wet and cool and he rolled and rolled, happy that he could still feel its cooling affects.

~~~

CHAPTER TWENTY-FOUR

Mickey's voice was frantic, but so far away. "Come on, Dutch! We have to keep moving!" The sound of more gunfire filled Dutch's ears as he sat up in the water. He realized he was alive, but not safe. More explosions could be heard near the hangars and the persistent whine of the jet.

"Get up, buddy. Let's go!" Mickey shouted, tugging on Dutch's good arm. The voice seemed closer, and Dutch started to move, or was someone dragging him. Flames from the gas tank climbed 100 feet in the air. In their run to safety, their weapons and packs were left behind. The squeal of brakes from the general direction of their previous location killed any thoughts of going back, so they pressed against the low sea wall and started moving toward the north end of the runway.

Mickey had made the water just as the tank exploded and was uninjured. He turned and looked at Dutch, seeing he was badly burned on the face and hands. He didn't say anything, just pushed him along the wall.

"Keep moving, buddy!"

Dutch stumbled along, his head down, following the edge of the water along the embankment. He couldn't tell if he was warm or cold. He had no feeling in his hands. He was starting to shiver.

"What the hell is that?" Mickey muttered as they walked along. He saw two silhouettes suddenly appear out of the black sky lazily flying into the light from the gas fire.

"Paratroopers!" he yelled at Dutch.

"Oh, great!" Dutch mumbled, looking up just in time to catch a glimpse of the two soldiers from the sky. "This guy's got an army in the sky, too!"

Meanwhile, Stoney, Dave and Azulmora watched the fiery havoc they had wrought from the Greyhound. Stoney banked for another pass. His sharp eyes spotted the two crewmembers against the embankment.

"Barney, this is Sky Blue, we're making one more pass from the north. I've got Dutch and Mickey in the water at this end."

"Roger that, Stoney," Barney answered. "Lenny's team with us. Everyone's okay. Can you stop that jet from taking off?"

"Stoney, ...th.....key!" the radio crackled, the transmission badly broken up.

"We're pi...d ..wn .. ..e ..rth end. Can ....p!"

Stoney recognized Mickey's voice through the breakup.

"Mickey, we're coming around again," Stoney radioed.

He turned behind him and shouted to Dave who was buckled in a safety harness, his feet braced against the lower frame of the open side door with the AGS-19 grenade launcher in between his legs. Azulmora was also tied in, helping him feed the grenade belts to the launcher.

"Cover Dutch and Mickey and go for the jet, Dave!"

Dave was popping grenades like snowballs out the side door, and just beginning to feel confident in his ability to solve the physics problem required to aim the launcher. He had to adjust the expected trajectory of the projectiles with the movement of the plane. The gas tank had been a lucky shot. He had actually aimed for the hangar, but misjudged badly.

"I'll try!" Dave shouted back.

The Greyhound banked hard left sending Azulmora tumbling against the side of the cabin. Her safety harness went taut, pulling her up short with one hand on the barrel of the grenade launcher, the other on the cabin door and her face in the middle of the door with a clear view of the chaos below. Dave grabbed at her harness and pulled her back to the cabin deck.

They made a complete circle over the water and approached from the north again. Dave could see four men along the top of the embankment. They turned their attention skyward and began firing at the Greyhound. Metallic pings surrounded Dave as the bullets hit the side of the plane. Dave began to fire back.

He sent a string of five grenades and prayed he had gauged the distance correctly. If they fell short and in the water near Dutch and Mickey...he didn't finish the thought. He needn't have worried. His aim was accurate and the grenades landed in a line of explosions that killed at least two of the men and sent the other two running back toward the hangar.

"Got them!" Dave shouted, then aimed at the jet, which had positioned itself on the north end of the runway. He only had seconds to aim as they approached at a sharp angle and let go another salvo of five, but they all missed, exploding around the plane, some on the parking tarmac and others harmlessly on the grass.

"Missed, dammit!" he shouted.

Stoney had already made up his mind that different action was needed as they flew directly behind and above the jet.

"Hold on, everyone. We're going down!" he shouted.

He turned the wheel of the Greyhound to the right, cut engine power dramatically and lowered the landing gear and flaps. The tough old plane, in the hands of the tough old pilot handled the stresses well.

Stoney came out of the tight turn and leveled off about 100 yards out from the end of the runway, lined up with the jet just as it began its takeoff roll. Still 200 feet high, Stoney let the bottom drop out. He pitched the nose down and gunned the engines. Over the runway threshold, he leveled out the controls and adjusted power again. He was keying on the lights of the moving jet and hoped he had enough momentum to get in front even as it accelerated.

Dave couldn't believe his eyes, but for a second they were so close to the jet he thought he could stand on its high T-tail section. But the Greyhound was moving slightly faster than the jet and soon Dave could clearly see the rivets across its camouflaged back. Then he caught a glimpse of the jet's cockpit windows as Stoney yelled from up front.

"Hold on, we're going hit hard!"

The Grumman C-2 Greyhound was built to handle the brutal shock of repeated aircraft carrier landings, and Stoney had made a few in his time, albeit in jet fighters. A second before they touched down, he wished he had a cable system to grab the hook hanging behind the Greyhound. But, there was no cable and the Greyhound hit hard, the landing gear shock absorbers depressed to their limit and beyond. The seals inside the shock tubes on the left side ruptured as the lower piston drove deep into the upper, spilling out hydraulic oil. The extreme pressure on the single, left tire blew it out.

Stoney felt it go and turned the nose wheel right, blipped the power throttle, trying everything he knew to correct the sudden pull to the left. He knew he needed to stay on the runway at least another few seconds or they were in danger of the damaged gear hitting the soft grass, which might start the plane cart wheeling. The Greyhound responded, a shower of sparks flying up from the left tire rim. The plane stayed dead center on the strip of asphalt.

In the cockpit of the BAe 146, the Peruvian Air Force colonel at the controls was first aware of the second plane when he saw the glow from her landing lights. Then he saw the nose wheel of the Greyhound as it sudden appeared not ten feet over his head, and then the rest of the plane's body dropped directly into the swath of brightness from the jet's own powerful lights. The jet had used up about 1500 feet of the 5000-foot runway and the speed dial read 70 knots and increasing, but still well short of the necessary takeoff speed.

He wondered who the hell was at the controls. He was a crazy man, for sure! He had the best seat in the house as the Greyhound hit hard, skittered left, and blew a tire. It lurched back to the right, in a shower of sparks about 100 yards in front of them. He saw the speed dial reading 80 knots out of the corner of his eye. They were closing in on the plane in front of them at 10 yards a second, and the closure speed was increasing dramatically as the jet accelerated while the Greyhound slowed. The colonel had no choice but to abort the takeoff or collide.

"Abort! Abort!" he shouted to his co-pilot as he reached for the controls to reverse thrust, and pressed down hard with both feet on the brake pedals. He was in Colombia because of the extra $20,000 he received from Colonel Acarapi Gonzales for each trip, but his life was still his first priority.

His co-pilot opened the special air dam brake on the tail and also stepped on the brake pedals. The empty plane with about 18,000 pounds of fuel, enough to fly the 1300 miles back to Peru, weighed about thirty-four tons and it responded slowly at first. Smoke came from the brake drums as they heated up, then the nose wheels locked up producing smoke from the tires. In front of them, the Greyhound slowed more dramatically. The colonel realized he had run out of space and swerved to the right.

Quickly, the jet went off the runway, the left wing tip missing the Greyhound by twelve inches. The jet hit the grass at sixty knots and began to skid on the slicker surface. The colonel fought the controls like a racecar driver, trying to keep the eighty-seven foot wingspan level and the plane upright. Their speed decreased, but the grass was about to run out as the plane skidded right through the burning guard tower, splintering the structure into burning embers. The colonel gave the controls a hard turn to the left and the plane responded reluctantly, lumbering, and bouncing across the grass.

Finally, the nose wheel dug in, the plane made a final lurch to the left, and came to a stop well to the right of the runway. Its right wing tip hung over the edge where the grass met rocks and where the steady waves of the Caribbean Sea spent their last bit of energy on the shoreline, oblivious to the drama taking place twenty feet above.

The Greyhound slid to a stop as well only seventy-five feet from the end of the runway. Stoney sat in the pilot's seat, his hand locked on the wheel. He realized the blown tire would prevent them from taking off again and began the methodical process of shutting down the plane's power systems, all the while vowing never to try something like that again.

"Whoa!" came the shout from Dave in back, as he let go of his grip on a cargo strap. "That was one hell of a landing, Stoney!" Dave looked at Azulmora, thought she was Kathryn for a second, and saw a terrified look in her eyes. He unbuckled his harness and moved to her.

"Are you okay, Kath...Azulmora?" he asked. She had never experienced anything like that and didn't respond to him or move. She just stared straight ahead, right through Dave, still holding tight to the horizontal wooden bar that ran between two bulkheads on the side of the cabin.

Dave gently reached over and put his large hand over her grip and slowly opened her fingers, freeing them from the bar. Her eyes moved and she looked at him, unsure of what had happened or what was going to happen next.

"It's all right, Azulmora. We're okay, we're on the ground," Dave said soothingly. She slowly nodded and then smiled.

"I don't want to do that again," she said quietly and then suddenly became alert. "Where are we?" she asked.

"On the runway. Come on, get ready to move." Dave said, pulling her up. He unbuckled her harness as Stoney jumped down from the cockpit. He had hooked up his radio, but didn't need it as PJ appeared suddenly in the side doorway. He climbed into the plane, Barney right behind him.

"Stoney, you're a maniac! I love you!" PJ yelled at his diminutive friend.

"Any landing you walk away from is a good one, right?" Stoney responded. He and PJ exchanged high fives.

Barney and Azulmora fell into each other's arms. She was plainly frightened still and began to sob against his chest.

"It's okay, my princess," he said soothingly, stroking her long black hair. "We're heading home."

"PJ, company!" came Lenny's cry from outside the plane. PJ moved to the doorway. Three sets of headlights were visible beyond the orange grove on the road to the hangar area, moving fast. Christina pointed back toward the hangars and everyone saw another set of headlights.

"Reinforcements! Damn, will it ever end!" PJ muttered under his breath.

"We can't take off, PJ, not with that blown tire!" Stoney said.

"Okay, everyone over the embankment. We make our stand there!" PJ shouted. "Move it! Move it! Let's go, Barney!"

They all scrambled out of the aircraft. Dave struggled with the AGS-19, finally maneuvering it through the door. Stoney grabbed a box of grenades and was the last one out. He had just slipped over the edge of the embankment when the gunfire started, aimed at the plane.

"Hold fire, let them get closer!" PJ yelled. "Don't give away our position yet!"

"Closer? Are you crazy!" Azulmora muttered, hovering low next to Barney, keeping her head below the edge of the embankment. She focused on the relentless sound of the sea lapping at the shore below them and pressed herself against the sand.

The three vehicles had stopped and PJ's heart sank. He could see at least twenty silhouettes coming from the trucks. They were outnumbered better than two to one. The reinforcements were spread out in a line, extending 100 yards and they slowly moved forward toward the Greyhound, their crouched figures clearly outlined by the colorful backdrop of the burning fire from the gas tank.

PJ felt the wind pick up behind him. He saw dark clouds moving in. They had already blocked out the stars in the northern sky. He thought he heard the drone of an engine, but couldn't zero in on the sound amid the other noises all around them, including the surf below.

He looked up and down the line at his crew and cursed the day he had decided to go sailing in San Francisco Bay.

"Wait until they are close, friends," he whispered down the line. He wondered about Dutch and Mickey and hoped they were alive. Kathryn's face appeared in his mind's eye and he smiled at her beauty and the warmth she had put in his heart. He knew he would fight to the last to rescue her, but thought the last was very near at hand.

Suddenly, there was an explosion at the right end of the advancing line, a bright, fiery one as if someone had ignited a gallon of gasoline. To everyone's horror, the figure of a man, his arms flailing, was clearly visible inside the flames. A moment later, night turned into day, as a white flare exploded in the air, casting the reinforcements into the spotlight, a suddenly illuminated tableau of soldiers in grey and brown uniforms, their rifles pointed forward, their heads instinctively looking up at the flare, which was blinding. PJ's crew also froze in the brightness, their heads and rifles sticking up above the top of the slope, revealed by the flare.

Another incendiary explosion occurred to PJ's left, sending up a burst of orange and black near the jet sitting about 300 yards away, her bright landing lights still shining into the darkness above the sea.

"Holy smoke! Do you see that!" Lenny said about fifteen feet to PJ's right.

"I can see everything now!" PJ snapped. "What the hell is going on?" The flare continued to burn overhead, slowly drifting down to the field. The line of reinforcements hit the ground as soon as they realized they were in the light. Then Stoney called out from the far right!

"Choppers!" he called.

PJ listened and sure enough the low, unmistakable *thunk thunk* of a Huey's rotors beating the air reached him. Approaching from downwind, to mask the noise, thought PJ. Smart.

One Huey appeared moving at top speed, its brown shape flying toward their hiding position at the end of the runway, passing not twenty feet over their heads. Then it executed a steep turn, coming back toward Quintaro's men still on the ground. The blast of the rotors could be felt as it zoomed over PJ's head. He thought he heard an unusual hissing noise as it went by.

The pilot executed a quick flare and the chopper hovered. Shots rang out from the guards lying exposed on the grass, not 100 feet from the copter. Unexpectedly, a roar joined the confusion as a stream of liquid fire came spewing from the nose of the chopper, lighting up the arena of battle. The stream of flame, riding the wind from behind, enveloped the prone guards and those not hit in the first blast began to retreat. The flame moved left and then back to the right following the retreating men.

Several were turned into running torches, their attempted escape ending after a few steps as they stumbled and fell in a fiery death. Others never had a chance and breathed their last while still on the ground, their fates marked by half a dozen small fires burning in the field.

As suddenly as it had appeared, the tongue of flame disappeared and the helicopter peeled off to the right. More sounds of blades beating the air reached PJ and three more Hueys appeared from the left. A fourth flew in from the far end of the runway. Flashes of light from a heavy machine gun filled its doorway as it covered the parking area with deadly fire.

The Hueys touched down briefly and half a dozen soldiers jumped out of each one, automatic weapons firing as they hit the ground. The last soldier was hardly out the door when the choppers took off again, disappearing into the night, leaving only the sound of their rotors signaling their nearby presence.

PJ couldn't move, marveling at the gruesome efficiency of their arrival.

"Whose side are they on?" Lenny asked.

"I think they have their own agenda," PJ said with a grim smile.

"PJ McDonough, I do believe that is Colonel Jesus Cesar's *Rapidero Fuego* force! Holy cow, would you look at that!" Barney was shouting. In a matter of 60 seconds, the soldiers from the sky had landed and the advancing column of Quintaro's reinforcements had been decimated, most of them killed in the fiery attack, others caught in a deadly crossfire from the hangar area and the runway.

More gunfire came from the left, near the jet, but it was quickly answered and quieted. Quintaro's guards had been routed. The big jet stopped. Minutes after the flare had ignited the sky, the remaining guards dropped their weapons and surrendered.

"No one move!" PJ commanded. "They probably don't know who we are! Just stay here and be ready for anything." He turned to Barney on his left.

"What do you think? How well do you know this Cesar?" PJ asked.

"He knows me, but his men don't," Barney said. He thought for a moment. "How about a white flag so they won't fire. Let them take us into custody."

"Are we sure these are Cesar's boys?" Stoney asked. PJ nodded. The idea of surrendering to someone who might not be sympathetic to their story worried him.

"Has to be. No other unit in Colombia could have done what they just did," Barney assured PJ.

"Plane landing!" Lenny called out, his eyes watching the scene playing out in front of them through the binoculars. "Looks like a small twin, PJ! I count at least two dozen soldiers on the ground...they're herding the guards toward the hangar. Uh, oh. Six heading this way!"

"Steady, everyone," PJ called. "Anyone got anything white? T-shirt or anything?"

Before anyone could react, gunfire sprayed the ground right next to PJ from behind. Stoney turned quickly and fired instinctually toward the muzzle flashes. His bullets cracked off the shoreline rocks.

The down slope protecting them from the soldiers coming across the field was suddenly a backstop trapping them on the embankment. Some of Quintaro's men must have slipped in behind them, thought PJ. Or was it Cesar's men who didn't know who they were? Either way, PJ realized they were sitting ducks.

"Move! Move!" PJ yelled at Barney and Azulmora next to him.

He jumped up and slipped up over the ledge as rocks splattered around him from more gunshots.

"Amigo! Amigo!" was all he could think to shout, hoping the shooters were Cesar's men.

The rest of the crew took PJ's lead and scrambled up the embankment and started running right toward the advancing soldiers in front of them. Stony was the last over the ledge, firing into the darkness behind him.

They had nowhere to run. Azulmora was waving a piece of white cloth she had ripped from her ruana, but the soldiers kept advancing. PJ looked back to see the shadows of two soldiers coming over the edge after them. He turned and set up in a crouch to fire when suddenly he heard a recognizable voice above the din.

"Pare! Pare! No matelos! Pare! Amigos! No matelos!"

"What the hell? Harold? Is that you?" PJ shouted in amazement watching a man in full battle gear come running out of the darkness and positioned himself between the crew and the two soldiers who had surprised them from the water's edge.

"Stop! Don't kill them! They are fiends!" Harold shouted. He bounced around like a maniac waving first at the two from behind and then at the advancing soldiers in front.

The soldiers heard and held their fire.

Another flare went off high in the sky and brightness returned to the dark field. Three of the helicopters landed on the parking area, another could be seen with a bright spotlight moving slowly over the ranch to the right. A fifth suddenly appeared over their heads, hovering with its own blinding spotlight aimed right on PJ and his crew as they stood between the soldiers.

The downwash from the blades took everyone's breathe away, forcing them to gulp for air, which was filled with sand and grass. The six approaching soldiers stopped about ten yards away, their weapons pointed right at the crew. The two from behind came right up and Harold went over to speak to one of them.

"Captain Pizzaro, these are my friends I spoke of," Harold said and the captain nodded. He looked at the group of Americans curiously as he moved toward his men approaching from the hanger.

"H, what the hell are you doing here?" cried out PJ.

"Looks like I'm saving your ass, buddy," laughed Harold. PJ gave him a big hug.

"I'm glad you weren't relying on a phone call this time," PJ said gratefully with a big smile.

Harold chuckled and gave PJ a big aw shucks smile. "Sometimes you got get your hands dirty, my friend."

"But, how the hell did you get here?" PJ asked.

"Ah, trade secret, PJ," Harold answered. He looked at PJ for a moment. "I actually helped train Cesar in the states a few years back. I tipped him off earlier today and hooked up with them just before they left."

"I thought you were a desk jockey, a phone guru, the master of negotiations," PJ smiled.

"And you should keep thinking that, PJ," was all Harold said.

PJ looked at Harold in full battle dress and realized he had another friend with a side story he had yet to hear.

"Look, H," he continued, the urgency returning to his voice. "Quintaro's kidnapped Kathryn and they were here." He held up Kathryn's earring from under the bed. "We're sure he's taken her to the mine and that's where we are going next."

Harold touched the earring for a moment and looked confused. He glanced over at Azulmora standing next to Barney.

"But, who is that?"

PJ explained to Harold's amazement.

"Sheeet! Bad timing, PJ" Harold exclaimed and turned away. He was visibly upset.

"You gotta help us!" PJ said.

"I can't, damn it!"

Harold started to walk away, when the line of soldiers around the crew parted and a tall man walked slowly toward them. His silhouette was distorted by the brightness of the nearby helicopter's searchlight. He came close, circling around the crew, carefully looking at them. When his face came into the light, PJ turned to follow his eyes. He saw a tired looking man of fifty, his brown face filled with lines, but his demeanor alert and erect.

"Captain Pizzaro, where is this McDonough person?" the man demanded in perfect English. The captain pointed to the circle.

"I'm McDonough," PJ said stepping forward. Cesar moved over to him and the two shook hands warmly.

"PJ, is it? Hello, I'm Colonel Jesus Cesar, Colombian Army. Looks like you got yourself into some deep shit, mister!"

"Colonel, your timing and execution were beautiful," PJ said. "My compliments to your men!"

"So, you are the leader here? And who are all these men?" He looked carefully at Christina and Azulmora.

"And women?" he corrected, nodding to Christina. She smiled, returning his nod. They were standing in a close-knit group, happy to be alive. "These are my friends, Colonel. My sailboat crew."

"Your sailboat crew!" Cesar said in amazement. "You must have one hell of a sailboat, Mr. McDonough!"

"Actually, Colonel, I have one hell of a problem and that's why we are here tonight."

"I know of your problem," Cesar answered, nodding his head. "Harold informed me of the situation."

"Yes, sir," PJ said looking around for Harold who had disappeared. "Ah, I have two men missing yet. I think they are near the other end of the runway. I'd like to send a search party for them," PJ spoke rapidly.

"Indeed, Mr. McDonough, I will give you several men to help," Cesar said. PJ quickly dispatched Lenny and Dave with three of the soldiers to search for Dutch and Mickey. There had been no radio transmissions since Stoney made his landing and PJ was blocking the worst possibility out of his mind.

"Tell me, who landed the C-2?" Cesar asked, his eyes searching those remaining.

"Stoney Bullard, Colonel," PJ answered. "Stoney, where are you, old man?"

Ray and Crash stepped back to reveal Stoney standing with his hands on his hips, a sly smile on his face, looking taller than is five-six height.

Cesar looked at him in the glow of the spotlight.

"Hello, Colonel," Stoney said quietly.

"Stoney Bullard, is it?" Cesar said. "You are one crazy son of a bitch! May I shake your hand?"

"Sure, Colonel. You did a nice job yourself," Stoney said and the two shook hands.

"That was some landing," the Colonel repeated.

The radio on Captain Pizzaro's belt crackled in Spanish and Cesar quieted to listen. PJ saw Barney give a thumbs up as the voice reported.

"*Incendiar!*" Cesar said deeply, nodding to Pizzaro when the report was finished. The Captain repeated the command into his radio.

"Well, it seems, Mr. McDonough, you are doing my job for me," Cesar said when the transmission was finished. He turned to PJ.

"Well, actually, sir, with all due respect, we don't have time for stories right now because our job isn't quite finished yet," PJ said.

The Colonel looked surprised, but Barney, who still had his radio plugged into his ear, interrupted his response.

"PJ, a message from Lenny. They've found Dutch and Mickey...they're both okay!" Barney reported, holding up his hand so he could hear over the shouts from Stoney, Christina and Ray. "Dutch may need some medical attention. He's been burned. But they're okay!"

"Great news, Barney," PJ smiled. He turned to Cesar, but the Colonel had already anticipated.

"Captain Pizzaro, send the medic to assist!" he ordered. Pizzaro spoke into his radio again and another man was dispatched to help out.

Just then, another explosion erupted from the nearby hangar. It had more light than noise.

"What's that?" PJ said in surprise.

"That is fire, Mr. McDonough. My men are burning what we estimate is 10,000 kilos of cocaine paste that apparently came off that jet, delivered by one Peruvian Air Force Colonel Acarapi Gonzales. A smuggling rogue familiar to my men and me. He was apparently Carlos Quintaro's main source of paste. I'm happy to say he is out of business."

"Will he go to jail?" PJ asked.

"No! I'm afraid not," Cesar said with a laugh. "He will burn in hell, I presume. Shot dead in his plane!" Cesar pointed toward the jet. "One less cockroach in the world. Now, Mr. McDonough, I am interested in your story?" Cesar continued without a pause.

PJ was a little taken aback by Cesar's ability to laugh at death. PJ was still sickened by the vision of the burning guards in front of the fire breathing Huey. He put it out of his mind for the moment and addressed Cesar's question.

"Sir, as you probably already know, Carlos Quintaro is the man responsible for all this and other crimes. I believe he is responsible for fifteen Indians who are missing from a mine my company owns in the Valley of Codazzi," PJ said.

"I don't know this valley, other than what Harold told me. I have heard of Pico Codazzi. What makes you so sure he is there?" Cesar asked.

"He would feel safe there, Colonel," said PJ. "I'm sure we will find his helicopter there if we use his tracking system in the main house. Probably track his entire fleet! Also, his brother is still there. Bernardo Quintaro might be willing to talk to a man of your rank and position," PJ smiled.

"I'm most interested, Mr. McDonough. Carlos Quintaro has a good reputation in Colombia, at least politically, but I think much has been hidden from official eyes by design. Let's move to the main house," he said, putting his hand on PJ's shoulder.

"There's one other thing, Colonel," PJ said as they moved off. "We are convinced a good friend is with Quintaro. Kathryn Byrnie accompanied us to Colombia, but she was kidnapped earlier tonight, ah, last night by Quintaro's men."

"That is not good news," Cesar said.

"Colonel, I have to go into the valley to get her out and I need your help," PJ said.

"You need my help?," Cesar smiled. "Excuse me, Mr. McDonough, but this is now a drug matter for Colombia and *Rapidero Fuego*. I cannot allow a band of commandos, American no less, to roam our countryside, taking the law into their own hands! It just can't be," Cesar said seriously, shaking his head as they walked.

PJ stopped short, grabbing the Colonels arm and turning him around so they were face to face.

"Colonel, this is a life and death matter," PJ said, quiet but tough. "As good as you and your men are, you cannot just fly into that valley without putting Kathryn in danger. I have a plan that gives us a chance to get her out. You can still have your way with Quintaro."

"Oh, you have a plan?" Cesar said skeptically.

"That's right, Colonel. I have a plan, but more than that, I have information that you need."

"He's right, Jesus," Barney interrupted.

Cesar looked at Barney. They had met fifteen years ago during an illegal weapons importing sting. Barney helped Cesar set it up. Their trust had grown in their half dozen contacts since.

"Hello, Devlin. Well? Information?" Cesar asked.

"First off, we know about the defenses Quintaro has set up to protect himself in the valley. Where they are. Number of men," Barney said.

"You would withhold information from an official government operation? From a friend?" he asked Barney.

"If you do not take the woman's safety into mind, I would, Jesus," he said. He looked at Azulmora and repeated himself. "I would."

"Go on," Cesar said after a moment.

"Colonel, we have reason to believe the hostage, while American, is a Kogi Indian by birth," PJ pleaded his case.

"A Kogi?" Cesar responded.

Azulmora stepped forward and spoke up

"Colonel, I am Azulmora Nevita and I work with the Indian Bureau from Santa Marta. It is my sister who is hostage in the Valley of Codazzi. You must listen to these men and help us."

Cesar listened intently.

"Colonel," PJ said, "There is only one way to fly into the valley."

"I'm sure your pilots can fly anywhere, Jesus, but I have the navigation numbers that can turn a suicide flight into only a tough flight," Barney smiled. "Look, we owe you a great debt for tonight. But, this woman is in danger. I think you should listen to PJ's plan and give us a shot."

"We have to do this together, Colonel," PJ urged. "I don't know if either of us can do it alone. Regardless, if you don't help us, I'm still going in to get Kathryn."

"And we're going with him," Stoney added. Cesar looked at him sharply. Ray and Crash stepped forward also.

"That's right," Crash said.

Cesar put his hands on his belt and smiled.

"Harold said it was personal. Still, you must be a crazy bunch to want to keep fighting," Cesar said, "and maybe get yourself killed."

"Not crazy, Colonel, just committed," PJ told him.

"When do you suggest we go in?" Cesar asked.

"Every minute we wait lessens our chances of success. We need to move before sunrise. Right now," PJ said emphatically. His watch read 3:15 in the morning.

"Before sunrise? Impossible! My men have just been through a fire fight," he looked at PJ driving home his point, "We have only enough fuel for another hour or so in the Hueys, enough to get back to our base in Mompos!"

"The valley is only fifty miles away, sir," PJ said, sensing that Cesar was coming around. "When word arrives in the valley about your success tonight, I'm not sure Kathryn will live much longer."

PJ moved up close to Cesar so they could look one another in the eye. "Colonel Cesar, I'm asking for your help based on the trust and friendship you have shared with Barney. And, apparently, Harold. Give me the chance to get Kathryn out before you go in there and burn the hell out of them!"

Cesar looked into PJ's blue eyes and saw the determination and the openness. The eyes were bright, they were brave and they were honest. He liked what he saw. And he was pleased with the success his *Rapidero Fuego* force had just enjoyed at Quintaro's ranch.

"Okay, PJ McDonough. We will help each other," Cesar said in a commanding voice. "But only this one time. If your hunch doesn't pay off, you will promise to leave matters to me?"

"I agree, Colonel, but I assure you, it's more than a hunch," PJ said with a smile.

"Okay, tell me about it on the way to the house," Cesar said.

The breeze had freshened. PJ estimated it was blowing over twenty knots, and he took several deep breaths. The sea air filled his lungs and cleared his mind. As they walked, PJ felt the pain in his body, but suppressed it as best he could. It was something he couldn't worry about until he had Kathryn at his side again.

~~~

CHAPTER TWENTY-FIVE

In a matter of minutes, the stillness of the Valley of Codazzi erupted into an angry symphony. It started as a hiss that slipped suddenly out of the darkness, its source unseen, a bed of sound upon which other sounds played. Sounds changing decibels and pitch, low like the roar of a train and high like a shrill whistle, noises that rose and fell and gave life to an invisible power. Funneled along rocky walls onto the open plateau, the power blanketed all, twisting and turning around every corner, enveloping every nook and cranny in the valley. There was no escape from its grasp.

Kathryn watched the ragged burlap curtains on the lone window dance like spirits in a nightmare. Their dark shapes billowed stiffly, the glow from some distant light giving shadow to their movement and substance to the unseen.

Violent bursts of pressure slapped at the wooden frame of the building. Beams creaked and shingles flapped. Her face felt the touch of air currents. Her nose smelled a familiar, fresh aroma, as it wafted through the half opened window and washed away the stale odor of the mattress she lay upon.

The winds of Codazzi had come alive, and as the whistling turned to howling, Kathryn felt their anger. She was surprised at how calm that made her feel.

Kathryn guessed she had been lying on the bed for over an hour, listening intently to every sound she could hear, trying to identify the activities of the people who had brought her to this small room. She knew she would need this information when she made her escape.

So far, she had identified the sounds of two guards, one outside her door and the other outside her window. A vehicle, probably a jeep, had driven by. She had counted at least six voices among those who had accompanied her and Carlos Quintaro on the harrowing trip from Santa Marta to Riohacha and then to this location she suspected was the Valley of Codazzi.

At Quintaro's ranch, she had been blindfolded, gagged, and tied on a bed, softer than the one she was on now. Then her hands and legs were bound and she had been carried to a helicopter.

Lying on the floor, she could feel every vibration as the aircraft climbed, tilted, rocked and dropped. She thought they had headed south, but was soon totally disoriented. After twenty minutes of flight they had suddenly begun to descend, straight down, as if a cable had snapped on an elevator.

They descended for several minutes before they slowed, moved forward, only to land softly moments later. As the whine of the engines drifted away, she heard Quintaro order the men to take her to "the barracks without harm."

Their strange hands had grabbed her body as they lifted her from the helicopter, placed her in a jeep and then took her to this tiny room. She felt totally exposed in her short sports coatdress and vowed never to wear it again. Once away from Quintaro, their hands had roamed over her freely and roughly, their voices cackling like schoolboys away from the teacher. She had fought them as best she could.

They threw her on a thin mattress, removed her blindfold and untied her. When they removed her gag she had directed a stream of Spanish curse words at the men, enough to make many a soldier blush. But they took sport in her disgust, laughing and touching her until the guard outside the room ordered them to leave.

One of the men, his hair long and stringy, his face covered with two day's growth of beard, leaned real close. His teeth were stained green from smoking bazuko, his breath the fragrance of burnt tires and dirty dishwater, and he whispered in her ear in Spanish.

"You want us, don't you, Chaquita? Don't you? We will be back soon. Get ready for some loving." He laughed through his green teeth, his smile revolting her. She assembled what little moisture there was in her mouth and spat forcefully in his face. He only laughed harder, wiping the spittle from his nose with his fingers and licking them with his tongue, a disgusting display that made her turn her head. Another guard pulled him away, turned off the table lamp and shut the door.

Her hard demeanor, a shield in the face of the rough treatment by the men, crumbled as soon as they left and she began to cry quietly on the bed, frightened and alone. She cried for PJ, for her mother and father, for her friends in San Jose and her new friends on the crew. Their faces flashed through her mind as if she were saying goodbye to them all.

PJ's face was the brightest, his reddish-brown hair falling over his ears and forehead, his gentle lips turned in a smile, his rounded chin set firm, and his blue eyes looking tenderly at her, the crinkles at the corners and the dimples on his cheeks telling her he was happy. And in love. She saw steel beyond his tenderness and clung to the belief he wouldn't abandon her.

She remembered the face in the water, the light form that tried to speak to her. She was sure it was Eduardo's face. And the statue of the Indian girl. She repeated the word "Zarzamora" again and tried to find hope in its sound. She could not. She realized she was totally helpless and cried herself to sleep.

She woke to the sound of the strengthening wind. Rain began to fall, lightly at first, then harder, the streaks of moisture showing in the dim light. Every now and again, the dark shape of a guard would pass by the window, close enough for her to see his constant grin.

She thought a weather front was passing through. She watched the rain fall at an angle from left to right, indicating the storm was coming from the left of the window, but she still had no reference to the compass. She wondered if she could detect a northerly wind from a southerly wind by sound alone.

The rain started to drip in the half opened window and she thought about getting up to close it. But as the storm continued, she took comfort in the open window and its connection to the outside. The smell of the air changed with the rain. Again it was familiar, but unidentified, like the smell of a childhood toy if it could be unearthed from under the thousands of smells of a thirty-five year lifetime.

The sound of a truck's throaty engine and squealing brakes reached her. It was a different vehicle than the others. It stopped outside and she heard the footsteps of men. They entered the building and conversed with another man, the inside guard she guessed. She couldn't quite make out what they were saying.

Suddenly, the door burst open and three men rushed in, joined in a moment by two more. She sat up on the bed, fearing the worst. Someone turned on the light, its erratic glow showed the wicked smiles on their faces as they stood in a semi-circle around the bed.

The men were wet, their hair matted from the rain, their clothes dirty, although each wore the brown pants and grey shirts she had seen on the guards at Quintaro's ranch. They carried a combination of weapons slung over their shoulders or in their hands. Two rifles, three sub machine guns, two with pistols in their belts. She recognized the grinning guard. He had a long knife. She pressed against the wall behind the bed, intensely aware of her vulnerability.

"Carlos will have your heads if you touch me!" she said grimly in Spanish.

Two of the men grimaced at the image, looking nervously at the one with the green teeth, who seemed to be the ringleader.

He grabbed his crotch and smiled.

"You can have me first, bitch!" he sneered. He moved closer to her and she swung her left leg at him, but he easily stepped aside and caught it, holding it tight even as she struggled. Any hope for modesty was forgotten as her short dress was soon above her hips, revealing her white panties.

"Help me, you idiots!" Green Teeth yelled as he held on to her flailing leg. Two men moved forward and grabbed her legs, holding them firmly, their wide eyes focused on her exposed thighs. Kathryn swung at Green Teeth with a free hand, striking a blow on his ear, but it didn't stop him.

She started to scream as loud as she could only to have a handkerchief stuffed in her mouth by a guard, who pulled his hand away quickly with a yell as she bit his finger.

Both her hands were pinned back and her struggles weakened, useless against the men's strength. Green Teeth reached for her dress and ripped it open, the double-breasted buttons popping free like candy wafers.

Her black eyes were on fire, a mixture of disgust, anger and terror as Green Teeth's fingers roamed over her body. She could do nothing as he ripped open her bra, exposing her breasts. The men let out a chorus of laughs, shouts and taunts, urging on Green Teeth while his hands roughly massaged her. She felt one of the men loosen his grip on her leg as he reached for her breasts and she broke free, smashing him in the mouth with her sandal before they were able to corral her again.

They twisted her body around, spreading her legs sideways on the bed. Green Teeth dropped his pants and knelt on the bed. He pulled aside the crotch of her panties, his knuckles rubbing against her.

Kathryn closed her eyes, her brain awash in terror. She reached deep inside and mustered all her strength to pull her right arm free from the grinning guard, distracted by her nakedness. She swung her body upright, bringing her fist down squarely on Green Teeth's erection only inches from her. The pain was instant and tremendous. It went right to his eyes which stared at her in agony, pitifully looking for sympathy like a little boy, as if he believed she could forgive him for his transgressions and then give him comfort for the pain that was shooting through his whole body.

He crumbled backward off the bed and fell to the floor, howling in agony. She pulled the gag from her mouth and began to scream again, as loud as she had ever screamed in her life.

"Help! Help! Rape! Rape! Help!"

She kept crying out until one of the men smashed her with the back of his hand across the face. Pain shot through her cheek and blood sprang from her lip. That silenced her for only a moment. She let out another

---

bloodcurdling scream and started to cry, big sobs, mixed with more screams and curses at the men, her head and hair shaking hysterically, her free arm swinging wildly at anything and anyone. They backed away from her as if she had gone mad. No one heard another vehicle pull up.

When they let go of her, she collapsed back on the bed, sobbing in terror, anger, fear, and knew she would kill these men right now if she could. She feared in the next instant they would kill her.

Green Teeth was on his knees, his pain intense. He stood and pulled up his pants, cinching the rope belt around his waist. He looked evil and moved around the bed to face her.

"You bitch!" he shouted, and reached for the knife in the belt of the grinning guard, pulling it from its sheath.

"I will show you pain!"

He raised the knife high as if to plunge it into Kathryn. A hand reached from behind him and grabbed his fingers clenched around the knife. Slowly the surprise visitor applied pressure to the fingers, peeling them backward until the knife fell, sticking into the wooden floor behind Green Teeth.

"You stupid son of a bitch, I will teach you to disobey my orders!" seethed the voice of Carlos Quintaro. Green Teeth's face contorted in surprise, then fear and now pain as Quintaro continued to apply pressure on the man's fingers until the bones of his middle two fingers broke with an audible snap.

He cried out and Quintaro let him fall to the floor.

"Take him out of my sight. Put him on the vats for a week, that should straighten out his head!" Quintaro spat, the coldness of his voice setting the other men into quick action. They dragged the moaning Green Teeth away, leaving just Quintaro with Kathryn.

She looked up at him, her sobs subsided to quiet tears, and tried to regain her composure. She pulled her dress tightly around her as best she could. He bent down and pulled the knife from the floor, holding it in his hand as he stood staring at her for a long time. He had a surprisingly calming influence on her.

"I am sorry for the actions of my men," he said, sitting on the edge of the bed. He watched as she rubbed her wrists and ankles where the men had held her. "They are animals and do not understand how to treat a beautiful lady like you."

"Thank you," she said simply, looking at his green eyes. She thought his expression seemed clouded, maybe confused. He gave her a slight smile then looked away and just sat there, staring at the blank wall.

She heard the wind, the still strong gusts shaking the building, but the rain had stopped. It was cool in the room and she started to shiver. He noticed and removed his suede jacket, placing it around her shoulders. It smelled slightly of rain, but it was a pleasing smell. They sat quietly for a few minutes.

"Carlos, why did you bring me here?" she said, sitting with her knees under her on the bed, trying to fit her whole body under the warming influence of his jacket.

"We are safe here," he said with reassurance.

"Safe from what?" she asked.

"Safe from trouble, my dear. Safe from the people who are trying to ruin my business."

She said nothing. In the quiet, she detected a new sound. More rain? Seeing no streaks through the window, she remembered the photographs of the Miller Mine. There was a stream alongside the runway. It must be very close, she thought, and in front of her. That meant north was to her left, she thought. She thought of PJ.

"He will come after me," she said to him after a moment.

"Your friend? Not if he is smart," he snapped and stood up. He held his hands apart as if he were a priest delivering a prayer to the faithful, with the noted exception of the knife still in has hand.

"Of course, if he chooses to act foolishly, I will be forced to kill you." His tone was straightforward and cold. He stuck the knife into the wooden bedpost at the foot of the bed to punctuate his statement.

"Kill me? You can't be serious!" she said, not wanting to believe it, though she knew he was capable of it.

"I have no choice, do I?" he said.

"Yes, you do! You can chose to let me go!" she said.

He laughed.

"And you can choose to stay! I can make you queen of the Sierra Nevadas. My *Indios de montanas.* You could enjoy riches beyond your imagination," he gestured grandly.

She couldn't believe he was asking her to willingly stay. She tore off his jacket, flinging it to the floor, and slid backward to the head of the bed, pressing herself against the wall.

"You're crazy!" she said.

He picked up the knife again and, with a swift overhand motion, threw it against the wall over her head. It stuck into the wooden panels, quivering on its point. He had moved so quickly, she didn't have time to react, but felt the blood drain from her face. The knife was a foot above her.

"It is not so crazy that I should want a dark beauty like you around me, is it, Kathryn Byrnie?" Quintaro said with a wicked grin.

"I am not yours to have, Señor," she answered.

"We shall see, my dear," he said and walked toward the bed. She pressed deeper against the wall as he reached over her head and pulled the knife from the wood. Her eyes were wide as he bent over her, placing the knife point an inch from her face. He brought the point to her cheek, lightly touching her skin two inches under her left eye. Kathryn dared not take a breath.

"You will find me preferable to death," he whispered and effortlessly pricked her skin, drawing a drop of blood. She pulled away, slapping his knife hand away from her. He was surprised for a second, but grabbed her by the hair and pulled hard, causing her to scream in pain.

"You cannot resist me, Kathryn Byrnie," he laughed, his powerful grip holding her head in front of the knife. She dared not resist this time, fearing he would kill her. Tears ran down her cheek from the pain of his grip and the terror in her heart.

After a moment, he let her go and stood up. She curled up in a ball and began to cry again. She felt like an abused toy, total helplessness. She heard his footsteps walking around the room. Then the radio worn by the guard outside the room crackled, followed a moment later by a pounding on the door.

"Señor Quintaro, a radio message from Riohacha," came the guards voice through the door.

"What is it?" he asked. He opened the door.

"Excuse me, jefe," the guard spoke rapidly. "Señor Quintaro...Bernardo radios the American has left Colombia."

Kathryn's heart sank. She couldn't believe PJ would leave her. Did he actually think that Quintaro would release her if he left? She convinced herself it was a trick.

"Well, that is good news, Juan, if it is true," Quintaro said. "Who heard the message?"

"I don't know, jefe. Señor Caron just radioed me to tell you."

"Good. I must see about this myself," Quintaro said and waved the guard out of the room. He turned to Kathryn and showed his lewd smile again.

"I will be back," he said. "Until then, relax and wait. There is nowhere to run in these mountains."

He turned, went out the door, said something to the guard and then left, his laugh trailing off behind him as he walked away from the building. Kathryn sat still until she couldn't hear him, her dress pulled close around her again.

The door opened a minute later and the young guard entered. He smiled at her with that same, lewd grin she had seen too many times in the last hour, but merely dropped some clothing on the bed and left, taking one last peek around the door before he shut it.

She picked up the clothing, a grey shirt and brown pants. They were clean and she quickly put them on, then put her dress over the top. The layers of clothing felt warm and she felt protected with the cloth against her skin. She shut off the light and went to the window, nearly falling down from her cramped legs, which had been literally manhandled the last hour. Her terror was beginning to subside and she became energized by the need to make an escape plan.

She had lost track of time, but it was still dark outside. She could plainly hear the river, it's banks swollen with the night's rain, and estimated it was about 50 yards in front of her. She could hear the echo of the water off the high canyon wall on the other side of the river as she remembered from the photos.

Another gust of wind, she estimated at over twenty knots, blew the curtains over her head as she crouched in the darkened room. The grinning guard walked by the window, fifteen feet away, bent forward in the breeze. The gust subsided. She guessed there was a steady breeze of about ten knots. Get the heavy number one genoa, she found herself thinking. It brought a small smile to her lips at the memory of her week sailboat racing with PJ.

She stayed by the window for several minutes, allowing her eyes to become accustomed to the dark. After a while she thought she could see the blackness of the canyon wall across from her, though it was only a darker shade of blackness compared to the ground.

She estimated the guard wouldn't appear for five minutes and stuck her head out of the window, finding the source of the dim light that allowed her to see bushes and rocks among the flatness outside. There were several large spotlights in front of another building to her left a quarter of a mile. She counted three fixed wing aircraft and Quintaro's helicopter. Two men seemed to be working on the largest plane, the one with four engines. A third man was moving back and forth between the building and the planes.

She recognized one of the planes as a Cessna Caravan, a single engine turbo prop with an overhead wing that could carry a ton of cargo. She knew the plane and had flown a version of it when it first appeared in the early '80's. She studied the airplane parking area and saw a fourth man armed with a rifle move toward the runway and then disappear into the dark.

She wondered again if PJ had left the country without her. She knew for certain she did not want to see Quintaro again. She moved back inside the window just as one of the plane engines starting up. It sputtered for a moment and then died. As she sat, she perceived slight variations begin to appear in the deep blackness around her. Escape was her only option and she realized she would have to act soon, while the fading darkness was still her ally.

~~~

CHAPTER TWENTY-SIX

P J willed his tired mind to shut down for a twenty minute power nap. The steady, throaty roar of the Starship helped him doze, her twin turbos biting into the thin air over the Sierra Nevada de Santa Marta mountains. There were no dreams this time and after what seemed a painfully short time a nudge at his elbow brought him instantly awake.

"Ten minutes, PJ" came the soothing voice of Azulmora Nevita. He opened his eyes and saw her crouched in the aisle. He nodded his head.

"Thanks, Azulmora."

She smiled and rose to go, but he grabbed her arm and gently pulled her back down. He looked into her black eyes, realizing she was the physical embodiment of the life he had committed his friends and himself to save.

"What does it feel like, that presence of your sister that you are aware of?" he asked.

"It's hard to say. It happens in different ways. A random memory, a temperature change in my chest, a sudden thought that someone is watching me, like she is in the same room," Azulmora answered, shrugging her shoulders. She smiled, the same crooked smile that Kathryn displayed when she smiled at herself.

"Sometimes I don't know who is creating those feelings. You have helped focus them with your stories about this Kathryn."

"I believe Kathryn is your sister, Zarzamora," PJ said quietly. "I'm going to bring her back. And we will find Eduardo, too," he said in a solemn voice.

She smiled at him.

"I can feel him, too, a presence that has never left," she said. Her eyes grew misty at the mention of his name.

"You have given me hope," she continued. "Even if she is not my lost sister, she is lucky to have a man as brave as you, PJ," and she touched his cheek gently. He squeezed her hand and let go, and she moved back forward to join Barney in the Starship's cockpit.

PJ closed his eyes again and couldn't help but smile at Harold's quick exit. While interrogating Bernardo at the ranch he suddenly slapped PJ on the back and said it was time for him to leave, again.

They walked outside and a Blackhawk helicopter with US markings appeared out of the dark sky and in short order, Harold was aboard and gone.

"This is your fight now, PJ," was the last thing Harold said to him.

He felt another hand tapping him on the shoulder and he opened his eyes to see Captain Jorge Pizzaro looking at him from across the aisle of the Starship. The Colombian smiled and gestured toward the parachutes lying on the seat across from him.

"It is time, no?" he said in his heavily accented English.

"Yes, it is time," PJ nodded and he reached for one of the packs. They put them on, helping each other adjust the straps for a tight fit.

"Looks good, Captain," PJ said. Pizzaro gave him a thumbs up. They both strapped GPS receivers above the reserve chutes on their chests, positioned so a downward glance would show them the navigation numbers they would need to reach their target. The power gain was turned up full, the glow of the display bright even under the Starship's cabin lights.

They next checked their packs filled with survival gear. Two days worth of food, extra ammo, explosives and detonators. The packs were attached to their utility belts and would hang from fifteen-foot nylon ropes once they opened their parawings.

They slipped on full helmets with goggles and oxygen masks, attached to a small green bottle with five minutes worth of oxygen if they needed it in the thin air. They were about to make what the Army calls a HALO jump - high-altitude, low opening. Their freefall would cover 17,000 feet in less than 100 seconds.

"Barney, wind check!" PJ yelled forward.

"Twenty-seven knots true, from 345 degrees," Barney answered immediately. He was piloting the Starship, and with Azulmora, would circle over the valley as a command center. They would monitor radio frequencies, relay information and keep track of the action on the ground as best they could. With nearly a full load of fuel, they could stay on station for three hours.

"Remember Barney, if you have to make an emergency landing in the valley, we'll have to turn the Starship into a bed and breakfast. The runway's too short for take off," PJ said with a good-natured grin.

Barney looked back and nodded. "I'm not planning to come anywhere near you guys. One firefight every ten years is all I can handle! Five minutes!" he shouted after a quick look at the instruments, holding open his hand to indicate the time to the jump.

PJ had convinced Colonel Cesar and Barney that he was the one who should parachute into the valley. They considered it suicide, but PJ insisted it was basically a math problem to hit a target a mile wide and nearly three miles long, regardless of how dark it was or how many clouds you had to fall through. The key was avoiding the mountains.

PJ had taken out his pocket calculator and worked out the numbers for the jump, combining vertical rate of fall with horizontal drift on the wind. The directional control provided by the parawings and the accuracy of the GPS receivers, programmed with co-ordinates from a topographical map, would enable him to navigate around the high peaks in the mountains and find the target, the south end of the runway in the Valley of Codazzi.

Pizzaro was the deciding factor when he volunteered to jump with PJ. Pizzaro had made sixty-five jumps in the last two weeks and was quite confident. Despite twenty-five sport jumps to his credit, PJ knew it had been four years since his last jump. He didn't believe that was a problem. Besides, no one else had volunteered and there was no time to enter the valley any other way.

"PJ, two minutes. Team One has just been dropped off," Barney relayed. "Team Two standing by for your call."

PJ looked out the porthole. From their altitude of 25,000 feet, he could see the first hint of sunrise. The sky was a light grey far to the east. There was enough light to make out the clouds that sat about 5000 feet below them. Another 15,000 feet below lay the Valley of Codazzi.

"One minute!" Barney warned.

PJ started silently counting backward from sixty and nodded over at Pizzaro. The Captain nodded back. He appeared calm. He handed PJ an M-16 and helped him secure it under his harness and across his back. PJ did the same for Pizzaro. PJ had traded his AK-74 for the American rifle so he and Pizzaro could share the same ammunition.

Barney turned and gave a thumbs up. Both he and Azulmora had donned oxygen masks for the depressurization of the cabin. PJ returned it, then pushed the door lever down and leaned on it to force it open. Hinged at the bottom, it slowly swung downward, the built in steps leading into the darkness. Barney had slowed to 130 knots, less than half the Starship's cruising speed. PJ held onto the door rail and pushed hard with his foot on the top step, riding it down with his weight. A line had been rigged so Azulmora could pull it shut from the safety of the cabin once PJ and Pizzaro were gone.

The wind tugged at PJ's jumpsuit as he backed down to the bottom step, threatening to throw him into the Starship's wing. He held tightly to the stair rails, his pack slung low behind his legs. Captain Pizzaro then backed out and stepped down to the second to last stair, his parachute in PJ's face.

They were out on the stairs less than ten seconds when the sound of the engines cut just as PJ reached five in his countdown. Without a second thought, he lifted his head up, and let go his grip on the railing, "giving up the ghost" as he liked to put it. His body fell backward away from the stair, and he was airborne. Pizzaro was right above him, twenty feet to his right.

The big black wing of the Starship zoomed over their bodies, but PJ never saw it. He was diving head down, his arms and legs swept behind him, falling at about 175 feet per second.

If PJ's mind was tired before, it was now fully alive. He and the wind became one. His plummeting mass warmly accepted the blanket of air and the inexorable pull of gravity. PJ's first thought was regret that he had gone four years between jumps, so fulfilling was the immediate sense of freedom.

His eyes were wide, taking in all they could, memorizing the colors of the sky to the east, just now brightening with a hint of pink appearing in the light grey. The edge of the white and grey clouds on the horizon cleanly separated from the blue-grey sky, a razor mark at the end of the earth.

The rush of the wind billowed his cheeks and pulled his lips back from his teeth, helped by the irrepressible smile that seemed to spread from ear-to-ear across his face. He was so enthralled; he realized he hadn't attached his oxygen mask over his face.

He took a breath but felt nothing in his lungs. He reached for the mask, flapping at the side of his helmet and it seemed to take him a long time to get a grip on it. The colors of the sky changed and he dimly realized he had entered the clouds. Below him there was only darkness and he was descending deeper into it. He did not know where Pizzaro was.

"PJ open your chute," came a voice in his ears, calm, almost quiet, clear as a bell. But he didn't recognize it.

He finally controlled the facemask and held it tight to his face, and inhaled. Nothing came out. He fumbled for the dial on the small bottle, spun it and inhaled. The sweet taste of the oxygen filled him. He looked at the altimeter readout on his chest pack and pulled his ripcord. A rumpling noise was heard dimly behind his ears, like clothes flapping on a line, and suddenly he felt a giant hand jerk him upwards.

PJ took another deep breath, then another and the darkness around him became very real. He looked over his head and could just make out the rectangular cloth parawing, fully opened. He took another and cursed himself for giving in to the euphoria of free fall and not controlling his breathing. He looked at his GPS and saw his altitude was 7000 feet, only 1700 feet above the mountains! He had fallen 1000 feet more than he wanted. He cursed himself again and pressed his radio switch.

"Pizzaro, this is PJ. I'm with you," he radioed. "Thanks."

"PJ, I read you," Pizarro's voice came on and PJ realized he was hearing it over the radio for the first time. "Thanks for what?"

"Ah, never mind," PJ answered, confused momentarily about the voice that urged him to open his parachute. Who had he heard?

"What's your location?" asked Pizarro.

"Target is bearing 175 degrees, distance 3.3 miles, altitude 6900, 1400 Above Ground Level," PJ read from the well-lit display of his GPS.

"You're a little low and away," Pizzaro suggested. "I'm at 177 degrees, 4.2 miles, altitude 7950, AGL 2650."

"Roger. Guess I had too much fun falling," PJ admitted. "Wind speed reads 15, I'm turning toward target now."

PJ's problem was similar to his dead stick landing in the Starship. He had to balance forward movement with rate of descent to land on the target. By dropping the extra thousand feet he was forced to cover the remaining distance with less altitude to work with than Pizzaro. The parawing had a forward speed of fifteen miles an hour, but it would not keep him aloft indefinitely. His only solution was to increase his forward speed or he would land in the mountains north of the valley.

PJ eyed the instrument display on his GPS. He turned downwind, so the wind speed would be added to the parawing's forward speed. The GPS now calculated his approach speed at twenty-five knots. That number did not excite him. It meant the true wind behind him was only ten knots. He needed more.

The darkness around PJ was nearly complete, and it was darker below than above, since the sun's rays would not reach the valley floor until later. He felt weightless, floating on the wind, but the altimeter continued its downward spiral.

The wisps of cloud vapor were just visible in the light of the GPS display, and the vapor was moving. He glanced at the constantly changing read-out, which indicated he was dangerously below a safe glide path. He let his pack extend to the end of the fifteen-foot line. It would hit first, he thought.

"I need a big puff, Captain," PJ calmly radioed to Pizzaro. He thought of Kathryn's comment about mountains at the end of the runway and laughed to himself. Mountains of the mind.

"Roger, PJ. I'm reading solid 20 knots tailwind at 7000. AGL 1700. Target 180 degrees, 1.7 miles. I'm increasing descent slightly. Glide slope looks good."

PJ's numbers weren't so good. He was at 5700 feet, to the right of the river and only 100 feet above the ground, a mile and a half from the runway. At this rate, he would not clear the flat top canyon wall at the north end of the valley. Then he saw a pinpoint of light ahead.

"Out of clouds at 5700, Captain," he quickly radioed. "I'm going to be way short. Stay with plan A."

"Roger, PJ. Hope for a puff," Pizzaro said.

The light suddenly disappeared and PJ realized the cliffs along his approach probably blocked it. He thought of releasing his pack to lighten the load and gain altitude, but decided against it. He didn't want to land without survival gear.

He turned left, hoping to slide over the river, invisible in the dark below. Feeling a little wind puff from behind, he pulled on the risers, flaring the chute and catching a thirty-foot ride upward. He saw the light again, this time to the right. He dared not venture any further left for fear of the high cliffs on the other side of the river.

His body loose, his mind alert, all PJ's senses focused on his predicament. He needed to take advantage of anything that would help him. He expected to hit rock any second, he just hoped he could cushion the blow and not break any bones. He felt the wind pressure through the chute's control handles, trying to tweak every inch of altitude he could from the gusts and puffs. His forward speed was now twenty knots, but he needed thirty to make it. He forgot about the instruments and tried to focus in the darkness, using the light as reference.

The outline of the ridge came up quickly, a variation in blackness, but he saw it. When he heard his pack hit, he pulled up his knees and flared the chute. The rock was hard, but he came up running in the dark, his feet feeling each step, hoping not to stumble over the pack and be dragged by the chute, which was still drawing air. He ran about four steps when a glow appeared ahead just beyond the sharply outlined edge of the black land, and in the next second, the glow was directly below him and he was flying again!

An updraft rising up the face of the canyon wall caught the chute and sent him climbing rapidly until he had gained another seventy-five feet. His knees ached, but he hardly noticed and felt like screaming out thanks to the wind gods.

But someone might have heard for he was over the valley. Less than

300 feet below, spotlights lit up an aircraft parking area. He saw Quintaro's helicopter plain as day and three other planes, including the four-engine plane he was sure he had seen in Quintaro's hanger. He saw two men working on a single prop with an overhead wing.

"Pizzaro upwind final...touchdown," came the captain's voice. Seconds later, another transmission. "100 meters from end. Taking up position along river. Your location, PJ?"

Pizzaro was a cool customer, PJ thought. Dead solid perfect, calm and professional.

"Captain, I'm over aircraft, got an updraft, but well to the right of runway. I'll try and bring it in."

PJ did a tight circle over the aircraft to get another look and, seeing the operations building next to the parking area, wondered if Kathryn was there. He would know soon enough, he thought.

The circle cost him some altitude and he realized it was time to make his landing approach. He could see the beginnings of the dirt runway and the river's edge in the light from the aircraft parking area. He steered for the darkness at the other end of the runway.

He saw several buildings to his right, the barracks he guessed, each with a light over a door. One hundred feet above the ground, he reached the runway and prepared for his landing. He crossed the strip at an angle and began to turn into the wind for his final approach. At that moment, the winds of Codazzi spoke again.

A strong gust blew straight out of the river canyon, its dull hiss turning into a powerful roar. PJ guessed it was a thirty knot gust and it pushed him sideways, and up. He quickly initiated several circles to kill altitude, but he realized he was being blown downwind faster than he could fly upwind. And he was going to miss the end of the runway and land in the lake!

Altitude was now only sixty feet and he continued to circle, pulling hard on the control lines, spinning almost horizontally, dropping fast, but not quick enough. The chute rode the last bit of the powerful gust, carrying PJ in a dizzying spiral beyond the orange cone that marked the end of the runway. And then the wind gave out. It left PJ to drift slowly into the water, one hundred feet from shore.

Pizzaro watched helplessly, crouched on the bank of the noisy river, dimly aware of the spinning parawing as it corkscrewed its way over his head and into the water. He heard a double splash, a small one from PJ's pack, followed a second later by the bigger splash as PJ himself made a wet touchdown. There was nothing Pizzaro could do but wait.

"PJ's landed in the water," he radioed to the circling Starship after thirty seconds. "No sign yet."

Radios with Team One, on a narrow mountain trail about a mile beyond the ridge at the south end of the valley, and Team Two, sitting in Huey One waiting to move into position, heard Barney relay the message. The crew also could do little but listen, wait and wonder.

* * *

Kathryn had no idea what was happening just a few hundred feet from her room. Her mind was focused on escape and she sat still on the bed, her muscles tensed, her eyes adjusted to the half-light and her ears tuned to the hallway. The two guards were talking near her door. She knew the first touches of dawn would reach the valley in a few minutes.

She had hoped to slip through the window when the two guards got to chatting, just as they were doing at that moment, but she had been unable to budge it. Opened only six inches from the sill, it was too narrow for her to crawl through. She could only sit and wish they would hurry up and finish!

The round piece of aluminum felt light in her hand. Too light, she thought. She had fashioned the weapon from the sparsely furnished room by jamming the bent wire frame of the lampshade into the hollow end of a broken piece of curtain rod. The other end of the wire formed a four-pronged instrument, each prong three inches long. She looked at the makeshift weapon and prepared herself to use it.

The two guards stopped talking and within a minute, the outside guard could be heard walking past the window. She went to the door, and called to the other guard in Spanish, softly.

"Hello. Hombre. Can you help me? I need water," she tried to sound weak.

"Quiet, bitch! There is no water!" the guard answered.

"Oh, please, my friend, I have a soreness on my leg. I need water to soothe the pain," she begged him.

She heard his chair scrape on the wooden floor and then the door opened, and his head appeared in the darkened room. He flashed his bright light on the bed where she was sitting, the light landing on her bare leg, the pant rolled up well above her knee, her hands supporting her as she leaned backward. He stepped farther into the room, moving the light up and down her body. His weapon, a CETME rifle, was slung over his left shoulder.

"What is your problem?" he asked, standing near the bed.

"The pain is in my legs, and my cheek, see here, where the blood is," she said. He shined the light on her face and saw the remnants of the blood where Quintaro had punctured her with the knife.

"That is nothing!" the guard said.

"But my leg. It is sore," she pleaded with him.

"Maybe you need it massaged," he said with a smile, placing his hands on her leg, just above the calf."

"How does a young boy like you know what a lady needs?" she asked coyly, her fingers tightening around the makeshift knife.

"Ha, I have been around before I came here," he boasted.

She nearly choked on her next words.

"You feel good, such strong hands," she murmured, letting her head fall backward. She placed her left hand on his right hand, which was moving under her pant leg and inside her thigh.

"Oh, you are one hot lady!" he sighed in excitement. His rifle slipped of his shoulder, the barrel falling against her leg. Kathryn laughed.

"Your gun is excited, yes?" she cooed to him. He laughed, too, slipping the weapon off his arm and leaning over to place it on the side table. The movement opened his body to her briefly. She held his right hand firmly against her thigh and lunged at him with the makeshift prong, aiming for his neck, and striking him just under the chin.

She felt the flimsy prongs penetrate his skin, and she rose up on the bed and put her weight behind the weapon, pushing against him. He grabbed her with both hands and tumbled backward, landing heavily on the floor with Kathryn on top. She pushed the prong one more time and then rolled off him. He lay there, gasping for breath, his hands reaching for the instrument in his throat. He began to bleed.

Kathryn crawled on the floor to his rifle and grabbed the barrel. Using it as a bat, she went after him, swinging blindly toward his head and kept swinging until she hit something hard. She heard a crack and he went silent.

Without a pause, the gun still in her hand, she raced out of the room, through the small hallway and quickly to the front door of the two-story building. She wasn't sure where the outside guard might be, but started running anyway, across the plateau. It was light enough now to see the black mountain walls on the edge of the valley outlined against the dark grey clouds. The light had not reached the floor of the valley yet and she felt safer after running out of the bright circle of the barrack's spotlight.

She ran in a crouch to her left, away from the glow of the aircraft parking area, circling toward the back of the operations building several hundred yards away. The terrain ran slightly uphill and she stumbled several times over football-sized rocks, hidden in the knee-high scrub brush.

She reached the back of the ops building, and hid in a small, attached shed. She felt a wooden floor under her feet and stacks of canvas duffel bags piled several feet high. She leaned against one pile and buried her head inside her white sport coat, hoping it would muffle the sound of her heavy breathing. She thought about ridding herself of the white coat, but dismissed that idea. Warmth was important.

She knew she didn't have much time before they discovered her and she squeezed deeper between the duffle bags planning her next move. Out front, she heard the sound of an airplane engine start up and this time it kept running.

* * *

PJ spiraled toward the cold water of The Lake of the Empty Emerald and prepared himself for the shock. As his pack hit, he pulled the cutaway handle on his parawing to enter the water free of the chute. Nothing happened.

He looked down at the handle, pulled it again and then saw his reflection as plain as day between his feet in the rippling water. His face grinned back at him, a dim light in a forbidding blackness, that dissolved as his feet crashed right into the floating image and then the rest of his body followed. PJ thought of the cold showers he enjoyed taking and drew in a deep breath an instant before his head slipped into the cold. The water was very cold, but he locked that last gulp of air in his lungs.

The padded release handle, attached to Teflon cables and designed to breakaway the nylon risers and the chute, proved stubborn and PJ tried it only twice more before he reached for his military knife. Sheathed under his parachute harness, he unbuckled the flap that kept it in place and calmly began slicing through the straps over his shoulder. He thanked Stoney for buying sharp knives as the first riser cut easily. He was still falling through the cold water when he cut through the second strap. Every movement seemed to be in slow motion. He replaced the knife carefully in the sheath, and snapped the strap over the handle to keep it in place. However, now free of the canopy's drag on top of the water, the fifteen-pound equipment pack dangling below him dragged him deeper and faster.

He began to frog kick, spreading his legs wide and then forcing them together, doing the same with his hands, reaching up over his head and sweeping them backward, alternating the strokes to keep force always working upward. The pull of gravity was as strong as in free fall, but his body slowed, then stopped and began to rise, reluctantly changing direction.

He thought about the oxygen mask he could feel, but not see, flapping in his face, but didn't think he needed it yet. To stop and use it would require at least one hand and that would surely kill his upward momentum and send him downward again, following the pack to the icy blackness below.

The water was colder than those cold showers, and he thought about his muscles turning to stone, followed by hypothermia and then asphyxiation - all roads he wished not to travel. The images motivated him upward, his arms and legs reaching and kicking through the liquid. The gulp of air grabbed seconds before splashdown was exhaled slowly, releasing pressure on his lungs as he climbed through the blackness. The pressure on his ears lessened. He knew he was rising through the black and cold, and he stroked again and again, determined not to stop until he could take another breath.

He broke the surface a minute from the moment he went down. There was jubilation for only a second, as he gulped mightily for air, then he feared the noise he was making would wake up the world of the valley and expose him to discovery and, worse, gunfire.

He started swimming quietly toward shore, using the distant lights of the ops buildings to guide him. The pack dragged behind. His gloves, which had kept him warm in the high altitude, were now soaked and added to the extra weight. His nose and his fingers were growing numb. Then the hard bottom hit his knees, and he crawled to the shore, tired and happy to feel the solid earth.

He heard the crunch of footsteps and tried to pull his rifle, still attached across his back, into position. He gave up quickly and reached for his knife as the footsteps came right up to him.

"Holy Mother of God, can't you do anything right!" Pizzaro whispered. PJ could see a smile on his face and realized it was getting lighter every second.

"Hell, only missed by a hundred feet," PJ protested weakly. He was still out of breath and panted mightily as he scrambled to his feet. He started to shiver and knew they had to move quickly, both to warm him up and to get back on schedule.

"I'm okay," PJ said to Pizzaro, removing his helmet and slipping out of the still attached harness. He looked at his watch. Five minutes behind schedule. In another minute, PJ was ready to move.

"It's been quiet so far," Pizzaro reported, keeping his voice low, close to PJ's ear. "They are working on an aircraft engine over there, starting and stopping it. There is one guard at the barracks and a light in the middle of the valley. Looks like that guard tower is operational."

He pointed directly opposite them, just to the left of the three barrack buildings. PJ could just make out a dark outline. The Kogi scouts had reported it was still under construction when they had reconned the valley. It was camouflaged by the blackness of the mountain wall on the far side of the valley, but there appeared to be a light in it. He estimated it was at least half mile away, across open ground.

"Let's go for the barracks first," PJ said, cinching up his soaking wet pack. PJ was gambling that Kathryn, and the missing Indians, were being held either in the barracks or the Ops building. The only other shelter in the valley was the storage building, but that was third on his list. Then there was the mine, which Cesar guessed housed the processing lab.

PJ inserted a full clip into his M-16 and switched the select lever to semi-automatic. His radio was useless, so he had Pizzaro call Barney.

"Barney, this is Pizzaro. PJ is okay. We are moving into position. Give Team Two the signal."

"Roger, Captain. Good news. Team Two moving now." There was genuine relief in Barney's voice and Teams One and Two began to move, the fear of PJ's demise lifted from their hearts.

* * *

As PJ and Captain Pizzaro moved stealthily across the end of the runway toward the barracks, Team Two sat in a Huey on a flat spot two miles south of the valley. Dave, Dutch, and Crash were on board with two pilots and a gunner from Colonel Cesar's *Rapidero Fuego* force.

Twenty minutes ago, though it seemed to Dutch as if it were hours, they had landed between two mountains, navigating by GPS, radar and a powerful searchlight, the noise of their approach masked by a large ridge between them and the valley.

They immediately unloaded Team One, namely, Lenny, Stoney, Ray and Mickey. Those four had already started their two-mile trek to the valley up a drainage saddle between two mountains, climbing two thousand vertical feet over the first mile.

"Come on, guys, climbing the front face of Stowe is tougher than this," Stoney laughed, referring to the Vermont ski resort.

"I'd rather we rode the ski lift up and skied down," Lenny answered.

Team One hoped to arrive above the south ridge guard post in thirty minutes and secure that end of the Valley of Codazzi. It was a lot to ask, but Stoney had led them away from the chopper with grim enthusiasm.

On the signal from Barney, Team Two lifted off and set course for the high canyon plateau that ran parallel with the runway and overlooked the valley. Dave planned to set up the AGS-17 grenade launcher and provide cover, with Dutch and Crash supporting him.

"It's getting lighter, isn't it," Crash shouted over the sound of the Huey, looking out the open door. They had climbed back into the clouds, but the blackness that had surrounded them when they landed was now a solid grey.

"At least we can see better," Dutch shouted back. "I don't think these guys particularly liked landing in the dark. I know I didn't."

"And you'll like it this time?" Dave said skeptically, "With Quintaro's buddies watching us?"

Dutch shrugged his shoulders, fully aware of the situation. He could have easily stayed behind, with the burns he sustained in the gas tank explosion. His hands were wrapped in bandages, and his face was covered with a gooey salve that eased the heat, though it didn't change the deep red color. He hoped the painkiller the Rapideros' medic had given him would hold. At least he could hold a pair of binoculars and spot for Dave from the canyon wall.

"I sure hope Kathryn's here," Crash said, almost to herself. She held her AK-74 across her lap, and two canisters of grenade belts between her feet. Her mind replayed over and over the scene in the house at the ranch where two men had died by her hand. She was thankful she would be a healthy distance from the close-in fighting this time. She smiled at the young soldier balanced in the doorway, his M-60 machine gun at rest, pointed straight down. He smiled back wondering what possessed the young American woman to be there.

The noise of the Huey was deafening and made it easy for the four of them riding in the back to stay within their own thoughts. The pilots up front were glued to the GPS receiver, and their radar, climbing over the mountain ahead of them. They both knew that once they climbed over the mountain, they would be heard in the valley, before they were seen. They hoped their downwind approach would delay discovery.

~~~

CHAPTER TWENTY-SEVEN

P J heard the steady sound of a generator running far off to his right. He guessed it was coming from near the mine entrance. And he heard the wind. It continued to blow in gusts and puffs, howling to thirty knots, he thought, then settling back into a dull hiss of white noise. Even at a steady ten knots, the sound seemed magnified by the high rocks around them. It chilled him even as it whisked away the moisture in his jumpsuit.

He and Pizzaro were pressed against the barracks farthest from the Ops building. The three buildings surrounded a courtyard fifty feet across, the open end facing the plateau and the guard tower. PJ looked at his watch. It was 5:55 in the morning and they were behind schedule. They had little time to search for Kathryn and the Indians before Cesar showed up with his forces. He heard the single engine plane start up again and then shut off moments later.

Using the plane's noise as cover, PJ and Pizzaro entered the barracks and searched both floors. Both had seen rough drawings from Jester's files and moved quickly through the eight rooms, all unoccupied. Guards, not Indians stayed there, PJ thought. They must be the overnight shift.

In a corner room on the ground floor, PJ pulled two small explosive charges from Pizzaro's pack and attached them to the walls. The detonators were set to go off in five minutes. PJ had no sooner activated the detonator than a man's shout froze them both. They scrambled to the window, but the courtyard was empty.

A light went on in the barrack directly across from them. A door slammed to the right, in the general direction of the initial shout and the same voice could be heard again, only louder. PJ didn't understand what he was yelling and still could not see anyone.

"The prisoner has escaped. Get the doctor," Pizzaro translated in a whisper to PJ. They exchanged glances.

"One prisoner?" PJ asked. Pizzaro nodded.

"Kathryn?"

Pizzaro shrugged. "Could be one of the Indians."

It had to be Kathryn, thought PJ! He was thrilled, but not sure what to do next. More noises came from the barracks and three men came running out the door, two heading toward the shouts, the third going the opposite direction to circle around. Soon, three more guards appeared, all carrying rifles.

"We can't stay here," PJ said.

They retraced their steps, slipping out the door on the far side. Crouched against the outside wall, PJ thought about their options. And Kathryn's.

If she had indeed escaped, where would she go? Toward open ground? Maybe the river? What's the quickest way out of the valley? By plane, of course! PJ liked that idea. It is exactly what he would try to do if in her shoes. PJ knew what they had to do next.

Pizzaro pointed toward the dark hint of an object about one hundred yards away, right on the edge of lake. It looked like a box and beyond it, more shadowy shapes on the ground. PJ nodded.

"Let's create a diversion," PJ whispered. "We can use that object by the lake for cover, then take out the tower."

"Wait," Pizzaro said, and turned PJ around, pulling one of the charges from his pack. Pizzaro activated the detonator, setting if for two minutes and laid it just inside the doorway.

"Good idea," PJ said and when the explosive was set, he ran directly toward the lake. He hoped the general confusion, which was growing behind them would cover their movement.

PJ was twenty yards from the shadowy shape before he realized what it was...a small bulldozer. He ducked behind it, joined a moment later by Pizzaro, both out of sight for the moment. The guard tower stood silent lost in the valley darkness.

Scales of rust flaked off as PJ ran his hand over the bulldozer's engine cover. The letters N and A could be seen on the body, the others in the name brand long since obliterated by exposure to mother nature. One track was missing, the hulk apparently left where it had last stopped to rot away. He wondered if old Klaus Luki had flown it in to improve the dirt runway.

The other shadows PJ had seen were the overturned hulls of the Sunfish sailboats he had bought for the Indians three years ago. He momentarily wished he was sailing, but turned his attention to the growing noise coming from the barracks.

Headlights bounced through the darkness from the Ops building. Another pair of lights could be seen moving from up the plateau by the mine.

"I think the valley is awake," PJ said. "We have to take out this tower."

"Right," Pizzaro agreed quickly. "We will be exposed as soon as we start firing," he added matter of factly.

Pizzaro trained his night goggles on the tower. The cloud cover overhead was a light grey and even without the night vision aid, PJ picked up the outlines of rocks, brush, and the tower, all emerging from the night.

"See anyone?" he asked.

"Two men, both looking toward the barracks. I see a heavy caliber machine gun, looks like it's mounted."

"What do you guess, 350 meters?" PJ said, gauging the distance to the tower even as he propped his rifle through the open engine compartment of the dead tractor.

"Yes, less than 400, I think," Pizzaro answered. He also took aim on the tower, using the rear fender for support.

"When the barracks blow, we fire," PJ said, looking at his watch. "Then, we move to the south ridge and let your boys take care of the rest."

Pizzaro nodded. He looked at his watch. "They are already late."

"Less than a minute for the charges," PJ whispered.

Suddenly, the sound of another airplane filled the valley and bright lights appeared over the south ridge. Both PJ and Pizzaro looked over their shoulders, surprised. They were suddenly very exposed to the single engine plane making its final approach to the valley runway.

"Who the hell is this?" PJ said aloud. He watched the plane float gently over the lake, its flaps and gear extended. Its engine went quiet and PJ picked up another sound. A distant thumping.

"The Huey! It has to be Major Salazar and Team Two," Pizzaro said.

Sure enough, the distinctive noise of a Huey helicopter filled PJ's ears. They were coming in from the east as planned, unseen as yet, still in the clouds. The white plane, however, was plainly visible and PJ was sure the pilot looked right at them just before he touched down at the end of the runway.

The intrusion of new sounds into the valley was completed when the two detonators ignited inside the barracks creating a brilliant white flash accompanied by a deadly loud bang. That was followed a few seconds later by the third explosion.

For a moment, everyone in the valley, including the dozen workers on the overnight shift in the mine, the half dozen guards at their posts around the valley, the dozen workers on the off shift still asleep in barracks number two, the three mechanics, three pilots asleep in the Ops building, even Carlos Quintaro, dozing in his room across from the pilots, and Kathryn Byrnie, hiding in the shed among the duffel bags of cocaine behind the same building, either woke up or stopped what they were doing to take note of the explosions.

Except Rex Simka, who, startled by the sight of two men in camouflaged uniforms with weapons near that old rusting hulk of a tractor, had hit the runway hard in his white TBM 700. Even as he wondered who they were, he fought for control of his plane as it bounced once, than twice, and threatened to skitter off to the right unless he regained directional stability. He wasn't half way down the runway when he heard the two explosions behind him.

"What the hell is going on?" he asked the man sitting next to him. The man just shrugged his shoulders, his face white. He was only a guard at Quintaro's ranch who had been pulled from his post several hours ago to accompany Simka to the Barranquilla military base. He was now holding on to anything he could grab, thinking he would never survive his first visit to the Valley of Codazzi.

Simka slowed the plane, turned it back to the left and taxied under control to the parking area. Carlos Quintaro came rushing out of the Ops building as Simka's plane came to a stop.

"Grab the boxes, unload quickly!" Simka shouted to his passenger as he stepped from the plane. A mechanic joined them and the three pulled, while Simka's passenger pushed, and the four olive green boxes that sat in the cabin of the TBM 700 were hurriedly stacked on the ground.

"Rex, we are under attack!" Quintaro yelled. "We must get the planes airborne...immediately! We have to get the shipments away!" The weekly shipment, three thousand kilos of cocaine, was already loaded on the DHC-7 and was scheduled to fly to Marib Cay later in the morning. Quintaro was not about to let his business stop in the face of the explosions that had interrupted his sleep.

"I saw two men in camouflage by the lake!" Simka responded. "Where are Caron and Rafael?"

A guard came running up to both of them, out of breath.

"The woman, she has escaped!" he shouted.

"What? You idiots!" Quintaro shouted. He stood still for a moment, sorting his priorities. "Forget about her for now, she has nowhere to run. We must get the planes away and prepare to defend!" He turned to Simka.

"You got them, I see," Quintaro smiled, his green eyes wide. Simka nodded as Caron drove up in his jeep, two men in back, one apparently injured. "Well, let's get ready to use them!" Quintaro ordered and turned on his heel, walking back into the building. He didn't even turn his head at the sound of semi-automatic weapons fire that rang out from the direction of the lake, beyond the barracks.

"What happened to him?" Simka asked Caron as the jeep skidded to a halt. The young guard, with a bloody cloth around his neck was barely conscious as two men helped him from the jeep and carried into the Ops building.

"The woman stabbed him, he's lost a lot of blood!" Caron said, but his eyes fell on the boxes stacked next to Simka's plane.

"Forget about him, for now," Simka shouted. "Shots are coming from behind the barracks. Who the hell's in the tower?" Simka asked, taking command. More guards came running and more shots rang out from the lake.

"Andre, do you read?" Caron radioed one of the guards in the tower. There was no answer on the radio, but the silence was broken by the sound of the tower machine gun. Its heavy caliber report resounded off the canyon walls. More semi-automatic rifle fire answered and then there was quiet.

"Andre! Andre! Answer me!" Caron shouted into the radio.

"Take some men and find out what the hell is going on, damn it!" Simka shouted. "Take one of these!" he said, gesturing for the men to load a box on the jeep.

Simka flipped open the lid to reveal four weapons that looked like short stove pipes with the fins of a rocket sticking out one end. They were LAW rocket launchers, a Light Anti-tank Weapon, made in Norway, supplied to NATO and purchased from a supply sergeant in Colombia's Barranquilla army barracks, who had acquired them from the Spanish army.

Simka grabbed one of the fiberglass tubes, about four inches across and eighteen inches long. He extended the tube to nearly three feet with a yank at both ends. Sights popped up front and back and then Simka settled it on his shoulder.

"A throw away bazooka, Luis," Simka said, "One shot each, make sure you make it a good one. They'll take out a plane."

Caron waved three men into his jeep and jumped in himself.

"Luis, you must control this situation. Where is Rafael? He must take the DHC-7 immediately!" Simka said. "Carlos wants the shipments away now!"

"I'll be right back," Caron laughed as he loaded the box in the back of the jeep and drove off with the three men. At Simka's direction, another box was carried to the guard post at the near end of the runway.

"Who can fly that Cessna, dammit!" Quintaro yelled at one of the mechanics, his voice on edge. He knew they might be able to taxi it, but none of them could fly. It, too, was loaded with cocaine destined for the ranch and eventually, Europe. There was only one other pilot available and that was Quintaro himself.

Simka started after Quintaro when the unmistakable sound of a helicopter turned him back toward the lake. Then he saw it, a military Huey dropping out of the clouds, still several hundred feet in the air.

"Damn, Rex, your timing is impeccable," he muttered under his breath, smiling about his decision to return to the valley at sunrise. It was almost as if his arrival had triggered the chaos.

"Quick, open that box!" he shouted at one of the mechanics and pulled out one of the LAW rockets. He popped it open and took aim. The Huey made a sudden change in course toward the canyon wall. Simka waited until it was closer, then aimed slightly to the left and squeezed the trigger. The stovepipe exploded in a roar, fire blasting out the back while a projectile traveling at 400 feet a second left through the front, aimed to intersect paths with the Huey carrying Team Two.

No one saw it on board the chopper. The two pilots were busy looking to their right at the top of the canyon wall, their landing zone. They were happy to be out of the clouds, but were a few hundred yards off target and went hard right as soon as they realized they were fully exposed over the valley. Unwittingly, the turn gave Simka a wider target.

The rocket hit the tail rotor square on, exploding on contact, disintegrating the last four feet of the tail section. Without the tail rotor, Major Salazar had nothing to counter-act the torque of the main rotors and the Huey began to spin violently out of control. Salazar cut power immediately, auto-rotating the blades, but the Huey pitched over out of balance.

PJ and Pizzaro, still hiding by the tractor, watched in frozen horror at the explosion. The Huey begin to spin and fall. From their angle on the ground it appeared to be heading right for the two hundred foot high canyon wall. But, the chopper cleared the wall and disappeared from their view. There was the distant sound of crunching metal as it crashed on top of the canyon. Debris thrown by the wildly spinning blades fell over the side and dropped lazily into the river.

PJ waited for the sound of an explosion, but it never came. His heart sank and the commitment to come into the valley suddenly seemed so foolish in the face of the sure death of his close friends.

Gilmartin

"We have to move, PJ. Now!" came Pizzaro's voice. He was next to PJ.

"Dutch...my friends," PJ said, as if in a trance. "Crash..." Pizzaro grabbed his arm.

"Salazar was my friend. But we may join them if we don't move," Pizzaro said sternly. He had seen a lot of friends die at the hands of the drug makers. It didn't make it any easier.

"We follow the plan, to the tower, then toward the ridge, now move, McDonough!" he shouted.

PJ fought the urge to give up and moved to the front of the tractor. It would be a long run, over open ground, but if they got to the tower, the machine gun might hold off the guards until.... He never finished the thought because ripples appeared in the lake, followed by the pop, pop, pop of gunshots coming from the left. He saw a lone guard several hundred yards away, moving quickly toward them. His first shots had been short, but PJ didn't wait any longer and took off, sprinting as fast as he could toward the tower, the sound of more gunfire in his ears.

He didn't have time to think of the worst as he picked his way over the rough ground. Pizzaro opened fire to cover him from behind. PJ reached the guard tower safely, putting it between himself and the new gunman. The structure was little more than a platform with sides and he climbed the short ladder to the gun level, trying not to think about the two dead men lying on the wooden floor.

He had never killed a man before. It had seemed so easy when these two had popped into his sights and he had squeezed off several rounds while they watched the action near the barracks. Maybe Pizzaro got them, he thought. He didn't know because they both fired at the same time.

The lone guard was still moving closer and now PJ could see him clearly, about 300 yards away, trying to blend in along the rock walls that formed the valley boundaries on the west side. He crouched behind the thick wooden sides of the platform and opened fire with his M-16. The man sudden changed direction and began to zigzag, looking for cover.

Pizzaro made his break for the tower and PJ kept firing until he used up his clip. He heard more firing behind him. Changing clips, he fired off a dozen more shots when Pizzaro arrived at the platform.

"Does the machine gun work?" Pizzaro asked, panting slightly.

"Don't know," PJ answered and turned to look at it. It had two handles and he grabbed them. It reminded him of the .50 caliber machine guns carried on U.S. Navy riverine boats, with a protective plate through which the gunner had to look. He swung the barrel toward the lone gunman, but couldn't find him at first. Then he noticed him lying still about 200 meters away.

"I think you got him," Pizzaro said. "But, here comes more trouble." He pointed back toward the barracks and sure enough, at least a half dozen men were moving in their direction, behind a jeep. A second vehicle, a pickup with men in the rear, was sending up a cloud of dust far to their left, also heading their way.

"Andre? Andre?" squawked the radio of one of the dead men on the floor.

Pizzaro picked it up and spoke into it.

"We got them. They are dead," he said, hoping to delay the approach of the guards.

"Andre?" came the radio. PJ heard the disbelief in the speaker's voice.

"Fight or run?" PJ asked.

"Run where?" Pizzaro answered, looking at the box of bullets under the machine gun. He grabbed the big machine gun from PJ, cocked the firing lever and swung it to face the guards moving through the knee high brush. He fired off a few rounds, kicking up dust and sending the guards for cover.

"Just to let them know we're here," Pizzaro said with a grim smile. The guards were up again in a moment and continued their advance.

"Give me your radio, Captain. We have to give Barney a status check," PJ said to Pizzaro. "And find out where the hell everyone else is?"

More sounds joined the confusion as one of the four engines on the DHC-7 coughed to life. A second engine followed immediately.

"That big plane is trying to leave!" PJ said, looking through his binoculars. "I bet it's loaded with coke!" They were too far away to have any affect on its departure. And even as PJ watched, the big plane started to roll, taxiing down the runway toward the lake end. Its third and fourth engines coughed to life before it pirouetted at the edge of the lake and began to roll.

PJ crouched down with the walkie-talkie and called Barney circling overhead. The news wasn't good from the ground. It was 6:05 in the morning. Team Two had crashed. Team One was late. So was Cesar. He wondered what had happened to Kathryn. Where were the Indians? He knew there was no way he could reach the Ops building now. He couldn't help but think his plan was nothing but a disaster.

* * *

A shaft of sunlight caught Kathryn's eye as she huddled in her new hiding place. It came through an opening in the clouds that looked no bigger than a thumbprint in the sky. If it were a ray of hope or a sign from above, Kathryn didn't take it as such.

She had moved to the far side of the Ops building, away from the open plateau. There, between the building and a rocky slope, she shivered among tens of dozens of barrels she guessed were filled with gasoline, all interconnected by hoses. From there, she could see the parking area in front of the building.

As the valley awoke with explosions and shouts of men, she had changed her mind about escape more than once. Was it PJ and the crew trying to rescue her? Would she be better off staying put? The sound of an aircraft arriving, and the growing fear that she would be found, had prompted her to move.

She immediately recognized the tall, thin man who stepped out of the white plane. He was the same man who first accosted her in the hallway at Quintaro's party in Santa Marta and invited her to the kitchen under the pretext that PJ was waiting for her there. He had been one of the three men who had carried her to the boat. Now, here he was again, talking with Quintaro!

She watched in horror a few moments later when the tall man fired the rocket at some unseen target and heard the explosion and distant crunching of metal crashing against rock. She was convinced an attack was underway on the valley and decided to stay low and stay put.

She held the rifle in her hands. The CETME was different than the AK-74, but she was able to read the markings on the rife and switched the shot selection lever to automatic, despite Stoney's instructions. She wanted a steady stream of fire for protection.

She heard more gunfire coming from the plateau and wondered who was firing at whom. Minutes later, the sound of four engines winding up at full throttle reached her and then the DHC-7 suddenly appeared about twenty feet in the air and climbing at full power. In an instant it was gone beyond the rocks, its sound fading away quickly.

Voices from behind gave her a start and she saw two men coming around the corner of the Ops building from the rear, heading right toward her. One of them was the guard with green teeth who tried to rape her. The other had held her leg down. She shuddered.

Her first instinct was to turn and run, but she didn't move. Instead, she made a split second decision that came from a place she had not know existed inside her. Her fingers gripped the weapon loosely in her hand and she popped up, surprising the two men not fifty feet from her hiding place. They didn't get off a single shot as she sent three short bursts their way, dispatching the bad guys to their destiny among the barrels.

The shots committed Kathryn to her original plan and, without pause, she ran for the Cessna parked thirty yards away. Two more men appeared from the Ops building, alerted by the gunfire. She sprayed them with a salvo, driving them back into the building without a return shot.

She kept firing at the doorway until she ran out of bullets and then threw the gun down, covering the last few yards to the plane in a panic. She expected a bullet in the back any moment, but reached the pilot side door before the gunfire started from the building.

She wasn't fully in her seat yet when she reached for the throttle and turned the key. The engine came to life instantly, still warm from its recent tests. She hoped the mechanics fixed what was wrong. She punched the throttle to full on and started to move, the engine loud enough to block out the sound of bullets hitting metal behind her.

Simka came to the door behind the two men firing at the plane, Quintaro directly behind him.

"Who the hell is that?" Simka shouted.

"It's the woman!" one of the guards yelled back as he switched magazine clips on his rifle and started to run after her.

"That *puta!*" Quintaro shouted. "Simka, I want her dead, do you hear me. I want her dead!"

Simka saw the anger in his eyes. The sporadic sound of the rifle fire from the plateau, counter pointed by the heavier sound of the Uirapuru machine gun, fueled his rage. Operation Snowmine was crumbling around them. Simka couldn't remember ever seeing Quintaro as angry as he was at that moment. In a booming voice, Quintaro gave Simka a final order.

"If you can't kill her, don't bother coming back!"

Simka thought about killing Quintaro right there. But, he still needed him. The operation wasn't defeated yet. There was still $100 million if they could get through this. He ran for his plane without looking back.

Quintaro turned to his own helicopter pilot next to him. "Get the chopper ready, we're leaving!"

He looked at a Beechcraft twin parked off to the right, its cabin filled with cocaine and he thought for a second he might be better off taking it. But the thought disappeared as a sudden explosion ripped off part of the twin's wing and opened up the gas tank, igniting the gasoline and causing a secondary explosion that tore through the plane.

Quintaro, knocked back by the explosion, watched $25 million worth of cocaine reduced to a burning mess. He looked for the source of the explosion, but couldn't see or hear anything unusual, except the gunfight

---

continuing on the plateau.

"Son of a bitch!" he shouted and ran back into the Ops building. He quickly gathered a small pack and a knife with an eight-inch blade, slipping its sheath onto his belt. He had run out of contingency plans, save one.

Outside, the guards stationed at the end of the runway reacted slowly to the moving Cessna. They at first didn't pay much attention to it, thinking it was one of their own pilots. When they saw Kathryn's long black hair and two of their own men running after the plane, shooting at it, they got the message. One guard opened the box of LAW rockets and quickly set one up on his shoulder.

"Wait until it turns into the wind for take off," his companion said with a slight smile. He had seen dozens of take offs since coming into the valley. "She has to fly right over us." His companion, giving way to his wiser partner, understood and laughed the laugh of a bully who has cornered his prey.

Kathryn had already made up her mind there was no way she was going to follow normal flight procedures. She only had one option. She bounced onto the runway with the throttle wide open, glad Cessna had designed a plane for rough strips, and hoped the prop didn't catch a rock. Straightening out on the runway center, she lowered her flaps slightly to increase the wing surface and watched the painfully slow upward creep of the airspeed indicator.

A quick glance over her shoulder and she realized the plane was fully loaded with duffel bags. While it acted as a shield from the gunshots, the heavy load would make it harder to get in the air. The open cargo door wouldn't help the plane's aerodynamics, either. She shook her head at how crazy and desperate she was, fully aware of the wind gusting behind her. Every reason for avoiding downwind takeoffs ran through her mind, but she never once thought there was any other way.

The lake raced toward her and she pulled back on the wheel, only to get a mushy response. She had that sickening feeling a pilot gets when his plane isn't ready to leave the earth even though the available runway is about to run out. Instantly, she leveled the controls.

A flash of orange light went rushing past her, the same color as the rocket she had seen earlier. The two guards had realized she wasn't going to turn around, but in their haste, the rocket missed, passing just under the wing and splashing harmlessly in the lake. On the ground ahead, looking very lonely at the end of the runway, she saw the orange cone. Past the point of no return, she was committed to flight or a watery grave.

The mass of air flowing over and under the wings was close to supporting flight. The airspeed continued to climb, knot by knot. A ground effect built up under the wings and that helped increase lift. Kathryn waited until the last possible instant, and just as the cone disappeared under the nose, she gave the wheel a nudge backward.

For a second she thought the water had turned into freshly rolled asphalt because the rough ride on the dirt runway changed to a smooth ride on water. She was airborne! She wished aloud she could raise the landing gear to cut windage, but they were permanently fixed.

As the prop churned the air, she held level flight to take advantage of the ground effect until her speed increased sufficiently to climb out. When she did pull back on the controls, the high ridge across the south end of the valley loomed ahead. There was no way she could make it over. To punctuate that realization, she saw pinpoints of light coming from the top of the ridge. More guards were shooting at her.

The lake was about a mile wide and she made a steep bank to the right, the plane sluggish but controllable. Now, the canyon wall to the west filled her windshield as she leveled out and flew across the valley's width. There was no way out this way, either, and she turned back left, banking steeply, still climbing for altitude, keeping the plane on the edge of a stall. The altimeter passed 100 feet above ground and edged upward.

She heard movement behind and glanced over her shoulder to see duffel bags falling toward the lake through the open door. Eight in all had succumbed to the pull of gravity. She smiled as the turn and climb continued, the turbo charged engine roaring steadily at full power. The lightened load made the plane more responsive in her hands. She completed a full circle over the lake, feeling as though she were flying inside a gigantic indoor arena, surrounded by rock walls on the sides and the cloud layer above. She completed another half circle, leveled off at 350 feet, just under the clouds, her course due east back across the lake.

Below she caught the white plane moving on the runway, also taking off downwind. Lighter and with a more powerful engine, it lifted off easily and climbed at a sharp angle.

"He's going to chase me!" she said out loud. Then she saw the wreckage of the Huey helicopter just ahead, sitting on a narrow plateau on top of the canyon wall about two hundred feet above the valley. The broken fuselage was upside down, its wreckage spread over the rocks, but she could see three people moving. She circled left, flying directly over the spot of the crash. She saw another person in camouflage not moving. She recognized the tiny Christina right near the cliff's edge and big Dave next to her with the grenade launcher. She was right! They were coming to rescue her!

A blast of white and orange silently appeared on the ground near Quintaro's helicopter. A second and third followed in quick succession and then a fourth that landed just in front of the nose. The rotors jerked and shook and appeared to collapse.

Kathryn's heart leaped for joy, but then immediately sank as she realized she was not doing her rescuers any good flying around in someone else's plane! She completed half a left hand circle and spotted the white plane climbing towards her from out of the lake. He flashed a small light at her from under one wing, or that is what she thought until holes started to appear in her left wing.

"He's got a gun on that thing!" she shouted in amazement. "Oh, my God, a dogfight!"

She did a right hand wingover and dived, working hard to control her terror and concentrate on flying the plane. She dropped straight down for a few seconds and then pulled out of the dive, only 50 feet from the valley floor, turned hard right again over the lake and then left, flying back over the runway in the opposite direction from which she had taken off. Another duffel bag fell out.

The canyon wall was on her right, it seemed only a few feet from her wingtip and she lined herself up with the riverbed. She tried to make herself a small target, constantly altering her altitude. At one point she looked back, and caught a flash from the gun molded under the body of her chaser.

An explosion went off just below her as she crossed over the north end of the runway and entered the river canyon. Suddenly, she was inside a rock-lined hallway, the riverbed in the middle, twisting gently left and right. She remembered from the charts the key to flying out of the valley safely was to follow the river for several minutes until the canyon walls fell away and the river turned due west. Only then was it safe to climb into the clouds.

It was brighter now and Kathryn thought the clouds were thinning, as if the sun would suddenly appear. Sure enough, a small hole opened to the right, revealing a spot of blue. She checked behind her as the Cessna banked slightly right to follow the river's bend and caught a glimpse of the sunlight off a windshield. He was still there.

She continued to alter her altitude, at one point she was only twenty feet above the river. She climbed again, this time above the canyon walls. More blue patches could be seen to her right. The sky was definitely clearing, revealing ragged slopes of rocks. Far ahead, the clouds were thin enough to see parts of a snowcapped summit.

The blue was so unexpected that Kathryn failed to see the sharp left hand turn of the riverbed until she had flown past it. She was forced to climb as the ground below rose up toward her. There was no way she could turn back because the white plane was still there, and she knew there was no way she could outrun him. The sound of metal pinging and ripping behind her confirmed it.

Acting instinctively, she killed the throttle and pulled back hard on the wheel, sending the Cessna straight up as if on an elevator. At the top of the climb, just as she was about to stall, she pushed the nose down and pulled on more power. Directly below her the white plane came into view. She had caught him by surprise, forcing him to overshoot. He recovered quickly and pulled into a climb, heading right for her.

More bullets peppered her plane, many absorbed by the dozen bags still in back. However, she heard two smash into the instrument panel from underneath, missing her leg by inches. Her airspeed indicator suddenly read zero, apparently knocked out by one of the bullets. She still had power in the engine and kept it on full.

The sky continued to clear and she now could see a good distance on each side of her. She turned hard left, planning to circle. She watched the white plane climbing inside her circle, and it passed her close enough to clearly see the thin mustache on Rex Simka, and the look of determination set on his face.

She reversed her circle, banking right, and went into a steep climb. She caught a glimpse of him above her and well to the right, but also circling around to come at her from behind again. Now she wanted clouds. A few puffballs surrounded her briefly, but nothing big enough to get lost in. Suddenly, matching her speed and angle of climb exactly, the white plane appeared on her left wing. The pilot was gesturing to her, pointing downward.

She stared back at him and knew he would kill her as soon as they landed, if he didn't do it up in the air. Hoping that PJ and the crew, or whoever was fighting in the valley, would be in control when she landed was not a good risk. She would rather take her chances in the sky. She chopped power, slipping in behind him. He immediately dove away to the left and Kathryn responded with full power and a slight turn to the right. She started to climb and saw a trail of clouds ahead, spilling off a mountain peak. It looked to be only a few miles away.

She went right for it, coaxing every knot she could out of the rugged plane. She clung to the hope that she would figure out something to shake the relentless pilot in the white plane. Just in case she didn't, however, she flipped on the Emergency Locator Transmitter. The ELT broadcast a signal on 121.5 MHZ and she hoped someone would be listening. They could track the signal and find her. Find her body, she allowed under her breath.

She had gained considerable altitude, nearly 12,000 feet, but the ground had risen too, gently at first, but now more sharply. Rocks appeared close by on both sides. She had flown into a broad canyon that rose toward a peak.

She looked behind and picked up the white plane a good way off, closing rapidly. She continued to alternate her course, banking from side to side, climbing, and hoping to reach the top of the mountain and the safety of its clouds.

She was almost there, maybe a mile away when the bullets from the white plane shred more metal. The rudder controls became ineffective, the engine coughed, missed a beat and the rpms began to decrease. She tried to enrich the mixture of gas and air, but to no avail. The engine kept running, but she was losing power. She looked behind, but could not see her pursuer. She looked ahead at the snowcapped peak and its surrounding ridges and realized the gradual rise in the land from a distance was deceiving, because up close, the land went steeply upward. She realized she wasn't going to make it over the mountain.

More shots ripped the wings and a piece of the right wing's trailing edge disappeared. The plane was beginning to come apart. A trace of white smoke came from the engine. Her temperature gauge read hot and she knew a crash was imminent. She aimed for the soft looking snow on the side of the peak, but now even that was impossible as the nose of the Cessna dropped below the ridge and she began to fall.

The mountain filled her vision, the rocks jagged and hard, the snow unreachable. She knew it would be a hard landing. Then she felt just a nudge, a force, as if life had returned to her dying engine. The sensation became stronger and she saw the snow line was getting closer, not farther away. An updraft, she thought! She babied the throttle, and the engine coughed and sputtered, gasping its last. Yet, the nose was rising!

As if carried by a gentle, giant hand, the Cessna reached the edge of the sharply angled snowfield, its white, billowy form rising toward the rocky peak. She was going to make it! Just before impact, she pulled back on the control wheel, and killed the throttle, trying to stand the plane on its tail so it would hit the snow at the same angle as the slope and soften the impact. Amazingly, the plane responded once more, flaring at a forty-five degree angle, which burned off the last remnants of speed just before reaching the side of the mountain. It was still a hard landing.

The tail section hit first, cocked the plane onto its left wing tip, which snapped on impact and the cockpit came crashing down on its left side, burrowing into the loose snow about ten feet.

She thought of PJ a second before she hit. His smiling face had made her smile. She was sorry she had screwed up his rescue attempt. Then the voice of a man filled her mind, strangely familiar, but so very distant. "Zarzamora," the voice said and then her head hit the side window frame and she blacked out.

Rex Simka saw it all. He had climbed higher and positioned himself above for a shallow dive for the kill shot. He let off a burst of gunfire and saw part of the wing's trailing edge disintegrate. Watching the Cessna lose altitude, he realized she would never get over the ridge, so he added some power and pulled out of his own dive, content to let the mountain finish his task, a smile of satisfaction filling his face.

He set his course to cross over the ridge by one hundred feet, but suddenly, as he approached the rocky top, he felt the controls moving in his hands, as though a giant hand was slapping his TBM 700. He started to lose altitude! "Damn it!", he said to himself.

Mountain winds often create updrafts on one side of a peak, but once over the top, the updraft turns into a downdraft, following the terrain on the other side. Approaching only fifty feet above the ridge, Simka was caught in a downdraft. He applied full power and tried to escape the deadly winds that now gripped his plane. The mountain peak, under his cockpit window a second ago, was now above it.

He tried to turn around, banking hard right, but a rocky growth of mountain batted his wing tip, ripped off a six-foot section, and pitched the plane downward fifty feet into the snow. The long nose of the TBM 700 hit first, then it cart wheeled end over end before coming to rest on its roof at the higher end of the same snowfield where Kathryn had crashed.

The impact smashed Simka's face against the windshield as his shoulder harness ripped from the bolts in the cabin frame. Both his legs were caught under the instrument panel, his body held in place by his lap belt. The violent twisting of the tumbling plane crushed both his kneecaps. When the plane came to a stop in the snow, he howled in pain. He could smell gasoline as he lay in a crumpled ball, his head bleeding and pressed against the cracked windshield, his legs pinned in the cockpit.

He released his lap belt and his legs fell outward through the crushed door opening. He was dizzy with pain, passing in and out of consciousness, but still alive. Fearing a fire more than anything, he managed to drag his broken body away from the wrecked fuselage, leaving a small trail of blood in the snow. It was cold and the wind was fierce, howling over the nooks and crannies of the rocky peak one hundred feet over his head. He dragged himself to a small lump in the snow and leaned backward on it, looking up at the sky.

He dreamed about the sunny Mediterranean and beautiful women on an expensive yacht, everyone sipping cocktails, snorting coke and thinking about the wild night ahead. He was delirious, feeling the hot touch of an adoring woman one moment, and in the next, the cold rocks hanging over his head. Time didn't matter. His mind was free. Quintaro was a fool. He laughed to himself, the taste of blood in the back of his mouth.

Gilmartin

The laugh cut sharply to a cry of pain. He admitted he was a fool as well and laughed again leaning back on a lump in the snow.

A small tornado descended upon him, everything going white in the swirling blizzard. It soon passed and his bloody eyes were drawn to the color of gold next to him in the snow. He used his last bit of energy to raise himself up onto his elbow and looked at what the wind had uncovered. The lump he was leaning on was, in fact, a body, frozen in the snow with a gold pendant hanging around the neck.

It sparked a memory in his delirious mind, distant, but real. He had seen that pendant before. He touched it. Suddenly, the snow around him began to rumble. He looked up toward the mountain peak where another cloud of snow was swirling. Then he realized the snow was moving down the steep slope toward him. Avalanche!

The body under him also started to move, seemingly brought to life by the wave of the advancing snow. It stiffly sat up and toppled over on top of Simka, who still had his hand on the pendant. In that instant, Simka's mind filled with realization, as clear as day, as searing as the snow was cold, and as final as the last breath he took.

The brown face stared with black, penetrating eyes, only inches from Simka's own. The snow tumbled around them. Whiteness was everywhere. Simka saw a slight grin on the man's face. For one brief instant, Rex Simka was whole again. Every sense worked perfectly, every emotional fiber was alive and receptive, and the full weight of understanding flashed in his consciousness and consumed his soul.

"The mine superintendent!" he exclaimed at the grinning face, the words riding on the final breath of his life. And he died in the swirling snows at the top of the Valley of Codazzi.

~~~

CHAPTER TWENTY-EIGHT

The battle for the Valley of Codazzi took a new turn with the first explosion from the grenade launcher of Dave Bender. PJ couldn't believe it came from the top of the canyon, but the successive explosions confirmed it had to be Team Two. The twin-engine plane was destroyed and Quintaro's helicopter badly damaged by the blasts.

PJ's heart sang, even as it ached for Kathryn, who surely was flying the Cessna Caravan. Just knowing she was alive was a thrill, and to hear and see the plane was a joy to behold, yet he was so far from her.

He didn't have much time to dwell on it because he and Pizzaro had their hands full with the advancing guards. The Uirapuru machine gun had kept the guards at bay, but bullets were now in short supply. They fired in short bursts to conserve ammo, Pizzaro on the Uirapuru alternating with PJ's M-16. Already one rocket had been launched at them, but it had landed short, harmlessly exploding on the ground.

Slowly, the guards had spread out in front of them. PJ counted a dozen as they slowly advanced, staying low among the rocks and brush. He and Pizzaro could not cover them all and they moved one at a time between salvos, to the point where their return fire was regularly ripping into the thick wooden sides of the platform and more than a few had pinged off the metal shield around the machine gun. PJ wished he could radio Dave to direct his fire, but there had been no answer moments ago when Barney had tried to contact Team Two.

Team One had reported they were still a few minutes away from their position. PJ knew they didn't have a few minutes. Where the hell was Cesar?

Then an explosion behind the advancing guards from the east gave PJ some hope. Dave had figured it out for himself from his high perch. A second and third exploded to the left and right of the first one. Then a fourth. The guards, momentarily stopped by the sudden fireworks behind them, continued on. Dave's grenades were falling short.

"NO! They're beyond his range!" PJ shouted when he realized what was happening. Pizzaro let go another salvo from the Uirapuru but silence broke the string in mid burst.

"That's it, PJ. Out of ammo," Pizzaro said simply as he dropped to the other side of the platform and picked up his own M-16. A rocket explosion hit close, just to the right, sending rocks and dirt onto them and knocking away part of the south side of the platform.

"I think it's time to make our move again," PJ said dryly. Pizzaro nodded. They both knew the next rocket wouldn't miss.

"I have four clips left," Pizzaro said, looking in his pack.

"I have one," PJ held up his magazine, "plus half loaded."

"Which way? We're nearly surrounded," Pizzaro asked, handing PJ a clip and smiling weakly.

"I think to the south, away from the mine, toward Team One. The other way is a box canyon," PJ said, reaching for the radio.

"Let's go," Pizzaro said and moved first, crawling to the back of the tower.

"Barney, this is PJ. We are moving from the tower to south ridge. Please alert Team One."

Pizzaro was already off the platform and hugging the ground. PJ followed through the blown away panels and landed heavily on the ground. They both scrambled on their hands and knees toward the canyon wall and hadn't gotten fifty feet when the next rocket hit dead on target, exploding under the tower and sending debris everywhere.

The concussion from the blast was so loud that PJ suddenly couldn't hear very well. It was as if the volume had been turned down. A chunk of wood that had supported the platform hit PJ flush in the back, knocking the breath from him. He went down as if shot and lay on his side, unable to move. Pizzaro, ten yards ahead, came back and began to drag him as the dim sound of a hundred guns seemed to fill the air.

"No, no," PJ was saying, but nothing was coming out. The pain was intense and he tried to move his muscles, but nothing was responding. He was gasping for air, every breath painful.

"Damn!" Pizzaro exclaimed and they both went down.

"I'm hit! Damn!" Pizzaro winced, holding on to his leg. PJ forced himself to the Captain's side and saw the blood oozing between his fingers that covered the wound in his right thigh. PJ numbly reached for a compress in a vest pocket and placed the wad of gauze under Pizzaro's fingers. PJ looked in his eyes and saw the pain, his lips tight, the face tense, holding it in. Then Pizzaro's eyes moved left and his expression changed.

They were laying exposed about twenty yards from the side of the valley, only a few rocks and bushes for protection. PJ grabbed his rifle and sat up, looking around. He expected to see the guards upon them, but instead he saw three Hueys in formation, fifty feet off the ground, charging across the lake. From the left, flying from the box canyon near the mine, another Huey moved in and as PJ watched a 150-foot stream of fire spewed from its nose.

The guards, already running from the attack from the lake, ran right into the fire, and turned back. With nowhere to go, they started for the runway, only to see several grenades exploding in that direction, launched from the top of the valley by Dave.

Suddenly, a rocket trail shot out from the vicinity of the Ops building, aimed for the fire breathing dragon of a Huey and it was right on target. A brilliant explosion fueled by 400 gallons of gasoline, incinerated pilot Alberto and his co-pilot Esteve, the *Acalorados*.

PJ grabbed for his binoculars and caught of glimpse of a man putting down the small launcher.

"That was Quintaro," PJ said.

Pizzaro watched in stunned silence at the wreck that used to be Alberto's helicopter, a column of black smoke rising from the fire. The battle seemed to pause for an instant, enough for PJ to notice the clouds over the valley were thinning, replaced by a blue sky and sunshine.

The guards, flattened by the explosion of the fire breather, started moving again, slowly at first, one by one, then more rapidly, running toward the mine, the way now cleared by the destroyed Huey.

The other Hueys landed and quickly unloaded their troops. One took off again and joined the chase from above, sliding sideways over the retreating guards to allow the right side gunner to make use of their M-60 machine gun. A dotted line of fire sprayed the retreat, every fifth bullet a tracer, pointing the way.

PJ brought his binoculars back on Quintaro and saw him running toward the barracks with a satchel on his back.

"Where is he going?" PJ asked himself. Two soldiers came running towards them. PJ raised his rifle, but Pizzaro's hand stopped him.

"It's okay, PJ. Cepeda, you lug, over here! Get a medic!" he shouted out, his face in pain, a grim smile on his lips.

Lieutenant Cepeda and a second man dropped down next to Pizzaro and began to immediately work on his leg. PJ, whose breath had returned, was back watching Quintaro who had disappeared behind the barracks.

"Captain, you're in good hands. I've got some unfinished business," PJ said, standing wearily. His legs felt weak and his back hurt.

"PJ, your plan, how you say...it stunk!" Pizzaro laughed.   "But, it worked!"

"Captain, we still don't have Kathryn. Or the Indians," he said.

"We will find them," Pizzaro said, wincing as the medic worked on his wound.

PJ smiled at the brave professional and gave him a short salute. He would not want his job. Besides, there was another job to do. He looked toward the lake and started after Quintaro.

PJ could see the *Rapidero Fuego* troops moving in a ragged line to his left. He thought he saw Colonel Cesar among them, crouching next to a radioman. Looking behind the Hueys, toward the lake, Quintaro had reappeared along the shoreline, moving skillfully among the rocks, heading toward the old tractor that PJ and Pizzaro had used for cover.

PJ dropped his pack and gave chase. At first he thought Quintaro was trying to get to the south ridge where the mountain trail was located. He angled to the right to cut him off. But, in a moment, it was clear Quintaro had other ideas.

Quintaro stopped at one of the overturned sailboats and flipped the fourteen-foot hull over and slid it into the water. He quickly rigged the sail, sticking the mast in the deck and hoisting the brightly colored cloth. It only took about half a minute and then another ten seconds to rig the mainsheet. With a glance over his shoulder right at PJ, Quintaro hopped on board. In seconds, he was accelerating on the lake.

"Where the hell is he going?" PJ asked as he ran toward the boats. He thought about using his rifle, but he wanted Quintaro alive and it seemed there was no place to sail. The lake was a mile wide, maybe two miles long, and there was nothing on the other side but mountains. PJ then realized the slope of the mountain across the lake was not as severe as the ones on either side. Was there a trail no one knew about?

By the time PJ reached the boats, Quintaro was already fifty yards off the shore.

"Well, looks like this is just another sailboat race after all," he thought to himself and quickly rigged one of the boats. He remembered Jester's reaction to the surprise gift on the third anniversary of the mine's opening.

"Teach the Indians how to sail?" Jester had said skeptically.

"Sure. Hell, I'll bet production drops once they start fooling around on these things," PJ remembered joking. "They'll want to sail instead of work."

Quintaro was 200 yards away by the time PJ pushed away from the land, jumped in and hauled in on the mainsheet. The wind was coming from his left at maybe ten knots. As he began to accelerate, he could see wind waves rippling across the lake that looked like gusts closer to twenty. The darkest ripples were to the left and PJ headed for them.

With a flat bottom, it didn't take much to get the Sunfish planing, especially for someone with PJ's sailing skill. Sitting sideways, he hooked his feet under the webbed straps in the small cockpit, trimmed in the sail and turned left to take the wind over his left shoulder.

As the breeze pushed on the sail, PJ used his weight on the edge of the boat to counterbalance, keeping the hull flat on the water. With his left hand on the mainsheet and his right on the tiller extension, the Sunfish responded like a young colt and soon he was screaming along, the spray splashing up in his face.

He knew the water would be cold and when it hit his face, he let out a grin that would have lit up the dark valley just a hour ago. It was as if he had stepped from the twilight zone of the last 24 hours into another afternoon of match racing with Dutch on Long Island Sound. The thought that his friend might be alive up on the top of the canyon made the smile all that much wider. The weariness faded from his brain and he clicked into sailing mode.

Quintaro was definitely heading across the lake to the southeast corner of the valley, where the mountain slope could be climbed. He had the boat steady, but did not look comfortable on it. He certainly didn't have the hull planing and the sail was eased well out. PJ was moving twice as fast.

He angled his course more easterly, keeping Quintaro to his right. In fifteen seconds, he reached the dark patch of ripples where the stronger wind was and turned right about ten degrees, bearing off to make the most of the wind gust. He tenderly adjusted the sail, easing slightly. His speed increased and he drew closer to Quintaro.

He rode the puff as long as it lasted and then hardened up toward the East again to maintain speed. Quintaro was now in the middle of the lake, while PJ was closer to the shore, a quarter of a mile from him, but now directly abeam. As PJ raced past the mouth of the river, he gybed, switching the sail to the other side and aimed directly at Quintaro.

Two more gybes, he thought, as he accelerated out of the turn. Back on a plane, the fiberglass hull skittered across the deep blue water. PJ constantly adjusted the sail and angle of his body hanging out over the water to keep the boat moving at its maximum speed and take best advantage of every puff of wind. He crossed about 100 yards behind Quintaro, eliciting a glance from the white haired man. When he gybed again, turning back to the left, he was only twenty yards behind.

Quintaro gybed also, turning right. PJ mirrored his actions and now was closing in from behind. The wind shadow of his sail was beginning to disrupt the airflow on Quintaro's sail. The distance closed to ten yards, and Quintaro gybed again. PJ was so caught up in the gybing duel that he didn't even think that Quintaro might have a gun until he was right on his tail.

"Give it up, Carlos!" PJ yelled out. "There is no place to go. And you're not going to out sail me." PJ sailed to Quintaro's left, only five yards apart.

"You are a complete nuisance, McDonough!" Quintaro shouted at him and gybed away, the boom swinging violently around, just missing Quintaro's head as he ducked under it. PJ followed and accelerated, edging closer, drawing even along the right side, their hulls overlapped. Their little gybing duel had carried them to the south end of the lake, the high ridge at the end of the valley sloping up sharply only 200 feet ahead.

PJ was content to just shadow Quintaro until they hit the shore. Quintaro was not and suddenly turned hard right, intent on ramming PJ. PJ reacted late, but pushed the tiller all the way over and his boat spun around, making a 270-degree turn, and PJ's stern passed just in front of Quintaro's bow. PJ accelerated away and then turned back toward his adversary. Quintaro's turn had faced his sail directly into the wind and he floundered for a few seconds before he bore off to get his boat moving again.

"Give it up, Carlos," PJ yelled, as both boats took opposite courses, heading right for each other. PJ thought it odd that the mountain behind Quintaro was moving, then realized both of them were actually moving sideways as well as forward. Current in a lake, he thought? Odd. He looked to his left, surprised that the land was now half as close as before.

As the two boats came together, Quintaro turned off first, just enough to have PJ's boat slide down his left side. The sail blocked PJ's view, but suddenly a knife blade appeared through the brightly colored material, tearing a three-foot section, before it disappeared.

"You're going to die, McDonough! I promise you that," Quintaro yelled, his voice filled with anger. PJ said nothing, more worried about the sail holding together. It did, but PJ knew it might not for long. He carefully tacked, turning back toward Quintaro who was now sailing away. The rip hurt PJ's speed, and he was reluctant to put pressure on it by sheeting it in tighter. But, in the next instant, he wasn't given much choice.

Sitting on the left side of the Sunfish, twenty yards behind Quintaro, PJ noticed little splashes began to appear just behind his own boat.

PJ understood immediately what the splashes were. The guard up on the ridge was shooting at him. He pulled on the mainsheet and accelerated even as the bullets walked their way right to him. Then he spotted the flash of the gun, coming from up high. San Francisco Bay crossed his mind and he cursed.

He steered for Quintaro, trying to stay close and hoped the guard wouldn't shoot the boss! The ripped sailcloth flapped in the breeze, and PJ saw the tear lengthening. He had no choice but to hold his speed.

Quintaro, knowing he couldn't out run PJ, suddenly turned and came right back at PJ. He brandished the knife in his left hand and PJ patted his own knife still in its sheath on his chest to make sure he could reach it quickly. He didn't relish a knife fight, but had to stay close to Quintaro.

He prepared to pass on Quintaro's right side, keeping both sails between him and the knife. But, his plan was short lived because the sail gave way completely, the three-foot tear ripping right to the edge. Like pulling up a shade, PJ now had a full view of the shore, only twenty feet away. He wondered briefly about the current, but Quintaro gained his attention again by ramming into the right side of PJ's boat. The bow rode up and over, and PJ reached out to fend it off.

Quintaro pressed the attack, leaping through the large gap in the torn sail and onto PJ, the eight-inch blade in his left hand slashing downward. PJ blocked the blow with his arm, but Quintaro landed on top of PJ and tipped the narrow hull over on its side.

PJ held onto Quintaro's left wrist, keeping the knife at bay, but his feet were hooked under the webbed straps and he was unable to move. As the boat capsized, PJ's head and shoulders went underwater and Quintaro's weight held him there.

With no leverage to pull himself up, all PJ could do was hold onto Quintaro's wrist. Quintaro, in excellent condition, continued to slash at PJ with the knife. The two thrashed in the water until PJ finally unhooked his feet from the hiking straps. Quintaro, still on the boat, now pushed down on PJ's head, holding him under. PJ needed air. He let go of Quintaro's wrist, twisted away from the knife and broke the surface, gasping. Quintaro was right there, those evil green eyes laughing as he raised his left arm and plunged the knife toward PJ again.

PJ heard a couple of noises in that instant. One was a gunshot, the distinctive report of an AK-74, but well in the distance. The second was like rushing water.

He slapped at the knife with his right hand, hitting the blade, and deflecting the blow. He didn't feel the pain, but blood started to flow from a gash across his palm. The slashing knife was now under water and PJ again grabbed Quintaro's wrist and with his other hand, grabbed the back of Quintaro's jacket.

Their struggle was unexpectedly interrupted as the strong current pulled the fiberglass hull under Quintaro against the rocks. The Sunfish hull started to break up as the bow was sucked under the rocks, a small outcropping that masked an underground stream that had been formed over the centuries. The stern lifted out of the water and the hull, already submerged by the weight of the two men, was literally pulled out from between PJ and Quintaro. Then the current worked on their bodies.

PJ felt it first with his legs, as if a fishing line were reeling him in feet first. Still struggling and not ready to let go, the two combatants were quickly swept under the rocks and into the underground passage.

It was pitch black and the two men were pulled through the wet cold. The passage narrowed and PJ let go his grip on Quintaro's jacket, but continued to hold his wrist, fearing it might be the last human contact he would experience. The knife was no longer PJ's main concern. Now he wondered if this passage was big enough for a human.

It was big enough for the hull of a Sunfish, but the walls, smoothed by centuries of nature's constant cleansing, forced the two men through in single file. PJ couldn't tell if he were facing up or down in the blackness, but he led the way feet first. They rubbed against the walls, as if they were sliding down a water slide at a nearby amusement park. However, this ride didn't let them breathe.

The steady, noiseless current pulled them through the tunnel for maybe half a minute when suddenly PJ felt airborne. He had never ridden a wave through the night, he thought. The change in movement caused him to lose his grip on Quintaro. He was suddenly alone, gasping for air, even as he flew through it. The sound of his lungs greedily sucking in oxygen creating an echo that was lost in the crashing, wildly gushing sound of a waterfall. PJ thought he heard a scream above him. By the time he realized he was falling, he crashed into the water again, hitting something with his boots. It was solid but gave way on impact. The sailboat hull, he guessed.

He heard a splash next to him, but then he was underwater again, struggling to surface. The blackness was complete, darker than inner space, the complete absence of light. Only his senses of touch and hearing could help him figure out where he was. He felt his hand come out of the water and his head followed. Air! He drank it greedily, lustily, happily. It tasted grand and the cold that crept through his body was not as important as the sweetness of breathing. The sound of the crashing water faded and he realized he was still riding a stream to who knows where.

"Quintaro!" he shouted, the sound resonating off the nearby walls. There was no answer. There was only cold. Rushing water. Unknown.

Did he fear the unknown? He feared losing his innate belief in his ability to handle any situation. Reactions were frozen by fear, he knew, and right now, reactions were all he had left to rely on. He would not let himself be afraid and did not allow himself the thought that he might be dead before he got to wherever he was going.

He sensed his speed increase, and in mid breath, he was back under water again. The cold continued to take feeling from his hands and legs. He tumbled along in the watery tunnel, helpless, the cold reaching for his mind.

There is no future, he thought, there is only now, and this is reality. The reality, McDonough, is simple - you are screwed, chewed and spewed! Nice going, you lead footed, gear head! Last time you go sailboat racing! Hey, no regrets, boys. We tried to do it right. This was the price we feared, though we never believed we would have to pay. Sorry, Jester. Sorry, Mom. Sorry, Kathryn. I am better for having known you.

PJ's boot hit something and he stopped moving. He could sense the water was still flowing past his body, but he was pinned against an opening. His mind and body were nearly sapped, but he felt around for the object he hit. It was the hull of the Sunfish, wedged in an opening. Was that light, he saw ahead? He moved around the hull. Everything was in slow motion, but he did see something.

He found the handle on the bow of the hull. He felt for the opening in the tunnel and braced his feet on each side. He pulled with his last bit of energy and the sailboat hull moved! He slipped into the opening, letting the current pull him through. He saw a light ahead.

"I hope it isn't a trick," he thought and that was the last thing he remembered before the water passage spit him out, sending him airborne again thirty feet down to a small pool that reflected the light from outside. He didn't feel the bump on the head and floated out from under the lip of a cavern and into the sunny river. He hit a rock on the shore and took a breath, and then another and another. Semi-conscious, spitting water, he wondered if the puffy clouds overhead were real.

~~~

CHAPTER TWENTY-NINE

Kathryn Byrnie saw the young boy playing by the river's edge and knew it was her brother, Eduardo. The image was a clear one, faded into her mind from blackness, the subdued colors of the mountains filling the view. The browns of the earth, the blues of the water, the greens of the trees and the whites of the snows formed a vision of her life, a moment from the past hidden deep in her subconscious.

Colorful, noisy birds provided the background sounds and the giggles of her sister playing in the dirt nearby provided the focus. Eduardo walked up to them both, proudly displaying a frog he had caught.

"I can be the master of these mountains, little ones," he said with a smile. Their father sat nearby and spoke to his young son. "Not master, Eduardo. You must be one with the mountains."

They didn't understand their father, being very young, but Kathryn knew her brother was happy. Then the vision changed and the air was filled with snow, powder dancing everywhere in spirals of white. She thought it odd she couldn't feel the cold.

When the snow cleared, Eduardo was standing before her, a small, but strong looking man. His deep, black eyes carried a calm, friendly look, as if he was at peace with himself and his world.

"Hello, Zarzamora," he said, a smile filling his brown face. "I have missed you." The way he pronounced the name, the tone of his voice, felt as much as heard. Then she understood!

He reached out with his hand and touched her cheek and the touch was warm. She just smiled and placed her hand on his, looking deeply into his eyes. It was his face she had seen in the waters off Ram Island, his voice she had felt from the water and heard at the statue.

"You are as lovely as our mother. And our sister," he said.

"You are as brave as I dreamt of you," she answered. "And as wise as our father."

"Our father understands the ways of pure thought and *aluna*," he answered. He gazed at her intently, as if trying to make up the missing years in just a few moments. "I cannot stay very long," he said.

"I am not going with you?" she asked. He shook his head and she nodded slowly, unsure if that was good or bad. "Then I will always carry you inside me," she finally said, holding his hand over her heart.

"Yes, you will," he answered and reached around his neck to remove the gold pendant of the Indian deity.

"Take this," he commanded and placed it in her hand, closing her fist over it with his own fingers. "It has been a part of our family for centuries and will always be a reminder of who you are and where you came from."

"And of you," she said softly, looking down at the gold figure in her hand. She felt sadness for a lost life of love from a brother and a family she never really knew.

"I will never let it go," she said, looking up at his open smile, slightly crooked like her own.

"Tell Azulmora I am one with the mountains and will be near her everyday." She nodded again.

Snow began to swirl around them and she heard a roaring noise, and the snow was soon overwhelming and she watched Eduardo melt into the whiteness, the look of peace still in his eyes.

A blast of cold air slammed into her face, forcing her to turn away. The sound was louder now and she recognized it as mechanical, manmade and of the world she knew. She looked up, the whiteness still swirling about her and she could make out the figures of two men walking toward her in the deep snow, dressed in uniforms, their helicopter the source of the blowing snow.

She realized she would never see Eduardo again.

~~~

CHAPTER THIRTY

Lenny, Stoney, Ray and Mickey came over the crest of the final ridge, looked down upon the deep blue lake and the stark Valley of Codazzi bathed in sunlight. They saw a scene none of them could have ever imagined. It looked like the bad dream of a rum-crazed sailor just back from a desert war.

Hueys on the ground, soldiers and guards on the run, billows of smoke and tongues of flame rising from a variety of buildings across the brown and green terrain and two colorful sailboats streaking across the lake in what appeared to be a fun loving race.

"I guess we're late," Lenny said.

Bad information in the form of an extra thousand-foot ridge on their march had nearly doubled the time it took for them to get to the valley. Ray had taken a bad fall, spraining his ankle to slow them down further. Awed, frustrated and angry, they stood overlooking the scene, not sure what to do next.

"Look, right below, a shooter in grey and brown," Stoney pointed at the south ridge in front of them. The ridge was at right angles to the mountain they had just crossed.

"That's PJ in one of the sailboats," Mickey shouted, binoculars to his eyes. "Other guy has white hair, could be Quintaro...man! They just collided!"

Stoney didn't hear the last because he had already moved down the slope fifty yards, positioned himself behind some rocks and took aim at the guard firing at the sailboats. Stoney estimated the range was about two hundred yards. The guard was hunched down in a circle of rocks and sandbags on the top of the ridge and had no idea that Team One was behind him.

Stoney opened fire. The first shots fell short, but close enough to get the guard's attention. He had time to only turn and look at the source of the bullets when the next salvo scored a direct hit and the guard and his gun were silenced.

Lenny joined Stoney, clambering down the hill in an avalanche of small rocks and stones.

"Nice shooting, old man," Lenny offered. "What the hell is PJ doing? Pre-start maneuvers?"

"No idea, Len," Stoney answered, watching intently.

Mickey hadn't moved, watching the sailing drama playing out on the lake from higher up on the slope. Ray was sitting next to him in pain.

"I don't believe it, I don't believe it," he shouted. He lowered the glasses and started running down to the other two. Ray started after him slowly.

"They've gone under the rocks!" he was shouting, even as he stumbled and fell, sliding the last twenty feet on his back. He landed at Stoney's side, still shouting.

"They've gone under the water and the rocks...I'm sure of it, I can't believe it," he winced, struggling to get up and resume watching.

Everyone took out binoculars and trained their eyes on the lake, but now there was nothing to see.

"What the hell is that?" Stoney asked, spotting two silver poles sticking out of the water, hard against the rock shore, blue, red and white tatters flapping in the breeze.

"Wow! It's the mast and sail rig," Lenny exclaimed. "Looks like its wedged against the shore, probably the boom stuck underneath."

"But where's the rest of the boat and PJ?" Stoney asked.

"I told you, they went under the rocks, like they were sucked down by a shark or a vacuum cleaner!" Mickey said in amazement. "Just sucked away...."

Stoney reached for his radio, his eyes showing concern. They were easily a quarter of a mile from the lakeshore where the rigging was wedged and that was line of sight. They still had to cover a steep slope dropping several hundred feet just to get off the ridge. There was no way they could get to the lake quickly.

"Barney, this is Stoney. We need a chopper and medic at the south end of lake immediately. We think PJ is under water. Hurry!" Stoney wasn't optimistic.

"Let's get down there," Stoney said as Ray arrived and dropped next to him.

"No, listen," Mickey said, grabbing Stoney by the arm. "The chopper can be there before we get a hundred yards. This is crazy, but I'm heading to the other side of the ridge...look, there's a stream at the bottom of that ravine."

"So?" said Stoney.

"You are crazy," Lenny said.

"PJ's done some amazing things, but swimming through rock is beyond even him," Ray offered.

"Unless there's already a path...hey, you've heard about underground streams. Fissures, cracks inside the mountains, years of water eroding away the rock...Discovery channel did a story on one in New Zealand that drops 600 feet inside a mountain."

Mickey looked at everyone. They all believed they had just witnessed the drowning of their good friend and leader.

"How does he breathe?" Lenny asked.

"What do we have to lose?" Mickey said. He didn't know how he would breathe, but he had said his piece and started moving down the slope to his right.

"He's right, Stone Man. It's one in a million, hell, its the only chance, come on!" Lenny urged, rising to his feet. Stoney and Ray looked at each other, shrugged their shoulders.

"Go ahead, I'll catch up," Ray said.

"Gimme your pack," Stoney said and pulled it off Ray and followed Lenny down the slope.

They had been scrambling down the mountain less than three minutes when Mickey started shouting from up ahead.

"There he is! There he is! Holy mother of God, I don't believe my eyes...he's right there!"

Mickey reached the narrow ledge above the river and started running to his right. He stopped above PJ's body lying about 100 feet below him, wedged between two rocks, half in and half out of the water.

He immediately removed his pack, and pulled out a coil of kevlar rope. Lenny was there next, took a look and did the same. They each had a fifty foot coil with them and soon Stoney, the lightest, was hooked to a makeshift harness configured by Lenny and was lowered down to PJ, the two others acting as the counterweight. Stoney was half way down the slope when Ray added his weight to the line.

Stoney found PJ semi-conscious, muttering under his shallow breath with lips purple and his face a grey, waxy color. Stoney carefully pulled him out of the water and wrapped him in a poncho.

The Huey with medic appeared over the ridge, alerted to the discovery by radio. However, the ravine was too narrow for it to land and, not designed for rescue work, it did not have a winch. Lenny improvised and shouted down instructions to Stoney, who rigged a harness for both him and PJ. The Huey hovered next to the ledge and Lenny tied the other end of the rope to the skids. Lenny never tied as good a knot on a sailboat as he tied to that skid and the chopper slowly lifted Stoney, his arms securely over the sling and around PJ.

In the air, hanging 100 feet below the Huey and three hundred feet above the valley, PJ opened his eyes again and looked at Stoney, not six inches from his face. A small smiled crossed PJ's discolored lips.

"I guess this isn't heaven if you're here," he said.

"Hey, be nice! You don't want me to drop you, do you?" Stoney grinned broadly, happy to see the first sign of life in PJ's blue eyes since they had found him.

"What about Kathryn?" he asked.

"Don't know yet. Barney said they had an ELT signal but were still looking," Stoney answered. He didn't know what else to say.

The sun felt good on PJ and he took it as a good sign that he could feel pain in his right hand where Quintaro had slashed him.

"Did you find Quintaro? He was right behind me," PJ asked. Stoney just shook his head. "We didn't find anyone else, PJ. We were lucky to find you!" Miraculous, Stoney thought.

"It was quite a ride, Stoney. Quite a ride," PJ said softly, looking back at the ridge and lake under them.

The chopper eased them into the waiting arms of soldiers around the Ops building, where the aircraft parking area had been turned into a field hospital. PJ was immediately stripped of his wet clothing, and dressed in dry clothes, ironically the grey and brown uniform of Quintaro's men. He suddenly grabbed at his pants, reaching into the pocket to pull something from it before they were tossed in a pile.

The medic wrapped him in blankets and placed him on one of several mattresses pulled from the buildings and arranged on the ground. He was shivering uncontrollably, but the blankets felt good as did the warm towels soaked in hot water that were applied to his feet and head. His slashed hand was bandaged and PJ started to feel little pains, as the shakes slowly disappeared.

There was a lot of activity around him. Several other soldiers were on mattresses. He saw Pizzaro about twenty feet away, Colonel Cesar crouched down by his side. Cesar worked his way toward PJ, stopping at each wounded man. PJ saw five men off to the side with blankets over them and realized they hadn't been so lucky. Cesar bent down next to PJ.

"I'm sorry about your men in the Huey, Colonel," PJ said as Cesar took his hand. The lines on his face seemed sharper than normal, his eyes more tired. He nodded his head.

"This war is a constant sacrifice, McDonough," he said. "But we have inflicted a heavy toll here." As if to punctuate his remarks, a muffled explosion came from beyond the Ops building back up the box canyon in the direction of the mine. Cesar closed his eyes for a moment, then let go a deep sigh.

"This drug maker is out of business," he pronounced and squeezed PJ's arm. "The Indians, PJ. There is no sign of them but, I have good news. They have found your woman friend, Kathryn. She is hurt, but she is alive."

"Where is she?" he asked, happily shocked by the news.

"They zeroed in on her ELT about ten miles north, up on Codazzi. I understand they found her and another person, but he didn't make it."

PJ couldn't speak, but his smile spoke volumes to Cesar who smiled back and moved on to the next wounded man. PJ's head lay back on the mattress, looking straight up at the blue sky and the puffy clouds. He had never felt such joy. A moment later, charged by the news, he took off the blankets and slowly sat up.

Another Huey was landing on the edge of the parking area and several men were moving toward it. Dave and Christina got off and slowly walked toward PJ. Dave was badly limping, helped by Major Salazar. Christina's face was partially covered with a bloody bandage.

The three were happy to see each other. PJ slipped under Dave's free shoulder and helped him to a mattress. He had apparently crushed his foot. Flying metal had cut Christina in the crash. She was crying and threw her arms around PJ's neck. He held her close. Her youthful tears were infectious and he could feel the tears of his own beginning to run.

"PJ, let's not do this ever again," she said choking back a cry.

"I promise," he laughed gently. "They found Kathryn!" he managed to say, but the helicopter caught his attention again behind them. The soldiers were lifting the body of one of their soldiers. It was the young machine gunner.

He looked at Dave, the first hint of realization in his voice. "Where's Dutch?" he asked.

Dave's lips were tight, his face sad and just shook his head and looked down. He couldn't say it. PJ was already moving toward the helicopter, his tears of joy vanishing, washed by a new emotion that was draining what little color had been restored in his face.

"Oh, PJ, he didn't make it!" Christina sobbed after him and then she turned to Dave and they held each other.

PJ found his buddy lying on the floor of the helicopter, the whole right side of his uniform soaked in blood. He picked up his head gently, the eyes closed, the blond hair still neatly in place. There was a look of determination frozen on his mouth, a look that PJ had seen before. It was the look of a fighter who went down swinging, as if his last act had been to reach out and hold back the earth as the tumbling helicopter fell toward it.

The tears flowed unashamedly from PJ, as he cradled his dead friend whose spirit had been so alive in him only minutes before. He knew he would carry that spirit with him wherever he went.

He felt a hand on his shoulder. It was one of Cesar's men explaining in Spanish they had to unload the chopper because it was needed to pick up others. PJ nodded absently and let go of Dutch, watching the men carry his friend's lifeless body away to the field hospital.

He found himself walking toward the river and stood there for a long time. The pain and anguish was intense, and filled every pore and nerve. He felt guilt and an immense sadness that overwhelmed him and unleashed a gruesome howl from deep in his soul that echoed off the hard canyon walls and sent a shiver down the spines of the soldiers who were busy in the parking area.

Later, sitting by the river, PJ was joined by Lenny, Stoney and Christina. They sat for a moment in silence.

"He told me to tell you, he was glad we came," Christina said. "He said if you can't fight for your friends, it's not worth having any."

PJ nodded his head. "He loved a fight, didn't he," he said. "That's what I loved about him."

Another Huey came thumping in from their left, out of the river canyon. PJ thought Kathryn might be on board. It landed on the runway just behind them and he walked toward it, shielding his eyes from the dust blown by the rotors.

He saw her sitting up by the doorway, wrapped in blankets, a bandage across her forehead and her left arm in a sling. Their eyes met across the distance and he hurried toward her. Her dark face was even darker, badly bruised on the side, but she managed a smile as he approached.

There was a calm in her eyes as he reached her. She was in pain, and he gingerly touched her face, his lips brushing her forehead, and her nose. She felt the side of his face with her good hand, their eyes moist, the touch of each other's skin a reaffirmation of their new love.

He easily found the strength to lift her off the seat and carried her a few feet, before Lenny joined him and lent a hand. He just smiled at the two of them. No words were needed to express the happiness of them being reunited. But PJ had words for Kathryn.

"I love you, Kathryn," he whispered in her ear as they carried her to the waiting medics.

"I love you, Peter," she said, her head resting on his shoulder, her good arm around him. She was clutching the gold pendant in her bandaged hand, shaped in the image of a man wearing a full headdress, his hands on hips, striking a defiant pose.

"Where did you get that?" PJ asked.

She looked at him, a small smile on her face, that deep look in her eyes, a look of understanding and revelation, a look he hadn't seen before in quite the same way.

"Eduardo," she said, her voice soothing and happy. "My brother."

"Eduardo? How in the world?" PJ started, but Kathryn put her hand to his lips.

"He was alive, his spirit is alive, it's in me, in all of us, right now, always," she was speaking softly, as if to herself. "I am his sister, Zarzamora," she said to PJ, a smile on her face.

"I know," he said. "I have met your twin sister, Azulmora." She nodded.

"I know. He told me. I will see her again soon," she continued to talk softly. "The Indians, PJ, they are with us also, they are alive in the mountains they love. Listen to them laughing and talking."

He heard nothing but the wind and the rush of the water in the nearby stream. It was a lively sound, he thought.

"I love you, Zarzamora," PJ said as they lowered her onto one of the mattresses. He reached into his pocket and pulled out the gold earring he had found under the bed at Quintaro's ranch. He closed her fingers around it and held her hand. She smiled up at him, hearing that name from his lips for the first time. She felt contented, the warm feelings of her love for PJ and his for her overwhelming the pain in her body. And she clutched tightly onto the gold pendant, and the earring, content that she finally knew the answers to those distant questions that had drawn her to Colombia.

It was two hours before PJ and his crew could be evacuated from the Valley of Codazzi. Colonel Cesar's remaining three choppers ferried the seriously wounded to Santa Marta first and then refueled. During the wait, PJ sat at Kathryn's side. She had three broken ribs, a broken arm and many bruises, but she insisted on staying. The other injured crew, Dave, Ray and

Christina, insisted they also would wait so the whole crew could be airlifted out together.

PJ listened carefully to Kathryn's story of her meeting with Eduardo. She didn't try to analyze it, rather accepted it as real. He believed she believed it had happened, and wondered if it wasn't Eduardo's voice that had spoken to him while he was falling, telling him to open up his parachute. He didn't pretend to understand the workings of the supernatural. He accepted the fact they were together and the events they had just experienced were very real. As was the sound of the wind and water.

It was after nine o'clock Friday morning when the crew lifted off from the Valley of Codazzi in a Huey. They had been up for thirty straight hours, much of it spent on an adrenalin rush, and the ride was a quiet one back to Riohacha. It was made all the more somber by the presence of their dead friend, wrapped in ponchos, lying at their feet between the two bench seats.

The eyes of each of the crew made contact with each other during the flight, their spirits and their lives bared to each other, too tired for pretense or bravado. Their friendships seemed stronger than before. Their shared feelings and memories of the last few days had changed their view of life forever.

Dave and Crash sat close together, their hands tightly clasped. Kathryn and PJ sat close and he reached over to Stoney with his bandaged hand and gripped his arm warmly, their eyes connecting. Lenny, Ray and Mickey joined hands and they flew on in silence, as if in a prayer meeting or a huddle, linked by their physical touch and the spirit of Dutch at their feet.

Their pain would never be healed completely, but time would at least bury it. New joys and new accomplishments would come to their lives. And the pain would rest under cover until a moment when they could reach for it to find strength, to find wisdom or to just relive a moment that would help make them feel happy to be alive.

~~~

EPILOGUE

F our days after the battle in the Valley of Codazzi, Dutch took his final sail and was buried at sea. It was a magnificent Tuesday in October, sunny, sixty degrees with a southwest breeze at fifteen knots. The kind of day that Dutch loved. The kind of day the entire crew loved. They were all aboard on a brisk three-hour reach from Mystic in a borrowed sixty-foot yacht, quietly trimming the sails. PJ steered. They were making over ten knots speed. White bandages and blue plastic casts were evidence of the crew's recent trauma. Stoney and Mickey were the only crew unscathed. A few of Dutch's other close friends also joined the waterborne cortege.

Barney and Azulmora had flown north to pay their respects to Dutch. They sat on the rail with Kathryn, their thoughts to themselves. It was one of the rare times Azulmora and Kathryn had not been talking since they were reunited. It seemed every minute had been taken up with the two catching up. Kathryn delighted in hearing about their brother, Eduardo and of Azulmora's work with the Indians. Azulmora listened intently to Kathryn describe the joys of sailing and flying. And life in America. They seemed intent on making up for lost time as sisters and were fast becoming friends.

Before leaving Colombia, Presidente Gomez offered private thanks to PJ and his crew for their part in shutting down Operation Snowmine. Colonel Cesar promised protection from the other cartels if PJ ever decided to reopen the Goshenite mine. PJ hadn't made up his mind about that yet.

The information from Quintaro's computers helped the U.S. Anti-Drug Network intercept three drug planes on Marib Cay and seize three tons of cocaine. The empty four engine DHC-7 was able to take off and make a dash for Cuban airspace. It was forced down by a Coast Guard jet, crashed and sank ten miles off Cuba. The pilot, Rafael, was last seen aboard a Cuban patrol boat.

One drug plane did get away, piloted by the eagle eyed Gabriel, and completed its afternoon trip to Fitchburg airport, north of Worcester. DEA agents and State Police were on hand that night to catch Mario Terrazi and his gang in the act of unloading the cocaine. They had been tipped off by a twice-retired old man who lived on Boylston Street and still wanted to feel useful.

Carlos Quintaro's body was never found along the river at the south end of the Valley of Codazzi and Colonel Cesar presumed he drowned.

PJ didn't feel good about Quintaro's death. Revenge proved not to be sweet. The whole episode had been costly. Two of his dearest friends, gone, just days apart. It wasn't worth it. But, we have life and we must go on, he thought.

They reached the chosen burial spot south of Block Island and the crew hove to, backing the jib with the rudder hard over so the boat would drift gently before the wind. PJ watched Dutch's naked body slide from its wrappings and slip into the water. That's the way Dutch wanted it. PJ knew a chapter of his life went with his friend. The crew offered their own silent thoughts as they watched the body disappear. The last ripples had gone, but no one wanted to leave.

"Let's get going," PJ said finally.

On the trip back, the crew was animated and they cracked a few beers in Dutch's name. Barney, Azulmora and Kathryn huddled close together in the cockpit as the afternoon sun slipped behind Fisher's Island. PJ marveled at the two women and their sameness, but knew quite clearly which one he had fallen for. They looked at each other and smiled. He found peace in her eyes. And hope.

The noise of the boat pushing through the water mixed well with the sounds of the friendly voices on deck. PJ watched and listened and steered the boat. It felt good to be with his crew.

About the same time, but across five time zones, in the darkness of the Atlantic Ocean, twenty miles west of Gibraltar, the cargo ship *Alma de Maria Vargas*, bound to Rotterdam from Santa Marta, rendezvoused with a Liberian registered freighter named *Freelander*. In gentle five-foot seas, a cargo container was hoisted from the *Maria Vargas* into the sea, floating on a specially rigged buoyancy collar. Within minutes, the Freelander picked up the container. It was a tricky operation at night, but the two experienced crews handled it with aplomb.

The container, loaded with 4500 kilos of pure cocaine processed in the Valley of Codazzi, was secured on deck and the *Freelander* picked up speed. Over the next few days, she would steam through the Mediterranean to her destination off the coast of Lebanon. There, the cocaine would be ferried to shore in small boats, to be exchanged for cash and weapons.

As the ships resumed their courses, it was not clear who would step forward and stop them.

The End

The Author

Greg Gilmartin is a writer, TV producer and director living in the Mystic region of Connecticut. His varied careers range from car wash specialist, USAF Russian linguist, journalist, talk show host, play by play announcer and the public address announcer for the once famous Hartford Whalers hockey team. He is a passionate member of the Mystic River Mudheads. His experiences with the crew of *Madcap* provided much of the inspiration for this first novel.

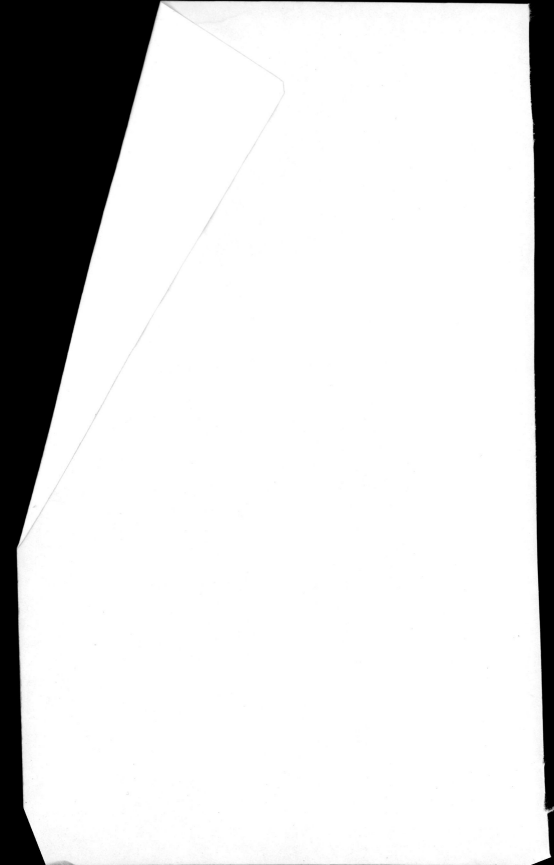